WHAT A WESTMORELAND WANTS

BY
BRENDA JACKSON

AND

STAND-IN BRIDE'S SEDUCTION

BY
YVONNE LINDSAY

MILLS & BOON

**He wasn't sure exactly when he de-
cided Gemma Westmoreland was
destined to be *his* woman.**

Probably the day she had arrived from college.
The moment she got out of her car and raced
over to her older brother's arms for a huge hug,
Callum had felt as if he'd been hit over the head
with a plank—not once but twice. And when she'd
turned that wonder-girl smile on him, he hadn't
been the same since.

Gemma, the one with the fiery temper. The one a
man would least be able to handle.

Yes, Callum was more than certain that Gemma
was the woman for him.

Now he had the job of convincing her of that…in
an unsuspecting way, since she was also a woman
who thought a serious relationship was not for her.
Gemma Westmoreland was determined never to
let a man break her heart.

But Callum knew that was the one thing she didn't
have to worry about.

Dear Reader,

When I first introduced Callum Austell in *Hot Westmoreland Nights,* I knew he would be a man to die for; a man who would know what he wanted and would do whatever it took to get it. I left no doubt in anyone's mind that Callum wanted Gemma Westmoreland, and in this very special story he plans to get what he wants.

But first he has to be gracious enough to give Gemma what she wants, or what she thinks she wants. Gemma and Callum's story is a special love affair that shows the love and devotion of a man determined to win the heart of the woman he loves, although that woman is determined to keep her heart to herself.

I hope all of you enjoy reading Callum and Gemma's story as much as I enjoyed writing it.

And I want to thank all of you who helped to make *Hot Westmoreland Nights* a *New York Times* bestseller!

Happy reading!

Brenda Jackson

WHAT A WESTMORELAND WANTS

BY
BRENDA JACKSON

Published in Great Britain 2011
by Mills & Boon, an imprint of Harlequin (UK) Limited,
Eton House, 18-24 Paradise Road, Richmond, Surrey TW9 1SR

© Brenda Streater Jackson 2010

ISBN: 978 0 263 88314 5

51-0911

Harlequin (UK) policy is to use papers that are natural, renewable and recyclable products and made from wood grown in sustainable forests. The logging and manufacturing processes conform to the legal environmental regulations of the country of origin.

Printed and bound in Spain
by Blackprint CPI, Barcelona

To my husband, the love of my life and my best friend,
Gerald Jackson, Sr.

To everyone who enjoys reading about the
Westmoreland family,
this one is for you!

Esteem her, and she will exalt you; embrace her,
and she will honour you.
—Proverbs 4:8

Brenda Jackson is a die "heart" romantic who married her childhood sweetheart and still proudly wears the "going steady" ring he gave her when she was fifteen. Because Brenda believes in the power of love, her stories always have happy endings. In her real-life love story, Brenda and her husband of thirty-eight years live in Jacksonville, Florida, and have two sons.

A *New York Times* bestselling author of more than seventy-five romance titles, Brenda is a recent retiree who now divides her time between family, writing and traveling with Gerald. You may write to Brenda at PO Box 28267, Jacksonville, Florida 32226, by e-mail at WriterBJackson@aol.com or visit her website at www.brendajackson.net.

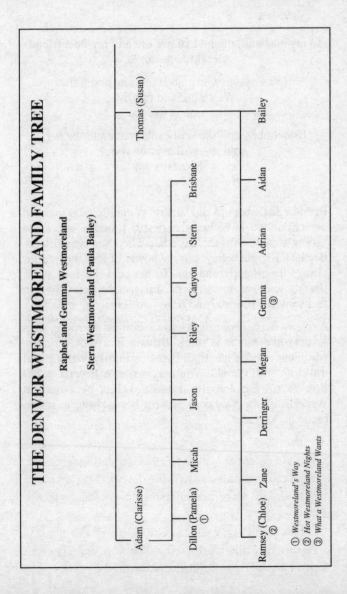

THE DENVER WESTMORELAND FAMILY TREE

Raphel and Gemma Westmoreland

Stern Westmoreland (Paula Bailey)

Adam (Clarisse) — Thomas (Susan)

Dillon (Pamela) ①

Micah — Jason — Riley — Canyon — Stern — Brisbane

Ramsey (Chloe) ② — Zane — Derringer — Megan — Gemma ③ — Adrian — Aidan — Bailey

① *Westmoreland's Way*
② *Hot Westmoreland Nights*
③ *What a Westmoreland Wants*

Prologue

Callum Austell sat in the chair with his legs stretched out in front of him as he stared at the man sitting behind the huge oak desk. He and Ramsey Westmoreland had become friends from the first, and now he had convinced Ramsey that he was the man who would give his sister Gemma the happiness she deserved.

But Callum knew there was one minor flaw in his plans. One that would come back to haunt him if Gemma Westmoreland ever discovered that the trip to Australia he would offer her would be orchestrated for the sole purpose of getting her off familiar turf so that she would finally come to realize just how much he cared for her.

"I hope you know what you're doing," Ramsey said, interrupting Callum's thoughts. "Gemma will give you hell when she finds out the truth."

"I'll tell her before then, but not before she falls in love with me," Callum replied.

Ramsey lifted a brow. "And if she doesn't?"

To any other woman Callum's intense pursuit might seem like a romantic move, but Ramsey was convinced his sister, who didn't have a romantic bone in her body, wouldn't see things that way.

Callum's expression was determined. "She will fall in love with me." And then the look in his eyes almost became one of desperation. "Damn, Ram, she has to. I knew the first moment I saw her that she was the one and only woman for me."

Ramsey took a deep breath. He wished he'd had the same thoughts the first time he set eyes on his wife, Chloe. Then he would not have encountered the problems he had. However, his first thoughts when he'd seen Chloe weren't the least bit honorable.

"You're my friend, Callum, but if you hurt my sister in any way, then you'll have one hell of an angry Westmoreland to deal with. Your intentions toward Gemma better be nothing but honorable."

Callum leaned forward in his chair. "I'm going to marry her."

"She has to agree to that first."

Callum stood. "She will. You just concentrate on becoming a father to the baby you and Chloe are expecting in a couple of months, and let me worry about Gemma."

<u>One</u>

Gem, I am sorry and I hope you can forgive me one day.

—Niecee

Gemma Westmoreland lifted a brow after reading the note that appeared on her computer after she'd booted it up. Immediately, two questions sailed through her mind. Where was Niecee when she should have been at work over an hour ago and what was Niecee apologizing for?

The hairs on the back of Gemma's neck began standing up and she didn't like the feeling. She had hired Niecee Carter six months ago when Designs by Gem began picking up business, thanks to the huge contract she'd gotten with the city of Denver to redecorate several of its libraries. Then Gayla Mason had wanted her mansion redone. And, last but not least, her sister-in-law, Chloe, hired Gemma for a makeover of the Denver branch of her successful magazine, *Simply Irresistible*.

Gemma had been badly in need of help and Niecee had possessed more clerical skills than the other candidates she'd interviewed. She had given the woman the job without fully checking out her references—something her oldest brother, Ramsey, had warned her against doing. But she hadn't listened. She'd figured that she and the bubbly Niecee would gel well. They had, but now, as Gemma quickly logged into her bank account, she couldn't help wondering if perhaps she should have taken Ramsey's advice.

Gemma had been eleven when Ramsey and her cousin Dillon had taken over the responsibility of raising their thirteen siblings after both sets of parents had been killed in a plane crash. During that time Ramsey had been her rock, the brother who'd been her protector. And now, it seemed, the brother she should have listened to when he'd handed out advice on how to run her business.

She pulled in a sharp breath when she glanced at the balance in her checking account. It was down by $20,000. Nervously, she clicked on the transaction button and saw that a $20,000 check had cleared her bank—a check that she hadn't written. Now she knew what Niecee's apology was all about.

Gemma dropped her face in her hands and felt the need to weep. But she refused to go there. She had to come up with a plan to replace that money. She was expecting invoices to come rolling in any day now from the fabric shops, arts and craft stores and her light fixtures suppliers, just to name a few. Clearly, she wouldn't have enough funds to pay all her debts. She needed to replace those funds.

She stood and began pacing the floor as anger consumed her. How could Niecee have done this to her? If she needed the money, all she had to do was ask. Although Gemma might not have been able to part with that much from her personal account, she could have borrowed the money from one of her brothers or cousins.

Gemma pulled in a deep frustrated breath. She had to file a police report. Her friendship and loyalty to Niecee ended the minute her former worker had stolen from her. She should have suspected something. Niecee hadn't been her usual bubbly self the last few days. Gemma figured it had to do with her trifling live-in boyfriend who barely worked. Had he put Niecee up to this? It didn't matter because Niecee should know right from wrong, and embezzling from your employer was wrong.

Sitting back down at her desk, Gemma reached for the phone and then pulled her hand back. Dang! If she called Sheriff Bart Harper—who had gone to school with both Ramsey and Dillon—and filed a report, there was no doubt in her mind that both Ram and Dillon would hear about it. Those were the last two people she wanted in her business. Especially since they'd tried talking her out of opening her interior design shop in the first place.

For the past year, things had worked out fairly well with her being just a one-woman show with her sisters, Megan and Bailey, helping out if needed. She had even pulled in her brothers, Zane and Derringer, on occasion, when heavy lifting had been involved. But when the big jobs began coming in, she had advertised in the newspapers and online for an administrative assistant.

She stood and began pacing again. Bailey was still taking classes at the university and wouldn't have that much money readily available, and Megan had mentioned just the other week that she was saving for a much-needed vacation. Megan was contemplating visiting their cousin, Delaney, who lived in the Middle East with her husband and two children, so there was no way she could hit her up for a loan.

Zane and Derringer were generous and because they were bachelors they might have that kind of ready dough. But they had recently pooled all their funds to buy into a horse-breeding and -training franchise, together with their cousin, Jason. She couldn't look in their direction now, due to that business venture. And all her other siblings and cousins were either in school or into their own businesses and investments.

So where was she going to get $20,000?

Gemma stood staring at the phone for a moment before it hit her that the thing was ringing. She quickly picked it up, hoping it was Niecee letting her know she was returning the money to her or, better yet, that the whole thing was a joke.

"Hello?"

"Hello, Gemma, this is Callum."

She wondered why the man who managed Ramsey's sheep farm would be calling her. "Yes, Callum?"

"I was wondering if I could meet with you sometime today to discuss a business proposition."

She lifted a brow. "A business proposition?"

"Yes."

The first thought that crossed her mind was that engaging in a business meeting was the last thing she was in the mood for today. But then she quickly realized that she couldn't let what Niecee did keep her from handling things with her company. She still had a business to run.

"When would you like to meet, Callum?"

"How about today for lunch."

"Lunch?"

"Yes, at McKay's."

She wondered if he knew that McKay's was her favorite lunch spot. "Okay, that'll work. I'll see you there at noon," she said.

"Great. See you then."

Gemma held the phone in her hand, thinking how much she enjoyed listening to Callum's deep Australian accent. He always sounded so ultrasexy. But then he was definitely a sexy man. That was something she tried not to notice too much, mainly because he was a close friend of Ramsey's. Also, according to Jackie Barnes, a nurse who worked at the hospital with Megan and who'd had a bad case of the hots for Callum when he first arrived in Denver, Callum had a girl waiting for him back in Australia and it was a very serious relationship.

But what if he no longer had that girl waiting for him back in Australia? What if he was as available as he was hot? What if she could forget that he was her oldest brother's close friend? What if…

Dismissing all such thoughts with a wave of her hand, she sat back down at her computer to figure out a way to rob Peter to pay Paul.

* * *

Callum Austell leaned back in his chair as he glanced around the restaurant. The first time he'd eaten here had been with Ramsey when he first came to Denver. He liked it then and now this would be the place where he would put into motion a plan some would think was way past due being executed. He would have to admit they were probably right.

He wasn't sure exactly when he decided that Gemma Westmoreland was destined to be *his* woman. Probably the day he had helped Ramsey build that barn and Gemma had arrived from college right after graduation. The moment she got out of her car and raced over to her older brother's arms for a huge hug. Callum had felt like he'd gotten hit over the head with a two-by-four, not once but twice. And when Ramsey had introduced them and she'd turned that wondergirl smile on him, he hadn't been the same since. His father and his two older brothers had warned him that it would be that way when he found the woman destined to be his, but he hadn't believed them.

That had been almost three years ago and she'd been just twenty-two years old. So he'd waited patiently for her to get older and had watched over her from afar. And each passing day she'd staked a deeper claim to his heart. Knowing how protective Ramsey was of his siblings, especially his three sisters, Callum had finally gotten up the nerve to confront Ramsey and tell him how he felt about Gemma.

At first Ramsey hadn't liked the idea of his best friend lusting after one of his sisters. But then Callum had convinced Ramsey it was more than lust and that he knew in his heart that Gemma was "the one" for him.

For six months, Ramsey had lived with Callum's family back in Australia on the Austell sheep ranch to learn everything he could so he could start his own operations in Denver. He had hung around Callum's parents and brothers enough to know how dedicated the Austell men were once they fell in love.

His father had given up on falling in love and was on his way back to Australia from a business meeting in the United States to marry an Australian woman when he'd met Callum's mother. She was one of the flight attendants on the plane.

Somehow the already engaged Todd Austell had convinced the Detroit-born Le'Claire Richards that breaking off with his fiancée and marrying her instead was the right thing to do. Evidently it was. Thirty-seven years later the two were still married, remained very much in love and had three sons and a daughter to show for it. Callum was the youngest of the four and the only one who was still single.

His thoughts shifted back to Gemma. Ramsey claimed that of his three sisters, Gemma was the one with the fiery temper. The one a man would least be able to handle. He'd suggested that Callum pray long and hard about making the right decision.

In the end, Callum had convinced Ramsey that he had made the right decision and that a hard-to-handle woman with a fiery temper was the kind he liked. He was more than certain that Gemma was the woman for him.

Now he had to convince Gemma… He'd have to be

stealthy about his pursuit. He knew Gemma had no intention of engaging in a serious relationship after she had witnessed how two of her brothers, and several of her womanizing cousins, had operated with women over the years, breaking hearts in their wake. According to Ramsey, Gemma Westmoreland was determined never to let a man break her heart.

Callum straightened up in his seat when he saw Gemma enter the restaurant. Immediately, the same feeling suffused his heart that always settled there whenever he saw her. He loved the woman. He no longer tried to rationalize why. It really didn't matter at this point.

As she walked toward him, he stood. She was probably 5'8", but just the right height for his 6'3" frame. And he'd always thought she had a rather nice figure. Her dark brown, shoulder-length hair was pulled back in a ponytail. He thought she had dazzling tawny-brown eyes, which were almost covered by her bangs.

Callum had worked hard not to give his feelings away. Because he'd always been on his best behavior around her, he knew she didn't have a clue. It hadn't been easy keeping her in the dark. She saw him as nothing more than her brother's best friend from Australia. The Aussie who didn't have a lot to say and was basically a loner.

He studied her expression as she got closer. She seemed anxious, as if she had a lot on her mind.

"Callum," she said and smiled.

"Gemma. Thanks for agreeing to see me," he said as he took her oustretched hand.

"No problem," she said, sitting down once he released her hand. "You said something about meeting to discuss a business proposition."

"Yes, but first how about us grabbing something to eat. I'm starving."

"Sure."

As if on cue, a waitress strolled over with menus and placed glasses of water in front of them. "I hope this place is acceptable," Callum said, moments later after taking a sip of his water.

"Trust me, it is," Gemma said smiling. "It's one of my favorites. The salads here are fabulous."

He chuckled. "Are they?"

"Yes."

"That might very well be, but I'm not a salad man. I prefer something a lot heavier. Like a steak and the French fries I hear this place is famous for."

"No wonder you and Ramsey get along. Now that he's married to Chloe, I'll bet he's in hog heaven with all those different meals she likes to prepare."

"I'm sure he is. It's hard to believe he's married," Callum said.

"Yes, four months tomorrow and I don't recall my brother ever being happier."

"And his men are happy, too, now that Nellie's been replaced as cook," he said. "She never could get her act together and it worked out well for everyone when she decided to move closer to her sister when her marriage fell apart."

Gemma nodded. "I hear the new cook is working out wonderfully, although most of the guys still prefer Chloe's cooking. But she is happy just being Ramsey's wife and a mother-in-waiting. She doesn't have long now and I'm excited about becoming an aunt.

"Are you an uncle yet?"

It was his turn to smile. "Yes. My two older brothers and one sister are married with a child each. I'm used to being around kids. And I also have a goddaughter who will be celebrating her first birthday soon."

At that moment the waitress returned. Callum resented the interruption.

Gemma appreciated the interruption. Although she had been around Callum plenty of times, she'd never noticed just how powerfully built he was. Her brothers and male cousins were all big men, but Callum was so much more manly.

And she had to listen carefully to what he said and stop paying so much attention to how he said it. His thick Australian accent did things to her. It sent a warm, sensual caress across her skin every time he opened his mouth to speak. Then there were his looks, which made her understand perfectly why Jackie Barnes and quite a number of other women had gone bonkers over him. In addition to being tall, with a raw, masculine build, he had thick chestnut-brown hair that fell to his shoulders. Most days he wore it pulled back into a ponytail. He'd made today an exception and it cascaded around his shoulders.

Gemma had once overheard him mention to her sister, Megan, that his full lips and dark hair came from his African-American mother and his green eyes and his square jaw from his father. She'd also heard him say that his parents had met on an airplane. His mother had been a flight attendant on his father's flight from the United States back to Australia. He'd told Megan it had been love at first sight, which made her wonder if he believed in such nonsense. She knew there was no such thing.

"So what do you think of Dillon and Pamela's news?"

Callum's question cut into her thoughts and she glanced up to meet his green eyes. She swallowed. Was there a hint of blue in their depths. And then there was his dimpled smile that took her breath away.

"I think it's wonderful," she said, suddenly feeling the need to take a sip of cold water. "There haven't been babies in our family in a long time. With Chloe expecting and now Pamela, that's two babies to spoil and I can't wait."

"You like children?"

She chuckled. "Yes, unfortunately, I'm one of those people who take to the precious darlings a little too much. That's why my friends call on me more often than not to babysit for them."

"You could always marry and have your own."

She made a face. "Thanks, but no thanks. At least no time soon, if ever. I'm sure you've heard the family joke about me never wanting to get serious about a man. Well, it's not a joke—it's the truth."

"Because of what you witnessed with your brothers while growing up?"

So he *had* heard. Any one of her brothers could have mentioned it, especially because she denounced their behavior every chance she got. "I guess you can say I saw and heard too much. My brothers and cousins had a reputation for fast cars and fast women. They thought nothing about breaking hearts. Ramsey usually had a steady girl, but Zane and Derringer were two of the worst when it came to playing women. As far as I'm concerned, they still are." Unfortunately, she'd overheard one of Zane's phone calls that very morning when she had stopped by to borrow some milk.

"I can clearly recall the times when Megan and I, and sometimes even Bailey, who was still young enough to be playing with her dolls, would be the ones to get the phone calls from love-stricken girls in tears after being mercilessly dumped by one of my brothers or cousins."

And they were females determined to share their teary-eyed, heart-wrenching stories with anyone willing to listen. Megan and Bailey would get them off the phone really quickly, but Gemma had been the bleeding heart. She would ease into a chair and take the time to listen to their sob stories, absorbing every heartbreaking detail like a sponge. Even to the point at which she would end up crying a river of tears right along with them.

She'd decided by the time she had begun dating that no man alive would make her one of those weeping women. And then there was this inner fear she'd shared with no one, the fear of falling in love and having the person abandon her one day…the way she felt whenever she thought about her parents. She knew she had no logical reason for feeling abandoned by them because she was certain if they'd had a choice they would have survived that plane crash. But still, as illogical as it might be, the fear was there for her and it was real. She was convinced there was no man worth a single Gemma Westmoreland tear or her fears, and intended to make sure she never shed one by never giving her heart to anyone. She would be celebrating her twenty-fifth birthday in a few months and so far she'd managed to keep both her heart and her virginity intact.

"And because of that you don't ever plan to get seriously involved with a man?"

She drew in a deep breath. She and her sisters had had this conversation many times and she was wondering why she was sitting here having it with Callum now. Why was he interested? It dawned on her that he probably wasn't; he was just asking to fill the time. "As far as I'm concerned that's a good enough reason. Those girls were in love with my brothers and cousins and assumed they loved them back. Just look what that wrong assumption did to them."

Callum took a sip of his water, deciding not to respond by saying that as far as he was concerned her brothers' behavior was normal for most men, and in some cases women. Granted, he hadn't been around Zane and Derringer while they had been in their teens and could just imagine some of the things they had gotten in to. Now, as grown men, he knew they enjoyed women, but then most hot-blooded men did. And just because a man might be considered a "player" somewhat before finally settling down with one woman—the one he chose to spend the rest of his life with—that didn't necessarily mean he was a man who totally disrespected women. In fairness to Zane and Derringer, they treated women with respect.

He wondered what she would think if she knew how his behavior had been before he'd met her. He hadn't considered himself a womanizer, although he'd dated a slew of woman. He merely thought of himself as a man who enjoyed life and wanted to have a good time with the opposite sex while waiting for the girl destined to share his life to come along. Once she had, he'd had no trouble bringing his fun-loving, footloose and fancy-free bachelor lifestyle to an end. Eventually, the same thing would happen to her brothers and cousins.

No wonder her brothers thought she was a lost cause, but he refused to accept that. He was determined to show her how things could be if she were to fall in love with a man committed to making her happy.

In a way, he felt he knew Gemma. He believed that beneath her rough and tough "I'll never fall in love" exterior was the heart of a woman who not only loved children but loved life in general. He also believed that she was a passionate woman. And that she was unknowingly reserving that passion for the one man capable of tapping into it. The same man destined to spend the rest of his life with her. Him.

The waitress delivered their food, and they engaged in chitchat while they ate their meal.

After they had finished eating and the waitress removed their plates, Gemma leaned back in her chair and smiled at Callum. "Lunch was wonderful. Now, about that business proposition?"

He chuckled, reached over and picked up the folder he had placed on an empty chair. He handed it to her. "This is information on the home I purchased last year. I would love you to decorate it for me."

Callum saw how her eyes lit up. She loved her work and it showed in her face. She opened the folder and carefully studied every feature, every detail of the house. He knew exactly what he was doing. He was giving her

9,200 feet of house to do with as she pleased. It was an interior designer's dream.

She lifted her gaze with a look of awe on her face. "This place is beautiful. And it's huge. I didn't know you had purchased a house."

"Yes, but it's still empty and I want to turn it into a home. I like what you did with Ramsey's place and thought you would be the ideal person for the job. I'm aware that because of the size of the house it will take up a lot of your time. I'm willing to pay you well. As you can see I haven't picked out any furniture or anything. I wouldn't know where to begin."

Now that much was true, Callum thought. What he didn't tell her was that other designers had volunteered to decorate his new house, but he had bought it with her in mind.

She glanced back down at the papers in front of her. "Umm, eight bedrooms, six bathrooms, a huge kitchen, living room, dining room, family room, theater, recreation room and sauna. That's quite a lot of space for a single man."

He laughed. "Yeah, but I don't plan on staying single forever."

Gemma nodded, thinking that evidently Callum had decided to settle down and send for that girl back home. She glanced down at the papers again. She would love taking on this project, and he was right in thinking it would take up a lot of her time. But then she definitely needed the money.

"So, what do you think, Gemma?"

She glanced back up at him and smiled. "I think you just hired yourself an interior designer."

The smile that touched his face sent a tingling sensation flowing through her stomach. "I can't wait to see it."

"No problem. When can you get away?"

She pulled out her cell phone to check her calendar and her schedule for this week. Once she saw the place and gave him an official estimate, she could ask for a deposit, which would make up some of what Niecee had taken from her. "What about tomorrow around one?"

"That might be a bit of a problem."

"Oh." She figured he would probably be tied up at Ram's ranch doing something at that time, so without looking up she advanced her calendar another day. "What about Wednesday around noon."

He chuckled. "Twelve noon on Monday would be the earliest availability for me."

She nodded when she saw that time was free for her, although she wished she could see it sooner. "Monday at noon will be fine."

"Great, I'll make the necessary flight arrangements."

She put her phone back into her purse and glanced over at him. "Excuse me?"

"I said that I will make the necessary flight arrangements if we want to see the house Monday at noon. That means we'll need to fly out no later than Thursday morning."

Gemma frowned. "Thursday morning? What are you talking about? Just where is this house located?"

Callum leaned back in his chair and gave her one kilowatt smile. "Sydney, Australia."

Two

Gemma didn't have to look in the mirror to know there was a shocked look on her face. And her throat felt tight, as if sound would barely pass through it if she tried to speak. To prove the point, she tried to utter a word and couldn't. So she just sat there and stared across the table at Callum like he had lost his ever-loving mind.

"Now that that's all settled, let's order some dessert," Callum said, picking up the menu.

She reached out, touched his hand and shook her head. "What's the matter?" he asked. "You don't want dessert?"

She drew in a deep breath, made an attempt to speak once more and was glad when sound came out. But to be absolutely sure he understood, she held up her hands in the shape of a T. "Time-out."

He lifted an eyebrow. "Time-out?"

She nodded. "Yes, time-out. You lost me between the flight on Thursday and Sydney, Australia. Are you saying this house that you want me to decorate is in Sydney, Australia?"

"Of course. Where else would it be?"

She fought hard not to glare at him; after all, he was a potential client. "I thought possibly in the Denver area," she said in what she hoped was a neutral tone.

"Why would you think that?"

She couldn't hold back her glare any longer. "Well, you've been in this country for almost three years now."

"Yes, but I've never said or insinuated to anyone that I wouldn't return home. I was here helping Ramsey out and now that he has the hang of things, I'm no longer needed. Now I can get back home and—"

"Get married," Gemma supplied.

He chuckled. "As I said earlier, I don't plan on staying single forever."

"And when do you plan on marrying her?"

"Her who?"

Gemma wondered why some men suddenly went daft when their girlfriends were mentioned. "The woman waiting for you back in Australia."

"Umm, I didn't know there was such a creature."

Gemma stared at him in disbelief. "Are you saying you don't have a fiancée or a sweetheart back in Australia?"

He smiled. "That's exactly what I'm saying. Where did you hear something like that?"

Normally Gemma wouldn't divulge her sources, but typically, Jackie knew what she was talking about, and that wouldn't be anything the woman would have made up. "Jackie Barnes. And everyone figured she got the information from you."

Callum shook his head. "She didn't get that from me, but I have an idea where it came from. Your brother, Zane. I complained about Jackie making a nuisance of herself and he figured the best way to get rid of a woman like Jackie was just to let her believe I was already taken."

"Oh." She could see Zane doing something like that. If for no other reason than to shift Jackie's interest from Callum to him. Her brother was a womanizer to the nth degree. And Derringer wasn't any better. It was a blessing that the twins, Adrian and Aidan, were away at college, where the only thing on their minds was making the grade. "I assume Zane's plan worked."

"It did."

"In that case you were lucky," Gemma decided to say. "Some women would not have cared that you were spoken for. They would have taken it as a challenge to swing your interest their way."

Callum couldn't help but think of just where his interest had been for the past three years and knew no one could have succeeded in doing that. The woman sitting across the table was the one he intended to marry.

"And you actually assumed I have someone of interest back home?"

She shrugged. "Hey, that's what we all heard and I had no reason to assume differently. As far as I knew, you weren't dating anyone and whenever we had events you always came alone."

And tried hanging around you every chance I got, he thought.

"You were almost as much of a loner as Ramsey," Gemma added. "If your goal was to keep the women away, then it evidently worked for you."

He took a sip of his drink, wondering if the reason she had yet to pick up on his interest in her was because she figured he was already taken.

"Callum, about this trip to Australia?"

He knew where she was about to take the discussion and was prepared with a spiel to reel her in. "What about it? If you're having second thoughts, I understand. No sweat. I've already contacted a backup in case you couldn't do it. Jeri Holliday at Jeri's Fashion Designs has indicated she would love the job and will have her bags packed for Australia before I can blink an eye."

Over my dead body, Gemma thought as she sat up straight in her chair. Jeri Holliday had been trying to steal clients from her for years.

"I think she liked the fact that I'm offering $50,000, and half of that upfront."

His words froze her thoughts. "Come again?"

He smiled. "I said, considering that I'm asking the decorator to give up at least six weeks, I'm offering $50,000, just as a starting price."

Gemma could only stare at him once again in disbelief. She leaned closer to the table and spoke in a hushed tone, as if anyone sitting in close range could overhear their top-secret conversation. "Are you saying that you're paying $25,000 on acceptance of the job and the other half on completion; and that $50,000 does not include any of the materials? That's just for labor?"

"Yes, that's what I'm saying."

Gemma began nibbling on her bottom lip. The $25,000 would definitely boost her bank account, replacing what Niecee had stolen. And then to think there would be another $25,000 waiting when she completed everything. However, as good as it sounded there were a few possible conflicts.

"What do you see as the time line for this project, Callum?" she decided to ask him.

He shrugged wide shoulders. "I'll tell you the same thing I told Jeri. I think it will take a month to six weeks to take down all the measurements and get things ordered. I'd also like that person there to coordinate the selection of all the furniture. However, there's no rush on that."

Gemma began nibbling on her lips again. "The reason I asked is because there are two babies who will be born within a few months of each other and I'd like to be here for both births. If I can't make it back at the time of delivery then at least within a few days."

"No problem. In fact, I'll spring for the flight."

Gemma couldn't help but wonder why he was being so generous and decided to ask him.

"I've always believed in being fair when it came to those who worked for me," he said.

"In any case, I'm going to need to return myself to help out because Ramsey will be busy with Chloe and the baby," he continued. "I don't want him to worry about the ranch during that time, so I've already promised him that I would return. And although Dillon probably won't need me to do anything, he and Pamela are like family and I want to be here for their baby's arrival, too."

Gemma felt relieved. But still—Australia? That was such a long way from home. And for a month, possibly six weeks. The only other time she'd been away from home for so long was when she left for college in Nebraska. Now she was considering trekking off to another country. Heck, it was another continent.

She was suddenly filled with an anticipation she'd never felt before. She'd never been a traveler, but if she took Callum's job offer, she would get to see a part of the world she'd only read about. That was exciting.

"So are you still interested or do you want me to go with Jeri Holliday?"

She didn't hesitate. "I don't have a problem traveling to Australia and will be ready to fly out on Thursday. I just need to get my business in order. I'll be gone for a while and I'll need to let my family know."

It then occurred to her that her family might not like the idea of her going so far away. Ramsey had a tendency to be overprotective. But he had his hands full with Chloe expecting their baby at the end of November. He would be too busy to try to micromanage her life…thank goodness.

"Terrific. I'll make flight arrangements and will let you know when I have everything in order."

"All right."

Callum lifted up his soda glass in a toast. "Here's to adventures awaiting you in the outback."

Gemma chuckled as she lifted her glass in a toast, as well. "Yes, here's to adventures in the outback."

A few hours later back at her house, despite her outer calm, Gemma was trying to keep things together on the inside while she explained everything to her sisters, Megan and Bailey, as they sat together at the kitchen table. Megan was the oldest at twenty-six and Bailey was twenty-two.

"And why didn't you file a police report? Twenty thousand dollars isn't a little bit of money, Gem," an angry Megan wanted to know.

Gemma drew in a deep breath. "I'm working with the bank's security team in trying to recover the funds. The main reason I didn't get Sheriff Harper involved is because he's close friends with both Dillon and Ramsey. He'll probably get a report of the incident from the bank, eventually, but I think he'd be more inclined to keep his mouth shut about it. It would appear more of an official matter then."

"Oh."

From the look on her sisters' faces and their simultaneous responses, she knew they had forgotten that one important piece of information. There wasn't too much a Westmoreland did in these parts that Dillon and Ramsey didn't know about. Sheriff Harper, who had gone to high school with Dillon and Ramsey, made sure of that.

"And I didn't want to hear, 'I told you so' from those two. Neither of them wanted me to start my own business when I did. So there was no way I was going to tell them what Niecee had done. Hiring her was my mistake and I'll have to deal with it in my own way."

"But will you make sure she doesn't get away with her crime? I'd hate for her to steal from some other unsuspecting soul."

"Yes, I'm going to make sure she doesn't do this

again. And to think that I trusted her," Gemma said with a nod.

"You're too trusting," Megan said. "I've always warned you about that."

And she had, Gemma thought. So had her older brothers. "So what do you think about me going to Australia?" She needed to change the subject.

Megan smiled. "Personally, I think it's cool and wish I could go with you, but I'm saving my time off at the hospital for that trip to visit Delaney in Tehran."

"I think that's cool, as well," Bailey said. "I'm still reeling over the fact that there's no woman waiting for Callum back in Sydney. If that's true, then why isn't he dating? I don't ever recall him having a girlfriend while he's been here in the States. He's nothing like Zane and Derringer."

"And he's such a cutie-pie," Megan added.

Gemma couldn't help smiling as she recalled how sexy he looked sitting across from her at lunch. "He'd already mentioned the job to Jeri Holliday, but it was contingent on whether or not I would accept his offer."

"And I'm sure she was ready to grab it," Bailey said with a frown.

"Of course she was. I wish the two of you could see the size of his house. I can't believe he'd buy such a place as a single man. Now that I've made up my mind about going to Australia, I need to let Ramsey know."

Gemma inhaled sharply at the thought of doing that, but knew it needed to be done. However, under no circumstances did Ramsey need to know that Niecee had embezzled $20,000 from her. She would let the bank's security team handle things.

"You don't have any appointments or projects sched-uled for the next six weeks?" Megan asked as they helped her pack.

"No. This job offer came at a good time. I had thought about taking a well-deserved vacation anyway, but now it's back to work for me. I'll take some time off during the holidays."

"If Callum bought a house in Australia, does that mean he's moving back home?"

Gemma glanced over at Bailey. That thought hadn't occurred to her. "I guess so."

"What a bummer. I've gotten used to seeing him," Bailey said with a pout. "I'd begun thinking of him as another big brother."

Gemma drew in a deep breath. For some reason she'd never thought of him as another big brother.

She'd never felt the need to become as friendly with him as Megan and Bailey had, but she never knew why she'd been standoffish with him. She'd only accepted that that was the way things were. Why now, all of a sudden, did the thought of him returning to Australia to live and her not seeing him ever again seem like such a big deal?

The very thought made her uneasy.

Three

"Are you okay, Gemma?"

Gemma turned her head to glance over at Callum. What had the pilot just said? They were now cruising at an altitude of 36,000 feet. Was Callum inquiring as to how she felt because she'd suddenly turned green?

Now was not the time to tell him that she had an aversion to flying. Although she'd flown before, that didn't mean she liked it. In fact, she didn't. She'd told herself while packing that she could handle the eighteen hours it would take to get to Australia. Now she was having some pretty serious doubts about that.

"Gemma?"

She drew in a deep breath. "Yes, I'm fine."

"You sure?"

No, she wasn't sure, but he would be the last person to know. "Yes."

She turned her head to look out the window and wondered if asking for a window seat had been a wise choice. All she could see were clouds and Callum's reflection. He smelled good, and she couldn't help wondering what cologne he was wearing. And he looked good, too. He had arrived to pick her up wearing a pair of jeans, a blue chambray shirt and Western boots. She'd seen him in similar outfits plenty of times, but for some odd reason he seemed different to her today.

"The attendant is about to serve snacks. Are you hungry?"

She turned and met his eyes. They were a beautiful green and she could swear that a strange expression shone in their dark depths. "No, I ate a good breakfast this morning with Ramsey and Chloe."

He lifted a brow. "You got up at five this morning to do that?"

She smiled. "Yes. All I had to do was set the alarm. I figured if I got up early, then by the time this plane leveled off in the sky I would be ready to take a nap."

He chuckled. "Does flying bother you?"

"Let's just say it's not one of my favorite things to do," she answered. "There're other things I prefer doing more. Like getting a root canal or something else equally as enjoyable."

He threw his head back and laughed, and she liked the sound of it. She'd known him for almost three years and this was the first time she recalled hearing him laugh. He'd always seemed so serious, just like Ramsey. At least that was how Ramsey used to be. She would be one of the first to say that marriage had changed her brother for the better.

"And then," she added in a soft, thoughtful tone. "My parents were killed in a plane crash and I can't help but think of that whenever I'm in the air." She paused a moment. "There was a time after their deaths that I swore I'd never get on a plane," she said quietly.

Callum did something at that moment she hadn't expected. He reached out and took her hand in his. His was warm and large and completely covered hers. "How did you overcome that fear?"

She shifted her gaze away from their joined hands to his face and sighed deeply. "I refused to live my life in fear of the unknown. So one day I went to Ramsey and told him I was ready to take my first plane ride. He was working with Dillon at Blue Ridge Land Management at the time and made arrangements to take me on his next business trip. I was fourteen."

A bright smile touched her lips. "He signed me out of school for a few days and I flew with him to New Mexico. My first encounter with turbulence almost sent me through the roof. But he talked me through it. He even made me write an essay on my airplane experience."

The flight attendant came around serving drinks and snacks, but Gemma declined everything. Callum took a pack of peanuts and ordered a beer. Gemma had asked for a pillow earlier and adjusted it against her neck as she reclined comfortably in her seat. She had to admit that the first-class seats on this international flight were spacious. And Callum had booked a double-seat row for just the two of them.

Gemma noticed that the attendant had given Callum one or two smiles more than was necessary. The attendant's obvious interest in her passenger made Gemma think of something. "Is it true that your parents met on a flight to Australia?"

He inclined his head to look at her. "Yes, that's true. Dad was actually engaged to someone else at the time and was returning home to Australia to help plan his wedding."

"And he fell for someone else when he was already engaged?"

Callum heard the shock in her voice. Considering what she thought about men deliberately breaking women's hearts, he decided to explain. "From what I was told, he had asked this woman to marry him and it was to be a marriage of convenience."

She lifted a brow. "A marriage of convenience for whom?"

"The both of them. She wanted a rich husband and he wanted a wife to start a family. They saw it as the perfect union."

Gemma nodded. "So love had nothing to do with it?"

"No. He didn't think such a thing could exist for him until he saw my mother. He was hit between the eyes with a ton of bricks." Callum chuckled. "Those are his words, not mine."

"And what happened to the other woman? The one he'd been engaged to at the time?"

He could hear pity in her voice. "Not sure. But I know what didn't happen to her."

Gemma lifted a curious brow. "What?"

A smile touched his lips. "She didn't get the wedding she planned."

"And you find that amusing?"

"Actually, yes, because it was discovered months later that she was pregnant with another man's child."

Gemma gasped sharply and leaned her head closer to Callum's. "Are you serious?"

"Very much so."

"The same thing almost happened to Ramsey, but Danielle stopped the wedding," Gemma said.

"So I heard."

"And I liked her."

"I heard that, too. I understand that your entire family did. But then that goes to show."

She looked over at him. "What?"

"Men aren't the only ones who can be heart-breakers."

Surprise swept across her face at his remark. Gemma leaned back against her seat and released her breath in a slow sigh. "I never said they were."

"You didn't?" he asked smiling.

"No, of course not."

Callum decided not to argue with her about it. Instead, he just smiled. "It's time for that nap. You're beginning to sound a bit grouchy."

To Callum's surprise, she took one, which gave him the opportunity to watch her while she slept. As he gazed at her, he experienced the same intense desire that he'd always felt whenever he was close to her. At the moment, he was close, but not close enough. He couldn't help but study her features and thought her moments of peaceful bliss had transformed her already beautiful face into one that was even more striking.

He would be the first to admit that she no longer looked like the young girl he'd seen that first day. In three years, her features had changed from that of a girl to a woman and it all started with the shape of her mouth, which was nothing short of sensuous. How could lips be that full and inviting, he wondered, as his gaze moved from one corner of her mouth to the other.

Callum's gaze drifted upward from her mouth to her closed eyes and the long lashes covering them. His gaze then moved to her cheekbones and he was tempted to take the back of his hand and caress them, or better yet, trace their beautiful curves with the tip of his tongue, branding her as his. And she *was* his, whether she knew it or not, whether she accepted it or not. She belonged to him.

He then noticed how even her breathing was, and how every breath drew his attention to the swell of her breasts that were alluringly hidden inside a light blue blouse. He'd always found her sexy, too sexy, and it had been hard not to want her, so he hadn't even bothered fighting the temptation. He had lusted after her from afar, which was something he couldn't help, since he hadn't touched another woman in almost three years. Once her place in his life had become crystal clear, his body had gone into a disciplined mode, knowing she would be the one and only woman he would make love to for the rest of his life. Now, the thought of that made his body go hard. He breathed in her scent, he closed the book he had been reading and adjusted his pillow. He closed his eyes and allowed his fantasies of her to do what they always did, take over his mind and do in his dreams what he couldn't yet do in reality.

* * *

Gemma slowly opened her eyes at the same moment she shifted in her seat. She glanced over at Callum and saw that he had fallen asleep. His head was tilted close to hers.

She would have to admit that at first his close proximity had bothered her because she assumed they would have to make a lot of unnecessary conversation during the flight. She wasn't very good at small talk or flirting. She'd dated before, but rarely, because most men had a tendency to bore her. She'd discovered that most liked talking about themselves, tooting their own horn and figured they were God's gift to women.

She pushed all thoughts of other men aside and decided to concentrate on this one. He was sitting so close that she could inhale his masculine scent. She had enough brothers and male cousins to know that just as no two women carried the same scent, the same held true for men. Each person's fragrance was unique and the one floating through her nostrils now was making funny feelings flutter around in her stomach.

Gemma found it odd that nothing like this had ever happened to her before, but then she couldn't recall Callum ever being this close to her. Usually they were surrounded by other family members. Granted, they weren't exactly alone now, but, still, there was a sense of intimacy with him sitting beside her. She could just make out the soft sounds of his even breathing.

She had been ready to go when he had arrived at her place. When she opened the door and he had walked in, her breath had gotten caught in her throat. She'd seen him in jeans more times than not, but there was something about the pair he was wearing now that had caused her to do a double take. When he'd leaned down to pick up her luggage, his masculine thighs flexed beneath starched denim. Then there were those muscled arms beneath the Western shirt. Her gaze had lingered longer than it should have on his body. She had followed him out the door while getting an eyeful of his make-you-want-to-drool tush.

She studied him now, fascinated by just what a good-looking man he was and how he'd managed to keep women at bay for so long. A part of her knew it hadn't just been the story Zane had fabricated about a woman waiting for him back in Australia. That tale might have kept some women like Jackie away, but it would not have done anything to hold back the bolder ones. It was primarily the way he'd carried himself. Just like Ramsey. In his pre-Chloe days, most women would have thought twice before approaching her brother. He radiated that kind of "I'm not in the mood" aura whenever it suited him.

But for some reason, she'd never considered Callum as unapproachable as Ramsey. Whenever they had exchanged words, he'd been friendly enough with her. A part of her was curious about why if he wasn't already taken; he'd held himself back from engaging in a serious relationship with a woman. Perhaps he wanted a wife who was from his homeland. That wouldn't be surprising, although it was ironic that his mother was American.

"Oh." The word slipped through her lips in a frantic tone when the plane shook from the force of strong turbulence. She quickly caught her breath.

"You okay?"

She glanced over at Callum. He was awake. "Yes. I hadn't expected that just then. Sorry if I woke you up."

"No problem," he said, straightening up in his seat. "We've been in the air about four hours now, so we were bound to hit an air pocket sooner or later."

She swallowed when the airplane hit a smaller, less forceful pocket of turbulence. "And they don't bother you?"

"Not as much as they used to. When I was younger, my siblings and I would fly with Mom back to the States to visit our grandparents. I used to consider turbulence as exciting as a roller-coaster ride. I thought it was fun."

Gemma rolled her eyes. "There's nothing fun about the feel of an airplane shaking all over the place like it's about to come apart."

He released a soft chuckle. "You're safe, but let me check your seat belt to be sure."

Before she could pull in her next breath, he reached out to her waist and touched her seat belt. She felt his fingers brush against her stomach in the process. At that precise moment, sensations rushed all through her belly and right up her arms.

She glanced over at Callum and found her gaze ensnared by the deep green of his eyes and those sensations intensified. She knew at that moment that something was happening between them, and whatever it was, she wasn't quite prepared for it.

She'd heard about sexual awareness, but why would it affect her now, and why with someone who was almost a total stranger to her? It wasn't as if this was the first time she and Callum had been around each other. But then…as she'd acknowledged to herself earlier, this was the first time they had been alone to this degree. She wondered if her new feelings were one-sided, or if he'd felt it, as well.

"You're belted tight," he said, and to her his voice seemed a bit huskier…or perhaps she was just imagining things.

"Thanks for checking."

"No problem."

Since they were both wide awake now, Gemma decided it was probably a good idea to engage in conversation. That would be safer than just sitting here and letting all kinds of crazy thoughts race through her mind, like what would happen if she were to check on his seat belt as he'd checked on hers. She felt heat infuse her face and her heart rate suddenly shot up.

Then her anxiety level moved up a notch when she thought his gaze lingered on her lips a little longer than necessary. Had that really been the case? "Tell me about Australia," she said quickly.

Evidently talking about his homeland was something he enjoyed doing if the smile tilting his lips was anything to go by. And they were a gorgeous pair. She'd noticed them before, but this was the first time she'd given those lips more than a passing thought.

Why all of a sudden was there something so compelling about Callum? Why did the thought of his lips, eyes and other facial features, as well as his hands and fingers, suddenly make her feel hot?

"You're going to love Australia," he said, speaking in

that deep accent she loved hearing. "Especially Sydney. There's no place in the world quite like it."

She lifted a brow and folded her arms across her chest. She didn't want to get into a debate, but she thought Denver was rather nice, as well. "Nicer than Denver?"

He chuckled, as understanding lit his eyes. "Yes. Denver has its strong points—don't get me wrong—but there's something about Sydney that's unique. I'm not saying that just because it's where I was born."

"So what's so nice about it?"

He smiled again and, as if on cue, those sensations in her stomach fluttered and spread through her entire midsection.

"I hate to sound like a travel ad, but Australia is a cosmopolitan place drenched in history and surrounded by some of the most beautiful beaches imaginable. Close your eyes for a moment and envision this, Gemma."

She closed her eyes and he began talking in a soft tone, describing the beaches in detail. From his description, she could all but feel a spray of ocean water on her lips, a cool breeze caressing her skin.

"There're Kingscliff Beach, Byron Bay, Newcastle and Lord Howe, just to name a few. Each of them is an aquatic paradise, containing the purest blue-green waters your eyes can behold."

"Like the color of your eyes?" Her eyes were still closed.

She heard his soft chuckle. "Yes, somewhat. And speaking of eyes, you can open yours now."

She slowly lifted her lids to find his eyes right there. He had inched his head closer to hers and not only were his eyes right there, so were his lips. The thoughts that suddenly went racing through her mind were crazy, but all she would have to do was to stick out her tongue to taste his lips. That was a temptation she was having a hard time fighting.

Her breathing increased and she could tell by the rise and fall of his masculine chest, that so had his. Was there something significantly dangerous about flying this high in the sky that altered your senses? Zapped them real good and sent them reeling off course? Filled your mind with thoughts you wouldn't normally entertain?

If the answer to all those questions was a resounding yes, then that explained why her mind was suddenly filled with the thought of engaging in a romantic liaison with the man who was not only her client, but also her oldest brother's best friend.

"Gemma…" It seemed he had inched his mouth a little closer; so close she could feel his moist breath on her lips as he said her name in that deep Australian accent of his.

Instead of responding, she inched her mouth closer, too, as desire, the intensity of which she'd never felt before, made her entire body shiver with a need she didn't know she was capable of having. The green eyes locked on hers were successfully quashing any thoughts of pulling her mouth back before it was too late.

"Would either of you like some more snacks?"

Callum jumped and then quickly turned his face away from Gemma to glance up at the smiling flight attendant. He drew in a deep breath before responding. "No, thanks. I don't want anything."

He knew that was a lie the moment he'd said it. He *did* want something, but what he wanted only the woman sitting beside him could give.

The flight attendant then glanced over at Gemma and she responded in a shaky voice. "No, I'm fine."

It was only after the attendant had moved on that Callum glanced at Gemma. Her back was to him while she looked out the window. He suspected that she was going to pretend nothing had happened between them a few moments ago. There was no doubt in his mind that they would have kissed if the flight attendant hadn't interrupted them.

"Gemma?"

It took her longer than he felt was necessary to turn around and when she did, she immediately began talking about something that he couldn't have cared less about. "I was able to pack my color samples, Callum, so that you'll get an idea of what will best suit your home. I'll give you my suggestions, but of course the final decision will be yours. How do you like earth-tone colors? I'm thinking they will work best."

He fought the urge to say that what would work best would be to pick up where they'd left off, but instead he nodded and decided to follow her lead for now. In a way he felt good knowing that at least something had been accomplished today. She had finally become aware of him as a man. And he was giving her time to deal with that. He wouldn't push her, nor would he rush things for now. He would let nature take its course and with the degree of passion they exhibited a short while ago, he had no reason to think that it wouldn't.

"I happen to like earth-tone colors, so they will

probably work for me," he said, although he truly didn't give a royal damn. The bottom line was whatever she liked would work for him because he had every intention of her sharing that house with him.

"That's good, but I intend to provide you with a selection of vibrant colors, as well. Reds, greens, yellows and blues are the fashionable hues now. And we can always mix them up to create several bold splashes. Many people are doing that now."

She continued talking, and he would nod on occasion to pretend he was listening. If she needed to feel she was back in control of things, then so be it. He relaxed in his seat, tilted his head and watched ardently as her mouth moved while thinking what he would love doing to that mouth if given the chance. He decided to think positive and concentrated on what he would do with that mouth *when* he got the chance.

A few moments after Callum closed his eyes, Gemma stopped talking, satisfied that she had talked him to sleep. She had discussed some of everything with him regarding the decorating of his home to make sure they stayed on topic. The last thing she wanted was for him to bring up what almost happened between them. Just the thought of how close they'd come to sharing a kiss, right here on this airplane, had her pulse racing something awful.

She had never behaved inappropriately with a client before and wasn't sure exactly what had brought it on today. She would chalk it up as a weak moment when she'd almost yielded to temptation. When she had noticed just how close their mouths were, it had seemed a perfectly natural thing to want to taste his lips. Evidently, he'd felt the same way about hers, because his mouth had been inching toward hers with as much enthusiasm as hers had moved toward his. She was grateful for the flight attendant's timely interruption.

Had the woman suspected what they had been about to do? The thought had made Gemma's head heat up with embarrassment. Her heart was racing and the palms of her hands felt damp just thinking about it. She readjusted the pillow behind her head, knowing she would have to regain control of senses jolted by too much turbulence. Callum was just a man. He was a client. A friend of her family. He was not someone she should start thinking about in a sexual way.

She had gone twenty-four years without giving any man a second thought and going another twenty-four the same way suited her just fine.

Four

Gemma glanced around the spacious hotel where she and Callum would be staying for the night—in separate rooms, of course. Once their plane had landed, she had given herself a mental shake to make sure all her senses were back under control. Fortunately, the rest of the flight had been uneventful. Callum had kept his lips to himself and she had kept hers where they belonged. After a while, she had begun feeling comfortable around him again.

They'd taken a taxi from the airport. Callum had informed her that a private car service would arrive the next morning to take them to his parents' home. Gemma assumed they would be staying with his parents for the duration of the trip.

She thought this hotel was beautiful and would rival any of the major chains back home. The suite was spacious with floor-to-ceiling windows that looked out onto Sydney, which at this hour was dotted with bright lights.

Because she had slept a lot on the plane, she wasn't sleepy now. In fact, she was wide awake, although the clock on the nightstand by the bed indicated that it was after midnight. It was hard to believe that on the other side of the world in Denver they were trailing a day behind and it was eight in the morning.

She strolled to the window and looked out. She missed Denver already, but she couldn't help being fascinated by all the things she'd already seen. Although their plane had landed during the night hours, the taxi had taken them through many beautiful sections of the city that were lit up, and showed just how truthful Callum had been when he'd said that there was no place in the world quite like Sydney.

Gemma drew in a deep breath and tried to ignore a vague feeling of disappointment. Even though she was glad Callum hadn't mentioned their interrupted kiss, she hadn't expected him to completely ignore her. Although they'd shared conversation since, most of it had been with him providing details about Sydney and with her going over information about the decorating of his home. The thought that he could control his emotions around her so easily meant that, although he had been drawn to her for that one quick instant, he didn't think she was worth pursuing. If those were his thoughts, she should be grateful, instead of feeling teed off. Her disappointment and irritation just didn't make any sense.

She left the window and crossed the hotel room to the decorative mirror on the wall to study her features.

Okay, so she hadn't looked her best after the eighteen-hour plane flight, but she had taken a shower and had freshened up since then. Too bad he couldn't see her now. But overall, she hadn't looked awful.

Gemma couldn't help wondering what kind of woman would interest Callum. She was totally clueless. She'd never seen him with a woman before. She knew the types Zane and Derringer preferred dating—women who were all legs, beautiful, sophisticated, shallow, but easy to get into bed. For some reason she couldn't see Callum attracted to that type of woman.

There were times she wished she had a lot of experience with men and was not still a twenty-four-year-old virgin. There had been a number of times during her college days when guys had tried, although unsuccessfully, to get her into bed. When they had failed, they'd dubbed her "Ice Princess Gemma." That title hadn't bothered her in the least. She'd rather be known as an ice princess than an easy lay. She smiled, thinking that more than one frustrated stud had given up on seducing her. Giving up on her because she refused to put out was one thing, but ignoring her altogether was another.

A part of her knew the best thing to do was to relegate such thoughts to the back of her mind. It was better that he hadn't followed up on what had almost happened between them. But another part of her—the one that was a woman with as much vanity as any other female—hadn't liked it one bit and couldn't let it go.

A smile swept across her lips. Callum had suggested that they meet in the morning for breakfast before the car arrived to take them to his parents' home. That was fine with her, because she would be meeting his parents and she wanted to look her best. The last thing she wanted was for them to think he'd hired someone who didn't know how to dress professionally. So tomorrow she would get rid of her usual attire of jeans and a casual top and wear something a little more becoming.

She would see just how much Callum could ignore her then.

Callum got up the next morning feeling as tired as he'd been when he went to bed past midnight. He had tossed and turned most of the night, frustrated that he hadn't taken the opportunity to taste Gemma's lips when the chance to do so had been presented to him.

Every part of his body hardened with the memory of a pair of luscious lips that had been barely a breath away from his. And when she had tilted her head even more to him, placing her lips within a tongue reach, he had felt the lower part of his body throb.

The desire that had flowed between them had been anything but one-sided. Charged sensations as strong as any electrical current had surged through both their bodies and he had fought back the urge to unsnap her seat belt and pull her into his lap while lapping her mouth with everything he had.

He remembered the conversations they'd shared and how she'd tried staying on course by being the consummate professional. While she'd been talking, his gaze had been fixated on her mouth. He couldn't recall a woman who could look both sexy and sweet at the same time, as well as hot and cool when the mood suited her. He loved all the different facets of Gemma, and he planned on being a vital part of each one of them. How could any man not want to?

Minutes later, after taking a shower and getting dressed, he left his hotel room to walk a few doors down to where Gemma had spent the night. Just the thought that she had been sleeping so close had done something to him. He wondered if she had gotten a good night's sleep. Or had she tossed and turned most of the night, as he had? Probably not. He figured she had no idea what sexual frustration was all about. And if she did, he didn't want to know about it, especially if some other man ruled her thoughts.

The possibility of that didn't sit well with him, since he couldn't handle the thought of Gemma with any other man but him. He pulled in a deep breath before lifting his hand to knock on her door.

"Who is it?"

"Callum."

"Just a moment."

While waiting, he turned to study the design of the wallpaper that covered the expanse of the wall that led to the elevator. It was a busy design, but he had to admit that it matched the carpet perfectly, pulling in colors he would not have normally paid attention to.

He shook his head, remembering that Gemma had gone on and on about different colors and how her job would be to coordinate them to play off each other. He was surprised that he could recall any of her words when the only thoughts going through his mind had been what he'd like doing to her physically.

"Come on in, Callum. I just need to grab a jacket," she said upon opening the door.

He turned around and immediately sucked in a deep breath. He had to lean against the doorframe to keep from falling. *His* Gemma wasn't wearing jeans and a top today. Instead, she was dressed in a tan-colored skirt that flowed to her ankles, a pair of chocolate-suede, medium-heeled shoes and a printed blouse. Seeing her did something to every muscle, every cell and every pore of his body. And his gut twisted in a knot. She looked absolutely stunning. Even her hair was different. Rather than wearing it in a ponytail she had styled it to hang down to her shoulders.

He'd only seen her a few other times dressed like this, and that had been when they'd run into each other at church. He entered the room and closed the door behind him, feeling a gigantic tug in his chest as he watched her move around the room. He became enmeshed in her movements and how graceful and fluid they were.

"Did you get a good night's sleep, Callum?"

He blinked when he noticed that she stood staring at him, smiling. Was he imagining things or did he see amusement curving her lips? "I'm sorry, what did you ask?"

"I wanted to know if you got a good night's sleep. I'm sure it felt good being back home."

He thought about what she said and although he could agree that it was good being back home, it felt even better having her here with him. He'd thought about this a number of times, dreamed that he would share his homeland with her. He had six weeks and he intended to make every second, minute and hour count.

Apparently, she was waiting for his response. "Sleep didn't come easy. I guess I'm suffering from jet lag. And, yes, I'm glad to be home," he said, checking his watch. "Ready to go down for breakfast?"

"Yes, I'm starving."

"I can imagine. You didn't eat a whole lot on the plane."

She chuckled. "Only because I wasn't sure I could keep it down. There was a lot of turbulence."

And he'd known how much that bothered her. He was glad when she'd finally been able to sleep through it. He had watched her most of the time while she'd done so.

"I'm ready now, Callum."

He was tempted to reach out and take her hand in his, but he knew that doing such a thing would not be a smart move right now. He needed her to get to know him, not as her brother's best friend, but as the man who would always be a part of her life.

"Hey, don't look at my plate like that. I told you I was hungry," Gemma said, laughing. Her stack of pancakes was just as high as Callum's. He had told her this particular hotel, located in downtown Sydney, was known to serve the best pancakes. They not only served the residents of the hotel but locals who dropped in on their way to work. From where Gemma sat, she could see the Sydney Harbour Bridge in the distance. It was a beautiful sight.

"Trust me, I understand. I remember my mom bringing me here as a kid when I did something good in school," he said while pouring syrup onto his pancakes.

"Wow, you mean this hotel is *that* old?" Her eyes twinkled with mischief.

He glanced over at her as amusement flickered in his gaze. "Old? Just what are you trying to say, Gemma?"

"Umm, nothing. Sorry. I have to remember that you're my client and I have to watch what I say. The last thing I want to do is offend you."

"And be careful that you don't," he warned, chuckling. "Or all that information you provided yesterday on colors and designs would have been for naught. How you can keep that stuff straight in your head is beyond me."

He paused a moment. "And I talked to Ramsey last night. Everything is fine back in Denver and I assured him all was well here."

Gemma smiled as she took a sip of her coffee. "Did you tell him we were on the flight from hell getting here?"

"Not quite in those words, but I think he got the idea. He asked me if you fainted when the plane hit the first pocket of turbulence."

She made a face. "Funny. Did he mention how Chloe is doing?"

"Yes, she's fine, just can't wait for November to roll around." He smiled. "She has two more months to go."

"I started to call them last night when we got in, but after I took a shower and went to bed that did it for me. I hadn't thought I'd be able to sleep so soundly, but I did."

During the rest of their meal, Gemma explained to him how they managed to pull off a surprise baby shower for Chloe last month right under her sister-in-law's nose, and how, although Ramsey and Chloe didn't want to know the sex of the baby before it was born,

Megan, Bailey and she were hoping for a girl, while Zane, Derringer and the twins were anticipating a boy.

Sipping coffee and sharing breakfast with Callum seemed so natural. She hadn't ever shared breakfast with him before…at least not when it had been just the two of them. Occasionally, they would arrive at Ramsey's place for breakfast at about the same time, but there had always been other family members around. She found him fun to talk to and felt good knowing he had noticed her outfit and even complimented her on how she looked. She had caught him staring at her a few times, which meant he couldn't ignore her so easily after all.

They had finished breakfast and were heading back toward the elevators when suddenly someone called out.

"Callum, it's you! I can't believe you're home!"

Both Callum and Gemma glanced around at the same time a woman threw herself at him and proceeded to wrap her arms around his waist while placing a generous smack on his lips.

"Meredith! It's good to see you," Callum said, trying to pry himself from the woman's grip. Once that was accomplished, he smiled pleasantly at the dark-haired female who was smiling up at him like an adoring fan. "What are you doing in town so early?"

The woman laughed. "I'm meeting some friends for breakfast." It was then that she turned and regarded Gemma. "Oh, hello."

The first thought that came into Gemma's mind was that the woman was simply beautiful. The second was that if it was the woman's intent to pretend she was just noticing Gemma's presence, then she had failed miserably, since there was no way she could have missed her, when she'd nearly knocked her down getting to Callum.

"Meredith, I'd love you to meet a good friend of mine," he said, reaching out, catching Gemma's hand and pulling her closer to his side. "Gemma Westmoreland. Gemma, this is Meredith Kenton. Meredith's father and mine are old school chums."

Gemma presented her hand to the woman when it became obvious the woman was not going to extend hers. "Meredith."

Meredith hesitated a second before taking it. "So, you're from the States, Gemma?"

"Yes."

"Oh."

She then turned adoring eyes on Callum again, and Gemma didn't miss the way the woman's gaze lit up when Callum smiled at her. "Now that you're back home, Callum, what about us doing dinner at the Oasis, going sailing and having a picnic on the beach."

For crying out loud. Will you let the man at least catch his breath, Gemma wanted to scream, refusing to consider that she was feeling a bit jealous. *And besides, for all you know, I might be his woman and if I were I wouldn't let him do any of those things with you. Talk about blatant disrespect.*

"I'm going to be tied up this visit," Callum said, easing Gemma closer to his side. Gemma figured he was trying to paint a picture for Meredith that really wasn't true—that they were a twosome. Any other time she might have had a problem with a man insinuating such a thing, but in this case she didn't mind. In fact, she welcomed the opportunity to pull the rug right out from under Miss Disrespect. Meredith was obviously one of those "pushy" women.

"And I'm only back home for a short while," he added.

"Please don't tell me you're going back over there."

"Yes, I am."

"When are you coming home for good?" Meredith pouted, her thin lips exuding disappointment.

Gemma looked up at Callum, a questioning look in her eyes. Was this the woman waiting for him that he told her didn't exist? He met her gaze and as if he read the question lingering there, he pulled her even closer to his side. "I'm not sure. I kind of like it over there. As you know, Mom is an American, so I'm fortunate to have family on both continents."

"Yes, but your home is here."

He smiled as he glanced down at Gemma. He then looked back at Meredith. "Home is where the heart is."

The woman then turned a cold, frosty gaze on Gemma. "And he brought you back with him."

Before Gemma could respond, Callum spoke up. "Yes, I brought her back with me to meet my parents."

Gemma knew the significance of that statement, even if it was a lie. To say he had brought her home to meet his parents meant there was a special relationship between them. In truth, that wasn't the case but for some reason he didn't want Meredith to know that, and in a way she didn't want Meredith to know it, either.

"Well, I see my friends have arrived now," she said in a cutting tone. "Gemma, I hope you enjoy your time here in Sydney and, Callum, I'll talk to you later." The woman then beat a hasty retreat.

With his hand on her arm, Callum steered Gemma toward the elevator. Once they were alone inside the elevator, Gemma spoke. "Why did you want Meredith to assume we were an item?"

He smiled down at her. "Do you have a problem with that?"

Gemma shook her head. "No, but why?"

He stared at her for a few moments, opened his mouth to say something, then closed it. He seemed to think for a minute. "Just because."

She lifted a brow. "Just because?"

"Yes, just because."

She frowned up at him. "I'd like more of a reason than that, Callum. Is Meredith one of your former girlfriends?"

"Not officially. And before you assume the worst about me, I never gave her a reason to think anything between us was official or otherwise. I never led her on. She knew where she stood with me and I with her."

So it was one of those kinds of relationships, Gemma mused. The kind her brothers were notorious for. The kind that left the woman broken down and broken-hearted.

"And before you start feeling all indignant on Meredith's behalf, don't waste your time. Her first choice of the Austells was my brother, Colin. They dated for a few years and one day he walked in and found her in bed with another man."

"Oh." Gemma hadn't liked the woman from the first, and now she liked her even less.

The elevator stopped. They stepped off and Callum turned to her and placed his hand on her arm so she wouldn't go any farther. She hadn't expected the move and sensations escalated up her rib cage from his touch.

"I want to leave you with something to think about, Gemma," he said in that voice she loved hearing.

"What?"

"I know that watching your brothers and cousins operate with girls has colored your opinion of men in general. I think it's sad that their exploits have left a negative impression on you and I regret that. I won't speak for your brothers, because they can do that for themselves, but I can speak for myself. I'd never intentionally hurt any woman. It's my belief that I have a soul mate out there somewhere."

She lifted a brow. "A soul mate?"

"Yes."

Gemma couldn't help but wonder if such a thing really existed. She would be the first to admit that her cousin Dillon's first wife hadn't blended in well with the family, nor had she been willing to make any sacrifices for the man she loved. With his current wife, Pam, it was a different story. From the moment the family had met Pam, they'd known she was a godsend. The same thing held true for Chloe. Gemma, Megan and Bailey had bonded with their sister-in-law immediately, even before she and Ramsey had married. And just to see the two couples together, you would know they were meant for each other and loved each other deeply.

So Gemma knew true love worked for some people, but she wasn't willing to suffer any heartbreak while on a quest to find Mr. Right or her soul mate. But as far as Callum was concerned, she was curious about one thing. "And you really believe you have a soul mate?"

"Yes."

She noted that he hadn't hesitated in answering. "How will you know when you meet her?"

"I'll know."

He sounded pretty confident about that, she thought. She shrugged. "Well, good luck in finding her," she said as they exited the building and headed toward the parking garage.

She noted that Callum appeared to have considered her comment, and then he tilted his head and smiled at her. "Thanks. I appreciate that."

Five

"Wow, this car is gorgeous, but I thought a private car was coming for us."

Callum looked over at Gemma and smiled as they walked toward the car parked in the hotel's parking garage. "I decided to have my car brought to me instead."

"This is your car?" Gemma studied the beautiful, shiny black two-seater sports car.

He chuckled as he opened the door for her. "Yes, this baby is mine." *And so are you,* he wanted to say as he watched her slide her legs into the car, getting a glimpse of her beautiful calves and ankles. "I've had it now for a few years."

She glanced up at him. "Weren't you ever tempted to ship it to Denver?"

"No," he said with a smile. "Can you imagine me

driving something like this around Ramsey's sheep farm?"

"No, I can't," she said, grinning when he got in on the other side and snapped his seat belt into place. "Is it fast?"

"Oh, yes. And you'll see that it has a smooth ride."

Callum knew she was sold on the car's performance moments later when they hit the open highway and she settled back in her seat. He used to imagine things being just like this, with him driving this car around town with the woman he loved sitting in the passenger seat beside him.

He glanced over at her for a second and saw how closely she was paying attention to everything they passed, as if she didn't want to miss anything. He drew in a deep breath, inhaling her scent right along with it, and felt desire settle into his bones. Nothing new there; he'd wanted Gemma since the first time he'd seen her and knew she would be his.

"This place is simply beautiful, Callum."

He smiled, pleased that she thought so. "More so than Denver?"

She threw her head back and laughed. "Hey, there's no place like home. I love Denver."

"I know." Just as he knew it would be hard getting her to leave Denver to move to Sydney with him. He would have returned home long ago, but he'd been determined not to until he had her with him.

"We're on our way to your parents' home?" she asked, interrupting his thoughts.

"Yes. They're looking forward to meeting you."

Surprise swept across her face. "Really? Why?"

He wished he could tell her the truth, but decided to say something else equally true. "You're Ramsey's sister. Your brother made an impression on them during the six months he lived here. They consider him like another son."

"He adores them, as well. Your family is all he used to write us about while he was here. I was away at college and his letters used to be so full of adventure. I knew then that he'd made the right decision to turn over the running of the family's real-estate firm to Dillon and pursue his dream of becoming a sheep rancher. Just as my father always wanted to do."

He heard the touch of pain in her voice and sensed that mentioning her father had brought back painful memories. "You were close to him, weren't you?"

When they came to a snag in traffic, he watched her moisten her lips before replying to his question. "Yes. I was definitely a daddy's girl, but then so were Megan and Bailey. He was super. I can still recall that day Dillon and Ramsey showed up to break the news to us. They had been away at college, and when I saw them come in together I knew something was wrong. But I never imagined the news they were there to deliver."

She paused a moment. "The pain wouldn't have been so great had we not lost our parents and Uncle Adam and Aunt Clarisse at the same time. I'll never forget how alone I felt, and how Dillon and Ramsey promised that, no matter what, they would keep us together. And they did. Because Dillon was the oldest, he became the head of the family and Ramsey, only seven months younger, became second in charge. Together they pulled off what some thought would be impossible."

Callum recalled hearing the story a number of times from Ramsey. He had hesitated about going to Australia because he hadn't wanted to leave everything on Dillon's shoulders, so he'd waited until Bailey had finished high school and started college before taking off for Australia.

"I'm sure your parents would be proud of all of you," he said.

She smiled. "Yes, I'm sure they would be, as well. Dillon and Ramsey did an awesome job and I know for sure we were a handful at times, some of us more than others."

He knew she was thinking about her cousin, Bane, and all the trouble he used to get into. Now Brisbane Westmoreland was in the Navy with dreams of becoming a SEAL.

Callum checked his watch. "We won't be long now. Knowing Mom, she'll have a feast for lunch."

A smile touched Gemma's lips. "I'm looking forward to meeting your parents, especially your mother, the woman who captured your father's heart."

He returned her smile, while thinking that his mother was looking forward to meeting her—the woman who'd captured his.

Surprise swept across Gemma's face when Callum brought his car to the marker denoting the entrance to his family's ranch. She leaned forward in her seat to glance around through the car's windows. She was spellbound, definitely at a loss for words. The ranch, the property it sat on and the land surrounding it were breathtaking.

The first thing she noticed was that this ranch was

a larger version of her brother's, but the layout was identical. "I gather that Ramsey's design of the Shady Tree Ranch was based on this one," she said.

Callum nodded. "Yes, he fell in love with this place and when he went back home he designed his ranch as a smaller replica of this one, down to every single detail, even to the placement of where the barns, shearing plants and lambing stations are located."

"No wonder you weren't in a hurry to return back here. Being at the Shady Tree Ranch was almost home away from home for you. There were so many things to remind you of this place. But then, on the other hand, if it had been me, seeing a smaller replica of my home would have made me homesick."

He keyed in the code that would open the electronic gate while thinking that the reason he had remained in Denver after helping Ramsey set up his ranch, and the reason he'd never gotten homesick, were basically the same. Gemma. He hadn't wanted to leave her behind and return to Australia, and he hadn't, except for the occasional holiday visit. And he truly hadn't missed home because, as he'd told Meredith, home is where the heart is and his heart had always been with Gemma, whether she knew it or not.

He put the car in gear and drove down the path leading to his parents' ranch house. The same place where he'd lived all his life before moving into his own place at twenty-three, right out of college. But it hadn't been unusual to sleep over while working the ranch with his father and brothers. He had many childhood memories of walks along this same path, then bicycle rides, motorcycle rides and finally rides behind the wheel of a car. It felt good to be home—even better that he hadn't come alone.

He fully expected not only his parents to be waiting inside the huge ranch house, but his brothers and their wives, and his sister and brother-in-law as well. Everyone was eager to meet the woman whose pull had kept him working in North America as Ramsey's ranch manager for three years. And everyone was sworn to secrecy, since they knew how important it was for him to win Gemma's heart on his turf.

She was about to start getting to know the real Callum Austell. The man she truly belonged to.

When Callum brought the car to a stop in front of the sprawling home, the front door opened and a smiling older couple walked out. Gemma knew immediately that they were his parents. They were a beautiful couple. A perfect couple. Soul mates. Another thing she noted was that Callum had the older man's height and green eyes and had the woman's full lips, high cheekbones and dimpled smile.

And then, to Gemma's surprise, following on the older couple's heels were three men and three women. It was easy to see who in the group were Callum's brothers and his sister. It was uncanny just how much they favored their parents.

"Seems like you're going to get to meet everyone today, whether you're ready to do so or not," Callum said.

Gemma released a chuckle. "Hey, I have a big family, too. I remember how it was when I used to come home after being away at college. Everyone is glad to see you come home. Besides, you're your parents' baby."

He threw his head back and laughed. "Baby? At thirty-four, I don't think so."

"I do. Once a baby always a baby. Just ask Bailey."

Just a look into his green eyes let her know he still wasn't buying it. He smiled as he opened the door to get out and said, "Just get ready for the Austells."

By the time Callum had rounded the car to open the door for her to get out, his parents, siblings and in-laws were there and she could tell that everyone was glad to see him. Moments later she stood, leaning against the side of his car, and watched all the bear hugs he was receiving, thinking there was nothing quite like returning home to a family who loved you.

"Mom, Dad, everyone, I would like you to meet Gemma Westmoreland." He reached out his hand to her and she glanced over at him a second before moving away from the car to join him where he stood with his family.

"So you're Gemma," Le'Claire Austell said, smiling after giving Gemma a hug. "I've heard quite a lot about you."

Surprise lit up Gemma's features. "You have?"

The woman smiled brightly. "Of course I have. Ramsey adores his siblings and would share tales with us about you, Megan, Bailey and your brothers, as well as all the other Westmorelands all the time. I think talking about all of you made missing you while he was here a little easier."

Gemma nodded and then she was pulled into Callum's dad's arms for a hug and was introduced to everyone present. There was Callum's oldest brother, Morris, and his wife, Annette, and his brother, Colin, and his wife, Mira. His only sister Le'Shaunda, whom everyone called Shaun, and her husband, Donnell.

"You'll get to meet our three grands at dinner," Callum's mom was saying.

"I'm looking forward to it," Gemma replied warmly.

While everyone began heading inside the house, Callum touched Gemma's arm to hold her back. "Is something wrong?" He looked at her with concern in his green eyes. "I saw the way you looked at me when I called you over to meet everyone."

Gemma quickly looked ahead at his family, who were disappearing into the house and then back at Callum. "You didn't tell your family why I'm here."

"I didn't have to. They know why you're here." He studied her features for a moment. "What's going on in that head of yours, Gemma Westmoreland? What's bothering you?"

She shrugged, suddenly feeling silly for even bringing it up. "Nothing. I just remember what you insinuated with Meredith and hoped you weren't going to give your family the same impression."

"That you and I have something going on?"

"Yes."

He watched her for a moment and then touched her arm gently. "Hey, relax. My family knows the real deal between us, trust me. I thought you understood why I pulled that stunt with Meredith."

"I do. Look, let's forget I brought it up. It's just that your family is so nice."

He chuckled and pulled her to him. "We're Aussies, eight originals and one convert. We can't help but be nice."

She tossed him a grin before easing away. "So you say." She then looked over at the car as she headed up the steps to the house. "Do you need help getting our luggage?"

"No. We aren't staying here."

She turned around so quickly she missed her step and he caught her before she tumbled. "Be careful, Gemma."

She shook her head, trying to ignore how close they were standing and why she suddenly felt all kinds of sensations flooding her insides. "I'm okay. But why did you say we're not staying here?"

"Because we're not."

She went completely still. "But—but you said we were staying at your home."

He caught her chin in his fingers and met her gaze. "We are. This is not my home. This is my parents' home."

She swallowed, confused. "I thought your home is what I'm decorating. Isn't it empty?"

"*That* house is, but I also own a condo on the beach. That's where we're staying while we're here. Do you have a problem with that, Gemma?"

Gemma forced herself to breathe when it became clear that she and Callum would be sharing living space while she was here. Why did the thought of that bother her?

She had to admit for the first time she was noticing things about him she'd never noticed before. And she was experiencing things around him that she hadn't experienced before. Like the way she was swept up in heated desire and the sensuous tickling in the pit of her stomach whenever he was within a few feet of her, like now...

"Gemma?"

She swallowed again as she met his gaze and the green eyes were holding hers with an intensity that she wasn't used to. She gave her head a mental shake. His family had to be wondering why they were still outside. She had to get real. She was here to do a job and she would do it without having these crazy thoughts that Callum was after her body, just because she'd begun having crazy fantasies about him.

"No, I don't have a problem with that." She pulled away from him and smiled. "Come on, your parents are probably wondering why we're still out here," she said, moving ahead and making an attempt to walk up the steps again.

She succeeded and kept walking toward the door, fully aware that he was watching every step she took.

Callum glanced around his parents' kitchen and drew in a deep breath. So far, things were going just as he'd hoped. From the masked smiles and nods he'd gotten from his family, he knew they agreed with his assessment of Gemma—that she was a precious gem. Even his three nephews, ages six, eight and ten, who were usually shy with strangers, had warmed up to her.

He knew that, for a brief moment, she had been confused as to why his family had taken so readily to her. What he'd told her hadn't been a lie. They knew the reason she was here and decorating that house he had built was only part of it. In fact, a minor part.

"When are you getting a haircut?"

Callum turned and smiled at his father. "I could ask you the same thing." Todd Austell's hair was just as long as his son's and Callum couldn't remember him ever getting his hair cut. In fact, it appeared longer now than the last time he'd seen it.

"Don't hold your breath for that to happen," his father said with joking amusement in his green gaze. "I love my golden locks. The only thing I love more is your mother."

Callum leaned against the kitchen counter. His mother, sister and sisters-in-law had Gemma in a corner and from their expressions he knew they were making *his woman* feel right at home. His brother and brothers-in-law were outside manning the grills, and his nephews were somewhere playing ball. His parents had decided to have a family cookout to welcome him and Gemma home.

"Gemma is a nice girl, Callum. Le'Claire and Shaun like her."

He could tell. He glanced up at his father. "And you?"

A smile crossed Todd Austell's lips. "I like her."

As if she felt Callum's gaze, she glanced over in his direction and smiled. His muscles tightened in desire for her.

"Dad?"

"Yes?"

"After you met Mom and knew she was the woman for you, how long did it take you to convince her of it?"

"Too long."

Callum chuckled. "How long was too long?"

"A few months. Remember, I had an engagement to break off and then your mother assumed that flying was her life. I had to convince her that she was sorely mistaken about that, and that I was her life."

Callum shook his head. His father was something else. Callum's was one of the wealthiest families in Sydney; the Austells had made their millions not only in sheep farming but also in the hotel industry. The hotel where he and Gemma had stayed last night was part of just one of several hotel chains that Colin was in charge of. Morris was vice president of the sheep-farm operation.

When Callum was home, he worked wherever he was needed, but he enjoyed sheep farming more. In fact, he was CEO of his own ranching firm, which operated several sheep ranches in Australia. Each was run by an efficient staff. He also owned a vast amount of land in Australia. He'd never been one to flaunt his wealth, although in his younger days he'd been well aware money was what had driven a lot of women to him. He had frustrated a number of them by being an elusive catch.

He glanced again at the group of women together and then at his father. "I guess it worked."

The older man lifted a brow. "What worked?"

"You were able to convince Mom that you were her life."

A deep smile touched his father's lips. "Four kids and three grandsons later, what can I say?"

A smile just as deep touched Callum's lips. "You can say that in the end Mom became your life as well. Because I think it's obvious that she has."

Six

The moment Gemma snapped her seat belt in place, a bright smile curved her lips. "Your family is simply wonderful, Callum, and I especially like your mom. She's super."

"Yes, she is," Callum agreed as he started the car's engine to leave his parents' home.

"And your dad adores her."

Callum chuckled. "You can tell?"

"How could I not? I think it's wonderful."

She was quiet for a moment. "I recall my parents being that way, having a close relationship and all. As I got older, although I missed them both, I couldn't imagine one living without the other, so I figured that if they had to die, I was glad they at least went together," she said.

Gemma forced back the sadness that wanted to cloud

what had been a great day. She glanced over at Callum. "And I love your parents' home. It's beautiful. Your mother mentioned that she did all the decorating."

"She did."

"Then why didn't you get her to decorate yours?"

"Mine?"

"Yes, the one you've hired me to do. I'm grateful that you thought of me, mind you, but your mother could have done it."

"Yes, she could have, but she doesn't have the time. Taking care of my dad is a full-time job. She spoils him rotten."

Gemma laughed. "Appears he likes spoiling her as well."

She had enjoyed watching the older couple displaying such a warm, loving attitude toward each other. It was obvious that their children were used to seeing them that way. Gemma also thought Callum's three nephews were little cuties.

"Is it far to the condo where you live?" she asked him, settling back against the car seat. When they walked out of Callum's parents' house, she noted that the evening temperature had dropped and it was cool. It reminded her of Denver just weeks before the first snowfall in late September. She then remembered that Australia's seasons were opposite the ones in North America.

"No, we'll be there in around twenty minutes. Are you tired?"

"Umm. Jet lag I think."

"Probably is. Go ahead and rest your eyes for a while."

Gemma took him up on his offer and closed her eyes

for a moment. Callum was right, the reason she wanted to rest had to do with jet lag. She would probably feel this way until she adjusted to the change in time zone.

She tried to clear her mind of any thoughts, but found it impossible to do when she was drawn back to the time she had spent at Callum's parents' home. What she'd told him was true. She had enjoyed herself and thought his family was wonderful. They reminded her of her siblings.

She was close to her siblings and cousins, and they teased each other a lot. She'd picked up on the love between Callum and his siblings. He was the youngest and it was obvious that they cared deeply about him and were protective of him.

More than once, while talking to Callum's mom, she had felt his eyes on her and had glanced across the room to have her gaze snagged by his. Had she imagined it or had she seen male interest lurking in their green depths?

There had been times when the perfection of Callum's features had nearly stopped her in her tracks and she found herself at several standstills today. Both of his brothers were handsome, but in her book, Callum was gorgeous, and was even more so for some reason today. She could understand the likes of Meredith trying to come on to him. Back in Denver on the ranch, he exuded the air of a hardworking roughneck, but here in Sydney, dressed in a pair of slacks and a dress shirt and driving a sports car, he passed the test as the hot, sexy and sophisticated man that he was. If only all those women back in Denver could see him now.

She slowly opened her eyes and studied his profile

over semi-lowered lashes as he drove the car. Sitting in a perfect posture, he radiated the kind of a strength most men couldn't fabricate, even on their best days. His hair appeared chestnut in color in the evening light and hung around his shoulders in fluid waves.

There was something about him that infused a degree of warmth all through her. Why hadn't she felt it before? Maybe she had, but had forced herself to ignore it. And then there was the difference in their ages. He was ten years her senior. The thought of dating a man in close proximity to her age was bad enough; to consider one older, she'd thought, would be asking for trouble, definitely way out of her league.

Her gaze moved to his hands. She recalled on more than one occasion seeing those hands that were now gripping the steering wheel handle the sheep on her brother's ranch. There was an innate strength about them that extended all the way to his clean and short fingernails.

According to Megan, you could tell a lot about a man by his hands. That might be true, but Gemma didn't have a clue what she should be looking for. It was at times like this that her innocence bothered her. For once—maybe twice—she wouldn't mind knowing how it felt to get lost in the depth of a male's embrace, kissed by him in a way that could curl her toes and shoot sparks of pleasure all threw her. She wanted to be made love to by a man who knew what he was doing. A man who would make her first time special, something she would remember for the rest of her life and not forget when the encounter was over.

She closed her eyes again and remembered that

moment on the plane when Callum had awakened and found her there, close to his face and staring at him. She remembered how he had stared back, how she had actually felt a degree of lust she hadn't thought she could feel and a swell of desire that had nearly shaken her to the core. She had felt mesmerized by his gaze, had felt frozen in a trance, and the only thing that would break it would be a kiss. And they had come seconds, inches from sharing one.

She knew it would have to be one of those kisses she'd always dreamed of sharing with a man. The kind that for some reason she believed only Callum Austell could deliver. Yes, the mind-blowing, toe-curling kind. A ripple of excitement sent shivers up her spine at the thought of being swept up in Callum's embrace, kissed by him, made love to by him.

She sucked in a quick breath, wondering what was making her think such things. What was causing her to have such lurid thoughts? And then she knew. She was attracted to her brother's best friend in the worst possible way. And as the sound of the car's powerful engine continued to roar under Callum's skillful maneuvering on the roadway, she felt herself fall deeper and deeper into a deep sleep with thoughts of Callum Austell getting embedded thoroughly into her mind.

Callum settled comfortably in the driver's seat as he drove the road with the power and ease he had missed over the years. Three in fact. Although he had returned home on occasion and had taken the car on the road for good measure whenever he did, there was something different about it this time. Because he had his future wife sitting beside him.

He smiled when he quickly glanced at her before returning his gaze to the road. She was *sleeping* beside him. He couldn't wait for the time when she would be sleeping with him. The thought of having her in his arms, making love to every inch of her body, filled him with a desire he didn't know it was possible to feel. But then Gemma had always done that to him, even when she hadn't known she was doing it.

Over the years he'd schooled himself well, and very few knew how he felt. Ramsey and Dillon knew, of course, and he figured Zane and Derringer suspected something as well. What had probably given Callum away was his penchant for watching Gemma the way a fox watched the henhouse, with his eye on one unsuspecting hen. It wasn't surprising that Gemma was totally clueless.

So far things were going as planned, although there had been a few close calls with his family when he thought one of them would slip and give something away. He wanted Gemma to feel comfortable around him and his family, and the last thing he wanted was for her to feel as if she'd deliberately been set up in any way. He wanted her to feel a sense of freedom here that he believed she wouldn't feel back in Denver.

For her to want to try new and different things, to embrace herself as a woman, topped his list. And for the first time, he would encourage her to indulge all her desires with a man. But not just any man. With him. He wanted her to see that not all men had only one thing in mind when it came to a woman, and for two people to desire each other wasn't a bad thing.

He wanted her to understand and accept that no matter what happened between them, it would be okay because nothing they shared would be for the short term. He intended to make this forever.

Callum pulled into the gated condo community and drove directly to his home, which sat on a secluded stretch of beach, prized for the privacy he preferred. He planned to keep this place even after their home was fully decorated and ready to move in. But first he had to convince Gemma that he was worth it for her to leave the country where she'd been born, the country in which her family resided, and move here with him, to his side of the world.

He brought his car to a stop and killed the ignition. It was then that he turned toward her, keeping one hand on the steering wheel and draping the other across the back of the passenger seat. She looked beautiful, sleeping as if she didn't have a care in the world—and in a way she didn't. He would shoulder whatever problems she had from here on out.

With an analytical eye he studied her features. She was smiling while she slept and he wondered why. What pleasing thoughts were going through her mind? It had gotten dark, and the lights from the fixtures in front of his home cast a glow on her face at an angle that made it look even more beautiful. He could imagine having a little girl with her mouth and cheekbones, or a son with her ears and jaw. He thought she had cute ears.

With a tentative hand he reached out and brushed his fingers gently across her cheeks. She shifted and began mumbling something. He leaned closer to catch what she was saying and his gut tightened in a ball of ravenous desire when she murmured in her sleep, "Kiss me, Callum."

Gemma felt herself drowning in a sea of desire she'd never felt before. She and Callum were not on the ranch in Denver, but were back on the plane. This time the entire plane was empty. They were the only two people onboard.

He had adjusted their seats to pull her into his arms, but instead of kissing her he was torturing her mouth inside, nibbling from corner to corner, then taking his tongue and licking around the lines of her lips.

She moaned deep in her throat. She was ready for him to take her mouth and stop toying with it. She needed to feel his tongue sucking on hers, tasting it instead of teasing it, and then she wanted their tongues to tangle in a delirious and sensual duel.

She began mumbling words, telling him to stop toying with her and asking that he finish what he'd started. She wanted the kiss she'd almost gotten before—a kiss to lose herself in sensual pleasure. Close to her ear she heard a masculine growl, sensed the passion of a man wanting to mate and breathed in the scent of a hot male.

Then suddenly she felt herself being gently shaken. "Gemma. Wake up, Gemma."

She lifted drowsy lids only to find Callum's face right there in front of hers. Just as it had been on the plane. Just as it had been moments earlier in her dream. "Callum?"

"Yes," he replied in a warm voice that sent delicious shivers up her spine. His mouth was so close she could taste his breath on her lips. "Do you really want me to kiss you, Gemma? You are one Westmoreland that I'll give whatever you want."

Seven

Gemma forced the realization into her mind that she wasn't dreaming. This was the real deal. She was awake in Callum's car and he was leaning over her with his face close to hers and there wasn't a flight attendant to interrupt them if he decided to inch his mouth even closer. Would he?

That brought her back to his question. Did she want him to kiss her? Evidently, she had moaned out the request in her sleep and he'd heard it. From the look in the depth of his green eyes, he was ready to act on it. Is that what she wanted? He did say he would give her whatever she wanted.

More than anything, she wanted to be kissed by him. Although it wouldn't be her first kiss, she believed it would be the first one she received with a semblance of passion and desire on both sides. Before guys had wanted to kiss her, but she hadn't really cared if she kissed them or not.

This time she would act first and worry about the consequences of her actions later.

Holding his gaze, she whispered against his lips, "Yes, I want you to kiss me." She saw him smiling and giving a small nod of satisfaction before he leaned in closer. Before she could catch her next breath, he seized her mouth with his.

The first thing he did was seek out her tongue and the moment he captured it in his, she was a goner. He started off slow, plying her with a deep, thorough kiss as if he wanted to get acquainted with the taste and texture of her mouth, flicking the tip of his tongue all over the place, touching places she hadn't known a tongue could reach, while stirring up even more passion buried deep within her bones.

For a timeless moment, heat flooded her body in a way it had never done before, triggering her breasts to suddenly feel tender and the area between her thighs to throb. How could one man's kiss deliver so much pleasure? Elicit things from her she never knew existed?

Before she could dwell on any answers to her questions, he deepened the kiss and began mating with her mouth with an intensity and hunger that made her stomach muscles quiver. It was a move she felt all the way to her toes. She felt herself becoming feverish, hot and needy. When it came to a man, she'd never been needy.

He slanted his head, taking the kiss deeper still, while tangling with her tongue in a way she had dreamed about only moments earlier. But now she was getting the real thing and not mere snippets of a fantasy. He wasn't holding back on anything and his tongue was playing havoc with her senses in the process. It was a work of art, a sensuous skill. The way he'd managed to wrap his tongue around hers, only letting it go when it pleased him and capturing it again when he was ready to dispense even more pleasurable torture.

She had asked for this kiss and wasn't disappointed. Far from it. He was taking her over the edge in a way that would keep her falling with pleasure. His mouth seemed to fit hers perfectly, no matter what angle he took. And the more it plowed her mouth hungrily, the more every part of her body came alive in a way she wasn't used to.

She moaned deep in her throat when she felt the warmth of his fingers on her bare thigh and wondered when had he slid his hand under her skirt. When those fingers began inching toward her center, instinctively she shifted her body closer to his. The move immediately parted her thighs.

As if his fingers were fully aware of the impact they were having on her, they moved to stake a claim on her most intimate part. As his fingers slid beneath the waistband of her panties, she released another moan when his hand came into contact with her womanly folds. They were moist and she could feel the way his fingertips were spreading her juices all over it before he dipped a finger inside her.

The moment he touched her there, she pulled her mouth away from his to throw back her head in one deep moan. But he didn't let her mouth stay free for long. He recaptured it as his fingers caressed her insides in a way that almost made her weep, while his mouth continued to ply her with hungry kisses.

Suddenly she felt a sensation that started at her midsection and then spread throughout her body like tentacles of fire, building tension and strains of sensuous pressure in its wake. Her body instinctively pushed against his hand just as something within her snapped and then exploded, sending emotions, awareness and all kinds of feeling shooting all through her, flooding her with ecstasy.

Although this was the first time she'd ever experienced anything like it, she knew what it was. Callum had brought her to her first earthshaking and shattering climax. She'd heard about them and read about them, but had never experienced one before. Now she understood what it felt like to respond without limitations to a man.

When the feelings intensified, she pulled her mouth from his, closed her eyes and let out a deep piercing scream, unable to hold it back.

"That's it. Come for me, baby," he slurred thickly against her mouth before taking it again with a deep erotic thrust of his tongue.

And he kept kissing her in this devouring way of his until she felt deliciously sated and her body ceased its trembling. He finally released her mouth, but not before his tongue gave her lips a few parting licks. It was then that she opened her eyes, feeling completely drained but totally satisfied.

He held her gaze and she wondered what he was thinking. Had their business relationship been compromised? After all, he was her client and she had never been involved with a client before. And whether she'd planned it or not, they were involved. Just knowing there were more kisses where that one came from sent shivers of pleasure down her spine.

Better yet, if he could deliver this kind of pleasure to her mouth, she could just imagine what else he could do to other parts of her body, like her breasts, stomach, the area between her legs. The man possessed one hell of a dynamic tongue and he certainly knew how to use it.

Heat filled her face from those thoughts and she wondered if he saw it. At least he had no idea what she was thinking. Or did he? He hadn't said anything yet. He was just staring at her and licking his lips. She felt she should say something, but at the moment she was speechless. She'd just had her very first orgasm and she still had her clothes on. Amazing.

Callum's nostrils flared from the scent of a woman who'd been pleasured in the most primitive way. He would love to strip her naked and taste the dewy essence of her. Brand his tongue with her intimate juices, lap her up the way he'd dreamed of doing more times than he could count.

She was staring at him as if she was still trying to figure out why and how this thing had happened. He would allow her time to do that, but what he wouldn't tolerate was her thinking that what they'd shared was wrong, because it wasn't. He would not accept any regrets.

The one thing he'd taken note of with his fingers

was that she was extremely tight. With most men that would send up a red flag, but not him because her sexual experience, or lack thereof, didn't matter. However, if she hadn't been made love to before, he wanted to know it.

He opened his mouth to ask her, but she spoke before he could do so. "We should not have done that, Callum."

She could say that? While his hand was still inside of her? Maybe she had forgotten where his fingers were because they weren't moving. He flexed them, and when she immediately sucked in a deep breath as her gaze darkened with desire, he knew he'd succeeded in reminding her.

And while she watched, he slid his hand from inside of her and moments later he brought it to his lips and licked every finger that had been inside her. He then raked one finger across her lips before leaning down and tracing with his tongue where his finger had touched her mouth before saying, "With that I have to disagree." He spoke in a voice so throaty he barely recognized it as his own.

Her taste sent even more desire shooting through him. "Why do you feel that way, Gemma?"

He saw her throat move when she swallowed with her eyes still latched on his. "You're my client."

"Yes. And I just kissed you. One has nothing to do with the other. I hired you because I know you will do a good job. I just kissed you because—"

"I asked you to?"

He shook his head. "No, because I wanted to and because you wanted me to do it, too."

She nodded. "Yes," she said softly. "I wanted you to."

"Then there's no place for regrets and our attraction to each other has nothing to do with your decorating my home, so you can kill that idea here and now."

She didn't say anything for a moment and then she asked, "What about me being Ramsey's sister? Does that mean anything to you?"

A smile skidded across his lips. "I consider myself one of Ramsey's closest friends. Does that mean anything to you?"

She nervously nibbled on her bottom lip. "Yes. He will probably have a fit if he ever finds out we're attracted to each other."

"You think so?"

"Yes," she said promptly, without thinking much about his question. "Don't you?"

"No. Your brother is a fair man who recognizes you as the adult you are."

She rolled her eyes. "Are we talking about the same Ramsey Westmoreland?"

He couldn't help but grin. "Yes, we're talking about the same Ramsey Westmoreland. My best friend and your brother. You will always be one of his younger sisters, especially since he had a hand in raising you. Ramsey will always feel that he has a vested interest in your happiness and will always play the role of your protector, and understandably so. However, that doesn't mean he doesn't recognize that you're old enough to make your own decisions about your life."

She didn't say anything and he knew she was thinking hard about what he'd said. To reinforce the meaning of his words, he added. "Besides, Ramsey knows I would never take advantage of you, Gemma. I am not that kind of guy. I ask before I take. But remember, you always have the right to say no." A part of him hoped she would never say no to any direction their attraction might lead.

"I need to think about this some more, Callum."

He smiled. "Okay. That's fine. Now it's time for us to go inside."

He moved to open the door and she reached out and touched his hand. "And you won't try kissing me again?"

He reached out and pushed a strand of hair away from her face. "No, not unless you ask me to or give me an indication that's what you want me to do. But be forewarned, Gemma. If you ask, then I will deliver because I intend to be the man who will give you everything you want."

He then got out of the car and strolled to the other side to open the door for her.

He intended to being the man who gave her everything she wanted? A puzzled Gemma walked beside Callum toward his front door. When had he decided that? Before the kiss, during the kiss or after the kiss?

She shook her head. It definitely hadn't been before. Granted, they'd come close to kissing on the plane, but that had been the heat of the moment, due to an attraction that had begun sizzling below the surface. But that attraction didn't start until… When?

She pulled in a deep breath, really not certain. She'd always noticed him as a man from afar, but only in a complimentary way, since she'd assumed that he was taken. But she would be the first to admit that once he'd told her he wasn't, she'd begun seeing him in a whole different light. But she'd been realistic enough to know that, given the ten-year difference in their ages and the fact he was Ramsey's best friend, chances were that even if she was interested in him there was no way he would reciprocate that interest.

Or had it been during the kiss, when he had shown her just what a real kiss was like? Had he detected that this was her first real kiss? She'd tried following his lead, but when that lead began taking her so many different places and had made her feel a multitude of emotions and sensations she hadn't been used to, she just gave up following and let him take complete control. She had not been disappointed.

Her first orgasm had left every cell in her body feeling strung from one end to the other. She wondered just how many women could be kissed into an orgasm? She wondered how it would be if she and Callum actually made love. The pleasure just might kill her.

But then, he might have decided that he was the man to give her whatever she wanted after the kiss, when she was trying to regain control of her senses. Did he see her as a novelty? Did he want to rid her of her naiveté about certain things that happen between a man and a woman?

Evidently, he thought differently about how her oldest brother saw things. Well, she wasn't as certain as he was about Ramsey's reaction. She was well aware that she was an adult, old enough to call the shots about her own life. But with all the trouble the twins, Bane and Bailey had given everyone while growing up, she had promised herself never to cause Ramsey any unnecessary grief.

Although she would be the first to admit that she had a tendency to speak her mind whenever it suited her and she could be stubborn to a fault at times, she basically didn't cross people unless they crossed her. Those who'd known her great-grandmother—the first Gemma Westmoreland—who'd been married to Raphel, said she had inherited that attitude from her namesake. That's probably why so many family members believed there was more to the story about her great-grandfather Raphel and his bigamist ways that was yet to be uncovered. She wasn't as anxious about uncovering the truth as Dillon had been, but she knew Megan and some of her cousins were.

She stopped walking once they reached the door and Callum pulled a key from his pocket. She glanced around and saw that this particular building was set apart from the others on a secluded cul-de-sac. And it was also on a lot larger than the others, although, to her way of thinking, all of them appeared massive. "Why is your condo sitting on a street all by itself?" she asked.

"I wanted it that way for privacy."

"And they obliged you?"

He smiled. "Yes, since I bought all the other lots on this side of the complex as buffers. I didn't want to feel crowded. I'm used to a lot of space, but I liked the area because the beach is practically in my backyard."

She couldn't wait to see that, since Denver didn't have beaches. There was the Rocky Mountain Beach that included a stretch of sand but wasn't connected to an ocean like a real beach.

"Welcome to my home, Gemma."

He stood back and she stepped over the threshold at the same exact moment that he flicked a switch and the lights came on. She glanced around in awe. The interior of his home was simply beautiful and unless he had hidden decorating skills she wasn't aware of, she had to assume that he'd retained the services of a professional designer for this place, too. His colors, masculine in nature, were well-coordinated and blended together perfectly.

She moved farther into the room, taking note of everything—from the Persian rugs on the beautifully polished walnut floors, to the decorative throw pillows on the sofa, to the style of curtains and blinds that covered the massive windows. The light colors of the window treatments made each room appear larger in dimension and the banister of the spiral staircase that led to another floor gave the condo a sophisticated air.

When Callum crossed the room and lifted the blinds, she caught her breath. He hadn't lied when he'd said the beach was practically in his backyard. Even at night, thanks to the full moon overhead, she could see the beautiful waters of the Pacific Ocean.

Living away from home while attending college had taken care of any wanderlust she might have had at one time. Seeing the world had never topped her list. She was more than satisfied with the one hundred acres she had acquired on her twenty-first birthday—an inheritance for each of the Westmorelands. The section of Denver most folks considered as Westmoreland Country was all the home she'd ever known and had ever wanted. But she would have to admit that all she'd seen of Sydney so far was making it a close second.

Callum turned back to her. "So what do you think?"

Gemma smiled. "I think I'm going to love it here."

Eight

The next morning, after taking his shower, Callum dressed as he gazed out his bedroom window at the beautiful waters of the ocean. For some reason he believed it was going to be a wonderful day. He was back home and the woman he intended to share his life with was sleeping under his roof.

As he stepped into his shoes, he had to admit that he missed being back in Denver, working the ranch and spending time with the men he'd come to know over the past three years. During that time Ramsey had needed his help and they'd formed a close bond. Now Ramsey's life had moved in another direction. Ramsey was truly happy. He had a wife and a baby on the way and Callum was happy for his friend.

And more than anything he intended to find some of that same happiness for himself.

As he buttoned up his shirt, he couldn't help but think about the kiss he and Gemma had shared last night. The taste of her was still on his tongue. He'd told her that he wouldn't kiss her again until she gave the word, and he intended to do everything within his power to make sure she gave it—and soon.

The one thing he knew about Gemma was that she was stubborn. If you wanted to introduce an idea to her, you had to make her think that it had been *her* idea. Otherwise, she would balk at any suggestion you made. He had no problems doing that. When he put his seduction plan into motion, he would do it in such a way that she would think she was seducing him.

The thought of such a thing—her seducing him—had his manhood flexing. Although his feelings for Gemma were more than sexual, he couldn't help those nightly dreams that had plagued him since first meeting her. He'd seen her stripped bare—in his dreams. He'd tasted every inch of her body—in his dreams. And in his dreams he'd constantly asked what she wanted. What she needed from him to prove that she was his woman in every way.

Last night after he'd shown her the guestroom she would be using and had brought in their luggage, she had told him she was still suffering from jet lag and planned to retire early. She had quickly moved into her bedroom and had been sequestered there ever since. That was fine. In time she would find out that, when it came to him, she could run but she most certainly couldn't hide.

He would let her try to deny this thing that was developing between them, but she would discover soon enough that he was her man.

But what he wanted and needed right now was another kiss. He smiled, thinking his job was to make sure she felt that she needed another kiss as well. And as he walked out of his bedroom he placed getting another kiss at the top of his agenda.

Gemma stood in her bare feet in front of the window in Callum's kitchen as she gazed out at the beach. The view was simply amazing. She'd never seen anything like it.

One year while in college, during spring break weekend, she and a few friends had driven from Nebraska to Florida to spend the weekend on the beach in Pensacola. There she had seen a real beach with miles and miles of the purest blue-green waters. She was convinced that the Pacific Ocean was even more breathtaking and she'd come miles and miles away from home to see it.

Home.

Although she did miss home, she considered being in Australia an adventure as well as a job. Because of the difference in time zones, when she'd retired last night, she hadn't made any calls, but she intended to try to do so today. Megan was keeping tabs on the bank situation involving Niecee. With the money Callum had advanced her, her bank account was in pretty good shape, with more than enough funds to cover her debts. But she had no intention of letting Niecee get away with what she'd done. She had yet to tell anyone else in the family, other than Megan and Bailey, about the incident and planned on keeping things that way until the funds had been recovered and were back in her bank account.

She took another sip of her coffee, thinking about the kiss she and Callum had shared last night. Okay, she would admit it had been more than off the chain and the climax was simply shocking. Just the thought gave her sensuous shivers and was making her body tingle all over. What Callum had done with his tongue in her mouth and his fingers between her legs made her blush.

It had been hard getting to sleep. More than once she had dreamed of his tongue seeking hers and now that she was fully aware of what he could do with that tongue and those fingers, she wanted more.

She drew in a deep breath, thinking there was no way she would ask for a repeat performance. She could now stake a claim to knowing firsthand what an orgasm was about with her virginity still intact. Imagine that.

She couldn't imagine it when part of her dream last night dwelled on Callum making love to her and taking away her innocence, something she'd never thought of sharing with another man. The thought of being twenty-four and a virgin had never bothered her. What bothered her was knowing that there was a lot more pleasure out there that she was missing out on. Pleasure she was more than certain Callum could deliver, with or without a silver platter.

All she had to do was tell him what she wanted.

"Good morning, Gemma."

She turned around quickly, surprised that she had managed to keep from spilling her coffee. She hadn't heard Callum come down the stairs. In fact, she hadn't heard him moving around upstairs. And now he stood in the middle of his kitchen, dressed in a way she'd never seen before.

He was wearing an expensive-looking gray suit. Somehow he had gone from being a sheep-ranch manager to a well-groomed, sophisticated and suave businessman. But then the chestnut-brown hair flowing around his shoulders gave him a sort of rakish look. She wasn't sure what to make of the change and just which Callum Austell she most preferred.

"Good morning, Callum," she heard herself say, trying not to get lost in the depths of his green eyes. "You're already dressed and I'm not." She glanced down at herself. In addition to not wearing shoes, she had slipped into one of those cutesy sundresses Bailey had given as a gift for her birthday.

"No problem. The house isn't going anywhere. It will be there when you're ready to see it. I thought I'd go into the office today and let everyone know that I'm back for a while."

She lifted a brow. "The office?"

"Yes, Le'Claire Developers. It's a land development company similar to Blue Ridge Land Management. But also under the umbrella of Le'Claire are several smaller sheep ranches on the same scale as Ramsey's."

"And you are…"

"The CEO of Le'Claire," he said.

"You named it after your mother?"

He chuckled. "No, my father named it after my mother. When we all turned twenty-one, according to the terms of a trust my great-grandfather established, all four of us were set up in our own businesses. Morris, being the firstborn, will inherit the sheep farms that have been in the Austell family for generations as well as stock in all the businesses his siblings control. Colin is CEO of the chain of hotels my family owns. The one we stayed in the other night is one of them. Le'Shaunda received a slew of supermarket chains, and I was given a land development company and several small sheep ranches. Although I'm CEO, I have a staff capable of running things in my absence."

Gemma nodded, taking all this in. Bailey had tried telling her and Megan that she'd heard that Callum was loaded in his own right, but she really hadn't believed her. Why would a man as wealthy as Bailey claimed Callum was settle for being the manager of someone else's sheep ranch? Granted, he and Ramsey were close, but she couldn't see them being *so* close that Callum would give up a life of wealth and luxury for three years to live in a small cabin on her brother's property.

"Why did you do it?" she heard herself asking.

"Why did I do what?"

"It's obvious that you have money, so why would you give all this up for three years and work as the manager of my brother's sheep ranch?"

This, Callum thought, would be the perfect time to sit Gemma down and explain things to her, letting her know the reason he'd hung around Denver for three years. But he had a feeling just like when his father had tried explaining to his mother about her being his soul mate and it hadn't gone over well, it wouldn't go over well with Gemma, either.

According to Todd Austell, trying to convince Le'Claire Richards it had been love at first sight was the hardest thing he ever had to do. In fact, she figured he wanted to marry her to rebel against his parents trying to pick out a wife for him and not because he was truly in love with her.

Callum was sure that over the years his mother had pretty much kissed that notion goodbye, because there wasn't a single day that passed when his father didn't show his mother how much he loved her. Maybe that's why it came so easily to Callum to admit that he loved a woman. His father was a great role model.

But still, when it came to an Austell falling in love, Callum had a feeling that Gemma would be just as skeptical as his mother had been. So there was no way he could tell her the full truth of why he had spent three years practically right in her backyard.

"I needed to get away from my family for a while," he heard himself saying, which really wasn't a lie. He had been wild and reckless in his younger years, and returning home from college hadn't made things any better. The death of his grandfather had.

He had loved the old man dearly and he would have to say that his grandfather had spoiled him rotten. With the old man gone, there was no one to make excuses for him, no one to get him out of the scrapes he got into and no one who would listen to whatever tale he decided to fabricate. His father had decided that the only way to make him stand on his own was to make him work for it. So he had.

He had worked on his parents' ranch for a full year, right alongside the other ranch hands, to prove his worth. It had only been after he'd succeeded in doing that that his father had given him Le'Claire to run. But by then Callum had decided he much preferred a ranch-hand bunk to a glamorous thirty-floor high rise overlooking the harbor. So he had hired the best management team money could buy to run his corporation while he returned to work on his parents' ranch. That's when he'd met Ramsey and the two had quickly become fast friends.

"I understand," said Gemma, cutting into his thoughts.

He lifted a brow. He had expected her to question him further. "You do?"

"Yes. That's why Bane left home to join the Navy. He needed his space from us for a while. He needed to find himself."

Brisbane was her cousin Dillon's baby brother. From what Callum had heard, Bane had been only eight when his parents had been killed. He had grieved for them in a different way than the others, by fighting to get the attention he craved. When he'd graduated from high school, he had refused to go to college. After numerous brushes with the law and butting heads with the parents of a young lady who didn't want him to be a part of their daughter's life, Dillon had convinced Bane to get his life together. Everyone was hoping the military would eventually make a man of him.

Callum decided that he didn't want to dig himself in any deeper than he'd be able to pull himself out of when he finally admitted the truth to Gemma. "Would you like to go into the office with me for a while today? Who knows? You might be able to offer me a few decorating suggestions for there as well."

Her face lit up and he thought at that moment, she

could decorate every single thing he owned if it would get him that smile.

"You'd give me that opportunity?"

He held back from saying, *I'll give you every single thing you want, Gemma Westmoreland.* "Yes, but only if it's within my budget," he said instead.

She threw her head back and laughed, and the hair that went flying around her shoulders made his body hard. "We'll see if we can work something out," she said, moving toward the stairs. "It won't take long for me to dress. I promise."

"Take your time," he said to her fleeting back. He peeped around the corner and caught a glimpse of long, shapely legs when she lifted the hem of her outfit to rush up the stairs. His body suddenly got harder with a raw, primitive need.

He went over to the counter to pour a cup of the coffee she'd prepared, thinking he hadn't gotten that kiss yet, but he was determined to charm it out of her at some point today.

"Welcome back, Mr. Austell."

"Thanks, Lorna. Is everyone here?" Callum asked the older woman sitting behind the huge desk.

"Yes, sir. They are here and ready for today's meeting."

"Good. I'd like you to meet Gemma Westmoreland, one of my business associates. Gemma this is Lorna Guyton."

The woman switched her smile over to Gemma, who was standing by Callum's side. "Nice meeting you, Ms. Westmoreland," the woman said, offering Gemma her hand.

"Same here, Ms. Guyton." Gemma couldn't help but be pleased with the way Callum had introduced her. Saying she was a business associate sounded a lot better than saying she was merely the woman decorating one of his homes.

She glanced around, taking mental note of the layout of this particular floor of the Le'Claire Building. When they had pulled into the parking garage, she had definitely been impressed with the thirty-floor skyscraper. So far, the only thing she thought she would change with respect to the interior design, if given the chance, was the selection of paintings on the various walls.

"You can announce us to the team, Lorna," Callum said, and placing his hand on Gemma's arm, he led her toward the huge conference room.

Gemma had caught the word *us* the moment Callum touched her arm and wasn't sure which had her head suddenly spinning more—him including her in his business meeting or the way her body reacted to his touch.

She had assumed that since he would be talking business he would want her to wait in the reception area near Lorna's desk. But the fact that he had included her sent a degree of pleasure up her spine and filled her with an unreasonable degree of importance.

Now if she could just stop the flutters from going off in her stomach with the feel of his hand on her arm. But then she'd been getting all kinds of sensations—more so than ever—since they had kissed. When he'd walked into the kitchen this morning looking like he should be

on the cover of *GQ* magazine, a rush of blood had shot
to her head and it was probably still there. She'd had
to sit beside him in the car and draw in his scent with
every breath she took. And it had been hard sitting in
that seat knowing what had happened last night while
she'd been sitting there. On the drive over, her body had
gone through some sort of battle, as if it was craving
again what it once had.

"Good morning, everyone."

Gemma's thoughts were interrupted when Callum
swept her into the large conference room where several
people sat waiting expectantly. The men stood and the
women smiled and gave her curious glances.

Callum greeted everyone by name and introduced
Gemma the same way he had in speaking to Lorna.
When he moved toward the chair at the head of the
table, she stepped aside to take a chair in the back of
the room. However, he gently tightened his grip on her
arm and kept her moving toward the front with him.

He then pulled out the empty chair next to his for her
to sit in. Once she had taken her seat, he took his and
smiled over at her before calling the meeting to order
in a deep, authoritative voice.

She couldn't help but admire how efficient he was and
had to remind herself several times during the course
of the business meeting that this was the same Callum
who'd managed her brother's sheep farm. The same
Callum who would turn feminine heads around town
when he wore tight-fitting jeans over taut hips and an
ultrafine tush, and sported a Western shirt over broad
shoulders.

And this was the same Callum who had made her

scream with pleasure last night…in his car of all places. She glanced over at his hand, the same one whose fingers were now holding an ink pen, and remembered just where that hand had been last night and what he'd been doing with those fingers.

Suddenly, she felt very hot and figured that as long as she kept looking at his hands she would get even hotter. Over the course of the hour-long meeting, she tried to focus her attention on other things in the room like the paintings on the wall, the style of window treatments and carpeting. Given the chance, she would spruce things up in here. Unlike the other part of the office, for some reason this particular room seemed a little drab. In addition to the boring pictures hanging on the walls, the carpeting lacked any depth. She wondered what that was all about. Evidently, no one told the prior interior designer that the coloring of carpet in a business often set the mood of the employees.

"I see everyone continues to do a fantastic job for me in my absence and I appreciate that. This meeting is now adjourned," Callum said.

Gemma glanced up to see everyone getting out of their seats, filing out of the room and closing the door behind them. She turned to find Callum staring at her. "What's wrong? You seemed bored," he said.

She wondered how he'd picked up on it when his full attention should have been on the meeting he was conducting. But since he had noticed…

"Yes, but I couldn't help it. This room will bore you to tears and I have a bucket full of them." She glanced around the room. "Make that *two* buckets."

Callum threw his head back and laughed. "Do you always say whatever suits you?"

"Hey, you did ask. And yes, I usually say whatever suits me. Didn't Ramsey warn you that I have no problem giving my opinion about anything?"

"Yes, he did warn me."

She gave him a sweet smile. "Yet you hired me anyway, so, unfortunately, you're stuck with me."

Callum wanted nothing more than to lean over and plant a kiss firmly on Gemma's luscious lips and say that being stuck with her was something he looked forward to. Instead, he checked his watch. "Do you want to grab lunch before we head over to the house you'll be decorating? Then while we eat you can tell me why you have so many buckets of tears from this room."

She chuckled as she stood up. "Gladly, Mr. Austell."

Nine

"Well, here we are and I want you to tell me just what you can do with this place."

Gemma heard Callum's words, but her gaze was on the interior of a monstrosity of a house. She was totally in awe. There weren't too many homes that could render her speechless, but this mansion had before she'd stepped over the threshold. The moment he'd pulled into the driveway, she'd been overwhelmed by the architecture of it. She'd known when she'd originally seen the design of the home on paper that it was a beauty, but actually seeing it in all its grandiose splendor was truly a breathtaking moment.

"Give me the history of this house," she said, glancing around at the elegant staircase, high sculptured ceilings, exquisite crown molding and gorgeous wood floors. And for some reason she believed Callum knew it. Just from her observation of him during that morning's meeting, she'd determined that he was an astute businessman, sharp as a tack, although he preferred sporting jeans and messing with sheep to wearing a business suit and tweaking mission statements.

Over lunch she'd asked how he'd managed to keep up with his business affairs with Le'Claire while working for Ramsey. He'd explained that he had made trips back home several times when his presence had been needed on important matters. In addition, the cottage he occupied in Denver had a high-speed Internet connection, a fax machine and whatever else was needed to keep in touch with his team in Australia. And due to the difference in time zones, six in the evening in Denver was ten in the morning the next day in Sydney. He'd been able to call it a day with Ramsey around five, go home and shower and be included in a number of critical business meetings by way of conference call by seven.

"This area is historic Bellevue Hills and this house was once owned by one of the richest men in Australia. Shaun told me about it, thought I should take a look at it and make the seller an offer. I did."

"Just like that?" she asked, snapping her fingers for effect.

He met her gaze. "Just like that," he said, snapping his.

She couldn't help but laugh. "I like the way you think, Callum, because, as I said, this place is a beauty."

He shifted his gaze away from her to look back at the house. "So, it's a place where you think the average woman would want to live?"

She placed her hands on her hips. "Callum, the

average woman would die to live in a place like this. This is practically a mansion. It's fit for a queen. I know because I consider myself the average woman and I would."

"You would?"

"Of course. Now, I'm dying to take a look around and make some decorating suggestions."

"As extensive as the ones you made at lunch regarding that conference room at Le'Claire?"

"Probably," she said with a smile. "But I won't know until I go through it and take measurements." She pulled her tape measure out of her purse.

"Let's go."

He touched her arm and the moment he did so, she felt that tingling sensation that always came over her when he touched her, but now the sensations were even stronger than before.

"You okay, Gemma? You're shivering."

She drew in a deep breath as they moved from the foyer toward the rest of the house. "Yes, I'm fine," she said, refusing to look at him. *If only he knew the truth about how she was feeling.*

Callum leaned against the kitchen counter and stared over at Gemma as she stood on a ladder taking measurements of a particular window. She had long ago shed her jacket and kicked off her shoes. He looked down at her feet and thought she had pretty toes.

They had been here a couple of hours already and there were still more measurements to take. He didn't mind if he could continue to keep her up there on a ladder. Once in a while, when she moved, he'd get a glimpse of her gorgeous legs and her luscious-looking thighs.

"You're quiet."

Her observation broke into his thoughts. "What I'm doing is watching you," he said. "Having fun?"

"The best kind there is. I love doing this and I'm going to love decorating this house for you." She paused a second. "Unfortunately, I have some bad news for you."

He lifted a brow. "What bad news?"

She smiled down at him. "What I want to do in here just might break you. And, it will take me longer than the six weeks planned."

He nodded. Of course, he couldn't tell her he was counting on that very thing. "I don't have a problem with that. How is your work schedule back in Denver? Will remaining here a little longer cause problems for you?"

"No. I finished all my open projects and was about to take a vacation before bidding on others, so that's fine with me if you think you can handle a houseguest for a little while longer."

"Absolutely."

She chuckled. "You might want to think about it before you give in too easily."

"No, you might want to think about it before you decide to stay."

She glanced down at him and went perfectly still and he knew at that moment she was aware of what he was thinking. Although they had enjoyed each other's company, they had practically walked on eggshells around each other all day. After lunch he'd taken her on a tour of downtown and showed her places like the Sydney Opera House, the Royal Botanic Gardens and St. Andrew's Cathedral. And they had fed seagulls in Hyde Park before coming here. Walking beside her seemed natural, and for a while they'd held hands. Each time he had touched her she had trembled.

Did she think he wasn't aware of what those shivers meant? Did she not know what being close to her was doing to him? Could she not see the male appreciation as well as the love shining in his eyes whenever he looked at her?

Breaking eye contact, he looked at his watch. "Do you plan to measure all the windows today?"

"No, I'd planned to make this my last one for now. You will bring me back tomorrow, though, right?"

"Just ask. Whatever you want, it's yours."

"In that case, I'd like to come back to finish up this part. Then we'll need to decide on what fabrics you want," she said, moving to step down from the ladder. "The earlier the better, especially if it's something I need to backorder."

He moved away from the counter to hold the ladder steady while she descended. "Thanks," she said, when her bare feet touched the floor. He was standing right there in front of her.

"Don't mention it," he said. "Ready to go?"

"Yes."

Instead of taking her hand, he walked beside her and said nothing. He felt her looking over at him, but he refused to return her gaze. He had promised that the next time they kissed she would ask for it, but she'd failed to do that, which meant that when they got back to his place he would turn up the heat.

"You all right, Callum?"

"Yes, I'm fine. Where would you like to eat? It's dinnertime."

"Doesn't matter. I'm up for anything."

He smiled when an idea popped into his head. "Then how about me preparing dinner tonight."

She lifted a brow. "Can you cook?"

"I think I might surprise you."

She chuckled. "In that case, surprise me."

Whatever you want, it's yours.

Gemma stepped out of the Jacuzzi to dry herself while thinking that Callum had been saying that a lot lately. She wondered what he would think of her if she were to tell him that what she wanted more than anything was another dose of the pleasure he'd introduced her to last night.

Being around him most of the day had put her nerves on edge. Every time he touched her or she caught him looking at her, she felt an overwhelming need to explore the intense attraction between them. His mouth and fingers had planted a need within her that was so profound, so incredibly physical, that certain parts of her body craved his touch.

She'd heard of people being physically attracted to each other to the point of lust consuming their mind and thoughts, but such a thing had never happened to her. Until now. And why was it happening at all? What was there about Callum—other than the obvious—that had her in such a tizzy? He made her want things she'd never had before. She was tempted to go further with him than she had with any other man.

In a way she had already done that last night. There was no other man on the face of this earth who could ever lay a claim to fingering her. But Callum had done that while kissing her senseless, stirring a degree of passion within her that even now made her heart beat faster just thinking about it.

She shook her head, and tried to get a grip but failed to do so. She couldn't let go of the memories of how her body erupted in one mind-shattering orgasm. Now she knew what full-blown pleasure was about. But she knew that she hadn't even reached the tip of the iceberg and her body was aching to get pushed over that turbulent edge. The thought that there was something even more powerful, more explosive to experience sent sensual shivers through her entire being.

There were a number of reasons why she should not be thinking of indulging in an affair with Callum. And yet, there were a number of reasons why she should. She was a twenty-four-year-old virgin. To give her virginity to Callum was a plus in her book, because, in addition to being attracted to him, he would know what he was doing. She'd heard horror stories about men who didn't.

And if they were to have an affair, who would know? He wasn't the type to kiss and tell. And he didn't seem bothered by the fact that his best friend was her brother. Besides, since he would be returning to Australia to live, she didn't have the worry about running into him on a constant basis, seeing him and being reminded of what they'd done.

So what was holding her back?

She knew the answer to that question. It was the same reason she was still a virgin. She was afraid the guy she would give her virginity to would also capture her heart. And the thought of any man having her heart was something she just couldn't abide. What if he were to hurt her, break her heart the way her brothers had done to all those girls?

She nibbled on her bottom lip as she slipped into her dress to join Callum for dinner. Somehow she would have to find a way to experience pleasure without the possibility of incurring heartache. She should be able to make love with a man without getting attached. Men did it all the time. She would enter into the affair with both eyes open and not expect any more than what she got. And when it was over, her heart would still be intact. She wouldn't set herself up like those other girls who'd fancied themselves in love with a Westmoreland, only to have their hearts broken.

It should be a piece of cake. After all, Callum had told her he was waiting to meet his soul mate. So there would be no misunderstanding on either of their parts. She wasn't in love with him and he wasn't in love with her. He would get what he wanted and she would be getting what she wanted.

More of last night.

A smile of anticipation touched her lips. She mustn't appear too eager and intended to play this out for all it was worth and see how long it would last. She was inexperienced when it came to seduction, but she was a quick study.

And Callum was about to discover just how eager she was to learn new things.

Callum heard Gemma moving around upstairs. He had encouraged her to relax and take a bubble bath in the huge Jacuzzi garden tub while he prepared dinner.

Since they'd eaten a large lunch at one of the restaurants downtown near the Sydney Harbour, he decided to keep dinner simple—a salad and an Aussie meat pie.

He couldn't help but smile upon recalling her expression when she'd first seen his home, and her excitement about decorating it just the way she liked. He had gone along with every suggestion she made, and although she had teased him about the cost, he knew she was intentionally trying to keep prices low, even though he'd told her that doing so wasn't necessary.

His cell phone rang and he pulled it off his belt to answer it. "Hello."

"How are you doing, Callum?"

He smiled upon hearing his mother's voice. "I'm fine, Mom. What about you?"

"I'm wonderful. I hadn't talked to you since you were here yesterday with Gemma, and I just want you to know that I think she's a lovely girl."

"Thanks, Mom. I think so, too. I just can't wait for her to figure out she's my soul mate."

"Have patience, Callum."

He chuckled. "I'll try."

"I know Gemma is going to be tied up with decorating that house, but Shaun and I were wondering if she'll be free to do some shopping with us next Friday," his mother said. "Annette and Mira will be joining us as well."

The thought of Gemma being out of his sight for any period of time didn't sit well with him. He knew all about his mother, sister and sisters-in-law's shopping trips. They could be gone for hours. He felt like a possessive lover. A smile touched his lips. He wasn't Gemma's lover yet, but he intended to be while working diligently to become a permanent part of her life—namely, her husband.

"Callum?"

"Yes, Mom. I'm sure that's something Gemma will enjoy. She's upstairs changing for dinner. I'll have her call you."

He conversed with his mother for a little while longer before ending the call. Pouring a glass of wine, he moved to the window that looked out over the Pacific. His decision to keep this place had been an easy one. He loved the view as well as the privacy.

The house Gemma was decorating was in the suburbs, sat on eight acres of land and would provide plenty of room for the large family he wanted them to have. He took a sip of wine while his mind imagined a pregnant Gemma, her tummy round with his child.

He drew in a deep breath, thinking that if anyone would have told him five years ago that he would be here in this place and in this frame of mind, he would have been flabbergasted. His mother suggested that he have patience. He'd shown just how much patience he had for the past three years. Now it was time to make his move.

"Callum?"

The sound of her voice made him turn around. He swallowed deeply, while struggling to stay where he was, not cross the room, pull her into his arms and give her the greeting that he preferred. As usual, she looked beautiful, but there was something different about her this evening. There was a serene glow to her face that hadn't been there before. Had just two days in Australia done that to her? Hell, he hoped so. More than anything, he wanted his native land to grow on her.

"You look nice, Gemma," he heard himself saying.

"Thanks. You look nice yourself."

He glanced down at himself. He had changed out of his suit, and was now wearing jeans and a pullover shirt. She was wearing an alluring little outfit—a skirt that fell a little past her knees, a matching top and a cute pair of sandals. He looked at her and immediately thought of one word. *Sexy*. Umm, make that two words. *Super sexy*. He knew of no other woman who wore her sexuality quite the way Gemma did.

His gaze roamed the full length of her in male appreciation, admiring the perfection of her legs, ankles and calves. He had to have patience, as his mother suggested and tamp down his rising desire. But all he had to do was breathe in, take a whiff of her scent and know that would not be an easy task.

"What are you drinking?"

Her words pulled his attention from her legs back to her face. "Excuse me? I missed that."

A smile curved her lips. "I asked what you're drinking."

He held up his glass and glanced at it. "Wine. Want some?"

"Sure."

"No problem. I'll pour you a glass," he said.

"No need," she said, walking slowly toward him. He felt his pulse rate increase and his breathing get erratic with every step she took.

"I'll just share yours," she said, coming to a stop in front of him. She reached out, slid the glass from his hand and took a sip. But not before taking the tip of her tongue and running it along the entire rim of the glass.

Callum sucked in a quick breath. Did she know how intimate that gesture was? He watched as she then took a sip. "Nice, Callum. Australia's finest, I assume."

He had to swallow before answering, trying to retain control of his senses. "Yes, a friend of my father owns a winery. There's plenty where that came from. Would you like some more?"

Her smile widened. "No, thank you. But there is something that I do want," she said, taking a step closer to him.

"Is there?" he said, forcing the words out of a tight throat. "You tell me what you want and, as I said yesterday and again today, whatever you want I will deliver."

She leaned in closer and whispered. "I'm holding you to your word, Callum Austell, because I've decided that I want you."

Ten

Gemma half expected Callum to yank her down and take her right there on the living room floor. After all, she'd just stated that she wanted him, and no one would have to read between the lines to figure out what that meant. Most men would immediately act on her request, not giving her the chance to change her mind.

Instead, Callum deliberately and slowly put his glass down. His gaze locked with hers and when his hands went to her waist he moved, bringing their bodies in close contact. "And what you want, Gemma, is just what you will get."

She saw intense heat in the depths of his eyes just seconds before he lowered his mouth to hers. The moment she felt his tongue invade her mouth, she knew he would be kissing her senseless.

He didn't disappoint her.

The last time they'd kissed, he had introduced her to a range of sensations that she'd never encountered before. Sensations that started at her toes and worked their way up to the top of her head. Sensations that had lingered in her lower half, causing the area between her legs to undergo all kinds of turbulent feelings and her heart all kinds of unfamiliar emotions.

This kiss was just as deadly, even more potent than the last, and her head began swimming in passion. She felt that drowning would soon follow. Blood was rushing, fast and furiously, through her veins with every stroke of his tongue. He was lapping her up in a way that had her entire body shuddering from the inside out.

Callum had encouraged her to ask for what she wanted and was delivering in full measure. He wasn't thinking about control of any kind and neither was she. He had addressed and put to rest the only two concerns she had—his relationship with her brother and her relationship with him as a client. Last night, he'd let her know that those two things had nothing to do with this— the attraction between them—and she was satisfied with that.

And now she was getting satisfied with this—his ability to deliver a kiss that was so passionate it was nearly engulfing her in flames. He was drinking her as if she were made of the finest wine, even finer than the one he'd just consumed.

She felt the arms around her waist tighten and when he shifted their positions she felt something else, the thick hardness behind the zipper of his jeans. When she moved her hip and felt his hard muscles aligned with her curves, the denim of his jeans rubbing against her bare legs, she moaned deep in her throat.

Callum released Gemma's mouth and drew in a deep breath and her scent. She smelled of the strawberry bubble bath she had used and whatever perfume she had dabbed on her body.

He brushed kisses across her forehead, eyebrows, cheeks and temples while giving her a chance to breathe. Her mouth was so soft and responsive, and it tasted so damn delicious. The more he deepened the kiss, the more responsive she became and the more accessible she made her mouth.

His hands eased from her waist to smooth across her back before cupping her backside. He could feel every inch of her soft curves beneath the material of her skirt and top, and instinctively, he pulled her closer to the fit of him.

"Do you want more?" he whispered against her lips, tasting the corners of her mouth while moaning deep in his throat from how good she tasted.

"Yes, I want more," she said in a purr that conveyed a little catch in her breathing.

"How much more?" He needed to know. Any type of rational thought and mind control was slipping away from him big time. It wouldn't take much to strip her naked right now.

He knew for a fact that she'd rarely dated during the time he'd been in Denver. And although he wasn't sure what she did while she was in college, he had a feeling his Gemma was still a virgin. The thought of that filled him with intense pride that she would give him the honor of being her first.

"I want all you can give me, Callum," she responded in a thick slur, but the words were clear to his ears.

He sucked a quick gulp of air into his lungs. He wondered if she had any idea what she was asking for. What he could give was a whole hell of a lot. If he had his way, he would keep her on her back for days. Stay inside her until he'd gotten her pregnant more times than humanly possible.

The thought of his seed entering her womanly channel, made the head of his erection throb behind his zipper, begging for release, practically pleading for the chance to get inside her wet warmth.

"Are you on any type of birth control?" He knew that she was. He had overheard a conversation once that she'd had with Bailey and knew she'd been taking oral contraceptives to regulate her monthly cycle.

"Yes, I'm on the pill," she acknowledged. "But not because I sleep around or anything like that. In fact, I'm…"

She stopped talking in midsentence and was gazing up at him beneath her long lashes. Her eyes were wide, as if it just dawned on her what she was about to reveal. He had no intention of letting her stop talking now.

"You're what?"

He watched as she began nervously nibbling on her bottom lip and he almost groaned, tempted to replace her lip with his and do the nibbling for her.

He continued to brush kisses across her face, drinking in her taste. And when she didn't respond to his inquiry, he pulled back and looked at her. "You can tell me anything, Gemma. Anything at all."

"I don't know," she said in a somewhat shaky voice. "It might make you want to stop."

Not hardly, he thought, and knew he needed to convince her of that. "There's nothing you can tell me that's going to stop me from giving you want you want. Nothing," he said fervently.

She gazed up into his eyes and he knew she believed him. She held the intensity in his gaze when she leaned forward and whispered. "I'm still a virgin."

"Oh, Gemma," he said, filled with all the love any man could feel for a woman at that particular moment. He had suspected as much, but until she'd confessed the truth, he hadn't truly been certain. Now he was, and the thought that he would be the man who carried her over the threshold of womanhood gave him pause, had him searching for words to let her know just how he felt.

He hooked her chin with his fingers as he continued to hold her gaze. "You trust me enough with such a precious gift?"

"Yes," she said promptly without hesitation.

Filled with both extreme pleasure and profound pride, he bent his head and kissed her gently while sweeping her off her feet into his arms.

When Callum placed her on his bed and stepped back to stare at her, one look at his blatantly aroused features let Gemma know that he was going to give her just what she had asked for. Just what she wanted.

Propped up against his pillow, she drank him in from head to toe as he began removing his shoes. Something—she wasn't sure just what—made her bold enough to ask. "Will you strip for me?"

He lifted his head and looked over at her. If he was shocked by her request, he didn't show it. "Is that what you want?"

"Yes."

He smiled and nodded. "No problem."

Gemma shifted her body into a comfortable position as a smile suffused her face. "Be careful or I'll begin to think you're easy."

He shrugged broad shoulders as he began removing his shirt. "Then I guess I'll just have to prove you wrong."

She chuckled. "Oooh, I can't wait." She stared at his naked chest. He was definitely built, she thought.

He tossed his shirt aside and when his hand went to the zipper of his jeans, a heated sensation began traveling along Gemma's nerve endings. When he began lowering the zipper, she completely held her breath.

He slid the zipper halfway down and met her gaze. "Something I need to confess before I go any further."

Her breath felt choppy. "What?"

"I dreamed about you last night."

Gemma smiled, pleased with his confession. "I have a confession of my own." He lifted his brows. "I dreamed about you, too. But, then, I think it was to be expected after last night."

He went back to slowly easing his zipper down. "You could have come to my bedroom. I would not have minded."

"I wasn't ready."

He didn't move as he held her gaze. "And now?"

She grinned. "And now I'm a lady-in-waiting."

He threw his head back and laughed as he began

sliding his pants down his legs. She scooted to the edge of the bed to watch, fascinated when he stood before her wearing a skimpy pair of black briefs. He had muscular thighs and a nice pair of hairy legs. The way the briefs fit his body had her shuddering when she should have been blushing.

All her senses suddenly felt hot-wired, her heart began thumping like crazy in her chest and a tingling sensation traveled up her nerve endings. She felt no shame in staring at him. The only thing she could think of at that moment was that *her* Aussie was incredibly sexy.

Her Aussie?

She couldn't believe her mind had conjured up such a thought. He wasn't hers and she wasn't his. At least not in *that* way. But tonight, she conceded, and whenever they made love, just for that moment, they would belong to each other in every way.

"Should I continue?"

She licked her lips in anticipation. "I might hurt you if you don't."

He chuckled as he slid his hands into the waistband of his briefs and slowly began easing them down his legs. "Oh my…" She could barely get the words past her throat.

Her breasts felt achy as she stared at that part of his anatomy, which seemed to get larger right before her eyes. She caught a lip between her teeth and tried not to clamp down too hard. But he had to be, without a doubt, in addition to being totally aroused and powerfully male, the most beautiful man she'd ever seen. And he stood there, with his legs braced apart, his hands on his hips and with a mass of hair flowing around his face, fully exposed to her. This was a man who could make women drool. A man who would get a second look whenever he entered a room, no matter what he was wearing. A man whose voice alone could make woman want to forget about being a good girl and just enjoy being bad.

She continued to stare, unable to do anything else, as he approached the bed. She moved into a sitting position to avoid being at eye level with his erection.

Gemma couldn't help wondering what his next move would be. Did he expect her to return the favor and strip for him? When he reached the edge of the bed, she tilted her head back and met his gaze. "My turn?"

He smiled. "Yes, but I want to do things differently."

She lifted a confused brow. "Differently?"

"Yes, instead of you stripping yourself, I want to do it."

She swallowed, not sure she understood. "You want to take my clothes off?"

He shook his head as a sexy smile touched his lips. "No, I want to strip your clothes off you."

And then he reached out and ripped off her blouse.

The surprised look on her face was priceless. Callum tossed her torn blouse across the room. And now his gaze was fixed on her chest and her blue satin push-up bra. Fascinated, he thought she looked sexy as hell.

"You owe me for that," she said when she found her voice.

"And I'll pay up," he responded as he leaned forward to release the front clasp and then eased the straps down her shoulders, freeing what he thought were perfect twin mounds with mouth-watering dark nipples.

His hand trembled when he touched them, fondled them between his eager fingers, while watching her watch him, and seeing how her eyes darkened, and how her breath came out in a husky moan.

"Hold those naughty thoughts, Gemma," he whispered when he released her and reached down to remove her sandals, rubbing his hands over her calves and ankles, while thinking her skin felt warm, almost feverish.

"Why do women torture their feet with these things?" His voice was deep and husky. He dropped the shoes by the bed.

"Because we know men like you enjoy seeing us in them."

He continued to rub her feet when he smiled. "I like seeing *you* in them. But then I like seeing you out of them, too."

His hand left her feet and began inching up her leg, past her knee to her thigh. But just for a second. His hand left her thigh and shifted over to the buttons on her skirt and with one tug sent them flying. She lifted her hips when he began pulling the skirt from her body and when she lay before him wearing nothing but a pair of skimpy blue panties, he felt blood rush straight to his heads. Both of them.

But it was the one that decided at that moment to almost double in size that commanded his attention. Without saying a word, he slowly began easing her panties down her thighs and her luscious scent began playing havoc with his nostrils as he did so.

He tossed her panties aside and his hands eased back

between her legs, seeing what he'd touched last night and watching once again as her pupils began dilating with pleasure.

And to make sure she got the full Callum Austell effect, he bent his head toward her chest, captured a nipple in his mouth and began sucking on it.

"Callum!"

"Umm?" He released that nipple only to move to the other one, licking the dark area before easing the tip between his lips and sucking on it as he'd done to the other one. He liked her taste and definitely liked the sounds she was making.

Moments later he began inching lower down her body and when his mouth came to her stomach, he traced a wet path all over it.

"Callum."

"I'm right here. You still sure you want me?" His fingers softly flicked across her womanly folds while he continued to lick her stomach.

"Oh, yes."

"Are there any limitations?" he asked.

"No."

"Sure?"

"Positive."

He took her at her word and moved his mouth lower. Her eyes began closing when he lifted her hips and wrapped her legs around his neck, lowered his head and pressed his open mouth to her feminine core.

Pleasure crashed over Gemma and she bit down to keep from screaming. Callum's tongue inside her was driving her crazy, and pushing her over the edge in a way she'd never been pushed before. Her body seemed to fragment into several pieces and each of those sections was being tortured by a warm, wet and aggressive tongue that was stroking her into a stupor.

Her hands grabbed tight to the bedspread as her legs were nudged further apart when his mouth burrowed further between her thighs and his tongue seem to delve inside her deeper.

She continued to groan in pleasure, not sure she would be able to stop moaning even when he ceased doing this to her. She released a deep moan when the pressure of his mouth on her was too much, and the erotic waves she was drowning in gave her little hope for a rescue.

And then, just like the night before, she felt her body jackknife into an orgasm that had her screaming. She was grateful for the privacy afforded by the seclusion of Callum's condo.

"Gemma."

Callum's deep Australian voice flowed through her mind as her body shuddered nearly uncontrollably. It had taken her twenty-four years to share this kind of intimacy with a man and it was well worth the wait.

"Open your eyes. I want you to be looking at me the moment I make you mine."

She lifted what seemed like heavy lids and saw that he was over her, his body positioned between her legs, and her hips were cupped in the palms of his hands. She pushed the thought out of her mind that she would never truly be his, and what he'd said was just a figure of speech, words just for the moment, and she understood because at this moment she wanted to be his.

As she gazed up into his eyes, something stirred

deep in her chest around her heart and she forced the feeling back, refusing to allow it to gain purchase there, rebuffing the very notion and repudiating the very idea. This was about lust, not love. He knew it and she knew it as well. There was nothing surprising about the way her body was responding to him; the way he seemed to be able to strum her senses the same way a musician strummed his guitar.

And then she felt him, felt the way his engorged erection was pressed against her femininity and she kept her gaze locked with his when she felt him make an attempt to slide into her. It wasn't easy. He was trying to stretch her and it didn't seem to be working. Sweat popped on his brow and she reached up and wiped his forehead with the back of her hand.

He saw her flinch in pain and he went still. "Do you want me to stop?"

She shook her head from side to side. "No. I want you to make it happen, and you said you'll give me what I want."

"Brat," he said. When she chuckled, he thrust forward. When she cried out he leaned in and captured her lips.

You truly belong to me now and I love you, Callum wanted to say, but knew that he couldn't. Instead, after her body had adjusted to his, he began moving. Every stroke into her body was a sign of his love whether she knew it or not. One day when she could accept it, she would know and he would gladly tell her everything.

He needed to kiss her, join his mouth to hers the same way their bodies were joined. So he leaned close and captured her mouth, kissing her thoroughly and hungrily, and with a passion he felt through every cell in his body.

When she instinctively began milking his erection, he deepened the kiss.

And when he felt her body explode, which triggered his to do likewise, he pulled his mouth from hers to throw his head back to scream her name. *Her name*. No other woman's name but hers, while he continued to thrust in and out of her.

His body had ached for this for so long, his body had ached for her. And as a climax continued to rip through them, he knew that, no matter what, Gemma Westmoreland was what he needed in his life and there was no way he would ever give her up.

Eleven

Sunlight flitting across her face made Gemma open her eyes and she immediately felt the hard muscular body sleeping beside her. Callum's leg was thrown over hers and his arms were wrapped around her middle. They were both naked—that was a given—and the even sound of his breathing meant he was still asleep.

The man was amazing. He had made love to her in a way that made her first time with a man so very special. He'd also fed her last night the tasty meal he'd prepared, surprising her and proving that he was just as hot in the kitchen as he was in the bedroom.

She drew in a deep breath, wondering which part of her was sorer, the area between her legs or her breasts. Callum had given special attention to both areas through most of the night. But with a tenderness that touched her deeply, he had paused to prepare a warm, soothing soak for her in his huge bathtub. He hadn't made love to her since then. They'd eaten a late dinner, and returning to bed, he had cuddled her in his arms, close to his warm, masculine body. His hands had caressed her all over, gently stroking her to sleep.

And now she was awake and very much aware of everything they'd done the night before. Everything she'd asked him for, he had delivered. Even when he had wanted to stop because last night was her first time, she had wanted to experience more pleasure and he had ended up making it happen, giving her what she wanted. And although her body felt sore and battered today, a part of her felt that last night had truly been worth it.

Deciding to get a little more sleep, she closed her eyes and immediately saw visions of them together. But it wasn't a recent image. She looked older and so did he and there were kids around. Whose kids were they? Certainly not theirs. Otherwise that would mean…

Her eyes sprang open, refusing to let such an apparition enter her mind. She would be the first to admit that what they'd shared last night had overwhelmed her, and for a moment she'd come close to challenging everything she believed about relationships between men and women. But the last thing she needed to do was get offtrack. Last night was what it was—no more, no less. It was about a curious, inexperienced woman and a horny, experienced man. And both had gotten satisfied to the nth degree. They had both gotten what they wanted.

"You're awake?"

Callum's voice sent sensations running across her skin. "Who wants to know?"

"The man who made love to you last night."

She shifted her body, turned to face him and immediately wished she hadn't. Fully awake he was sexy as sin. A half asleep Callum, with a stubble chin, drowsy eyes and long eyelashes, could make you come just looking at him.

"You're the one who did that to me last night, aren't you?"

A smile curved his lips. "I'm the one who plans to do that to you every night."

She chuckled, knowing he only meant every night she remained in Australia. She was certain he knew that when they returned to Denver things would be different. Although she had her own little place, he would not be making late-night booty calls on her Westmoreland property.

"You think you have the stamina to do it every night?"

"Don't you?"

She had to admit that the man's staying power was truly phenomenal. But she figured, in time, when she got the hang of it, she would be able to handle him. "Yes, I do."

She then reached out and rubbed a hand across his chin. "You need a shave."

He chuckled. "Do I?"

"Yes." Then she grabbed a lock of his hair. "And…"

"Don't go there. I get my hair trimmed, never cut."

She smiled. "That must be an Austell thing, since I see your father and brothers evidently feel the same way. Don't be surprised if I start calling you Samson."

"And I'll start calling you Delilah, the temptress."

She couldn't help but laugh. "I wouldn't know how to tempt a man."

"But you know how to tempt me."

"Do I?"

"Yes, but don't get any ideas," he said. "Last night you made me promise to get you to your new office by ten o'clock."

Yes, she had made him promise that. He'd told her she could set up shop in the study of the house. He would have a phone installed as well as a fax machine and a computer with a high-speed Internet connection. The sooner she could get the materials she needed ordered, the quicker she could return to Denver. For some reason, the thought of returning home tugged at her heart. This was her third day here and she already loved this place.

"You do want to be on the job by ten, right?"

A smile touched her lips. "Yes, I do. Have you decided when and if you're returning to Denver?" She just had to know.

"Yes, I plan to return with you and will probably stay until after Ramsey and Chloe's baby is born to help out on the ranch. When things get pretty much back to normal for Ramsey, then I'll leave Denver for good and return here."

She began nibbling on her bottom lip. This was September, and Chloe was due to deliver in November, which meant Callum would be leaving Denver a few months after that. Chances were there would be no Callum Austell in Denver come spring.

"Umm, let me do that."

She lifted her gaze to his eyes when he interrupted her thoughts. "Let you do what?"

"This."

He leaned closer and began gently nibbling on her lips, then licking her mouth from corner to corner. When her lips parted on a breathless sigh, he entered her mouth to taste her fully. The kiss grew deeper, hotter and moments later, when he pulled his mouth away, he placed his fingers to her lips to stop the request he knew she was about to make.

"Your body doesn't need me that way, Gemma. It needs an adjustment period," he whispered against her lips.

She nodded. "But later?"

His lips curved in a wicked smile. "Yes, later."

Callum was vaguely aware of the information the foreman of one of his sheep ranches was giving to him. The report was good, which he knew it would be. During the time he'd been in Denver, he'd pretty much kept up with things here as well as with Le'Claire. He'd learned early how to multitask.

And he smiled, thinking how well he'd multi-tasked last night. There hadn't been one single part of Gemma he hadn't wanted to devour—and all at the same time. He'd been greedy, and so had she. His woman had more passion in her body than she knew what to do with, and he was more than willing to school her in all the possibilities. But he also knew that he had to be careful. He didn't want her to start thinking that what was between them was more lust than love. His goal was to woo her every chance he got, which is why he'd hung up with the florist a few moments ago.

"So as you can see, Mr. Austell, everything is as it should be."

He smiled at the man who'd been talking for the past ten minutes, going over his sheep-herding records. "I figured they would be. I appreciate the job you and your men have done in my absence, Richard."

A huge grin covered the man's face. "We appreciate working for the Austells."

Richard Vinson and his family had worked on an Austell sheep ranch for generations. In fact, upon Callum's grandfather's death, Jack Austell had deeded over five hundred acres of land to the Vinson family in recognition of their loyalty, devotion and hard work.

A few minutes later, Callum was headed back to his car when his phone rang. A quick check showed it was a call from the States, namely Derringer Westmoreland. "Yes, Derringer?"

"Just calling to see if you've given any more thought to becoming a silent partner in our horse-breeding venture?"

Durango Westmoreland, part of those Atlanta Westmorelands, had teamed up with a childhood friend and cousin-in-law named McKinnon Quinn, and bought a very successful horse-breeding and -training operation in Montana. They had invited their cousins, Zane, Derringer and Jason, to become part of their outfit as Colorado partners. Callum, Ramsey and Dillon had expressed an interest in becoming silent partners. "Yes. I'm impressed with all I've heard about it, so count me in."

"Boy, you're easy," Derringer teased.

His words made Callum think about Gemma. She had said the same thing to him last night, but during the course of the night he'd shown her just how wrong she was. "Hey, what can I say? Are you behaving yourself?"

Derringer laughed. "Hey, now what can I say? And speaking of behaving, how is that sister of mine? She hasn't driven you crazy yet?"

Callum smiled. Gemma had driven him crazy but in a way he'd rather not go into with her brother. "Gemma is doing a great job decorating my place."

"Well, watch your wallet. I heard her prices can sometimes get out of sight."

"Thanks for the warning."

He talked to Derringer a few moments longer before ending the call. After he married Gemma, Ramsey, Zane, Derringer, the twins, Megan and Bailey would become his in-laws, and those other Westmorelands, including Dillon, his cousins-in-law. Hell, he didn't want to think about all those other Westmorelands, the ones from Atlanta that Ramsey and his siblings and cousins were just beginning to get to know. It didn't take the Denver Westmorelands and the Atlanta Westmorelands long to begin meshing as if they'd had a close relationship all their lives.

Callum's father had been an only child and so had his father before him. Todd Austell probably would have been content having one child, but Le'Claire had had a say in that. His father had known that marrying the American beauty meant fathering at least three children. Callum chuckled, remembering that, according to his father, his birth had been a surprise. Todd had assumed his daddy days were over, but Le'Claire had had other ideas about that, and Todd had decided to give his wife whatever she wanted. Callum was using that same approach with Gemma. Whatever this particular Westmoreland wanted is what she would get.

After Callum snapped his seat belt in place, he checked his watch. It was a little past three and he would be picking Gemma up around five. He'd wanted to take her to lunch, but she'd declined, saying she had a lot of orders to place if he wanted the house fully decorated and ready for him to move in by November.

He really didn't care if he was in that house, still living in his condo on the beach or back in Denver. All that mattered to him was that Gemma was with him—wherever he was. And as he turned the ignition to his car, he knew that making that happen was still his top priority.

"Will there be anything else, Ms. Westmoreland?"

Gemma glanced up at the older woman Callum had introduced her to that morning, Kathleen Morgan. "No, Kathleen. That's it. Thanks for all you did today."

The woman waved off her words. "I didn't do anything but make a lot of phone calls to place those orders. I can just imagine how this place is going to look when you finish with it. I think Mr. Austell's decision to blend European and Western styles will be simply beautiful. One day this house will be a showplace for Mr. Austell and his future wife. Good bye."

"Goodbye." Gemma tried letting the woman's words pass, but couldn't. The thought of Callum sharing this house with a woman—one he would be married to—bothered her.

She tossed her pencil on the desk and glanced over at the flowers that had been delivered not long after he'd dropped her off here. A dozen red roses. Why had he sent them? The card that accompanied them only had his signature. They were simply beautiful, and the fragrance suffused her office.

Her office.

And that was another mystery. She had assumed she would have an empty room on the main floor of the house with a table and just the bare essentials to operate as a temporary place to order materials and supplies. But when she'd stepped through the door with Callum at her back, she had seen that the empty room had been transformed into a work place, equipped with everything imaginable, including a live administrative assistant.

She pushed her chair back and walked across the room to the vase of flowers she'd placed on a table in front of a window. That way she could pause while working to glance over at them and appreciate their beauty. Unfortunately, seeing them also made her think of the man who'd sent them.

She threw her head back in frustration. She had to stop thinking of Callum and start concentrating on the job he'd hired her to do. Not only had he hired her, he had brought her all the way from Denver to handle her business.

But still, today she'd found herself remembering last night and this morning. True to his word, he had not made love to her again, but he had held her, tasted her lips and given her pleasure another way. Namely with his mouth. He had soothed her body and brought it pleasure at the same time. Amazing.

She turned when her cell phone rang and quickly crossed the room to pick it up. It was her sister, Megan. "Megan, how are you doing?" She missed her sisters.

"I'm fine. I have Bailey here with me and she says hello. We miss you."

"And I miss you both, too," she said honestly. "What time is it there?" She placed her cell phone on speaker to put away the files spread all over her desk.

"Close to ten on Monday night. It's Tuesday there already, right?"

"Yes, Tuesday afternoon around four. Today was my first day on the job. Callum set a room up at the house for me to use as an office. I even have an administrative assistant. And speaking of administrative assistants, has the bank's security team contacted you about Niecee?"

"Yes, in fact I got a call yesterday. It seems she deposited the check in an account in Florida. They are working with that bank to stop payment. What's in your favor is that you acted right away. Most businesses that are the victims of embezzlement don't find out about the thefts until months later, and then it's too late to recover the funds. Niecee gave herself away when she left that note apologizing the next day. Had she been bright she would have called in sick a few days, waited for the check to clear and then confessed her sins. Now it looks like she'll be getting arrested."

Gemma let out a deep sigh. A part of her felt bad, but then what Niecee had done was wrong. The woman probably figured that because Gemma was a

Westmoreland she had the money to spare. Well, she was wrong. Dillon and Ramsey had pretty much drilled into each of them to make their own way. Yes, they'd each been given one hundred acres and a nice trust fund when they'd turned twenty-one, but making sure they used that money responsibly was up to them. So far all of them had. Luckily, Bane had turned his affairs over to Dillon to handle. Otherwise, he would probably be penniless by now.

"Well, I regret that, but I can't get over what she did. Twenty thousand dollars is not small change."

A sound made Gemma turn around and she drew in a deep breath when she saw Callum standing there, leaning in the doorway. And from the expression on his face, she knew he'd been listening to her and Megan's conversation. How dare he! She wondered if he would mention it to Ramsey.

"Megan, I'll call you back later," she said, placing her phone off speaker. "Tell everyone I said hello and give them my love."

She ended the call and placed the phone back on her desk. "You're early."

"Yes, you might say that," he said, crossing his arms across his chest. "What's this about your administrative assistant embezzling money from you?"

Gemma threw her head back, sending hair flying over her shoulders. "You were deliberately eavesdropping on my conversation."

"You placed the call on speaker and I just happened to arrive while the conversation was going on."

"Well, you could have let me know you were here."

"Yes, I could have. Now answer the question about Niecee."

"No. It's none of your business," she snapped.

He strolled into the room toward her. "That's where you're wrong. It *is* my business, on both a business and a personal level."

A frown deepened her brow. "And how do you figure that?"

He came to a stop in front of her. "First of all, on a business level, before I do business with anyone I expect the company to be financially sound. In other words, Gemma, I figured that you had enough funds in your bank account to cover the initial outlay for this decorating job."

She placed her hands on her hips. "I didn't have to worry about that since you gave me such a huge advance."

"And what if I hadn't done that? Would you have been able to take the job here?"

Gemma didn't have to think about the answer to that. "No, but—"

"No, buts, Gemma." He didn't say anything for a minute and it seemed as if he was struggling not to smile. That only fueled her anger. What did he find so amusing?

Before she could ask, he spoke. "And it's personal, Gemma, because it's you. I don't like the idea of anyone taking advantage of you. Does Ramsey know?"

Boy, that did it! "I own Designs by Gems—not Ramsey. It's my business and whatever problems crop up are *my* problems. I know I made a mistake in hiring Niecee. I see that now and I should have listened to

Ramsey and Dillon and done a background check on her, as they suggested. I didn't and I regret it. But at least I'm—"

"Handling your business." He glanced at his watch. "Ready to go?" he asked, walking away and heading for the door, turning off the light switch in the process. "There's a nice restaurant not far from here that I think you'll like."

Gemma spun around to face him. "I'm not going anywhere with you. I'm mad."

Callum flashed her a smile. "Then get over it."

Gemma was too undone…and totally confused. "I won't be getting over it."

He nodded. "Okay, let's talk about it then."

She crossed her arms over her chest. "I don't want to talk about it, because it's none of your business."

Callum threw his head back and laughed. "We're back to that again?"

Gemma glared at him. "We need to get a few things straight, Callum."

He nodded. "Yes, we do." He walked back over to her. "I've already told you why it's my business and from a business perspective you see that I'm right, don't you?"

It took her a full minute, but she finally said, "Yes, all right. I see that. I'll admit that you are right from a business perspective. That's not the way I usually operate but…"

"You were robbing Peter to pay Paul, I know. However, I don't like being Peter or Paul. Now, as far as it being personal, *you* were right."

She lifted a brow. "I was?"

"Yes. It was your business and not Ramsey's concern. I admitted it and told you that you handled it. That was the end of it," he said.

She gave herself a mental shake, trying to keep up with him. He had scolded her on one hand, but complimented her way of handling things on the other. "So you won't mention it to Ramsey?"

"No. It's not my place to do that…unless your life is in danger or something equally as dire, and it's not." He looked down at her and smiled. "As I said, from the sound of the conversation you just had with Megan, you handled this matter in an expeditious manner. By all accounts, you will be getting your money back. Kudos for you."

A smile crossed Gemma's lips. She was proud of herself. "Yes, kudos for me." Her eyes narrowed. "And just what did you find amusing earlier?"

"How quickly you can get angry just for the sake of doing so. I'd heard about your unique temperament but never experienced it before."

"Did it bother you?"

"No."

Gemma frowned, not sure how she felt about that. In a way she liked that Callum didn't run for cover when her temper exploded, as it did at times. Zane, Derringer and the twins were known to have had a plate aimed at their heads once or twice, and knew to be ready to duck if they gave her sufficient cause.

"However, I would like you to make me a promise," he said, breaking into her thoughts.

She lifted a curious brow. "What?"

"Promise that if you ever find yourself in a bind again, financial or otherwise, you'll let me know."

She rolled her eyes. "I don't need another older brother, Callum."

He smiled and his teeth flashed a bright white against his brown skin. "There's no way you can think we have anything close to a brother-sister relationship after last night. But just in case you need a little reminder…"

He pulled her into his arms, lowered his head and captured her mouth with his.

Twelve

Gemma's face blushed with anticipation as she walked into Callum's condo. Dinner was fantastic, but she liked being back here alone with him.

"Are you tired, Gemma?"

He had to be kidding. She glanced over her shoulder and gave him a wry look. He was closing the door and locking it. "What makes you think that?"

"You were kind of quiet at dinner."

She chuckled. "Not hardly. I nearly talked your ears off."

"And I nearly talked yours off, too."

She shook her head. "No, you didn't. You were sharing how your day went, and basically, I was doing the same." *While sitting there nearly drooling over you from across the table.* Now that they were alone, she wondered if she would have to tell him what she wanted or if he already had a clue.

"So Kathleen worked out well for you?"

"Yes," she said, easing out of her shoes. "She's a sweetheart and so efficient. She was able to find all the fabric I need and the cost of shipping won't be bad. I really hadn't expected you to set up the office like that. Thanks again for the roses. They were beautiful."

"You thanked me already for the flowers, and I'm glad you liked them. I plan to take you to the movies this weekend, but how would you like to watch a DVD now?"

She studied his features as he walked into the living room. Was that what he really wanted to do? "A movie on DVD sounds fine."

"You got a favorite?"

She chuckled as she dropped down on the sofa. "And if I do, should I just assume you have it here?"

He sat in the wingback chair across from her. "No, but I'm sure it can be ordered through my cable company. As I said, whatever you want, I will make it happen."

In that case. She stood from the sofa and in bare feet she slowly crossed the room and came to a stop between his opened legs. "Make love to me, Callum."

Callum didn't hesitate to pull Gemma down into his lap. He had been thinking about making love to her all day. That kiss in her office had whet his appetite and now he was about to be appeased. But first he had to tell her something before he forgot.

"Mom called. She's invited you to have lunch and go shopping with her, my sister and my sisters-in-law next Friday."

Surprise shone on Gemma's face. She twisted around in his arms to look up at him. "She did?"

"Yes."

"But why? I'm here to decorate your house. Why would they want to spend time with me?"

Callum chuckled. "Why wouldn't they? You've never been to Australia and I gather from the conversations the other day they figured you like to shop like most other women."

"The same way men like watching sports. I understand that sports are just as popular here in this country as in the States."

"Yes, I played Australian rules football a lot growing up. Not sure how my body would handle it now, though," he said, adjusting her in his lap to place the top of his chin on the crown of her head. "I also like playing cricket. One day I'm going to teach you how to play."

"Well, you must have plans to do that during the time I'm here, because once I return home it's back to tennis for me."

Callum knew Gemma played tennis and that she was good at it. But what stuck out more than anything was her mentioning returning home. He didn't intend for that to happen, at least not on a permanent basis. "How can you think of returning to Denver when you still have so much to do here?"

She smiled. "Hey, give me a break. Today was my first full day on the job. Besides, you hired Kathleen for me. She placed all the orders and I even hired the company to come in and hang the drapes and pictures. Everything is moving smoothly. Piece of cake. I'll have that place decorated and be out of here in no time."

He didn't say anything for a moment, thinking he definitely didn't like the sound of that. Then he turned her in his arms. "I think we got sidetracked."

She looked up at him. "Did we?"

"Yes. You wanted to make love."

She tilted her head. "Umm, did I?"

"Yes."

She shook her head, trying to hide a grin, which he saw anyway. "Sorry, your time is up."

He stood with her in his arms. "I don't think so."

Callum carried her over to the sofa and sat down with her in his arms. "We have more room here," he said, adjusting her body in his lap to face him. "Now tell me what you want again."

"I don't remember," she said, amusement shining in her gaze.

"Sounds like you need another reminder," he said, standing.

She wrapped her arms around his neck. "Now where are you taking me?"

"To the kitchen. I think I'd like you for dessert."

"What! You're kidding, aren't you?"

"No. Watch me."

And she did. Gemma sat on the kitchen counter, where he placed her, while he rummaged through his refrigerator looking for God knows what. But she didn't mind, since she was getting a real nice view of his backside.

"Don't go anywhere. I'll have everything I need in a sec," he called out, still bent over, scouring his fridge.

"Oh, don't worry, I'm not going anywhere. I'm

enjoying the view," she said, smiling, her gaze still glued to his taut tush.

"The view is nice this time of night, isn't it?" he asked over his shoulder.

She grinned as she studied how the denim of his jeans stretched over his butt. He thought she was talking about the view of the ocean outside the window. "I think this particular view is nice anytime. Day or night."

"You're probably right."

"I know I am," Gemma said, fighting to keep the smile out of her voice.

Moments later Callum turned away from the refrigerator and closed the door with his hands full of items. He glanced over at Gemma. She was smiling. He arched a brow. "What's so funny?"

"Nothing. What you got there?"

"See for yourself," he said, placing all the items on the counter next to her.

She picked up a jar. "Cherries?"

A slow smile touched his lips at the same time she saw a hint of heat fill his green eyes. "My favorite fruit."

"Yeah, I'll bet."

She picked up another item. "Whipped cream?"

"For the topping."

She shook her head as she placed the whipped cream back on the counter and selected another item. "Nuts?"

"They go well with cherries," he said, laughing.

"You're awful."

"No, I'm not.

She picked up the final item. "Chocolate syrup?"

"That's a must," he said, rolling up his sleeve.

Gemma watched as he began taking the tops off all the containers. "So what are you going to do with all that stuff?"

He smiled. "You'll see. I told you that you're going to be my dessert."

She blinked when she read his thoughts. He was serious.

"Now for my fantasy," he said, turning to her and placing his hands on her knees as he stepped between them, widening her legs as he did so. He began unbuttoning her shirt and when he took it off her shoulders he neatly placed it on the back of the kitchen chair.

He reached out to unsnap the front of her bra, lifting a brow at its peach color. He'd watched her put it on this morning and when he asked her about it, she told him she liked matching undies.

"Nice color."

"Glad you like it."

Gemma couldn't believe it a short while later when she was sitting on Callum's kitchen counter in nothing but her panties. He then slid her into his arms. "Where are we going now?"

"Out on the patio."

"More room?"

"Yes, more room, and the temperature tonight is unusually warm."

He carried her through the French doors to place her on the chaise longue. "I'll be back."

"Okay." Anticipation was flowing through her veins and she could feel her heart thudding in her chest. She'd never considered herself a sexual being, but Callum was proving just how passionate she could be. At least with him. She had a pretty good idea just what he planned to do and the thought was inciting every cell in her body to simmer with desire. The thought that couples did stuff like this behind closed doors, actually had fun being together, being adventurous while making love, had her wondering what she'd been missing all these years.

But she knew she hadn't been missing anything because the men she'd dated in the past hadn't been Callum. Besides being drop-dead gorgeous, the man certainly had a way with women. At least he had a way with her. He had made her first time memorable; not only in giving her pleasure but in the way he had taken care of her afterwards.

And then there were the flowers he'd sent today. And then at dinner, she had enjoyed their conversation where not only had he shared how his day had gone, but had given her a lot of interesting information about his homeland. This weekend he had offered to take her sailing on his father's yacht. She was looking forward to that.

While sitting across from him during dinner, every little thing had boosted up her desire for him. She couldn't wait to return here to be alone with him. It could be the way he would smile at her over the rim of his wineglass, or the way he would reach across the table and touch her hand on occasion for no reason at all. They had ordered different entrées and he had hand-fed her some of his when she was curious as to how his meal tasted.

Callum returned and she watched as he placed all the items on the small table beside her. The patio was dark, except for the light coming in from the kitchen and the moonlight overhead. They had eaten breakfast on the patio this morning and she knew there wasn't a single building on either side of them, just the ocean.

He pulled a small stool over to where she lay on her back, staring up at him. "When will you be my dessert?" she tried asking in a calm voice, but found that to be difficult when she felt her stomach churning.

"Whenever you want. Just ask. I'll give you whatever you want."

He'd been telling her that so much that she was beginning to believe it. "The ocean sounds so peaceful and relaxing. You'd better hope I don't fall asleep," she warned.

"If you do, I'll wake you."

She looked up at him, met his gaze and felt his heat. She'd told him last night there were no limitations. There still weren't. It had taken her twenty-four years to get to this point and she intended to enjoy it for all it was worth. Callum was making this a wonderful experience for her and she appreciated him for being fascinating as well as creative.

He moved off the stool just long enough to lean over her to remove her panties. "Nice pair," he said, while easing the silky material down her thighs and legs.

"Glad you like them."

"I like them off you even better," he said, balling them up and standing to put them into the back pocket of his jeans. "Now for my dessert."

"Enjoy yourself."

"I will, sweetheart."

It seemed that her entire body responded to his use of that endearment. He meant nothing by it—she was certain of it. But still, she couldn't help how rapidly her heart was beating from hearing it and how her stomach was fluttering in response to it.

While she lay there, she watched as Callum removed his shirt and tossed it aside before returning to his stool. He leaned close and she was tempted to reach out and run her fingertips across his naked chest, but then decided she wouldn't do that. This was his fantasy. He'd fulfilled hers last night.

"Now for something sweet, like you," he said, and she nearly jumped when she felt a warm, thick substance being smeared over her chest with his fingers and hands in a sensual and erotic pattern. When he moved to her stomach the muscles tightened as he continued rubbing the substance all over her belly, as if he was painting a design on her.

"What is it?"

"My name."

His voice was husky and in the moonlight she saw his tense features, the darkness of the eyes staring back at her, the sexy line of his mouth. All she could do was lie there and stare up at him speechlessly, trying to make sense of what he said. He was placing his name on her stomach as if he was branding her as his. She forced the thought from her mind, knowing he didn't mean anything by it.

"How does it feel?" he asked as his hand continued spreading chocolate syrup all over her.

"The chocolate feels sticky, but your hands feel good," she said honestly. He had moved his hands down past her stomach to her thighs.

He didn't say anything for a long moment, just continued to do what he was doing.

"And this is your fantasy?" she asked.

His lips curved into a slow smile that seemed to heat his gaze even more. "Yes. You'll see why in a moment."

When Callum was satisfied that he had smeared enough chocolate syrup over Gemma's body, he grabbed the can of whipped cream and squirted some around her nipples, outlined her belly button, completely covered her feminine mound, and made squiggly lines on her thighs and legs.

"Now for the cherries and nuts," he said, still holding her gaze.

He then proceeded to sprinkle her with nuts and place cherries on top of the whipped cream on her breasts, navel and womanly mound. In fact, he placed several on the latter.

"You look beautiful," he said, taking a step back and looking down at her to see just what he'd done.

"I'll take your word for it," she said, feeling like a huge ice-cream sundae. "I just hope there isn't a colony of ants around."

He laughed. "There isn't. Now to get it off you."

She knew just how he intended to do that, but nothing prepared her for the feel of his tongue when he began slowly licking her all over. Every so often he would lean up and kiss her, giving her a taste of the concoction that was smeared all around his mouth, mingling his tongue with hers. At one point he carried a cherry with his teeth, placed it in her mouth and together they shared the taste.

"Callum…"

Callum loved the sound of his name on her lips and as he lowered his mouth back down to her chest, he could feel the softness of her breasts beneath his mouth. And each nipple tasted like a delicious pebble wrapped around his tongue. Every time he took one into his mouth she shivered, and he savored the sensation of sucking on them.

He kissed his way down her stomach and when he came to the area between her legs, he looked up at her, met her gaze and whispered, "Now I will devour you."

"Oh, Callum."

He dropped to his knees in front of her and homed in to taste her intimately. She cried out his name the moment his tongue touched her and she grabbed hold of his hair to hold his mouth hostage. There was no need, since he didn't plan to go anyplace until he'd licked his fill. Every time his tongue stroked her clitoris, her body would tremble beneath his mouth.

She began mumbling words he was certain had no meaning, but hearing her speak incoherently told him her state of mind. It was tortured, like his. She was the only woman he desired. The only woman he loved.

Moments later when she bucked beneath his mouth when her body was ripped by a massive sensual explosion, he kept his tongue planted deep inside her, determined to give her all the pleasure she deserved. All the pleasure she wanted.

When the aftershocks of her orgasm had passed, he pulled away and began removing his jeans. And then he moved his body in position over hers, sliding between her open legs and entering her in one smooth thrust.

He was home. And he began moving, stroking parts of her insides that his tongue hadn't been able to reach, but his manhood could. And this way he could connect with all of her now. This way. Mating with her while breathing in her delicious scent, as the taste of her was still embedded in his mouth.

The magnitude of what they were sharing sent him reeling over the top, and he felt his own body beginning to explode. He felt his release shoot straight into her the moment he called out her name.

Instinctively, her body began milking him again, pulling everything out of him, making him moan in pleasure. And he knew this was just a part of what he felt for her. And it wasn't lust. It was everything love was based on—the physical and the emotional. And he hoped she would see it. Every day she was here he would show her both sides of love. He would share his body with her. He would share his soul. And he would continue to make her his.

He was tempted to tell her right then and there how he felt, let her know she was his soul mate, but he knew he couldn't. Not yet. She had to realize for herself that there was more between them than this. She had to realize and believe that she was the only woman for him.

He believed that would happen and, thankfully, he had a little time on his side to break down her defenses, to get her to see that all men weren't alike, and that he was the man destined to love her forever.

"So what do you think of this one, Gemma?" Mira Austell asked, showing Gemma the diamond earrings dangling from her ears.

"They're beautiful," Gemma said, and truly meant it.

The Austell ladies had picked her up around ten and it was almost four in the afternoon and they were still at it. Gemma didn't want to think about all the stores they had patronized or how many bags they had between the five of them.

Gemma had seen this gorgeous pair of sandals she just had to buy and also a party dress, since Callum had offered to take her to a club on the beach when she mentioned that she enjoyed dancing.

This particular place—an upscale jewelry store—was their last stop before calling it a day. Le'Claire suggested they stop here, since she wanted a new pair of pearl earrings.

"Gemma, Mira, come look at all these gorgeous rings," Le'Shaunda was saying, and within seconds they were all crowded around the glass case.

"I really like that one," Annette said, picking out a solitaire with a large stone.

"Umm, and I like that one," Le'Claire said, smiling. "I have a birthday coming up soon, so it's time to start dropping hints."

Gemma thought Callum's mother was beautiful and could understand how his father had fallen in love so fast. And no wonder Todd gave her anything she wanted. But then Callum gave her anything she wanted as well. Like father, like son. Todd had trained his offspring well. Last weekend Callum had treated her to a picnic on the beach, and another one was planned for this weekend as well. She had enjoyed her time with him and couldn't help but appreciate the time and attention he gave to her when he really didn't have to do so.

"Gemma, which of these do you like the best?" Le'Claire asked.

Gemma pressed her nose to the glass case as she peered inside. All the rings were beautiful and no doubt expensive. But if she had to choose...

"That one," she said, pointing to a gorgeous four-carat, white-gold, emerald-cut ring. "I think that's simply beautiful."

The other ladies agreed, and each picked out their favorites. The store clerk even let everyone try them on to see how each ring looked on their hands. Gemma was amused by how the others said they would remind their husbands about those favorites when it got close to their birthdays.

"It's almost dinnertime, so we might as well go somewhere to get something to eat," Le'Shaunda said. "I know a wonderful restaurant nearby."

Le'Claire beamed. "That's a wonderful idea."

Gemma thought it was a wonderful idea as well, although she missed seeing Callum. He had begun joining her for lunch every day at her office, always bringing good sandwiches for her to eat and wine to drink. They usually went out to a restaurant in town for dinner. Tonight they planned to watch a movie and make love. Or they would make love and then watch a movie. She liked the latter better, since they could make love again after the movie.

"Did Callum mention anything to you about a hunting trip in a couple of weeks?" Annette asked.

Gemma smiled over at her. "Yes, he did. I understand all the men are leaving for a six-day trip."

"Yes," Mira said as if she was eager for Colin to be

gone. The other woman glanced over at Gemma and explained. "Of course I'm going to miss my husband, but that's when we ladies get to do another shopping trip."

Everyone laughed and Gemma couldn't keep from laughing right along with them.

Thirteen

"Hello," Gemma mumbled into the telephone receiver.

"Wake up, sleepy."

A smile touched Gemma's lips as she slowly forced her eyes fully open. "Callum," she whispered.

"Who else?"

She smiled sleepily. He had left two days ago on a hunting trip with his father and brothers and would be gone for another four days. "I've been thinking about you."

"I've been thinking about you, too, sweetheart. I miss you already," he said.

"And I miss you, too," she said, realizing at that moment just how much. He had taken her to a party at his friend's home last weekend and she had felt special walking in with him. And he'd never left her side. It was nice meeting some of the guys he'd gone to college with. And the night before leaving to go hunting he'd taken her to the movies again. He filled a lot of her time when she wasn't working, so yes, she did miss him already.

"That's good to hear. You had a busy day yesterday, right?"

She pulled herself up in bed. "Yes, but Kathleen and I were able to make sure everything would be delivered as planned."

"Don't forget, you promised to take a break and let me fly you to India when I get back."

"Yes, and I'm looking forward to it, although I hope there isn't a lot of turbulence on that flight."

"You never know, but you'll be with me and I'll take care of you."

Her smile widened. "You always do."

A few moments later they ended the call, and she fluffed her pillow and stretched out in the bed. It was hard to believe that she had been in Australia four weeks already. Four glorious weeks. She missed her family and friends back home, but Callum and his family were wonderful and treated her like she was one of them.

She planned to go shopping with his mother, sister and sisters-in-law again tomorrow, and then there would be a sleepover at Le'Claire's home. She genuinely liked the Austell women and had had some rather amusing moments when they'd shared just how they handled their men. It had been hilarious when Le'Claire even gave pointers to Le'Shaunda, who claimed her husband could be stubborn at times.

But nothing, Gemma thought, could top all the times she'd spent with Callum. They could discuss anything.

When she'd received the call that Niecee had been arrested, she had let him handle it so that her emotions wouldn't stop her from making sure the woman was punished for what she had done. And then there were the flowers he continued to send her every week, and the "I'm thinking of you" notes that he would leave around the house for her to find. She stared up at the ceiling, thinking that Callum was definitely not like other men. The woman he married would be very lucky.

At that moment a sharp pain settled around her heart at the thought of any other woman with Callum, sharing anything close to what they had shared this past month. To know that another woman, his soul mate, would be living with him in the house she was decorating almost made her ill.

She eased to the edge of the bed, knowing why she felt that way. She had fallen in love with him. "Oh, no!"

She dropped back on the bed and covered her face with her hands. How did she let that happen? Although Callum wouldn't intentionally break her heart, he would break it just the same. How could she have fallen in love with him? She knew the answer without much thought. Callum was an easy man to love. But it wasn't meant for her to be the one to love him. He had told her about his soul mate.

She got out of bed and headed for the bathroom, knowing what she had to do. There was no way she would not finish the job she came here to do, but she needed to return home for at least a week or two to get her head screwed back on straight. Kathleen could handle things until she returned. And when she got back, she'd be capable of handling a relationship with Callum the way it should be handled. She would still love him, but at least she would have thought things through and come to the realization she couldn't ever be the number one woman in his life. She'd have to be satisfied with that.

A few hours later she had showered, dressed and packed a few of her things. She had called Kathleen and given her instructions as to what needed to be done in her absence, and assured the older woman that she would be back in a week or so.

Gemma decided not to call Callum to tell him she was leaving. He would wonder why she was taking off all of a sudden. She would think of an excuse to give him when she got home to Denver. She wiped the tears from her eyes. She had let the one thing happen to her that she'd always sworn would never happen.

She had fallen in love with a man who didn't love her.

Callum stood on the porch of the cabin and glanced all around. Nothing, he thought, was more beautiful than the Australian outback. He could recall the first time he'd come to this cabin as a child with his brothers, father and grandfather.

His thoughts drifted to Gemma. He knew for certain that she was his soul mate. The last month had been idyllic. Waking up with her in his arms every morning, making love with her each night, was as perfect as perfect could get. And he was waiting patiently for her to realize that she loved him, too.

It would be then that they would talk about it and he

would tell her that he loved her as well, that he'd known for a while that she was the one, but had wanted her to come to that realization on her own.

Callum took a sip of his coffee. He had a feeling she was beginning to realize it. More than once over the past week he'd caught her staring at him with an odd look on her face, as if she was trying to figure out something. And at night when she gave herself to him, it was as if he would forever be the only man in her life. Just as, when he made love to her, he wanted her to believe that she would forever be the only woman in his.

"Callum. You got a call. It's Mom."

Morris's voice intruded on his thoughts and he reentered the cabin and picked up the phone. "Yes, Mom?"

"Callum, it's Gemma."

His heart nearly stopped beating. He knew the ladies had a shopping trip planned for tomorrow. "What's wrong with Gemma? What happened?"

"I'm not sure. She called and asked me to take her to the airport."

"Airport?"

"Yes. She said she had to return home for a while, and I could tell she'd been crying."

He rubbed his forehead. That didn't make any sense. He'd just spoken to her that morning and she was fine. She had two pregnant sisters-in-law and he hoped nothing had happened. "Did she say why she was leaving, Mom? Did she mention anything about a family crisis?"

"No, in fact I asked and she said it had nothing to do with her family."

Callum pulled in a deep breath, not understanding any of this.

"Have you told her yet that you're in love with her, Callum?"

"No. I didn't want to rush her and was giving us time to develop a relationship before doing that. I wanted her to see from my actions that I loved her and get her to admit to herself that she loved me, too."

"Now I understand completely," Le'Claire said softly.

"You do?"

"Yes."

"Then how about explaining things to me because I'm confused."

He heard his mother's soft chuckle. "You're a man, so you would be. I think the reason Gemma left is because she realizes that she loves you. She's running away."

Callum was even more confused. "Why would she do something like that?"

"Because if she loves you and you don't love her back then—"

"But I do love her back."

"But she doesn't know that. And if you explained about waiting for a soul mate the way you explained it to me, she's probably thinking it's not her."

The moment his mother's words hit home, Callum threw his head back in frustration and groaned. "I think you're right, Mom."

"I think I'm right, too. So what are you going to do?"

A smile cascaded across Callum's lips. "I'm going after my woman."

Fourteen

Ramsey Westmoreland had been in the south pasture most of the day, but when he got home he'd heard from Chloe that Gemma was back. She'd called for Megan to pick her up at the airport. And according to what Megan had shared with Chloe, Gemma looked like she'd cried during the entire eighteen-hour flight.

He was about to place a call to Callum to find out what the hell had happened when he received a call from Colin saying Callum was on his way to Denver. The last thing Ramsey needed in his life was drama. He'd had more than enough during his affair with Chloe.

But here he was getting out of his truck to go knock on the door to make sure Gemma was all right. Callum was on his way and Ramsey would leave it to his best friend to handle Gemma from here on out because his sister could definitely be Miss Drama Queen. And seeing that she was here at Callum's cabin and not at her own place spoke volumes, whether she knew it or not. However, for now he would play the dumb-ass, just to satisfy his curiosity. And Chloe's.

He knocked on the door and it was yanked open. For a moment he was taken aback. Gemma looked like a mess, but he had enough sense not to tell her that. Instead, he took off his hat, passed by her and said in a calm tone. "Back from Australia early, aren't you?"

"Just here for a week or two. I'm going back," she said in a strained voice, which he pretended not to hear.

"Where's Callum? I'm surprised he let you come by yourself, knowing how afraid you are of flying. Was there a lot of turbulence?"

"I didn't notice."

Probably because you were too busy crying your eyes out. He hadn't seen her look like this since their parents' funeral. Ramsey leaned against a table in the living room and glanced around. He then looked back at her. "Any reason you're here and not at your own place, Gemma?"

He knew it was the wrong question to ask when suddenly her mouth quivered and she started to sob. "I love him, but he doesn't love me. I'm not his soul mate. But that's okay. I can deal with it. I just didn't want to ever cry over a man the way those girls used to do when Zane and Derringer broke up with them. I swore that would *never* happen to me. I swore I would never be one of them and fall for a guy who didn't love me back."

Ramsey could only stare at her. She actually thought Callum didn't love her? He opened his mouth to tell her just how wrong she was, then suddenly closed it. It was not his place to tell her anything. He would gladly let Callum deal with this.

"Sorry, Ram, but I need to be alone for a minute." He then watched as she quickly walked into the bedroom and closed the door behind her.

Moments later Ramsey was outside, about to open the door to his truck to leave when a vehicle pulled up. He sighed in relief when he saw Callum quickly getting out of the car.

"Ramsey, I went to Gemma's place straight from the airport and she wasn't there. Where the hell is she?"

Ramsey leaned against his truck. Callum looked like he hadn't slept for a while. "She's inside and I'm out of here. I'll let you deal with it."

Callum paused before entering his cabin. Ramsey had jumped into his truck and left in a hurry. Had Gemma trashed his place or something? Drawing in a deep breath, he removed his hat before slowly opening the door.

He strolled into the living room and glanced around. Everything was in order, but Gemma was nowhere in sight. Then he heard a sound coming from the bedroom. He perked up his ears. It was Gemma and she was crying. The sound tore at his heart.

Placing his hat on the rack, he quickly crossed the room and opened his bedroom door. And there she was, lying in his bed with her head buried in his pillows.

He quietly closed the door behind him and leaned against it. Although he loved her and she loved him, he was still responsible for breaking her heart. But, if nothing else, he'd learned over the past four weeks that the only way to handle Gemma was to let her think she was in control, even when she really wasn't. And even if you had to piss her off a little in the process.

"Gemma?"

She jerked up so fast he thought she was going to tumble out of the bed. "Callum! What are you doing here?" She stood quickly, but not before giving one last swipe to her eyes.

"I could ask you the same thing, since this is my place," he said, crossing his arms over his chest.

She threw her hair over her shoulder. "I knew you weren't here," she said as if that explained everything. It didn't.

"So you took off from Australia, left a job unfinished, got on a plane although you hate flying to come here. For what reason, Gemma?"

She lifted her chin and glared at him. "I don't have to answer that, since it's none of your business."

Callum couldn't help but smile at that. He moved away from the door to stand in front of her. "Wrong. It is my business. Both business and personal. It's business because I hired you to do a job and you're not there doing it. And it's personal because it's you and anything involving you is personal to me."

She lifted her chin a little higher. "I don't know why."

"Well, then, Gemma Westmoreland, let me explain it to you," he said, leaning in close to her face. "It's personal because you mean everything to me."

"I can't and I don't," she snapped. "Go tell that to the woman you're going to marry. The woman who is your soul mate."

"I am telling that to her. You are her."

She narrowed her eyes. "No, I'm not."

"Yes, you are. Why do you think I hung around here for three years working my tail off? Not because I needed the job, but because the woman I love, the woman who's had my heart since the first day I saw her, was here. The woman I knew the moment I saw her that she was destined to be mine. Do you know how many nights I went to this bed thinking of you, dreaming of you, patiently waiting for the day when I could make you belong to me in every possible way?"

He didn't give her a chance to answer him. Figured she probably couldn't anyway with the shocked look on her face, so he continued. "I took you to Australia for two reasons. First, I knew you could do the job, and secondly, I wanted you on my turf so I could court you properly. I wanted to show you that I was a guy worth your love and trust. I wanted you to believe in me, believe that I would never break your heart because, no matter what you thought, I was always going to be there for you. To give you every single thing you wanted. I love you."

There, he had his say and he knew it was time to brace himself when she had hers. She shook her head as if to mentally clear her mind and then she glanced back up at him. And glared.

"Are you saying that I'm the reason you hung around here and worked for Ramsey and that you took me to Australia to decorate your house and to win me over?"

She had explained it differently, but it all came down to the same thing. "Yes, that about sums it all up, but don't forget the part about loving you."

She threw her hands up in the air and then began angrily pacing the room while saying, "You put me through all this for nothing! You had me thinking I was decorating that house for another woman. You had me thinking that we were just having an affair that would lead nowhere."

She stopped pacing and her frown deepened. "Why didn't you tell me the truth?"

He crossed the room to stand in front of her. "Had I told you the truth, sweetheart, you would not have been ready to hear it, nor would you have believed it. You would have given me more grief than either of us needed," he said softly.

A smile then crossed his lips. "I had threatened to kidnap you, but Ramsey thought that was going a little too far."

Her eyes widened. "Ramsey knew?"

"Of course. Your brother is a smart man. There's no way I could have hung around here for three years sniffing around his sister and he not know about it."

"Sniffing around me? I want you to know that I—"

He thought she'd talked enough and decided to shut her up by pulling her into his arms and taking her mouth. The moment his tongue slid between her lips he figured she would either bite it or accept it. She accepted it and it began tangling with hers.

Callum deepened the kiss and tightened his hold on Gemma and she responded by wrapping her arms around his neck, standing on tiptoes and participating in their kiss the way he'd shown her how to do. He knew they still had a lot to talk about, and he would have to go over it again to satisfy her, but he didn't care. He would always give her what she wanted.

Callum forced his mouth from hers, but not before taking a quick lick around her lips. He then rested his forehead against hers and pulled in a deep breath. "I love you, Gemma," he whispered against her temple. "I loved you from the moment I first saw you. I knew you were the one, my true soul mate."

Gemma dropped her head to Callum's chest and wrapped her arms around his waist, breathing in his scent and glowing in his love. She was still reeling from his profession of love for her. Her heart was bursting with happiness.

"Gemma, will you marry me?"

She snatched her head up to look into his eyes. And there she saw in their green depths what she hadn't seen before. Now she did.

"Yes, I'll marry you, but…"

Callum chuckled. "There's a but?"

"Yes. I want to be told every day that you love me."

He rolled his eyes. "You've hung around my mom, sister and sisters-in-law too much."

"Whatever."

"I don't have a problem doing that. No problem at all." He sat down on the bed and pulled her down into his lap. "You never answered my question. What are you doing here and not at your place?"

She lowered her head, began toying with the buttons on his shirt and then glanced up and met his gaze. "I know it sounds crazy, but I came home to get over you, but once I got here I had to come here to feel close to you. I was going to sleep in this bed tonight because I knew this is where you slept."

Callum tightened his arms around her. "I got news for you, Gemma. You're *still* sleeping in this bed tonight. With me."

He eased back on the bed and took her with him, covering her mouth with his, kissing her in a way that let her know how much love he had for her. He adjusted their bodies so he could remove every stitch of her clothing and then proceeded to undress himself.

He returned to the bed and pulled her into his arms, but not before taking a small box from the pocket of his jacket. He placed his knee on the bed and pulled her into his arms to slide a ring on her finger. "For the woman who took my breath away the moment I saw her. To the woman I love."

Tears clouded Gemma's eyes when she gazed down at the beautiful ring Callum had placed on her finger. Her breath nearly stopped. She remembered the ring. She had seen it that day when she'd gone shopping with the Austell women and they had stopped by that jewelry store. Gemma had mentioned to Le'Claire how much she'd liked this particular one.

"Oh, Callum. Even your mom knows?" She had to fight back tears as she continued to admire her ring.

"Sweetheart, everybody knows," he said, grinning. "I had sworn them to secrecy. It was important for me to court you the way you deserved. You hadn't dated a whole lot, and I wanted to show you that not all guys were heartbreakers."

She wrapped her arms around his neck. "And you did court me. I just didn't know that's what you were doing. I just figured you were being nice, sending me those flowers, taking me to the movies and those picnic lunches on the beach. I just thought you were showing me how much you appreciated me…"

"In bed?"

"Yes."

"And that's what I was afraid of," he said, pulling her closer to him. "I didn't want you to think it was all about sex, because it wasn't. When I told you I would give you anything and everything you wanted, Gemma, I meant it. All you had to do was ask for it, even my love, which is something you already had."

She rested her head on his bare chest for a moment and then she lifted her head to look back at him. "Do you think you wasted three years living here, Callum?"

He shook his head. "No. Being here gave me a chance to love you from afar while watching you grow and mature into the beautiful woman you are today. I saw you gain your independence and then wear it like a brand of accomplishment in everything you did. I was so proud of you when you landed that big contract with the city, because I knew exactly what you could do. That gave me the idea to buy that house for you to decorate. That will be our home and the condo will become our private retreat when we want to spend time at the beach."

He paused a moment. "I know you'll miss your family and all, and—"

Gemma reached up and placed a finger to his lips. "Yes, I will miss my family, but my home will be with you. We will come back and visit and that will be good enough for me. I want to be in Sydney with you."

Callum didn't say anything for a moment and then asked. "What about your business here?"

Gemma smiled. "I'm closing it. I've already opened another shop in Sydney, thanks to you. Same name but different location."

Her smile widened. "I love you, Callum. I want to be your wife and have your babies and I promise to always make you happy."

"Oh, Gemma." He reached out and cupped her face with both hands, lightly brushing his lips against hers before taking it in a hard kiss, swallowing her breath in the process.

He shifted to lie down on the bed and took her with him, placing her body on top of his while he continued to kiss her with a need that made every part of his body feel sensitive.

He tore his mouth away from hers to pull in a much-needed breath, but she fisted her hands in his hair to bring his face closer, before nibbling on his lips and licking around the corners of his mouth. And when he released a deep moan, she slid her tongue into his mouth and begin kissing him the way she'd gotten used to him kissing her.

Callum felt his control slipping and knew this kiss would be imprinted on his brain forever. He deepened the kiss, felt his engorged sex press against the apex of her thighs, knowing just what it wanted. Just what it needed.

Just what it was going to get.

He pulled his mouth away long enough to adjust her body over his. While staring into her eyes, he pushed upward and thrust into her, immediately feeling her heat as he buried himself deep in her warmth. He pulled out and thrust in again while the hard nipples of her breasts grazed his chest.

And then she began riding him, moving her body on top of his in a way that had him catching his breath after every stroke. Together, they rode, they gave and took, mated in a way that touched everything inside of him; had him chanting her name over and over.

Then everything seemed to explode and he felt her body when it detonated. He soon followed, but continued hammering home, getting all he could and making her come again.

"Callum!"

"That's it, my love, feel the pleasure. Feel our love."

And then he leaned up and kissed her, took her mouth with a hunger that should already have been appeased. But he knew he would always want this. He would always want her, and he intended to never let her regret the day she'd given him her heart.

Totally sated, Gemma slowly opened her eyes and, like so many other times over the past weeks, Callum was in bed with her, and she was wrapped in his embrace. She snuggled closer and turned in his arms to find him watching her with satisfied passion in the depth of his green eyes.

She smiled at him. "I think we broke the bed."

He returned her smile and tightened his arms around her. "Probably did. But it can be fixed."

"If not, we can stay at my place," she offered.

"That will work."

At that moment the phone rang and he shifted their

bodies to reach and pick it up. "That's probably Mom, calling to make sure things between us are all right."

He picked up the phone. "Hello."

He nodded a few times. "Okay, we're on our way."

He glanced over at Gemma and smiled. "That was Dillon. Chloe's water broke and Ramsey rushed her to the hospital. Looks like there's going to be a new Westmoreland born tonight."

It didn't take long for Callum and Gemma to get to the hospital, and already it was crowded with Westmorelands. It was almost 3:00 a.m. If anyone was curious as to why they were all together at that time of the morning, no one mentioned it.

"The baby is already here," Bailey said, excited. "We have a girl, just like we wanted."

Callum couldn't help throwing his head back and laughing. Good old Ram had a daughter.

"How's Chloe?" Gemma asked.

"Ramsey came out a few moments ago and said she's fine," Megan said. "The baby is a surprise."

"Yes, we didn't expect her for another week," Dillon said grinning. He glanced over at his pregnant wife, Pam, and smiled as he pulled her closer to him. "That makes me nervous."

"Has anyone called and told Chloe's father?"

"Yes," Chloe's best friend, Lucia, said smiling. "He's a happy grandpa and he'll be here sometime tomorrow."

"What's the baby's name?" Callum asked.

It was Derringer who spoke up. "They are naming her Susan after Mom. And they're using Chloe's mom's name as her middle name."

Gemma smiled. She knew Chloe had lost her mother at an early age, too. "Oh, that's nice. Our parents' first grand. They would be proud."

"They *are* proud," Dillon said, playfully tapping her nose.

"Hey, is this an engagement ring?" Bailey asked loudly, grabbing Gemma's hand.

Gemma glanced up at Callum and smiled lovingly. "Yes, we're getting married."

Cheers went up in the hospital waiting room. The Westmorelands had a lot to celebrate.

Zane glanced over at Dillon and Pam. "I guess now we're depending on you two to keep us male Westmorelands in the majority."

"Yeah," Derringer agreed.

"You know the two of you could find ladies to marry and start making your own babies," Megan said sweetly to her brothers. Her suggestion did exactly what she'd expected it to do—zip their lips.

Callum pulled Gemma closer into his arms. They shared a look. They didn't care if they had boys or girls—they just wanted babies. There were not going to be any hassles getting a big family out of them.

"Happy?" Callum asked.

"Extremely," she whispered.

Callum looked forward to when they would be alone again and he bent and told her just what he intended to do when they got back to the cabin.

Gemma blushed. Megan shot her sister a look. "You okay, Gem?"

Gemma smiled, glanced up at Callum and then back at her sister. "Yes, I couldn't be better."

Epilogue

There is nothing like a Westmoreland wedding, and this one was extra special because guests came from as far away as Australia and the Middle East. Gemma glanced out at the single ladies, waiting to catch her bouquet. She turned her back to the crowd, closed her eyes and threw it high over her head.

When she heard all the cheering, she turned around and smiled. It had been caught by Lucia Conyers, Chloe's best friend. She glanced across the room and looked at the two new babies. As if Susan's birth had started a trend, Dillon and Pam's son, Denver, came early, too.

"When can we sneak away?"

"You've waited three years. Another three hours won't kill you," she jokingly replied to her husband of two hours.

"Don't be so sure about that," was his quick response.

Their bags were packed and he was going to take her to India, as they'd planned before. Then they would visit Korea and Japan. She wanted to get decorating ideas with a few Asian pieces.

Callum took his wife's hand in his as they moved around the ballroom. He had been introduced to all the Atlanta Westmorelands before when he was invited to the Westmoreland family reunion as a guest. Now he would attend the next one as a bona fide member of the Westmoreland clan.

"How soon do you want to start making a baby?"

Gemma almost choked on her punch. He gave her a few pats on the back and grinned. "Didn't mean for you to gag."

"Can we at least wait until we're alone?"

"To talk about it or to get things started?"

Gemma chuckled as she shook her head. "Why do I get the feeling there will never be a dull moment with you?"

He pulled her closer to him. "Because there won't be. Remember I'm the one who knows what a Westmoreland wants. At least I know what my Westmoreland wants."

Gemma wrapped her arms around his neck. "I'm an Austell now," she said proudly.

"Oh, yes, I know. And trust me—I will never let you forget it."

Callum then pulled her into his arms and in front of all their wedding guests, he kissed her with all the love flowing in his heart. He had in his arms everything he'd ever wanted.

* * * * *

"Nice perfume. It's different from your usual."

Rina swallowed against the gasp of irritation that rose in her throat. She hadn't even thought about what perfume Sara had been wearing. It was yet another example of how careful she was going to have to be if she was to carry this off properly.

She turned and smiled at Rey, slipping on a pair of sunglasses as she did so, so he couldn't see the lie in her eyes. "It's something I picked up while I was away. Do you like it?"

From behind her, Rey leaned in and inhaled again, his lips mere centimeters from the curve of her neck.

"Mmm, yeah, I do."

A frisson of awareness shot down Rina's spine with the velocity of lightning, leaving a fierce sizzle throbbing in its wake.

What was it she had told herself only minutes ago? About handling things provided it didn't get too personal? Right now it looked as if that was to be her biggest obstacle, because despite everything, she was left fighting a desire to get very personal indeed.

Dear Reader,

One of the things I do before I start writing my books is spend time finding pictures of people who, to me, embody my characters. The picture I had in my mind of Reynard del Castillo was a good one, but the photo I found of the male model I ended up using as my inspiration for Reynard was beyond even my expectations. Choosing which photos *not* to use as visual prompts was a serious problem. I tell you, it's a tough job sometimes being a writer, but someone's got to do it.

In this story, set on my fictional Mediterranean island, Isla Sagrado, Reynard del Castillo gets more than he bargained for with his engagement to Sara Woodville. Especially when the fiancée in question turns out to be none other than her identical twin sister, Rina. This is the first time I've worked with a sister-swap story line and I loved working with both Rina's conscience and Reynard's determination to protect his family. I particularly loved the tug-of-war they each battled with as they found their path to love.

I hope you enjoy *Stand-In Bride's Seduction* and that you look forward to my next book, where the youngest del Castillo brother, Benedict, finds that what he thought was lost forever was really just on the opposite side of the world. How he's going to keep it is quite another story.

Happy reading and very best wishes,

Yvonne Lindsay

STAND-IN
BRIDE'S
SEDUCTION

BY
YVONNE LINDSAY

Published in Great Britain 2011
by Mills & Boon, an imprint of Harlequin (UK) Limited,
Eton House, 18-24 Paradise Road, Richmond, Surrey TW9 1SR

© Dolce Vita Trust 2010

ISBN: 978 0 263 88314 5

51-0911

Harlequin (UK) policy is to use papers that are natural, renewable and
recyclable products and made from wood grown in sustainable forests. The
logging and manufacturing processes conform to the legal environmental
regulations of the country of origin.

Printed and bound in Spain
by Blackprint CPI, Barcelona

New Zealand-born to Dutch immigrant parents, **Yvonne Lindsay** became an avid romance reader at the age of thirteen. Now married to her "blind date" and with two surprisingly amenable teenagers, she remains a firm believer in the power of romance. Yvonne feels privileged to be able to bring to her readers the stories of her heart. In her spare time, when not writing, she can be found with her nose firmly in a book, reliving the power of love in all walks of life. She can be contacted via her website, www.yvonnelindsay.com.

This book is dedicated to the fabulous writers' organizations around the world, and the volunteers who run them, who provide support and encouragement and learning to wannabe writers everywhere.

One

"Rina! Over here!"

Sarina Woodville turned her head to the sound of her twin sister's voice. A huge smile spread across her tired features as she picked out the vibrant redhead in the crowd of faces in the airport's arrivals hall. Clearing customs and immigration had been smooth and efficient, a fact she was very grateful for at this stage of her journey. Tugging her suitcase along behind her, Rina crossed the short distance to her sister's waiting arms.

"It's so good to see you," Rina said.

"How was your trip? Absolute hell, I bet. It's so long, isn't it?" Sara bubbled along, not really listening for a response.

Despite how obviously happy her twin was to see her, Rina couldn't help but notice the strain on her face and the dark rings around her eyes.

"Sara, is everything okay? You're still all right with me staying with you, aren't you?"

She really hoped Sara hadn't changed her mind. When Rina's engagement had unexpectedly come to an ignominious end last week and Sara had suggested she come to Isla Sagrado for some much needed cosseting, she'd jumped at the chance to get away for a while. But now she was afraid she might be in the way. Sara had only recently become engaged herself, to some guy called Reynard del Castillo. Just privately, Rina thought the name a little on the pretentious side but then again, from what she'd heard from Sara, the family was virtually royalty here on this tiny Mediterranean island republic.

The del Castillos had sponsored the equestrian event trials Sara had participated in here after a successful tour in France. Her e-mails had been full of effusive praise for the beauty of the island—and the men on it. It hadn't taken a Mensa-rated IQ to see where her flighty sister was leading when her e-mails had mentioned Reynard del Castillo on several occasions. Their rapid engagement, though, had come as a huge surprise. This Reynard must be quite a man to have pinned Sara down.

Sara flashed her a weak smile. "Come to the cafe over here and we can talk."

"Can't we talk on the way to your place?" Rina asked, confused.

Right now she wanted nothing more than a shower, maybe a hot drink and then about ten or twelve uninterrupted hours of sleep. By tomorrow morning she was certain she'd be feeling human again. The journey between New Zealand and Isla Sagrado, with all its painfully necessary stopovers and airport transfers, was hitting around thirty-seven hours now, and counting. She was ready to drop on her feet.

"It's complicated and I don't have much time. I'm really sorry. I *will* explain later, I promise, but right now I have to get back to France."

"You what?" Rina's heart plummeted.

She knew Sara had recently been visiting some friends in the South of France, people she'd met on the event circuit, but had been due back today. Hence Rina's arrival here, timed to coincide with Sara's.

"Back to France? But didn't you fly in just now?"

Sara nodded, and wouldn't meet Rina's eyes. Instead she glanced at the departures board against the far wall.

"I did, but I'm just not ready to be back here yet. I thought I would be, but I need more time. Here." She reached into her handbag to grab an envelope and thrust it across the small, round table at Rina. "I wrote this for you just in case we missed one another this afternoon. Look, I'm really sorry. I wish I wasn't so strapped for time. I know you came here for support, but I really need *your* help. I've laid it all out in the letter and I promise to be back here for you as soon as I've sorted things out.

"Go to the cottage, I've given you the key in here." She tapped the envelope. "Settle yourself in, then when I get back we'll have a good old bitch-and-gossip session and get all our man-worries out of our systems, okay?"

The public address system suddenly crackled to life, announcing a final call for passengers to Perpignan.

"Oh, that's me. I'm so sorry, Reeny-bean," Sara said, using the pet name she'd always used when she needed to cajole or coerce her sister into a favor. "I know I said I'd be here for you but—"

Sara rose from her seat and reached forward to envelop Rina in her arms.

"I'll make it up to you soon, I promise. Love you!"

And then, she was gone. Stunned, Rina sat at the tiny

table and watched as her sister disappeared in the direction of her departure gate. When it finally penetrated her shell-shocked, jet-lagged, sleep-deprived mind that Sara had really gone and left her here, her fingers clenched reflexively around the envelope in her hand. The crinkle of paper reminded her that the only way she was going to get an answer from her sister right now was to open the envelope.

It was bulkier than she'd expected and she ripped away the seal to tip out the letter and a key—and something else that tumbled with a brilliant flash and landed on the coffee-cup-rim-stained table in front of her. Rina reached quickly to pick it up, barely stifling a gasp of shock as she did so. A massive princess-cut diamond solitaire set on an ornately chaste platinum band winked back at her.

It was typical Sara to put something so valuable in something as innocuous and insecure as an envelope. Rina stifled the sudden surge of irritation that flooded through her at Sara's careless actions, and unfolded the single sheet of paper. As she read her sister's looped handwriting, her fingers fisted tight around the ring in her hand.

Rina groaned out loud. Sara hadn't. She couldn't have. It was beyond belief and way beyond anything her sister had ever done before. No wonder she hadn't wanted to admit any of this face-to-face and had run the instant she'd had the opportunity. Rina scoured the words again, hoping against hope that she'd misread something, but no.

Darling Rina, I'm so sorry I can't be there with you. I know it's a tough time for you but at least you're away from him—and can take some time to heal. Thing is, I think I've made a big mistake and I really need some space to think long and hard about whether I'm doing the right thing. Please, can you be me for a few days while I sort things out? Reynard will never need to know. Just put on my engagement ring and wear some of my stuff—you know, like we used to before we grew up. Well, before you grew up anyway. My maturity is probably still under question.

Sara went on to list a few hints and tips about Reynard, things like how they'd met, what his favorite beverage was, where they'd been together.

Beneath her exhaustion and the shock of her sister's outrageous request, Rina felt anger begin to swell from deep inside.

How dare Sara ask her to do this? Had she no compassion for anyone but herself? How could she expect her twin, fresh from a painful broken engagement, to slide straight into another and pretend to be someone she wasn't? It was totally and completely wrong. Let alone what it was expecting of Rina, it certainly wasn't fair to Reynard del Castillo, either.

Rina crushed the letter in her hand as her anger inflamed and grew. The words Sara had used imprinted on her mind.

I think I've made a big mistake.

She heard almost exactly the same words play in her head from when she'd last heard them. Not from Sara, but from her ex-fiancé, Jacob.

Despite the warmth in the airport terminal, Rina felt suddenly and unutterably cold. She was back there in that restaurant. Their favorite. Sitting across from the man she'd planned to spend the rest of her life with and hearing him tell her that he had fallen in love with someone else. How he'd been putting off telling her for months but with their wedding only a week away, he could put it off no longer.

Rina shook her head to rid it of the images lodged there. After the deception Jacob had practiced all those months, the thought of deceiving someone else made her feel physically ill. There was no way she was doing this. Not even for her twin. No way.

She shoved the letter, key and ring into the envelope and pushed them deep inside her handbag before hoisting the bag back onto her weary shoulder and getting up from the table. She reached for the handle on her suitcase and pulled it along behind her. She was going to find a taxi, go to the cottage where Sara had been staying, get showered, get dressed and, somehow, find this Reynard del Castillo and tell him what her sister was obviously too afraid to. No one deserved to be lied to as Sara had suggested. No one.

Reynard del Castillo studied the court report that had sat on his office desk now for six months. He'd kept it there as a reminder to be ever-vigilant of the opportunists who frequently targeted his family as a fast ticket to easy street.

He opened the report and stared at the name marked in bold ink. Estella Martinez. The woman had worked for him here in his office. Vivacious, beautiful and intelligent, he'd almost been tempted into indulging in an affair with her. Almost, but not quite, because instinct warned him she was not what she painted herself to be. When Estella had attempted to stage a scene between them, one where he would be seen to be breaching employer-employee protocols, he'd spun into action to ensure that her claims of sexual harassment and her offers to keep things quiet— both from his family and the tabloids, for several hundred thousand Euros—fell flat in the dust.

Estella Martinez's pitiful grasping attempt at her

moment of fame, her attempts at extortion—all of it had been exposed in the closed court trial. He'd used every one of his contacts and the weight of his family name and position to see that her charges were brought before the Court within the minimum amount of time and that there was no public access to either the proceedings or the results of those proceedings.

To avoid a prison sentence for the extortion attempt, she had agreed to the gag clause his attorneys had so cleverly worded as well as the restraining order to remain well away from Isla Sagrado and any member of the del Castillo family, wherever they might be traveling.

He slid the concisely written papers back into the envelope in which they'd been delivered and sent the entire package through his shredder. There, gone as effectively as she had been escorted to the airport and off the island. He needed no such reminders now.

While the experience had left a bad taste in his mouth, his recent engagement to Sara Woodville was all the more sweet. She made few demands upon their relationship, which was exactly the way he wanted it to be, and helped to serve the purpose for which the engagement was intended: to keep his grandfather off his back about the curse of the governess. The old story of the curse dated back hundreds of years to a time of myths and superstitions which was where, in Reynard's opinion, nonsense like that belonged. But his grandfather, *Abuelo,* had recently fixated on it, and to ensure the old man stopped worrying about Rey and his brothers being the last of the family line, as the curse predicted, Reynard and his brothers had taken steps to ease his fears.

It had been bad enough when *Abuelo*'s unnecessary tension and worry had led to a stroke last month. His manservant had acted swiftly and *Abuelo* had received the vital medical care he needed to begin a strong recovery. Neither Rey nor his brothers, Alexander and Benedict, wanted to go through that again. They'd already resolved to do whatever it took to put the family patriarch's mind at rest, to ensure his final years were as comfortable as they could be.

Alex had gone so far as to revisit a twenty-five-year-old engagement promise made when he was only a boy and the woman involved was but three months old. Rey smiled as he thought of his new sister-in-law, Loren. She'd looked so frail and feminine—so young when she'd returned to Isla Sagrado to be Alex's bride. Who could have known a backbone of pure steel ran through her tiny frame?

She'd fought hard for her marriage. Fought and won. And strangely enough, she and Alex no longer scorned the idea of the curse. If anything, in their happiness, they were all the more determined for him and Benedict to settle down.

Settling down wasn't really something Reynard was ready for, but in the meantime, being engaged to Sara was working out quite nicely when it came to soothing *Abuelo*'s mind. And that, ultimately, was all Reynard was concerned with. Reynard would do whatever it took to protect his family—to ease every fear and to eliminate, utterly and completely, any threat. And women like Estella Martinez—well, they would get their just deserts every time.

Sarina lifted her face to the warm Mediterranean sun as she stepped outside Isla Sagrado's airport terminal. The contrast between the golden kiss of heat on her cheeks and the icy chill of rain, sleet and snow back home in the South Island of New Zealand was unbelievable. No wonder

Sara had chosen to stay here rather than come home to a southern hemisphere winter.

And if all had gone as it was supposed to, Rina would have been not far from here on a Greek island for her honeymoon. She remembered going to the travel agency with Jacob and poring over the brochures, weighing and balancing the charms of each destination to find the perfect place to celebrate the start of their new life together.

Rina absently rubbed the ring finger of her left hand with her thumb. An old habit, and one she would train herself to stop as she became all too aware of the deficit there and the faint indentation in her skin.

She tilted her head back a little, and closed her eyes against the brightness of the sun. Funny how her eyes watered even behind her sunglasses.

So what if Jacob had wanted someone more spontaneous, someone who wasn't afraid to spice things up? Rina bit back tears at the memory of the emotional hurt he'd inflicted. And here she'd thought she'd chosen a life partner who was stable and secure—someone the complete antithesis of her parents and their fiercely intense, competitive and oftentimes combative relationship. Just went to prove how wrong a girl could be. She'd have felt better if she and Jacob *had* fought—if he'd simply told her that she wasn't what he wanted, rather than stringing her along for all that time, long after he'd stopped loving her.

Rina forced from her mind the memory of Jacob's unrepentant and abrupt withdrawal from the relationship they'd developed over the past five years. She'd promised herself she wouldn't shed another tear over him. And she wouldn't. Not a single one.

She swallowed hard against the lump in her throat. Why were promises so darn hard to keep?

The crowd of travelers she'd arrived with had long since

dispersed, and the sidewalks outside the terminal building were nearly empty. Worse, so were the taxi stands. Half an hour later Rina was beginning to wilt as the concentrated afternoon heat continued to build around her. Mindful of her fair skin—the curse of a natural redhead—she'd sought some shade near the side of the building.

A trickle of perspiration ran down Rina's back, as she flicked another glance at her watch—a gift from Sara and her only really frivolous piece of jewelry with its crystal embedded bezel and bracelet-style strap. Finally, thankfully, a green-and-white taxi pulled up. Tucking her shoulder bag securely against her side, Rina tightened her grip on the extended handle of her practical black suitcase and rolled it to the curbside.

"The Governess's Cottage, please," Rina said through the open passenger window.

Was it her imagination or did the driver surreptitiously cross himself as he got out of the taxi and walked around to lift her suitcase into the trunk of his car? Either way, she was too tired to care right now. She could only focus on one thing. Sorting out this wretched mess her sister had left her in.

Rina watched the departing taxi speed down the road for a few minutes, more than a little startled by the haste with which the driver had taken off. Goodness only knew why he was in such a hurry.

She grabbed her suitcase handle for what she hoped would be the last time in the next four weeks and trudged wearily through the pretty iron gate set within a stone wall that surrounded the cottage. "Quaint" really was the only word to describe the ancient structure, Rina decided as she followed the path to the tiny front porch with its stone steps worn by the passage of years of foot traffic.

Pale ocher-plastered brick here and there, the plaster crumbling away, revealing the ancient brick beneath—and with a darker orange tiled roof, it looked like an old-fashioned watercolor. Deep-set mullioned windows, sashed with faded blue wooden trim, gave an insight into sparse, but adequate, furnishings inside. Not entirely Spanish in style, yet not entirely French either, the cottage was a delightfully eclectic mixture of both.

Inside, she thought she could hear a phone ring before the strident chime shut off abruptly for a few moments then started all over again.

Rina dug in her handbag for the envelope Sara had left her. The heavy old key fit neatly into the ancient black lock, and the door swung smoothly open. The telephone, coincidentally, fell silent once more as she stepped inside.

She didn't take so much as a second to admire the exposed beam ceiling of the main rooms of the cottage, nor the pristine perfection of the charming blue and white tiled bathroom. And she didn't allow herself more than a single longing glance at the all-too-tempting bed in the room where she'd stowed her suitcase. She was a woman on a single-minded mission. To tell Sara's fiancé exactly what she'd done. Surely he'd be reasonable. After all, they'd met and become engaged in such a short space of time. They barely knew one another. A certain amount of second thought was bound to occur.

After her shower, Rina grabbed the first thing off the top of her open suitcase and dragged it over her barely dry body, and headed into the open-plan sitting room where she searched for a phone.

Ten minutes later she had exactly what she needed. Thanking Isla Sagrado's multilingual culture, and the high profile of the del Castillo family, not to mention the helpfulness of the information operator, for making the process so straightforward, she made another quick call and ordered a taxi to collect her and take her into the city, Puerto Seguro, and Reynard's offices.

By the time Rina arrived at the tasteful high-rise in the downtown section of the port city, she was running on pure nerves. Having been the recent recipient of such a break in relations, she was wary of how to approach this. What did you say to someone you'd never met before when you wanted to tell him that his engagement was very likely on shaky ground?

She smoothed trembling hands over the sleeveless beige silk dress she'd pulled on in such a hurry and hoped her hair wasn't already escaping the casual twist. She'd secured it with a couple of topaz-colored jeweled clips she'd found scattered, in typical Sara-like fashion, on the bathroom vanity.

A quick scan of the floor directory next to the bank of elevators gave her the last bit of information she needed. Rina stepped into one of the elevator cars and pressed the button for the twenty-first floor. Her stomach lurched as the car started its upward journey, and all the while she ran through her head what she needed to say.

The corridor that faced her as she stepped out was vast and empty. The muted tones of elegant piped music filtered through discreetly placed ceiling speakers. Directly ahead of her was a matched pair of large wooden doors, each one displaying an ornate carving that was, no doubt, the del Castillo family crest. Rina stepped forward and ran her fingertips over the raised edges of the stylized shield divided into three sections. In one was an intricately carved sword, in another a scroll or parchment of some description and the bottom section held an ornate heart. Her patchy Spanish translated the words.

Honor. Truth. Love.

She swallowed. If the man she was coming to see lived by the ancient code of his family, then she was definitely doing the right thing by coming here and telling him the truth. It was the only thing she could do.

Rina pushed against the brass doorplate at the very same moment the door in question swung abruptly away from her. With all her energy moving forward, she stumbled and suddenly fell against an immovable rock of a hard male body clad in a perfectly tailored charcoal gray suit.

Large, warm hands swiftly cupped her elbows and steadied her. Balanced on her feet now, Rina summoned a smile and looked up. Instantly, her heart skittered in her chest as she took in the perfection of male beauty in the face above hers.

A broad, tanned forehead, strong dark brows over clear hazel eyes edged with short, dark lashes. A perfectly balanced face bisected by a straight nose that had obviously never been on the wrong end of a tackle in a rugby game, and finely chiseled lips that were even now curving in a smile that held a strange combination of recognition and relief.

"Thank God you're here," he murmured, his voice a deep caress that she felt as though it was a stroke of velvet across her skin.

"Mr. del Castillo. Your brother says he'll meet you at the hospital," the receptionist at the vast modern desk behind him said.

The young woman's words sank slowly into Rina's mind. Mr. del Castillo? This man, who looked like he'd be better suited to the cover of *GQ* magazine than a conference room, was her sister's fiancé, Reynard del Castillo?

Two

Before she realized what was happening, Rina found herself spun around and, her hand firmly locked in his, was marched swiftly toward the elevators.

"Sara! I've been trying to reach you for the past hour! I tried both your cell and your home phone because I wasn't sure you were back on the island. I don't know why you refused to tell me the details on your flight information. I could have picked you up from the airport. Why didn't you call me?"

"I—" she began. Her mind raced to catch up with him. Cell phone. Of course, Sara must be ignoring his calls. With her own number being New Zealand based, on global roaming, she knew she couldn't just say she'd changed numbers. *Think,* she told herself, *what would Sara do or say?* Rina latched onto the easiest response. "I'm sorry—I lost my phone while I was away. You know what I'm like."

"It doesn't matter now. I'm just glad you're here."

"But I—"

The look on his face sent a chill down through her. His eyes, which only a moment ago had been warm and welcoming, were suddenly bleak—a small frown creasing the smooth skin between his brows.

"I've got bad news. Benedict's been involved in an accident. Alex just called me. We're meeting him and *Abuelo* at the hospital. Thank goodness you came here, saves time for us both."

"Benedict?"

"The idiot." Reynard shook his head slowly. "You know how he drives. Seems the coast road out to the vineyard got the better of him, and that high performance pile of metal he calls a car."

"Is he okay?"

"No, he's not. We're not sure how long he was trapped in the car but it took emergency services nearly an hour to free him from the wreck. He's in surgery now."

Reynard's voice broke on the words and Rina instinctively curled her fingers tighter around his.

"I'm sure he'll be okay," she said with as much calm encouragement as she could muster.

Inside, though, her stomach knotted on the news. How on earth could she tell Reynard that she wasn't who he thought she was now? Benedict was the younger of the del Castillo brothers; she remembered that much from one of Sara's e-mails. She also remembered Sara mentioning that Benedict ran the winery division of the family business.

"I'm glad you're here," Reynard said, his hand all but squeezing hers now.

"I'm glad I'm here, too," she whispered in response, and in a strange way she really was.

The last thing he needed right now was an absentee

fiancée. Tomorrow would be soon enough to tell him the truth, once they knew that Benedict would be all right.

Reynard fell silent for the balance of the journey in the elevator. Rina could feel the tension and worry radiating off him in tangible waves and her heart twisted. She knew how she'd be feeling right now if it was Sara in the same position as Benedict. She'd barely be able to function.

Finally, the elevator doors sprang open to reveal a basement parking garage. Reynard reached into a trouser pocket and she saw the lights flash on a vehicle across the way. Even in the basement lighting, the low sleek car shone as if its surface was mirror finished. The rearing horse symbol on the front grill spoke to its expensive origins.

Confusion swirled around her. So far Reynard del Castillo hit every one of her sister's hot buttons. He was deliciously tall, exquisitely handsome and clearly money was no object. Rina had been unable to detect a single thing about him that wouldn't appeal to her sister on any level. So why was Sara wondering if she'd made a mistake? And why did she feel she had to leave to figure things out? It wasn't like Sara to run away from anything, either. She was usually more up-front about things than this. So why had she done so?

Despite his obvious anxiety about his brother, and his eagerness to get to the hospital, Reynard took the time to open the passenger door for her and waited until she was settled before closing her door and coming around to the driver's side. It took her by surprise. She was staunchly independent, and more than used to taking care of herself. She expected and administered equality in all the spheres of her life. However, the old-fashioned courtesy was strangely appealing.

And that wasn't all that was appealing about the man. In the close confines of the car, her senses became finely tuned to everything about him. The warmth that emanated from his body despite the car's air-conditioning, the capable movement of his hands on the steering wheel and the gear stick as he maneuvered out of the car park and into the blinding sunlight outdoors—not to mention the subtle blend of his fragrance.

She closed her eyes and slowly inhaled, mentally picking apart the different layers of the scent. It reminded her of the decadence of consuming a succulent mango, slice by luscious slice, and underlying that sensual fruitiness was another scent. Something spicy. Patchouli, maybe? Whatever it was, it was doing crazy things to her insides. Things that her insides shouldn't be doing given that she'd just been cast off by her own fiancé and was thinking these thoughts about her sister's!

Rina forced her eyes open. This was ridiculous. She'd never been the type to be so easily swayed by a man's appearance and presence. Passionate attraction went against every reasonable, logical instinct she had—and it scared her a little. Even at the height of her relationship with Jacob, when she'd agreed to spend the rest of her life with him, she'd never felt as drawn to him as she now did to the stranger sitting beside her.

She tried to shake it off. She was just overtired…and maybe a little emotionally vulnerable, after everything that had happened. Yes, that was definitely what was wrong with her. She'd get some sleep tonight and tell Reynard the truth tomorrow, and everything would go back to normal. She allowed her lips to part and forced herself to breathe lightly through her mouth in a vain attempt to rid herself of the disquieting sensation burgeoning to life deep inside her. Suddenly, telling him the truth tomorrow seemed a long, long time away.

When they pulled up outside the hospital, Rina alighted

from the car before Reynard could come around to her side and open the door for her. He did, however, ensure her hand was tucked in the corner of his arm as they walked toward the hospital doors.

It was all too easy to see why her sister had fallen so quickly for this man. He was what they'd always referred to between them as the whole package. She was no shortie, standing at five feet ten inches in bare feet, but he topped that by almost half a foot and had an air of command intriguingly entwined with an aura of sophisticated sexuality. It was enough to make a grown woman's mouth water.

Focus, Rina growled to herself, as they entered the pristine hospital reception area and Reynard made straight for the elevators. All the signs here were in three languages—Spanish, French and English—so she knew they were headed for the surgical floor.

Sudden nerves assailed her. What if another member of the family recognized her for a fraud? What would she do then? She forced herself to breathe calmly. Why should anyone suspect anything? she rationalized. If Reynard himself, supposedly Sara's fiancé, didn't immediately see the difference, then it made sense that no one else would, either.

On the surgical floor they were shown to a private waiting room. Immediately Rina spotted another handsome man who she assumed was Reynard's elder brother, Alexander. He stood near a window, his arm around a slender woman of average height, offering her comfort even as his own face bore the ravages of the worry they were all going through. Although his hair was darker than Reynard's, the family resemblance was still incredibly strong. On closer inspection, Rina realized that, converse to her original impression, the woman at his side was supporting him, rather than the other way around.

As soon as Alex saw his younger brother, he pulled away from his wife and came across the room. The affection the del Castillo brothers bore for each other was evident in the way they clasped in a long and silent embrace.

"Any news?" Reynard said as they pulled apart.

"Nothing," Alex said, his voice hoarse.

"The doctor said it could be a few hours," the other woman volunteered gently. Suddenly, she seemed to notice Rina standing near the door and crossed the room toward her. "You must be Sara. I'm so sorry our first meeting should be under these circumstances."

First meeting? Had Sara never met Reynard's family?

"She's only just returned from visiting friends in France. I haven't even given her time to take a breath yet." Reynard turned to Rina and pulled her to his side. "Alex, Loren, this is Sara Woodville, my fiancée."

"Welcome to the family," Alex said, taking her hand and leaning in to kiss her on the cheeks in European fashion. "As Loren said, I'm sorry we had to meet you like this, but I am glad you are here for Reynard."

"Thank you," she answered, but before she could say any more a commotion outside the waiting room distracted them.

A volley of voluble Spanish rent the air as the door opened. The del Castillo imprint was obvious on the face of the elderly gentleman who pushed into the room, leaning heavily on a highly polished wooden cane, soon followed by a middle-aged man who looked both worried and apologetic at the same time.

"I went to visit him at the nursing home to tell him the news in person, and he took my car keys and tried to hijack my car. I tried to stop him, *señors*, but he would not listen," the younger man said. "He said he would drive himself here if I did not bring him."

"Listen? Pah!" the white haired gentleman spat. "You think I am too old to give support to my grandchildren when they need me?"

"Don't worry, Javier, *Abuelo* will be fine with us. Why don't you see if you can find us all some decent coffee to drink, hmm?" Reynard suggested while smoothly stepping forward and taking his grandfather's arm.

"I know everyone else's preferences but, *señorita*, how do you take your coffee?" Javier asked.

"Strong and milky, thank you," Rina replied with a smile.

"You are forgetting your manners," the old man chastised his grandson. "Who is this young lady?"

His slightly quavering voice in heavily accented English belied the sharply inquisitive gleam in his eyes as he assessed Rina. For a moment she wondered if he could see right through her, see the falsehood she was perpetrating by masquerading as her twin.

"This is Sara Woodville, my fiancée," Reynard responded smoothly.

"It's about time she came back. I was beginning to think she was a figment of your imagination. The governess, she won't wait, you know. You mark my words. This accident of Benedict's," he stated as he waved a mottled hand through the air, "it is no accident, I tell you."

"*Abuelo,* enough!" Alex's voice was sharp. "Benedict endangered his own life every time he got behind the wheel of a car. It was bound to catch up with him sooner or later. It had nothing to do with—"

"You can deny it all you wish, my boy, but the facts remain in front of your face as clear as your nose. Now, where is my grandson? I wish to see him."

He imperiously stamped the cane he clutched in one gnarled hand on the vinyl floor, and Rina suddenly realized why the brothers had not wanted him at the hospital. He had no idea just how seriously hurt Benedict was.

She looked from the elderly man to his two grandsons, especially Reynard. His face was a mask of concern, his hazel eyes clouded. Clearly Benedict's injuries were life threatening. Why else would he and Alex be so determined to keep the information from their grandfather? And now, with him demanding to see his youngest grandson, and with the obvious respect they had for him so apparent in their demeanor, how could they tell him the truth?

Without a second thought, Rina stepped forward and tucked her hand in the crook of the older man's arm.

"Mr. del Castillo, I've been traveling all day and I'm exhausted. I need to sit down. Why don't you come and sit with me over here on one of these chairs and we'll get to know one another a little better?"

It wasn't an exaggeration. She *was* exhausted, and she'd been traveling, or on her feet now, for the better part of two days.

"What is this?" he bristled.

Rina immediately threw a worried glance toward Reynard who merely lifted his eyebrows a fraction.

"I'm sorry. Did I say something wrong?" she apologized.

"Rey, explain the meaning of this. Why does your fiancée call me *Meester* del Castillo?"

A small smile pulled at the sensual curve of Reynard's lips, giving Rina little insight into what had upset his grandfather.

"Should I have said *señor?* I'm sorry, my Spanish is—" she broke off. What if Sara's Spanish had improved past the basic minimum they'd both learned in their late teens on their big overseas experience?

"It is my mistake—I should have introduced the two of you properly instead of only doing half a job. Sara, this is my grandfather, Aston del Castillo," Reynard interjected.

"You must call me *Abuelo*," the old man replied, with a sudden twinkle in his eye. "If you're serious about marrying my grandson, that is."

Across the room Rey watched Sara blanch at his grandfather's words, and felt a brief surge of panic. Surely she wouldn't expose the capricious nature of their engagement now. He knew they'd entered into the thing as a bit of a lark, neither of them serious about it for now. Even Sara had said they should see where the wind blew them.

Her attitude had been what had made her perfect for the role as his fiancée. He'd needed an engagement that would require little true commitment from him while still keeping his grandfather off his back about getting married. He doubted that Sara had any more intention of them actually getting married right now than he did, himself. If *Abuelo* would just stop harping on about that wretched curse, they could all get back to normal again. And then, in a few months, he and Sara could part ways gracefully and without any hard feelings.

Of course, *Abuelo* was arguing even harder in favor of the curse now in light of the success of Alex and Loren's marriage. There was no denying that things had improved financially for the family business and economically on Isla Sagrado as a whole, even in the short time since the two had married, supporting *Abuelo*'s claims that marriage for all three of the brothers would break the curse, and bring prosperity back to the family.

Reynard still had his doubts though, about the curse of the governess. *Abuelo* had become unhealthily obsessed with the subject in recent months, even claiming to see her ghost. If the old man were to be believed, the scorned woman's final words to her del Castillo lover were solely responsible for every sudden death in the family, not to mention the downturn in the economy of Isla Sagrado. In itself, the thought was ridiculous, but Reynard and his brothers loved their grandfather deeply and had been prepared to do whatever it took to ensure his final years remained happy. Even if, on Reynard's part, it meant faking an engagement.

Suddenly Rey became aware of the extended silence in the room. He stepped forward to Sara's other side and kissed the tip of her lightly freckled nose, and was amused to see a faint flush of color flood her cheeks.

"Of course she's serious about marrying me, *Abuelo*. Who wouldn't want to be a del Castillo bride?"

"Bueno," the old man said then nodded and allowed himself to be drawn over to a bank of chairs in the room where he pulled Sara down alongside him.

Before long, their heads were together and Rey felt a sense of reprieve that his grandfather was distracted, at least for now. He moved over to Alex and Loren.

"She did that well," Alex commented, nodding to where Sara and their grandfather were conversing in a combination of Spanish and English.

Rey nodded, "Thank goodness. What were you going to tell him?"

Alex's face grew bleak. "The truth?"

"No," Loren murmured. "You can't. Not while he's still recovering from his stroke. He's not even well enough to be back home at the castillo yet. I'd be terrified he'd suffer a setback and never be allowed home—and you know what that would do to him."

"You're right," Rey agreed. "We don't want a repeat of that night."

"So what then? Keep him waiting with us until the surgeons are finished?"

"Surgeons?"

Rey felt ill. So there was more than one surgeon working on his brother. Working to save his life. The deep hollow ache that had manifested in his chest during Alex's first call sharpened and ached that little bit harder. He sent a silent prayer that his brother's strength and health would be enough to see him through this and that the skill of Isla Sagrado's best doctors would ensure his return to his family fold, where he belonged.

He gathered his fears in a tight knot and thrust them to the back of his mind.

"Did they say how long?"

Alex shook his head. "Could be hours yet."

Rey looked back toward Sara. "*Maybe* if Sara takes him, *Abuelo* will agree to go back to the home. Javier can drive them both and then take her back to the cottage."

"It's a good idea, but," Alex suggested as he curled his arm just that little bit tighter around his wife's slender waist, "are you sure you don't need her here?"

Need her here? Rey's mind was fogged for a moment but then he realized what his brother was getting at. Of course, under normal circumstances, if his had been a normal engagement, he'd want his fiancée here with him. But would Sara agree to play along? The one time she'd needed medical attention during the event trials where he'd met her, she'd all but run screaming from the first aid tent. All because they'd wanted to examine her when she'd bumped her head after fainting in the heat. He'd have guessed that, under any circumstances, a hospital was the last place on earth she'd choose to be. Besides, their relationship was hardly one where he would expect her emotional support at a time like this.

He quickly recovered his scattered thoughts. "Perhaps later. She's tired, just returned from Perpignan." *And God only knows where else judging by the exhaustion dragging at her lithe body.* "I didn't even give her time to say hello before we were on our way here. I'll suggest it to them after Javier has brought coffee."

It must have taken a minor miracle but Javier eventually returned with a series of steaming hot paper cups in varying sizes and handed each to its recipient, the shortest and darkest brew going to *Abuelo.*

"Ah, thank goodness. Finally, a decent cup of coffee." The old man sighed his pleasure as he savored the aromatic beverage.

"I thought it would be okay, just this once," Javier said by way of explanation to the brothers. "What they serve him in the convalescent home is…" Javier's expression left nothing to the imagination.

"That's fine," Rey replied and watched as Sara lifted the top off her cup and blew on the milky contents before taking a sip. *Abuelo* had distracted him when she'd given Javier her coffee order earlier, but now Rey looked at her in surprise. He knew for a fact that she took her coffee black, when she drank it. In the past couple of weeks, though, she hadn't touched any, saying she was on a health kick or something like that. Looked like the health kick was over, if the way she obviously enjoyed the coffee now was any indicator.

Rey watched as her throat slowly swallowed, the muscles moving sinuously beneath her pale skin, and suddenly he was jolted with a burst of sexual awareness that completely blindsided him.

Their relationship to date had been more platonic than passionate. Sure, they'd exchanged a few kisses in the moonlight, but overall he hadn't been fixated on getting her into his bed. They had fun together—kept things light and carefree—and that was the way he'd planned on keeping it before eventually carefully deconstructing the engagement and withdrawing with no hurt feelings. Right now, though, he wanted nothing more than to lose himself, and what was happening to his family, in the soft scents of her skin and the sensations of being entwined with her body.

She looked up at him over the rim of her cup, her gray eyes widening at what he could only assume was the burning hunger reflected in his own. Her hand shook slightly as she tipped her cup straight again and lowered it onto the table next to her. Her pink tongue swept away the trace of moisture left behind by the coffee on her lips.

Inside, whatever had taken hold of him tightened and sharpened into something totally inappropriate for a hospital waiting room. Remembering that somewhere on this floor his younger brother fought for his life beneath a surgeon's blade brought Rey painfully back into the here and now.

"*Querida,* you look weary. Perhaps you should go back to the cottage. I can call you there—let you know when we hear any news." Before she could answer he turned to his grandfather. "Would you escort her back for me, *Abuelo?* I promise, we will let you know every ten minutes, if necessary, if there are any updates, but for now, I would prefer it if Sara was taken home. Clearly she's worn out and needs rest."

He looked at Sara, his eyes locking with hers and willing her to agree, as he waited for his grandfather's blustering refusal. He saw the instant she understood his intention and watched as she turned to the old man.

"Would you? I always feel better if someone sees me to the door, and I'm really drooping here," she said, clasping his grandfather's hand between both of hers.

"I see what you are doing," the old man grumbled at Rey, "but for this young woman, I will do the gentlemanly thing and escort her home."

He slowly rose to his feet, slapping away at Rey's hand as he reached to support him.

"I'm not completely incapable yet."

He straightened to his full height and stared Rey straight in the eye. "You will tell me. The minute you hear anything."

"*Sí, Abuelo*. I promise."

Rey turned to Sara and took both her hands in his. "Go home, rest, I will call you when I hear anything."

"I'll be back in the morning," she promised, reaching up to kiss him lightly on the cheek.

It was a butterfly-light touch but every nerve in his body centered on that one spot. As she left the room with his grandfather and Javier, he pressed his fingers to the exact place her lips had touched.

"You've got it bad, *mi hermano*. If I hadn't seen it myself, I wouldn't have believed it. I was worried when you announced your engagement to us and implied you weren't serious about it. I'm pleased to see you were only joking." Alex's voice broke the brief spell that had captured him in its net.

Rey was momentarily lost for words. Of course he and Sara had kissed before, kissed but nothing more. The engagement was a smoke screen only. A ruse to keep *Abuelo* from getting even more upset about the three-hundred-year-old legend that had become his obsession.

At least that's all it was supposed to be. Maybe it was just the extreme situation they found themselves in with Benedict's accident, some age-old instinct to survive at all costs, but right now he wanted a whole lot more than kisses from Sara.

He pushed aside his reaction with a laugh. It was merely the tension of the situation—the worry over Benedict—and very probably, the length of time since he'd last taken a woman to his bed. It couldn't be anything more than that. Could it?

Three

Rina sat in the backseat of the sleek dark limousine next to the eldest del Castillo, yet her mind was filled with the image of her sister's fiancé. She fully understood the attraction. In fact, she was left fighting it herself.

It was all wrong. She and Sara had never been attracted to the same kind of guy before. Ever. While physically, both Rina and Sara's tastes had run to the tall, dark and handsome guys, Sara was all about presence. She fell for men with as much charisma as swagger. Rina's men had always been quiet achievers. The kind of guys who were strong and successful but not necessarily right up there on the podium announcing their achievements—the sort you might not look at twice, but if you did, you didn't regret it. Men like Jacob, although his quiet achievements hadn't exactly led them along the path she'd expected. Especially not when he'd told her the woman he now loved was his boss.

"It's the curse, you know," Aston del Castillo's voice interrupted her reverie.

"The curse?"

"I see he hasn't told you about it yet. Of course, he doesn't believe in it, but it's real."

Her curiosity piqued, Rina started to ask what the curse was, exactly, but instead the old man muttered something in Spanish and seemed to doze off.

Rina leaned forward and tapped Javier on the shoulder. "Is he okay? He just fell asleep."

She saw Javier's eyes in the rearview mirror and then a smile split his face. "*Sí*, the *señor* is fine. He is tired and refuses to admit he is not as strong as he used to be."

At the cottage, Javier saw her to the front door and waited until she was inside and had turned the iron key in the large black lock before returning to the car. Rina turned around and faced the main room, this time really seeing it properly.

Uneven beams ran the length of the cottage ceiling. Rather than being dark or daunting, the warmth of the wooden spines that gave the structure its strength was friendly and welcoming combined with the pale creamy apricot-tinted plaster between each. The low rays of the last of the evening sun speared in through the multipaned, deep-set windows. The simple wooden dining suite, and the chintz-covered sofas in the sitting room area, were clearly not new, but retained the patina of time and wear like badges of honor.

Shelves were built into a recess along one wall, and beneath them a modern television cabinet and stereo unit lounged side-by-side. Rina flicked on the TV, suddenly anxious to disperse the silence of being alone.

She dropped her bag onto the wooden tabletop and made her way through the open-plan living area to the small kitchen. A gas stove, with a shiny new chrome kettle on one of the burners caught her attention. She filled it and set it on the stove to boil. An old-fashioned coal range dominated the space beside the stove.

Her stomach growled as she opened the small refrigerator tucked in beneath the bench and was relieved to see her sister had left some food behind. Cheese, some slightly limp vegetables, eggs and a little leftover milk. The expiry date on the milk bottle suggested it was well overdue.

Rina's brow furrowed. Her sister could be erratic but she'd always been very particular about food safety after a serious bout of food poisoning when they were first flatting together in their late teens. It wasn't like Sara not to clean out perishables before going somewhere—she was a stickler for observing expiry dates. This whole situation just got more and more confusing. Had Sara first gone to France in a bit of a rush, expecting to return sooner than today? But then why would she have gone back again? Just trying to make sense of it was making Rina's head hurt.

Another rumble from the pit of her belly reminded her it had been a good eight or more hours since her last meal. As slender as she was, Rina had a high metabolism and usually ate regularly.

She grabbed the eggs and the best of all the vegetables from the fridge and whipped up a frittata for her supper. Tomorrow she'd have to find some way of gathering more groceries to replenish Sara's supply—especially if there would be the two of them here soon.

Rina had not long finished her meal and had cleaned up her dishes when she heard a car approach on the road to the cottage. She had the door open as the now familiar Ferrari pulled to a stop outside.

Her heart hammered in her chest as Reynard unfolded from the driver's seat and walked through the gate. The suit coat was gone, as well as the immaculately knotted rich burgundy silk tie he'd worn earlier in the day. With his face cast in relief by the setting sun, she couldn't make out his expression but weariness and dejection pulled at every line of his body. Each step was slow and deliberate. Rina felt unexpected tears prick at her eyes. Clearly the news about his brother was not good.

"Benedict? Is he going to be okay?" she asked softly as he reached the front porch.

"He's made it through surgery and he's in intensive care. Only one of us is allowed in at a time, and only for short periods. Alex and Loren will stay at the hospital tonight and I'll head in first thing in the morning."

His voice was flat, as if he couldn't believe the day his family had endured. Instantly, the urge to provide comfort flooded through Rina's veins. She opened her arms to him as he entered the cottage and without hesitation he clasped her to him.

He was lean muscle from top to toe, and fraught with a tension that held his body tight like a bow.

"He'll be all right, Rey," she murmured into the broad warmth of his shoulder.

"They've done everything they can—now it's up to him."

His voice was a guttural whisper. Rina was rocked by the strength of emotion she felt pouring from him. The three brothers had to be close, judging by how distraught he was. She couldn't even begin to imagine what they were all going through. She struggled to find the words that might provide him with some comfort.

"He's young and he's strong, and with you and Alex there for him, he'll pull through."

"I don't know what I'll do if he doesn't."

Rina closed her eyes against the building moisture there.

The fear in Rey's voice struck her to her core. She knew if it was Sara there in the ICU, she'd be frantic with worry herself. Slowly she edged from his embrace and pulled away to close the front door.

"Come in, I'll make you a warm drink—unless you'd like something stronger?"

"No, coffee will be fine. I want to have my wits about me should Alex call."

Rina nodded and went through to the kitchen and busied herself measuring coffee for the old-fashioned stovetop percolator she'd found in a cupboard earlier in the evening. She sent a silent prayer of thanks skyward that Sara had thought to include in her letter that Reynard took his coffee black and sweet. In her peripheral vision she saw Rey drop into one of the fabric covered sofas, his tall frame all but dwarfing the feminine piece of furniture. He leaned forward and rested his elbows on his knees, rubbing at his eyes with long, tanned fingers.

Once the coffee had percolated, she poured it into a mug and placed it, a spoon and a sugar bowl on a small tray and carried it to Rey.

"Thanks," he said, taking the mug off the tray and dropping two cubes of sugar into the steaming liquid and stirred—the clink of the spoon against the ceramic mug loud in the quiet of the room.

Rina settled onto the facing sofa and watched as he drained the mug in a series of slow pulls. "More?" she asked as he put the mug down on the coffee table between them.

"No, thanks. I suppose I should head back into town, to my place." He gave a massive yawn. "Sooner, rather than later."

"You could stay here," Rina offered, even though she had no idea if the cottage boasted more than one bedroom.

An unsettling thought occurred to her. Wouldn't he expect to sleep in the same bed with her? What if he wanted to be intimate—to seek comfort from the shock of his brother's near death in her arms? He was her sister's fiancé—wouldn't that be normal under the circumstances? What on earth had she been thinking inviting him to stay?

Rey shot her a heavy-lidded look. "Are you sure?"

Oh God, what had she done? She could always plead a headache, a period, or tiredness herself, she supposed. But what if this ridiculous attraction she felt for him enticed her into doing something she knew she shouldn't?

Reason overcame fear. He was shattered, and she knew firsthand the physical toll emotional exhaustion took on a person. She doubted he'd have the energy to do anything more than hold her while she slept. A prospect that she had to admit, she found almost too appealing. But it wouldn't go beyond that. Above all, he was her sister's fiancé—she could never betray Sara's trust like that. Ever.

"Hey, I think one del Castillo in the hospital right now is enough, don't you?"

He smiled a sweet, crooked smile. "Two, if you count *Abuelo* at the convalescent home."

"Good point," she agreed with a smile. "They say three's a charm but let's not tempt fate, shall we?"

"I'll get my things from the car."

His things? Did he often sleep over?

"I always keep a set ready in case I stay with one of my brothers," he explained, in response to the obvious surprise on her face.

"I'll, um…I'll go use the bathroom while you settle in, then."

Rina bolted for the bedroom and shoved her suitcase in a small closet, then rifled through her sister's chest of drawers for a nightgown, praying she still possessed at least one or two that were halfway decent. If he had slept here before, he'd know about things like that, wouldn't he?

She fervently wished, not for the first time today, that Sara hadn't put her in this position. Her fingers closed around an old, oversize T-shirt. She lifted it from the drawer and shook it out. Should be long enough, she surmised—and not sexy enough, which was even more important. Rina bunched the fabric in one fist and made it to the bathroom even as she heard Rey come back in through the front door.

The old metal lock clicked into place, the sound echoing through the tiny cottage like a knell of some sort. She swallowed against the sudden knot of tension that lodged in the base of her throat. What she wouldn't give for a chance to talk to Sara right this minute.

She swung the bathroom door shut behind her and reached for the toiletries she'd scattered around the bathroom before her shower. It only took a couple of minutes to wash her face free of makeup and brush her hair. She took her time over her teeth, even as she promised herself it didn't make any difference. It wasn't as if she and Reynard del Castillo would be indulging in anything other than sleep tonight.

By the time she pulled the soft, worn T-shirt over her head, her heart was beating erratically. If she didn't get a hold of herself soon she'd be the next one in hospital. Rina forced herself to breathe slowly; her fingers curled tight around the cool, white porcelain pedestal basin as if it was her only anchor in the world. She could do this. All she had to do was fall asleep. Should be simple, right? Forget that the time at home was something ridiculous like seven or eight in the morning—her body clock was so out of whack she should be on the verge of falling asleep on her feet.

But instead all she could think about was how it had felt to be pressed hard up against the strength of Reynard's body. How his scent had filled her nostrils. Not just the scent of the male fragrance he wore, but *him*. The man exuded pheromones, if her body's reaction was any judge. Any poor judge, she reminded herself. But the desperate truth was that she craved to be held like that again—to be made to feel precious and treasured. Safe. Wanted.

She blinked and slowly peeled her fingers from the basin. He'd be waiting to use the bathroom by now. She forced herself to turn and pick up her clothes from the tiled floor and open the door.

In the bedroom Reynard sat quietly on the edge of the bed, a small, black leather toilet bag between his hands. He looked up as she entered.

"Are you sure you're all right with this?" he asked.

"Of course I am," Rina breezed, with what she hoped was the right amount of savoir faire.

"I won't be long," he replied, rising from the bed and heading for the bathroom. "I can sleep on the sofa if you'd rather."

"As if you'd fit." Rina forced a smile. "Don't be silly. It's fine, really."

Rey gave a short nod and went through to the bathroom and closed the door. Rina scuttled under the crisp white sheets on the bed and inhaled the faint scent of lavender. Maybe he'd take his time. Maybe she'd even be asleep before he got into bed with her.

She lay facing the edge of the bed, closed her eyes and tried to let her head sink into the pillow, but every tense muscle in her body had other ideas and she felt as if she was rigidly surfing on top of the scented cotton. By the time she heard Reynard come back into the bedroom, switch off the bedside lamp and felt the mattress depress under the weight of his body, she could barely breathe again.

"This isn't how I imagined we'd spend our first night together," Reynard's voice murmured from close behind her.

Their *first* night together? It was true in more ways than he knew. Rina mumbled something indistinct in response. Beneath the sheets she could already feel the heat of his body only inches from hers. He shifted and she felt the weight of his arm over the top of the sheets and the thin bed cover as it draped across her body. The muscles in his arm bunched as he drew her up against his length. His bare chest seared through the thin cotton of her shirt and she felt his warm breath against the exposed skin of her shoulder.

"Sleep well," he said softly. "And thank you. It's good not to be alone with my fears tonight."

Rina remained silent. Sleep well? It was ironic. The last thing she wanted right now was sleep. His body, curled around hers, felt so right, yet everything about this was so very wrong. She listened carefully, her eyes burning in the darkened room. Soon his breathing settled into a deeper rhythm. His body relaxed against hers.

In the distance she could hear the sea. It was as if each breath from Rey's lungs matched the slow susurration of the waves as they caressed the coastline. Inch by slow inch she felt her body begin to relax, felt her own breathing slide into the gentle flow of the tide and the man behind her.

Rey knew the exact instant Sara accepted his presence behind her and slid into sleep. Her soft curves nestled against the planes of his body. It felt good to hold her, too good, he acknowledged as a certain part of his body showed no immediate signs of wanting to rest. He reminded himself why he was here—of the circumstances that had led to him being in Sara's bed tonight. It was as effective as a bucket of ice in his lap.

The memory of Benedict in that hospital bed, tubes and pipes snaking out from his body to various machines and apparatus—the knowledge that without them he wouldn't even be breathing on his own—was almost more than he could bear.

Rey's arm tightened around Sara's sleeping form and she instinctively snuggled closer against him, her neatly curved buttocks firm against his groin.

Dios, under any other circumstances he'd delight in waking her again. In losing himself, and the events of today, in the softness of her feminine curves. In spite of his plans to keep their relationship platonic to ease the sting when it ended, there was no denying that for the time being, they were engaged, even if it was mostly just for show. They were still a pair of normal healthy adults with normal healthy appetites.

But a del Castillo had more honor than that, he reminded himself. He'd been relieved at Sara's old-fashioned attitudes—allowing no more than a few kisses, a little light petting—because they'd given him the comfort of knowing that when they went their separate ways, there would be no serious heartbreak or recriminations. Tonight, however, he'd needed to hold her in his arms, and the realization shocked him on a new level. He hadn't expected to need her.

She seemed different today, he thought, even taking into account that the circumstances were completely out of sync with their normal lives. He couldn't quite put his finger on what it was. It was more than the coffee she'd drunk at the hospital, when he hadn't seen her drink the beverage since before she went to France. There was a sense of calm about her that was at odds with the party girl he'd first been attracted to.

Sure, he knew she could be focused. The accolades she'd earned on the dressage and other equestrian event circuits were mute proof of that. But her attitude today had been more. It was something that went beyond the superficial, something that spoke to him, instead, on a deeper level. A level that drew him to her for the comfort he now hungered for. How had that happened in the space of a few hours when before he'd had no difficulty keeping his emotional distance?

Whatever it was, he acceded—as sleep finally drew him under and he lost himself in the soft and slightly unfamiliar fragrance of Sara's hair as it streamed over her pillow—she had been exactly what he'd needed today.

Four

Reynard woke as sunshine streamed through the unshuttered windows. For a moment he was disoriented—both by the furnishings around him and the warm, lithe body sprawled across his. One part of his body, however, suffered no such disorientation.

In fact, that particular part of his body was creating undue influence on the state of his mind, particularly with the soft scent of Sara's hair filling his nostrils and the exposed creamy skin of her legs entangled with his.

She'd lost some of her light golden tan, he noticed. He fought the urge to stroke his hand over the delicious length of thigh exposed by her nightshirt riding up over the gentle round globes of her buttocks. And a little weight, too, he'd wager. What on earth had she been up to while she was away?

Reynard closed his eyes and breathed in a slow, steady breath—but even as he did so, the blend of fragrance from her hair and the feminine scent of her skin intoxicated him, stirring his body even more. His eyes flashed open again. The deprivation of that sensory input had only served to sharpen everything else. Painfully so, if his current condition was any indicator.

He let his eyes wander over her slumbering form again. Whatever the changes in Sara, he couldn't help but enjoy a certain voyeuristic pleasure in taking an eyeful while she still slept. Their open-ended engagement hadn't covered morning talk, or morning anything, for that matter, until now. Perhaps it would be worth exploring things a little further by coaxing her awake the most pleasurable way he knew how.

The discreet chirp of his cell phone in the main room of the cottage was a stark reminder to keep himself in check. There were more serious considerations in his life right now than whether or not Sara tasted as good as she smelled.

He eased his body out from under hers, freezing for a moment as she muttered something in her sleep and then repositioned herself on the pillow he'd used. There were still purple shadows under her eyes and her face was still as pale as she'd been ever since the previous afternoon when she'd come to his office. Whatever she'd been doing recently, it hadn't been restful, that much was certain. He adjusted his boxers and slipped from the room to answer his phone.

The news about Benedict, while not brilliant, was hopeful and it was time he relieved Alex and Loren in their vigil. He quickly showered and dressed into the change of clothes he'd brought last night and left a brief note explaining where he'd gone on the kitchen countertop.

She was still sleeping when he returned to the bedroom—he hadn't been quite able to resist one last glance before he headed to the hospital. She'd moved again, and beneath the sheet he could see her foot stroking back and forth—a tiny movement, even as she slept—across the sheets. So she was a sensualist, he surmised, feeling the tight knot that hadn't quite left him intensify low in his gut. Texture, sensation—he really had to stop torturing himself but he couldn't tear his gaze away.

The edge of her shirt now rode even higher on those long slender legs, exposing the gentlest hint of the curve of her buttocks as she lay half-sprawled on her stomach, one arm pushed far under the pillow. The fabric of the top was thin, and pulled tight under her arm and across the swell of one breast.

Even as he watched, she shifted again. Rolling onto her back. His mouth dried. She was like a ripe peach. Her dark red hair spread in spiraling disarray around her face. Her eyelids flickered—no doubt she'd be awake soon. He debated crossing the short distance to the bed and placing a fleeting kiss on the lush pale pink width of her lips. Just the thought of doing so was enough to make his fingers tighten on the brass handle of the bedroom door.

He shook his head slightly. Rey quickly drew the bedroom door closed with a faint "snick" of sound. How did she do that, all of a sudden? How did she make him forget so quickly, so effortlessly, when before it had been she who had been so easily blurred from his thoughts?

Rina stretched against the cotton sheets and yawned—then sat bolt upright. Reynard? Where was he? She grabbed at the hem of her nightshirt and pulled it down hard, then, realizing how it stretched the material against her upper body, let it go again. She slipped from the bed and to the bedroom door, listening carefully for sounds of movement. Nothing.

Cautiously, she opened the door and listened again. While the noise of birds chattering wildly filtered through from outside, the cottage merely reflected an echo of emptiness.

Muscles she didn't even know she'd tensed, eased as she realized he really was gone. She didn't know just how well she'd have been able to keep up the charade. Which reminded her, she needed to get a hold of Sara and find out exactly when she planned to be back.

Rina found her BlackBerry and dialed her sister's number. A frown pulled at her eyebrows as the call went straight through to voice mail. For a second she was tempted to hang up and just try again and again until Sara eventually answered, but she tempered that with the knowledge that her sister had never willingly and actively avoided her before, so she left a message.

"There's been an accident. Benedict's hurt. I'm sure they're expecting me—or rather, *you*—at the hospital again today and I don't know how long I can fake this. Please call me, Sara. Please?"

With an exasperated sigh she ended the call and walked across the cool tiled floor to the kitchen. On the bench she saw Rey's note. Her eyes skimmed the words, written in a bold, slashing script. So he'd send a car for her about ten, would he? She looked at the wall clock above the kitchen stove. That gave her about two hours to get ready. And two hours to figure out how to tell him the truth about Sara. The prospect settled in her stomach like congealed oatmeal—heavy and completely unappetizing.

Rina gathered a set of fresh clothes and went to shower and get dressed. With any luck, she'd make it to the nearest town to get some much-needed groceries, and back, before facing Rey again for what, depending on his reaction, might be the last time ever.

* * *

The huge black bicycle, with a basket attached to the front, had Rina scratching her head for a few moments. Dare she risk it? There was no helmet, no chain guard, not even a set of gears on the thing—and judging by the cobwebs draping the frame it hadn't moved past the lean-to shelter at the back of the cottage in some time.

She shuddered. She hated spiders. But as much as she hated spiders, she liked eating more, and her light breakfast had pretty much taken care of the remainder of the perishables in the house. She picked up a twig from a pile of kindling that was stacked just inside the lean-to, next to a larger pile of split wood, and carefully removed the spider webs before rolling the behemoth out into the sunlight and checking the tires.

The old bicycle pump, set on a bracket on the cross beam of the bike, thankfully lived up to its designated task of filling the tires with much-needed air. She cocked her head and listened. No telltale hiss anywhere. Deciding to err on the side of caution, Rina did a few short circuits up and down the road outside the cottage. Satisfied that the tires would hold, she gathered her wallet from inside, and the key, and popped them in the basket before rolling up the hem of her cotton trousers. Maybe white wasn't quite the best choice, she thought as she straddled the bike and wobbled her way up the road.

She'd been pedaling for no more than a couple of kilometers when a dust cloud approached her from the distance. Since she'd figured out this was a private road, she was surprised to see another vehicle coming her way. And quickly, too, if the smear of dust particles in the air was any indicator.

As the vehicle drew closer, she recognized Reynard's Ferrari. He slowed down and wheeled to a halt in the dirt road. Rina waited a moment for the dust to settle before getting closer.

His window rolled down and he leaned one arm along the open frame.

"What on earth are you doing?" he asked.

Rina bristled. It didn't take a rocket scientist to figure it out, surely.

"I'm riding a bike. I need some supplies."

"Since when did you ride a bike to get them?" he commented as he thrust open his door and unfolded his length from the car.

Her eyes drank in the sight of him. He was dressed in pale gray trousers, teamed with a long-sleeved, lightweight white knit sweater, with the sleeves pushed up to expose tanned muscled forearms with a light sprinkling of dark hair. His hazel eyes were obscured by a dark pair of designer sunglasses and his hair was swept off his forehead by the light breeze. Altogether he was a mouthwatering sight.

Realizing he was standing there waiting for an answer, she scoured her memory for what he'd just said and grabbed at the first thought that sprang to mind.

"I'm running out of a few things."

"So why didn't you just do as you always do and leave a list for the cleaner?"

Rina stifled a groan and mentally shook a fist at her sister for neatly landing her in it. She felt as if she had to walk on eggshells from here on in.

"I needed the exercise," she explained with a shrug. "Besides, it's a lovely morning and I wasn't expecting you for a while yet. How's Benedict today?"

"The doctors are talking about bringing him out of the induced coma today. *Abuelo* and Javier are at the hospital now so I thought I'd come and collect you early."

"Right, well, you'd better follow me, then," Rina suggested as she turned the bike around and hopped up on the worn saddle.

"Or we could just leave the bike here, and collect it when we come back," Rey said with one eyebrow quirked as if all his humor at the sight on her on the bike was hidden behind those dark lenses of his.

"No, I couldn't do that. It might get stolen. What would the owners say?"

"Sara, stop pulling my leg. I am the owner—of the cottage and everything in it. Or at least my family is, anyway. You know that."

Rina suddenly put it all together. The beautiful golden castillo she'd seen through the kitchen window by the cliff tops only a mile or two away. Reynard's surname. That whole sense of entitlement and privilege that she'd sensed about him and his brother from the minute she'd laid eyes on them. That also explained why Sara was staying at the Governess's Cottage. It was a family property; where else would one's fiancée stay if they weren't actually staying with you?

"Well, I'd still rather put it away. Don't want to get on the wrong side of you or anything," she half joked.

The tiny pull at the corner of his lips sent a zing straight to her chest. Serious faced, he was handsome as sin, but with that quirky little half smile he was devastating. She began to pedal, hoping that she wouldn't do anything stupid like wobble right off the road and into a ditch. She heard the slow purr of his car's engine as he cruised along behind at a snail's pace.

Every time her feet depressed the pedals she was conscious of how her backside must look to him. Of how the cotton pants she wore stretched tight across her buttocks and thighs. By the time she reached the cottage she was hot and flustered. Noticing that she'd smeared some chain grease on her pants leg, despite her efforts to the contrary, she excused herself to change before they left for the hospital.

Eschewing her own suitcase, she thrust open the doors to Sara's wardrobe and grabbed the first thing she found on a hanger. The fact it was a light floral dress with a background of mint green and a designer label on it that shrieked a budget far higher than Rina usually allowed herself for clothing was merely a side benefit, she decided as she yanked off her shirt and trousers and then shimmied into the dress. Sara always did prefer to spend her money rather than sock it away for a rainy day, and for once, Rina wholeheartedly approved.

She knew Sara wouldn't begrudge Rina borrowing her clothes, had in fact even suggested it, but Rina had the feeling this particular dress was special. It certainly felt that way as the deliciously soft fabric whispered across her legs as she slid her feet into a pair of matching open toe pumps.

She quickly stepped into the bathroom to freshen her makeup and to check her phone surreptitiously. At last! A text from Sara. Rina groaned under her breath in frustration. Was it too much to ask for her runaway sister to have finally responded at a time when Rina could call or text her back? Rina scanned the message.

Sori I hvn't been in touch. I hope things r ok with Ben. Pls, whateva u do, don't tell Rey wot I've done. Will call u soon. Luv u sis. Sx

Rina's heart sank. She'd geared herself up to give Reynard the full story and now here was Sara once more begging her not to. It made her sick to her stomach but despite her own feelings on the matter she decided to give Sara that little extra leeway. With any luck, she'd be back in a day or so and everything would be fine.

Reluctantly, she switched the phone to silent mode. If Sara called now she'd have to go to voice mail. Rina sincerely doubted she'd be able to carry off a phone conversation with her twin while said twin's fiancé sat next to her in the close confines of his car. And, of course, the hospital expected cell phones to be switched off in the high dependency unit where Benedict was currently being cared for. Rina remembered that much at least from when their father had suffered his last, fatal heart attack.

"Sara? Are you ready? We really need to get back now."

Rey's voice outside the bathroom door made her start. She turned on a faucet and let cool water splash over her wrists for a second before snapping it off.

"Just a minute. I'm nearly done," she called over her shoulder.

She grabbed her perfume and spritzed a tiny amount behind each ear before grabbing the length of her hair and twisting it up into a loose knot secured with a handful of Sara's pins. There was one advantage in having the same untamed mass of long red hair—they both tended to wear it in very similar styles. There. She could handle anything, she decided as she looked at herself in the mirror. Anything that didn't get too personal, at least.

As they left the cottage she heard Rey inhale softly.

"Nice perfume. It's different from your usual."

Rina swallowed against the gasp of irritation that rose in her throat. She hadn't even thought about what perfume Sara had been wearing. Her sister had always preferred the spicier floral, oriental-based perfumes while she herself was more a light floral fragrance person. It was yet another example of how careful she was going to have to be to carry this off properly.

She turned and smiled at Rey, slipping on a pair of sunglasses so he couldn't see the lie in her eyes. Sara always warned her that she gave too much away.

"It's something I picked up while I was away. Do you like it?"

From behind her, Rey leaned in and inhaled again, his lips mere centimeters from the curve of her neck.

"Mmm, yeah, I do."

A frisson of awareness shot down Rina's spine with the velocity of lightning, leaving a fierce sizzle throbbing in its wake. She stumbled a little, steadying as Rey's hands shot out to anchor her.

"I'm okay," she hastened to say, pulling from his light clasp before she could enjoy getting too close.

What was it she had told herself only minutes ago? About handling things provided it didn't get too personal? Right now, it looked as if that was to be her biggest obstacle because despite everything, she was left fighting against a desire to get very personal indeed.

Five

The updated news at the hospital wasn't good. Rather than attempt to bring Benedict out of his coma, Rey was shocked to learn the doctors had reassessed his condition and elected to keep him in that suspended state for at least two more days. While his air bags had deployed and saved him from more serious head injuries, there was still some swelling on the brain that was causing concern. Another forty-eight excruciating hours of hoping against hope their brother would find the will to fight his way out of the pain and darkness, and survive.

Rey leaned back on the hard, vinyl-covered seat in the private waiting room and exchanged a look with Alex. Somehow they had to get through this—more importantly, somehow they had to get *Benedict* through this. Rey didn't need words to know that he and Alex were remembering their last evening with the three of them together.

It had been weeks ago, the night of *Abuelo*'s stroke, and

they'd all gathered at the castillo for dinner together. Rey had announced his engagement to Sara to his brothers, and Ben had seen right through his plans. Despite the agreement they'd made three and a half months prior, to find brides to calm *Abuelo*'s fears, Benedict knew Rey had no intention of seeing the engagement through to marriage. *Abuelo*'s constant harping about the governess's curse was making him ill and had caused huge concern among the brothers—so much so, it had forced Alex to go ahead with the archaic arranged marriage he'd never planned to take seriously, and both Rey and Benedict to agree to do whatever it took to keep *Abuelo* well and happy.

The fact that Alex's marriage to Loren had turned out to be a whole lot happier than anyone had anticipated was beside the point. It certainly had come close to failing completely because of his brother's pride and stubbornness—a pride and stubbornness that was bred in all the del Castillo men, it would seem.

Rey felt a cold trickle of unease creep under his skin. Perhaps his grandfather had been right. Perhaps the curse really was coming full circle and Benedict's accident had been yet another reminder that the surviving del Castillo sons had to abide by honor, truth and love with their whole hearts in order to keep the family alive for another generation. His rational side rejected the thought emphatically, but who knew now how much truth there remained in the legendary curse, especially given the problems Alex and Loren had originally faced in their marriage, *Abuelo*'s stroke and now Benedict's life-threatening injuries?

Could the crazed words of a scorned woman really have such an effect nine generations later—with theirs reputed to be the last if they didn't get their act together? Again, that finger of disquiet stroked a chilling line down his neck. He huffed a sigh in frustration and shifted again on his chair. All this inactivity made him uncomfortable. It left him too much time to think.

The doctors only permitted one family member in with Benedict at a time, and only for about ten minutes each hour, at that. Loren had just returned from being with him now and Rey recognized the shell-shocked expression on her face as mirroring his own after his visit with Ben. He had found it both terrifying and frustrating to see his younger sibling so pale and bruised, his body covered with dressings over wounds, tubes and wires coming out everywhere—even a machine that aided his breathing.

Neither he nor Alex felt they could leave the hospital after this morning's news. Benedict's condition was too fragile. They had to remain, even if they couldn't be in the same room with their injured brother, they just had to be *here*. Their sentiments were strongly echoed by *Abuelo* who had stubbornly fought to stay at the hospital all day also, but whose exhaustion had finally seen him reluctantly agree to return to his room in the convalescent home for some much needed rest.

Rey shifted again on the seat. *Dios,* they were so uncomfortable. No wonder the old man tired so quickly. And where the hell had Sara gone? She'd left him a couple of hours ago, with Javier and *Abuelo*, on the pretext of "sorting some things out." Just what did she have to sort out, he wondered irritably. Her place was at his side—or at least to be seen at his side.

Now she was back from France, he was even more firmly reminded of the need to portray to his family that he was following the terms all the brothers had agreed upon. That they'd do whatever it took to give their grandfather the peace of mind he needed to stop worrying about the blasted curse. Well, he was doing his part, together with

Sara. Now it was up to Benedict to get well and do the very same.

A sound at the door to the waiting room caught his attention and he and Alex exchanged a puzzled look before they both rose to their feet to see what the commotion was about. If it kept up, then soon the charge nurse on the floor would be along, exhorting them to be quiet with her usual quelling glare. To Rey's surprise the door opened to reveal a crew of maintenance staff with large trolleys—one empty and the others stacked with covered, bulky loads. The men came into the room, closely followed by Sara who had a very smug smile on her face.

"Thank you, gentlemen. Yes, these are the ones to go and then you can bring in the new furniture."

"New furniture?" Rey asked, looking askance at his fiancée. What on earth was she thinking? New furniture in a hospital waiting room?

"Yes," she said, stepping out of the way of the two men as they stacked up the vinyl-coated chairs and loaded them onto the empty trolley before bringing in a very comfortable-looking three-seater sofa and two recliners, together with a set of highly polished side tables and a small credenza. "New furniture. No one can possibly be comfortable on those things." She gestured to the trolley outside the door. "Besides, if I'd only gotten the one recliner for *Abuelo* he would have refused to use it, wouldn't he?"

There was no argument there. The old man would have sat on the floor rather than admit that his age and infirmity granted him the privilege of a more comfortable seat than anyone else.

"Of course, you are right," Rey acknowledged, side-stepping one of the maintenance crew who was positioning the credenza against a wall near a power socket. "He most definitely would have refused it."

It was astute of Sara to have picked up that so quickly— she'd only met the del Castillo patriarch yesterday—astute and caring of an old man's need for comfort. Rey gave her a narrowed glance. Since when did she get so perceptive? When she smiled back in response, he felt an unexpected rush of something new toward Sara, something warm and heart deep. The sensation took him by surprise and made him a little uncomfortable at the same time. He was unused to feeling this way about a woman. Usually he indulged in what became a mutually satisfying physical affair. He always played all the right moves to ensure that each of his companions were made to feel special and treasured for however long he planned to spend with them. With Sara it had been no different, until she'd returned from France, that is.

It was as if she was two different people, or as if the Sara he'd asked to become his fiancée, carefully couching the proposal as "let's get engaged" so there was no actual mention of marriage, had changed while she'd been away. The differences were both disconcerting and appealing at the same time.

It was because of Benedict's accident, he told himself. It couldn't possibly be anything else. She hadn't changed, it was just his perception of her that was different, given his state of mind. His emotions were all over the place at the thought that one of his beloved brothers, no matter their occasional differences, could be lost to them.

But even as he tried to convince himself of this, he couldn't help asking himself whether the Sara he'd known before would have thought so far ahead to an elderly man's comfort, not to mention his pride, let alone to have conjured up an espresso machine together with a small refrigerator to store fresh, healthy snacks and milk for all the family.

Maybe he'd misjudged her. Even as he thought of it, the notion refused to make sense. Reynard trusted his people sense. It was an indispensable business skill that he'd spent years developing. He knew what Sara was like—had known ever since he'd met her at the annual del Castillo–sponsored equestrian trials. But how could one woman be so completely different? On the one hand, the life of the party—fun and flirtatious—then on the other, kind and compassionate and imbued with a warmth that went straight to people's hearts. It wasn't logical. The Sara he knew was taking her responsibility to him and his family far more seriously than he'd ever intended. Now, he was starting to believe that she was hardly the type to simply laugh and brush off a broken engagement, either. While he had no desire to actually marry her, a sudden protective surge warned him that he had no desire to hurt her, either.

What if he really married her, a little voice asked from deep inside. No, he quelled the thought immediately. That wasn't part of the plan. He didn't believe in the curse so it shouldn't matter whether he was engaged or married, or anything for that matter. He'd never given the state of marriage a great deal of thought—it was just something he knew would happen "one day"—but he did know that when he finally embarked on such a course, he'd be doing it because *he* was ready, not at the behest of a frightened old man, no matter how much he loved his grandfather. Despite his inner demons he had to acknowledge that he had begun to crave Sara in ways he'd never done before.

He reached for her, noting briefly the expression of surprise that danced across her beautiful face, and drew her into his arms. She held herself stiffly for a moment, before her body melted against his. Soft against hard. Feminine against the masculine. And it felt right. Shockingly, amazingly right. Every part of his body attuned to hers. His breathing slowed and steadied and it was almost as if his heart now beat to the same rhythm as that of the woman in his arms. For the first time in hours, he actually relaxed.

"Thank you," he murmured against the top of her fiery head. "You have been amazing."

"I aim to please," she said teasingly, clearly trying to make light of the situation. "Besides, I only arranged a short-term lease on the items, but I thought your family might like to make the furnishings a permanent donation to the hospital for other families that are going through what you guys are."

She pulled free of his arms and walked over to the coffee machine, and picked up the instruction booklet. Even though she made a show of reading it, he could tell their brief contact had unsettled her. Unsettled *her?* It had totally unsettled *him,* as well. His blood pumped with a new demand through his veins. His senses were totally in sync with her and her alone. Not even Loren and Alex's quiet appreciation of the new furniture, as they cuddled at one end of the couch totally lost in one another, broke through the focus that was Sara's and hers alone.

Rina felt the hairs on the back of her neck prickle under Rey's sharp regard. It had been all too easy to flow into his arms just then. She hadn't wanted to pull away but had forced herself to do so before she became altogether too comfortable. She kept reminding herself this was only temporary and that once the crisis with Benedict had passed, and she fervently hoped it would, she'd be able to tell Reynard the truth about why she was here instead of her sister.

A part of her wished she hadn't agreed to Sara's plans. Or that she'd insisted on telling Reynard the truth the moment she'd met him at his office. But seeing what all the members of the family were going through, she couldn't do that to him, as well. She knew firsthand how it felt to be rejected by the person you'd promised to marry. How much worse would it be if that happened while another person you loved fought for their life at the same time?

No, what she'd do instead was what she did best and what she made her living doing as a contract "Girl Friday" back home. Already, her knowledge and experience in publicity and problem solving was standing her in good stead in her self-appointed mission to make sure the family was taken care of as they dealt with Benedict's crisis. She'd make certain that every aspect of the del Castillos' time at the hospital went as smoothly as possible so they could focus on the person who needed them most. Whether it was organizing nutritious meals to be brought to their waiting room, or changes of clothes and access to a shower and bathroom, she'd make it happen.

And the truth? Well, she'd face up to that as soon as she could. As unpalatable as that would be.

The next two days passed painfully slowly. The family appeared to be trapped in a fugue of uncertainty until finally, at midday on the third day, Benedict's doctor came to the waiting room. Rina was almost too afraid to hope for good news as the man entered, his face looked so severe. But then, to everyone's great relief, a smile spread across his features.

"Señor del Castillo has made great progress in the past two days. He is coming out of the induced coma and all the indicators are looking strong at this stage. Of course, his full recovery will be demanding, but I am sure that with the support of his family, he will make it."

Rey and Alex peppered the doctor with questions after that but Rina noticed that *Abuelo* remained in his chair, his eyes suddenly awash with tears. She dropped to her knees and took his gnarled hands in her own.

"It's good news, *Abuelo*. Benedict will be all right. He's strong, he will make it."

Aston del Castillo lifted a hand to stroke her hair gently. "Thank you, I know he will survive. He is a del Castillo. Now we must fight the curse before it is too late."

Rina had overheard mutterings of the curse before but still no one had told her exactly what was involved.

"Too late?" she asked. "Tell me, why would it be too late?"

"They are running out of time. They refuse to believe it. Even Reynard." The old man shook his head slowly before fixing her with a slightly manic stare. "But you can make it work. You can help break the curse. She will not wait forever."

"*Señor,* you mustn't worry the *señorita* so," Javier interrupted before Aston could say anymore. "Thank you, Mees Woodville, you have made our vigil here so much more comfortable for two old men."

"Pah, old men. Speak for yourself," Aston said with a chuckle to his manservant.

Rina slowly rose to her feet. She wouldn't hear any more from *Abuelo* about the curse today, and now with Benedict's improvement and the promise he'd be out of intensive care in the next day or two, she knew they probably didn't need her here quite as much as they had. She was happy for Benedict—happy for all the del Castillo family—but suddenly it made facing reality just that much harder.

After the doctor had left and everyone had agreed to head to their respective homes for a break before taking shifts to return in the evening, Rina went up to Rey and lightly touched him on the arm.

"I'll go back to the cottage now. See you later, perhaps?"

"Let me drive you home," Reynard said smoothly, coming forward to take her by the hand.

"No, that's okay, I'm used to taking the taxi."

"And you shouldn't be. You're my fiancée and I should have been taking better care of you instead of the other way around. Thank you for all you've done."

"You're welcome, Rey, but seriously, it's what I do b—" She faltered before continuing. "It's what I'd do for anyone in this situation. You needed to keep your focus on Benedict."

For a minute she thought he'd press her on what she'd been about to say before she'd corrected herself, but thankfully he didn't. Instead, they made their goodbyes to the family and Javier before Rey led her out into the corridor, his fingers still lightly clasping her hand.

The contact sent a steady buzz of warmth up her arm. She still couldn't quite get used to this intensity of reaction every time he touched her. It wasn't normal, she was sure. Even with Jacob, whom she'd loved—still loved, she reminded herself sharply—she hadn't felt this tingling sense of attraction every single time their skin met.

The drive back to the cottage went swiftly. It was as if now that the pressure of worrying if Benedict would live or die had passed, Rey was in an all-fired hurry to resume his normal life. As they pulled up outside the cottage, Rina turned to him to thank him for the ride home but he was already getting out of the car and coming around to her door to open it for her.

"Thank you," she said, as he held the door and offered his hand to help her.

As he did, she noticed his eyes narrow, and his thumb stroked along her ring finger, particularly across the slightly paler band of skin there.

"Where is your ring?" he asked. "Why aren't you wearing it?"

Oh hell, she thought frantically. She hadn't stopped to think about the envelope Sara had given her on the day she'd arrived, or its obscenely valuable contents.

"I…I, um, I took it off the other night when I came back. I didn't want to get it dirty when I did the dishes and with everything that's been going on, I forgot to put it back on."

She fished in her bag and took out the key to the cottage, before swiftly inserting it in the ancient lock and pushing the door open. A few short steps took her to the table where she'd left Sara's envelope. She cursed herself for her stupidity. Rey could have seen it at any time and wondered what it was there for, and who this "Rina Woodville" was that it had been addressed to. And what if he'd read Sara's note?

She tipped the envelope and the ostentatious diamond solitaire fell into her hand. She slid the ring onto her finger, the cool metal a chilling brand against her skin and a reminder of the lie she'd agreed to perpetuate.

"There, see? Back where it belongs."

She smiled but to her surprise Reynard did not smile back. Oh Lord, had he guessed the truth? Did he realize now, for some reason, that she was not Sara?

Reynard looked at the ring upon Sara's finger and at the envelope from which she'd taken it, which still lay on the table. He'd only caught a glimpse of the front of the envelope, but that had been enough to see that it had her handwriting on it. Had she been on the verge of breaking things off with him? he wondered. Why else would she have put her ring in an envelope? An envelope that even now she was scrunching in the fist of one hand. Had it been addressed to him?

He couldn't let her do it. He couldn't let her back out. Especially not now. Aside from what it would do to *Abuelo*, he suddenly realized that he wasn't ready to let her go. If he was going to keep this working for as long as he needed, it was time to pull out all the stops. His responsibility to his family to project a united facade together with his brothers was primary. There was no room for second thoughts. The hell with keeping things platonic—if it took seducing her to make her stay then he'd do it.

So what if doing so was no great hardship. Rey closed his eyes for a second, refusing to admit, even to himself, that the prospect of seducing Sara held more allure than he wanted to acknowledge. He was doing this for his family.

"Would you like some coffee before you head home?" she said, although her voice sounded strained, as if what she really wanted was for him just to leave.

Well, he wasn't having that. Oh no. No one withdrew from Reynard del Castillo without his permission. Keeping his suspicions locked deep inside, Rey took a step toward her and was surprised to see her back away in response. He smiled. She could run, but she couldn't hide—not now he'd made up his mind about just what direction this engagement of theirs was to turn to next.

"No, thank you. I do not want coffee."

He deliberately let his gaze drop from her eyes to her lips, where he saw the tip of her tongue suddenly dart out to moisten their lush surface, before letting his view drop farther to her breasts. Her chest rose and fell quickly, betraying her nerves as he took another slow careful step toward her. He could see the outline of her nipples as they pressed against her softly patterned dress. Small sharp distended points begging for his touch.

"Something else then?" she persisted, her backside now against the edge of the table, one hand reaching out into the space between them as if she could somehow halt his advance.

"*Sí,* something else."

He flicked his eyes back up to hers, noting her dilated pupils before closing the distance between them completely. The hand she'd held in front of her brushed against his belly, then rode up the surface of his shirt to his chest, leaving an electric trail of heat. Rey slid one arm around her slender waist, and pulled her against his hips before lowering his head and taking her lips with his own. The instant his lips touched hers he knew it was not Sara Woodville in his arms.

Six

Kissing Sara had always been pleasant—fun, even. But this, this was something else altogether. It was all-consuming and lit a fire inside him that burned brighter and hotter than anything he'd experienced before. And, as it continued, drove all rational thought and conscience from his mind leaving him only open to glorious sensation.

The taste of her generous mouth filled his senses, stoking his hunger to flaming levels of demanding need. And because he could, he took more. His tongue stroked the seam of her lips until they parted, then swept inside her to lay claim without dispute. Logically, he knew he should stop—should demand to know who she was and what she was doing pretending to be Sara—but logic had no place here and now.

Her body melded against his, her hips meshed against his lower body, her mound pressing against his hardness and inciting an ache that threatened to consume him. While he continued to hold her firm against his body, his other hand reached up and tangled in her glorious hair, and he coaxed her head back a little more, allowing him a clear angle to the smooth curve of her throat.

Even her skin tasted like more. A subtle blend of sweetness and flowers that made heat pool heavily in his groin. His lips blazed a trail from the corner of her mouth down across her jawline until he reached the tiny hollow behind her ear. His tongue flicked over her skin and she moaned—an uncontrolled, instinctive sound that reverberated through his ears and sent his heart rate soaring.

He felt her hand on his chest, her fingers clenched in the fabric of his shirt, her other hand now curled behind his neck, holding him to her, anchoring him.

Dios, he wanted more than this. He wanted to taste all of her. To discover if her hidden places were as deliciously sweet as those he'd tasted now.

Tremors shook his body as he left a hot path of kisses down her throat and the hollow at the base of her neck. Again, he flicked his tongue against her skin. As before, the intoxicating elixir of the flavor of her sent hunger clawing through him.

Both her hands were now knotted in the short strands of his hair and the pleasure/pain of it added a new dimension to their embrace. He lifted his head and captured her mouth once more. Starving now for the taste of her, for the softness of her lips, the heat and wetness of her tongue as it met his and tangled in a duel that knew no losers.

This was passion. This was absolute. His body knew it even as his mind struggled to equate the reality of the ardent, hotblooded woman pressed against him—her hunger equal to his own—with the skittish creature who'd kept him at arm's length for weeks.

He couldn't stop kissing her, consuming her. He just couldn't get enough of the taste and texture and feel of her. The hand he'd kept at the small of her back coasted lower, over the curve of her buttocks. She felt different from the Sara he knew. The same general size, yet there was a hardness missing from her body. The tensile strength of an event rider gone, and in its place an enticing edge of softness. Not that there was anything out of condition about her body. To the contrary. She felt lithe and strong, yet yielding in all the right places.

No. This was definitely not Sara Woodville. It couldn't be. But then who was she?

Slowly, he loosened his embrace and tempered the heat in his caresses until he could gently push her away. Her eyelids slowly fluttered open, her gray eyes reminding him of a stormy, turbulent sky right before a storm. Her lips were slightly swollen, still moist and parted. Still inviting him to sup at their softness.

Reynard fought with his instincts, overcoming them with the cold reality that she was not who he'd thought, and driven by the need to find out exactly who she really was. His family had been the target of scammers before—people who thought, for whatever reason, that they deserved a slice of the wealth that made up the del Castillo fortune. He'd developed an instinct for them. One that had saved him and his family much heartache. The fact she had slipped under his radar was disconcerting, but he knew he daren't show his hand too early.

"I have to go, but I'll see you tomorrow, yes?"

"Yes," she said, her voice slightly hoarse, as if words were more than she could handle right now.

Somehow he found the strength to tear his gaze from her face and to drop his hands back to his sides and walk to the front door. As he drove away, he tried to make sense of what had just happened. It was difficult with his heart still racing, his blood still hot in his veins and an erection that demanded to be assuaged.

She looked like Sara, sounded like Sara—even moved the same way—but she was definitely not Sara. He'd wager his life on it.

He racked his memory, trying to think of what he knew of Sara Woodville beyond her talent as an equestrian, beyond her flaming beauty that drew looks and turned heads wherever she went. She'd mentioned family in New Zealand, he was sure of it. A sister, perhaps? Yes, a sister. They'd both competed in equestrian events as teenagers but Sara had stayed with the sport, going so far as to qualify to represent her country—as she had done while here on Isla Sagrado, when he'd met her. But the sister? He shook his head as he tried to force the memory from his brain.

By the time he'd pulled into the underground car park at his apartment building and ridden the lift to the penthouse—overlooking Puerto Seguro's harbor lights—his blood had finally begun to cool, but he was no closer to an answer. Still, how difficult could it be in this wonderful Internet age, he wondered, to find out just how close a sister Sara Woodville had?

It was only a matter of minutes before he had the information he needed. He stared at the search results on his computer screen and sipped slowly at the delicious red del Castillo Tempranillo wine he'd poured for himself while his computer booted up.

An identical twin.

He oughtn't to have been surprised, yet somehow the news still came as a shock to him. So, *Sarina* Woodville was standing in for her twin sister—an engaged Sarina Woodville at that, if the notice showing her and her fiancé in a local paper was any indicator. So why was she here instead; and where the hell was Sara? What scheme lay behind those identically beautiful faces? The web information he'd attained showed they came from fairly humble beginnings. Clearly, money was an enticement—how else would they maintain the kind of lifestyle and extravagance he'd seen Sara indulge in? Her riding sponsorship could only go so far and eventing was an expensive sport.

Even though the del Castillo wealth had diminished somewhat over the years—the result of the curse in action, as *Abuelo* would insist, Reynard thought with an ironic curve of his lips—the family was very well-placed in Sagradan society. And they were definitely wealthy enough to attract a scam. Estella Martinez had been a perfect example of that. Maybe in this case, the twins had decided that two scammers were better than one?

Anger welled from deep within. Slow and determined and gathering momentum until his body vibrated with suppressed energy. How dare they assume they could hoodwink his family? There was one thing he knew they would learn—no del Castillo would ever tolerate being played for a fool. No scandal had previously destroyed them; it had only made them stronger.

He thought for a moment of *Abuelo*, of his current infirmity and the ever present risk of another stroke. Was that going to be their angle? he thought. Were they going to somehow lure him into trouble and then threaten to expose him to his grandfather? Risk an old man's health, his fears of an ancient curse and the ghost of a governess who'd been dead three hundred years, for the sake of money?

What was their aim? Did they think they could use their switch to make him look a fool? Engaged to one woman while possibly bedding another? Was that how they planned to use their switch for financial gain? The papers would lap it up, paying huge money for exclusive rights to the story. Or was their aim like Estella's? To threaten to expose the story in a bid to get more money to keep quiet?

Anyone who knew his family knew that they would do anything to protect their own. And that was exactly what he was going to do. Protect his family—and if that meant ensuring he became a great deal closer to this Sarina Woodville, he'd do whatever it took.

Reynard took another sip of his wine, savoring the flavor, and allowing his mind to roam. Yes, he knew exactly what tack he'd take now that he had the upper hand in this charade the Woodville sisters were employing. They would discover they had met their match, and as his lethal anger came under control, he began to find himself strangely exhilarated by the upcoming challenge.

Rina looked at her reflection through bleary eyes. Last night had been the worst she'd had since arriving on the island. The worst since Jacob had broken off their engagement, actually.

Sara had called late in the night. The line had been bad, reception patchy at best, but her message had been quite clear. Whatever she was going through was taking a massive emotional toll on her and she was relying on Rina to keep things together in Isla Sagrado for her. To keep up the charade until she was strong enough to come back. Wracked with guilt over the kiss she had shared with Rey, a kiss she'd wished could go on forever, Rina had promised she'd do whatever it took.

Her sister had called upon her for help, albeit in typical Sara fashion with all too little notice and even less detail, and Rina had betrayed her. Worse, she'd actively enjoyed it.

Rina pressed her fingers to her lips, the memory of

Rey's mouth against hers still too vivid in her mind. She'd succumbed to his touch as if she'd been made for him and him alone, and in doing so she'd broken every unwritten law of sisterhood. She'd kissed her sister's fiancé and, God help her, she wanted to do it again. In fact, she wanted more than that. She wanted all of him, over and over again.

She reached for the taps over the white porcelain sink and turned on the cold water with a sharp twist of a shaking hand. This was all wrong. She and Sara had never been attracted to the same man before. They hadn't even so much as liked the same type, let alone ever had to worry about poaching on one another's ground.

But she'd done more than poach now and, somehow, without letting the truth come out, Rina had to find a way to step back and prevent anything like last night's kiss ever happening again. If it did, Rina knew she could never forgive herself.

She bent over the basin and splashed liberal amounts of cold water directly over her face, scrubbing at her skin with her bare hands until her cheeks tingled. She reached for a towel and wiped her face dry before looking at herself in the mirror once more. It was no good. She looked just as tired and disgusted with herself as she had when she'd woken.

The sound of the cottage's phone ringing in the sitting room stirred her to action. Please, please, let it be Sara calling to put her out of her misery, she prayed silently.

"Hello?" she answered, lifting the near museum quality handset from its cradle.

"Good morning, *mi corazon*."

Rey's voice flooded through the phone, as rich and liquid as warm dark chocolate. Instantly, she felt every nerve in her body react and hone in on the deliciously deep timbre—as if just the sound of his voice could reach through the telephone wires and stroke the surface of her skin.

Her nipples pebbled into tight aching buds against the surface of the old T-shirt she'd continued to wear to bed each night—the soft fabric a caress as light as a lover's touch against the taut peaks. Heat streaked, like lightning, through her body, centering low and deep in her body. Creating a throbbing need that all the cold water in the world could not extinguish.

"I trust you slept well last night," Rey continued, oblivious to her traitorous body's reaction. "I thought that you might like to see a little more of the island today. Perhaps in the late afternoon?"

Rina gathered her scattered thoughts and forced them into words through lips that were suddenly dry and uncooperative.

"Late afternoon?"

"Sí," he replied. "I will see Benedict this morning for a while, and again this afternoon, but I must also now attend to my office for some hours. I thought to pick you up around four or five and we could drive along the coast before coming back to my apartment for dinner. What do you say?"

His apartment? Dinner? Was that all he asked? She knew that he and Sara had not yet been intimate together; a fact that still surprised her given their engagement. But did he plan to change all that tonight? And if he did, would she have the strength, let alone the will, to discourage him?

"Sara?" he prompted, and she could hear the smile in his voice.

"Yes…yes, that sounds lovely," she finally spoke. At least she would have the day to herself. Time enough, hopefully, to shore up her defenses against her forbidden attraction to him. "Um, should I wear anything special?"

"Good question," he answered. "We might go out for a drink along the harborside, first, so something a bit dressy, perhaps. What about what you wore the night I proposed? You always look beautiful in that. Until this afternoon, then. *Hasta luego*."

Even after he'd hung up, Rina still stood there holding the phone to her ear. Her fingers clenched around the old black plastic, which creaked in protest at her white-knuckled grip. The dress she wore the night he proposed—the dress *Sara* wore, that is. What on earth was she to do? She had no idea which one it was and, without any contact from Sara, no way of finding out, either.

Numbly, she replaced the phone in its cradle and walked back to the bedroom to throw open the wardrobe doors. Given its rather frugal size, and the number of clothes Sara had kept here, it shouldn't be impossible to narrow it down—but what if her twin had taken the dress with her?

Rina slumped onto the edge of the bed and stared unseeingly at the contents of her sister's closet. Her eyes began to burn with unexpected tears. Suddenly this stupid charade was all too much. She loved her sister with an affection that transcended most sibling boundaries—would give her life for Sara's if necessary—but continuing to masquerade as her twin this time around was taking a toll she'd never anticipated.

Maybe she should come clean. Tell Reynard the truth about what had happened. Let him know that Sara was suffering cold feet and that she'd asked Rina to stand in for her—after all, he deserved the truth. As one who'd been lied to and cheated on, she knew with personal understanding how cruel that type of behavior was.

But Sara had her reasons for wanting to perpetuate this falsehood. Reasons she hadn't seen fit to disclose yet to

Rina. And blood was thicker than water. Rina had never had any cause to doubt her sister's choices before—had never been in open conflict with her, ever. Regardless of her original intention to stop this charade in its tracks, Sara needed her to do this for her and do it she must, whatever the price, because, if their situation had been reversed, Rina had no doubt Sara would step in for her.

She got up off the bed and fingered the clothes hanging neatly in the closet, wondering which dress it was that Sara had worn when she'd accepted Rey's proposal—or if it was even in here at all. She shook her head. She was being silly. She didn't have to worry. It would be a simple matter to say the dress was at the cleaners or that she'd spilled makeup on it or something like that.

She could do this. For Sara she could do anything. She just had to remind herself of the mini-adventures they'd conducted when they were younger, standing in for one another. Though, this felt entirely different. This time, for the first time, she wanted what her sister had with a longing she had never experienced with such intensity. Walking away from Reynard after this, and leaving him to Sara, was going to be the toughest thing she'd had to do, ever.

Rina spied her suitcase shoved in the bottom of the wardrobe and knew exactly what she'd wear tonight. The dress she'd bought once she'd made her mind up to come here to lick her metaphorical wounds, supported by her sister's tender love and care, was an aberration to her usual style. If anything, it was far more like something her party-mad sister would have chosen for herself.

Shorter than the type of dress she'd worn since she'd started going out with Jacob, the dark periwinkle blue fabric skimmed her thighs with flirty layers of hand painted chiffon and the softly draping cowl neck dropped from tiny spaghetti straps to give a hint of the swell of her breasts.

She'd even bought a special strapless bra to wear with it, and in a fit of extravagance, matching G-string panties. The second she'd tried on the dress in the store, she'd known it was perfect for her. She'd instantly felt empowered again, feminine and strong. Certainly not like a woman whose fiancé had only thought to let her know he'd be marrying someone else a week out from their proposed wedding date.

Yes, she might be pretending to be someone else, but she'd be doing it in her own clothes and wearing her own silver-strapped high-heeled sandals at the same time. And she'd do it with all the flair she could muster. Even as she made the decision to be herself, she felt conflicted. In the past, pretending to be her sister had been all about exactly that—being Sara. Was she treading too fine a line now?

Seven

By the time four o'clock rolled around, Rina was just about climbing the walls with frustration. The day had stretched out for what felt like forever and, with the cottage being as isolated as it was, there was little she could do to fill her time.

In the end, she'd taken out her frustration on the weeds along the front wall and in the gardens that bordered the front of the house—moving a sun umbrella along with her as she worked. At least she could see she'd been effective at something through the course of the day. The dry soil had made pulling weeds easy, though, and the job hadn't taken as long as she'd expected. Not even a long pampering session in the cottage's bathroom had filled enough hours before she could begin to expect Rey's arrival.

As the hands on the mantel clock had wound their way slowly between four and five o'clock, Rina found herself straining her ears to listen for the sound of Rey's car approaching. She smoothed the skirt of her dress for what was probably the twentieth time and checked the mantel clock again.

Finally, as the clock delicately chimed the quarter hour, she heard the muted roar of Rey's car as it pulled up outside the cottage. She grabbed her silver clutch bag and secured the cottage's front door before meeting him on the path at the front.

"You've been busy today," Rey commented, looking at the evidence of her work in the gardens.

Rina shrugged. "I had to do something or I'd have gone mad. I'm not used to doing nothing."

"I thought that was the purpose of a holiday? Especially one on a Mediterranean island," he said with a quirk of one brow.

Inwardly, she cringed. Sara would never have worked in the garden. It wasn't as if she wasn't prepared to work hard at the things that interested her, especially her horses, but gardens? She'd made a terrible faux pas in finding a relief for her boredom today.

Hoping like mad that she could carry it off, she gave Rey a bright smile and waved a hand in the general direction of the garden. "Well, you know me. Once I get my mind fixed on something I won't let up."

Rey gave a short laugh. "Isn't that the truth," he agreed. "Come here and let me see you properly. I haven't seen you wear that color before. It really suits you. Especially with the color you've caught in your skin today."

He took one of her hands in his and gave her a gentle twirl—not an easy feat in her high heels on the cobbled path.

"There was a stain on my other outfit, so I improvised," Rina said, averting her eyes and hoping a telltale flush wouldn't blotch her chest and neck at the lie.

"I'm glad," he said giving her a longer, more appreciative look that sent a sizzle of awareness straight through her. "I like this better. The color—" he paused a moment "—is more you."

Rina felt a trickle of unease creep along her spine. His ever so slight emphasis on the word "you" made her wonder if she'd taken too much of a risk in choosing to wear something that so completely reflected her real personality. Not something that Jacob would have approved of, not something that Sara, in her flamboyance, would have chosen—something that was unmistakably her. But then Rey tugged her hand and pulled her along the path to the car waiting outside the gate and settled her into the passenger seat.

She was being fanciful, she rationalized. Her own guilt at taking advantage of him, and his relationship with her sister, was making her see things in statements that were simply not there at all.

Rina cast a sideways glance at him as he dropped into his seat and put on his seat belt. He was wearing sharply creased black trousers that tautened across his thighs as he eased the car into gear. Beneath the finely woven fabric she could almost make out the delineation of his quad muscles, their lean strength a fluid movement beneath the material. In normal circumstances, as his real fiancée, she'd have the palm of her hand resting just there—be feeling the flex and release of those muscles as he changed gears on the high performance engine.

Her palm tingled just thinking about it, and she forced herself to turn her head away and stare out the side window at the scenery as they passed by. Sara would kill her. It wasn't part of the plan that she should be so powerfully attracted to him. It made no logical sense at all. He wasn't her type. He was too…too everything.

She tried to pull a picture of Jacob into her mind, to overprint the finely boned features of Rey's face and his fascinating hazel eyes with Jacob's fairer skin, broader forehead and pale blue eyes. It had only been three weeks since they'd shared that last meal together, since they'd ended their plans to marry on such a painfully civilized note.

Rina couldn't imagine Rey being quite so civilized if the situation had been his. There'd be fire in his eyes, rather than relief that she hadn't made a scene. There'd be challenge—demand. He wouldn't have made their five year relationship sound like a board meeting when encapsulating the reasons why he'd found it necessary to have a last minute fling. A fling that had rapidly turned into something more. A fling that had signaled the end of the plans they'd so painstakingly made together.

No, Reynard del Castillo was a different kettle of fish altogether. Rina risked another glance in his direction, and a warm flush of something she didn't want to name pulsed through her as he met her gaze and gave her a half smile before giving his attention back to the road.

For the first time in days she realized that thinking about Jacob didn't hurt anymore and that, despite her initial shock and pain, he'd done the right thing in ending their engagement. Of course, his method and timing still left a great deal to be desired, but could she honestly tell herself that a single glance from him had ever—in all the time they'd been together—had the power to elicit a reaction like the one still thrumming through her from Rey's smile? She'd be lying if she said yes.

Which left her in a very precarious position. Clearly, Sara's engagement to Reynard had been a fresh new thing for them both. Rina knew full well how alluring Sara could be; she'd watched her in action often enough. But Sara and

Rey hadn't even slept together, for goodness' sake. Who got engaged on what had apparently been such a platonic relationship to date? Was Sara playing hard to get? Was that what had coaxed the proposal from Rey all along? And if she was having second thoughts, why on earth had she simply not said so to him, rather than indulge in this subterfuge?

Something just didn't ring true, but until Sara divulged more details, there really was nothing she could do but continue the pretense—no matter the travesty it made of her own feelings.

"You're very quiet today. Everything all right?" Rey's voice broke into her thoughts.

"Just thinking, really. Nothing important."

"We will be at the waterfront soon. We'll leave the car at my apartment building and we can walk there for a predinner drink."

"That sounds lovely. I'm looking forward to it."

"As am I."

He gave her a slow wink and again that throbbing pulse beat through her, accompanied this time by a pull from deep within her body. She gave herself a mental shake. This wasn't for her benefit, it was for Sara's, she told herself sternly. She had no right to feel this way, to react this way, to wish that things could be different and that she could explore these new sensations he elicited in her.

"I don't know how well these shoes will bear up to much walking, though. I hope it's not far."

Rey cast a quick glance at her feet and gave a short laugh. "Don't worry, I'll be there to carry you if necessary."

The thought of his strong arms around her, holding her, carrying her—it was getting to be too much. She forced an answering laugh from a throat that had suddenly grown too tight.

"I don't think it'll have to come to that," she said, slightly breathless.

"Pity," Rey responded, his voice deep and intimate in the close confines of the car.

It was definitely time to get their conversation back onto a safer track, Rina decided and scoured her mind for something they could discuss without it entering into waters she had no desire to swim. Well, no right to swim anyway.

"Do you mind if I ask you something?" she said, keeping her voice light.

"Sure, what is it?"

"This curse your grandfather kept talking about. What's it all about?"

"Ah, yes. Not one of our family's best moments in history," Rey replied enigmatically. "I tell you what. I'll explain over our drinks, after we've done some dancing."

"Dancing?"

"Didn't I mention it? The restaurant is built over the water and the dance floor is one of the most popular in all of Puerto Seguro."

Dancing she could handle, high heels or not. It was something both she and Sara loved and did equally well. Although, she hadn't had the opportunity to indulge while she and Jacob had been together. He'd been uncomfortable on the dance floor and to keep him happy, she'd thought it was a small thing to forgo her own love of dancing. To be able to indulge tonight sent her pulse thrumming in anticipation.

"Sounds like fun," she responded with a smile that stretched from ear to ear. She couldn't wait.

And it was fun. Despite the relatively early hour for entertainment in the Med, the dance floor was crowded. To her delight, Rey was equally as skilled a dancer as her, even more so perhaps, she decided as he deftly twirled her out from his arms and back again in tune to the heady beat of the music playing from the discreetly placed speakers. She'd half expected the restaurant to be empty, being a week night, but the place was humming with activity. The tapas bar was doing a particularly fast trade on wines and beer and the delicious tapas menu which featured a lot of the local seafood as well as what Rey referred to as "foreign imports."

By the time they found a table, overlooking the harbor, Rina was feeling far more relaxed.

"Phew, that was great. Thank you for bringing me here," she said, catching her breath before taking a long, cold sip of the iced water that had just been delivered to their table.

"*De nada*. We were supposed to come here the night before you went to France, remember? You'd been begging me for days."

"Ah, yes, of course." And just like that her happy mood shattered into a million shards. How many other metaphorical land mines would she step straight into before Sara came back? she wondered.

"Did you want to look at the tapas menu, or do you prefer to leave the choice in my hands?" Rey asked.

Rina waved a hand at the sheet he held between his long elegant fingers. "Oh, you go ahead. Surprise me."

Rey beckoned to a waiter who came swiftly to take their order.

"And do you wish to have wine with your meal, also, *señor?*" the waiter asked politely.

"Sara? Do you want wine, or did you want to stay with your water?" Rey asked.

Rina had the impression he was expecting her to refuse

wine. She thought it strange when she knew Sara enjoyed quality sparkling wines over anything else.

"Oh, wine, please. Do they have any of the Catalonian Cavas?"

There, even though her preference was for a full-bodied red, she could be more like Sara if she needed to be. She'd even remembered the district Sara had mentioned, in one of her e-mails, where she'd discovered a new favorite. Rey raised an eyebrow at her and placed the order with the waiter who nodded before leaving them at the table.

"I was beginning to wonder if there was something wrong. You haven't taken wine for a couple of weeks now."

"Me? Oh, no. I'm fit as a horse." Rina tried to keep a smile plastered on her face.

Sara had stopped drinking wine? That wasn't like her at all. Maybe Rey was right. When Rina saw her at the airport, Sara had been a bit off-color. Ah, well, hopefully she would be able to get to the root of everything when she finally caught up with her twin. Rina settled back into her seat and decided a subject change was definitely in order. It was all too easy to slip unwarily into dangerous waters, like the wine.

"You were going to tell me about the curse?" she prompted.

"Ah, yes, the curse." Rey sighed and leaned back in his chair, fixing his gaze at something in the distance across the harbor. "As I said before, it is not one of my family's greatest moments. In fact, most of us would quite happily forget about the whole thing, but for some reason *Abuelo* has become fixated on the topic. It would probably be of benefit to all of us if you understood the background and helped to head him off from his ramblings."

"Is it really that bad?" Rina asked, leaning forward to

prop her elbows on the table and rest her chin on interlaced fingers.

Rey snorted. "As bad as it gets, though I have nothing else to compare it to. So, where to begin?"

"At the beginning, I suppose," she encouraged softly. "Who made the curse, and why?"

"That bit's easy. Three hundred years ago, one of my ancestors hired a governess to teach his three daughters. It's the old story, I suppose. His wife was often sickly, and largely absent from his daily life. The governess was young and beautiful. The Baron was handsome and virile—a typical del Castillo trait," he teased.

Rina felt her lips curve in an answering smile and she rolled her eyes at him. "And was he modest, too? Another del Castillo trait, I suppose?"

"Oh, of course." Rey's smile widened. "Anyway, to cut a long story short, over the years, he fathered three sons with her. At the same time, his long-suffering wife bore him three more daughters. He was determined to acknowledge his male heirs—his infant sons from the governess. So he forced his wife to acknowledge them as her own children, while substituting the girls for the governess's babes.

"As a token of his esteem for his lover, and as the only way he could show his thanks for the gift of his sons, he set her up in the cottage where you now stay and gave her a necklace set with a massive ruby, known as *La Verdad del Corazon*."

"The Heart's Truth? Have I got that right?"

"*Sí*, it was a family heirloom."

"He must have loved her very much to give her the necklace."

"Well, that is under dispute. Apparently, the necklace—or more particularly the stone itself—was supposed to represent the family's strength and prosperity. It was a gift which was to be endowed upon each new bride. Why he gave it to his lover, well, that is anyone's guess."

"Why is it under dispute? Surely the fact he gave it to her should be enough proof of his love?"

"One would have thought so, however when the boys were in their teens, the baron's wife died and he entered into a new marriage contract with a woman from a high-ranking French family. Some say it was for financial and political gain, but there was no need, then, for him to continue to advance the family fortunes. He was already the wealthiest man on Isla Sagrado, and one of the wealthiest in all of Spain and France."

"He married someone else?" Rina was shocked. "After she'd waited for him all that time?"

"Ah, I see you're a romantic at heart. You think he, a Baron, should have married his daughters' governess?"

"Well, of course he should!"

Reynard shook his head gently. "Such was not the way of things then. A commoner, while good enough to warm the sheets of the noble classes, could never marry above their station."

"That's just disgusting." Rina reached for the glass of cava that had appeared during Rey's storytelling. "He owed it to her."

"Well, it appears she felt much as you do. According to legend, she was apparently crazed with grief at what she saw as his betrayal, so she broke into the wedding festivities at the castillo and publicly accused the Baron of stealing her sons. Of course, he decried her statement but what is said to have made matters worse was her own sons refuting her claim as well—saying she was not their mother. She became uncontrollable and the Baron ordered his soldiers to take her below the castillo, to the cliff caves where cells were kept for unfortunates such as her.

"But before they could drag her away she cursed the Baron and his children, all nine of them, swearing that if in nine generations they could not learn to marry and live their lives by honor, truth and love, the family and all its branches would die out forever."

"She cursed her own children?"

Rey shrugged. "She was mad, what can I say?"

"Driven mad, more like. And then to have her own flesh and blood turn their backs on her?" Rina nodded slowly. "I can see why she'd have done it. But I imagine she regretted it with every bone in her body."

"We will never know if she felt regret. They say she broke free of her captors once they reached the tunnels below the castillo and ran down one in particular that led to an opening in the cliff face above the rocks. The legend says that as the soldiers closed in behind her, she ripped *La Verdad del Corazon* from her neck and cast it into the sea, saying it would only return to the family once the curse was broken. Then she followed the necklace into the savage ocean below."

"Oh, no. That's awful."

"Tragic, yes. Her body was washed up by the waves within days, but the necklace was never seen again."

"And her curse? Has it really happened?"

Rey shrugged. "Who is to say if she has seen her wishes come true or not? The family lines have certainly diminished over the past three hundred years. But that is only normal given the circumstances of wars, ill health and general bad luck. From the direct line of the sons, reputed to be hers—remember, there is no proof—only *Abuelo,* Alex, Benedict and myself remain. And my brothers and I are the ninth generation."

"Honor, truth and love. Those are the words on your family crest aren't they?" Rina took another sip of her wine, enjoying the dance of bubbles across her tongue before she swallowed.

"They are. I didn't know you'd seen that," Rey nodded.

"I saw it on the doors to your office, the day of Benedict's accident. I suppose it makes sense that she'd have chosen those three provisos if she felt her lover had not abided by them. So, have *you?*"

"Have I what?"

"Have you abided by them? Is the curse broken?"

Eight

She had the nerve to sit there and judge him? Rey bit back his instinctive response and schooled his features into a pleasant smile.

"Now what would make you think we del Castillos would live any other way?"

Sara—no, Sarina, he corrected himself—twirled the long stemmed champagne flute on the tabletop in front of her, eyeing him from beneath her long, dark lashes as if considering her reply very carefully. As well she should, he thought. She wasn't who she said she was, so she could hardly harp on about truth now, could she?

"Well, I was just thinking about what the governess said and how she phrased her curse. It's as if she wanted to remind her lover of his family's creed. Clearly, she felt he had not lived by it."

"She had gone mad. Who knows what she was thinking any more? Now, enough of history." Rey leaned forward and fixed her with a stare. "How about you tell me a little about your family? We've had so little opportunity to learn about ourselves beyond the obvious. I think it's time we got to know one another a little better, don't you?"

Her pupils dilated somewhat, before settling back to normal—the only visible sign of any fear. Oh, she was very good at this, he reluctantly acknowledged. If his suspicions hadn't been roused and if the damning information on the Internet hadn't been available, he'd never have suspected any different.

"What do you want to know?"

She was hedging; he knew it as surely as he knew the sun rose and fell each day. He reached across the table and gathered her left hand in his, his thumb gently swinging the diamond solitaire he'd put on her sister's finger, back and forth.

"Siblings? Parents? What sort of things did you get up to growing up?"

To his surprise she smiled. "One sibling—a sister, one surviving parent and mischief, generally. What about you?"

So she was already trying to turn the tide of conversation back to him. He hid his irritation behind a laugh.

"Oh, mischief also, most definitely. My parents died in an avalanche many years ago. *Abuelo* had the joy of seeing my brothers and me through our teenage years. No doubt that has aged him unfairly."

"I doubt that. If anything, I would imagine trying to keep you three in line kept him youthful. And from the way he is with you and your brothers, I'm sure he wouldn't have it any other way. I am very sorry to hear you lost your parents so young, though."

"Thank you. What about you? Tell me about your parents." It would be too obvious if he asked about her sister right away—he wanted to ease her in to it. Get her to open up, let her guard down, perhaps show her true colors.

She smiled and her eyes took on a faraway look. "For as long as I can remember, they were constantly competing with one another. I suppose, to an outsider, it was a rather strange marriage but it seemed to work for them. They fed on one another's need to be the best at everything. I think that's why they encouraged my sister and me into competitive sport. Winning was everything. It didn't matter if it was a game of cards, or the best vegetables, sport or anything. Sometimes they worked together to win against someone else, sometimes apart to compete against one another.

"It wasn't always…easy at home. Anyway, Dad died suddenly a couple of years ago, complications from pneumonia. It came as a heck of a shock to us all but while Mum still grieves for him, she's come to accept his death—and, with him gone, there's no further fierce competition. She seems more settled than she did before. Happier to take life at a slower pace, I guess."

"And your sister? What is she doing?"

Sarina's lips parted and she started to speak but then hesitated. Obviously gathering her thoughts together.

"This and that. She was recently engaged but it didn't work out."

That was interesting—the newspaper article he'd read gave the impression that she was still engaged. Was she lying? No, it seemed more likely that the engagement had truly ended—perhaps because she didn't manage to successfully fleece the poor idiot who'd asked her to marry him, Rey thought.

"She's been working as a kind of Girl Friday for the past couple of years, basically a problem solver for people—she has a knack for sorting things out, raising business profiles where necessary and creating calm where there's chaos—she's a bit of a Jill of all trades, but I think she's ready for a change now."

"You two are close?"

"Very close," she agreed and reached for her nearly empty wine glass.

"More wine?" he asked. Perhaps he could encourage her to be less guarded with her responses if she had a little more to drink.

"Thank you, that would be lovely."

Their waiter chose that moment to return to their table with a selection of the local tapas the restaurant specialized in. Reynard chose several of them and after the waiter set the dishes out, and explained each one in turn, he took their order for another glass of Cava for Sarina and a Tempranillo for Reynard.

He nodded his acceptance to the waiter before leaning forward to select a crisp golden croquette and hold it to Sarina's lips.

"Here, try this. I think you'll like it."

She obediently opened her mouth and he popped the tiny croquette inside, allowing her lips to close over his fingers before he withdrew them. He saw the surprise on her face at his lingering touch on her lips before the flavors of the morsel of food exploded in her mouth. An expression of sheer pleasure crossed her face, an expression not unlike that of a woman deep in the throes of lovemaking. Despite his simmering anger, passion pooled deep in his gut, sending blood to one particular extremity where it pulsed with demanding need. He'd been a fool to be taken in by her pretense for so long. He should have known from the first moment he had touched her that she wasn't Sara. While the twins were uncannily identical, his response to the two of them couldn't be more different. The woman he'd proposed to had never fired his blood the way the woman sitting before him now did with every gesture, every touch.

"That is divine," she said after a few moments. "What was it, again?"

"*Croquetas de gambas,* translated, prawn croquettes."

He was relieved she'd finished the morsel. Watching her eat it, watching the cascade of delight pass across her features, had been a torture all in itself.

"I think I like the Spanish term best. Hmm, *croquetas de gambas.* Yes, I like the way it rolls off the tongue almost as much as it rolls onto it."

Rey helped himself to one of the minicroquettes and let his teeth sink into the crispy coating before the soft filling spilled across his taste buds. Yes, he could understand why she'd gone into such raptures over the snack. It was truly delicious.

"You've got a crumb, just there."

Sarina reached across the table and wiped the bottom edge of his lip with her thumb, her touch leaving a flame of heat against his skin. She sat back suddenly, her eyes a little glazed. Had she felt that same burn along her skin as he had? He hoped so. She deserved as much torment as he could possibly put her through.

"Thanks," he said, with a slow smile calculated to both put her at ease with the intimacy of her touch and her reaction to it.

He steered the conversation into more desultory topics as they enjoyed the rest of the tapas selection. She had one more glass of wine, while he nursed his single glass, mindful of the dinner he had planned back at the apartment, the necessity to keep a clear head. Aside from the importance of keeping his wits about him while he figured out her angle, he also had to be sober enough to drive her home to the cottage again tonight.

Unless, of course, he could persuade her to stay the night at his apartment.

The thought of luring secrets from her while between his Egyptian cotton sheets had merit, he thought, but would she play along? Sara had kept him at arm's length, flirting with him but never letting it go too far. For some reason he'd never felt the urge to press the issue with her, especially as he'd never held the intention of following through on the engagement. With Sarina, however, there was an inexplicable difference. Almost a yearning. From the minute she'd appeared outside his offices, he'd felt a physical connection between the two of them, and it would be all too tempting to explore it further.

The idea took a firmer hold in his mind. How hard could it be to seduce the truth from her? he wondered. She had no idea he was onto whatever cunning plan the sisters had hatched between them.

The sun was low on the water and a new crowd of people had entered the bar. Noisier, more flamboyant and with an edge of careless fun he had no mood to indulge in.

He downed the last of his wine and stood, taking Sarina's hand and encouraging her to her feet.

"Come, it is time we went to my apartment. I have a special evening planned for us both."

"I don't know if I could eat another thing after those delicious bites," she halfheartedly protested as she tucked her clutch bag under her free arm.

He smiled in return and leaned closer to her, his lips almost grazing the shell of her ear as he spoke.

"I think I can tempt you to more, just you wait and see."

Even in the subdued lighting of the bar, he saw the flush

creep across her cheeks and noted the change in pitch in her breathing.

They strolled back toward his apartment building, a mere ten minutes away, and he allowed the silence between them to continue. Far better to allow her to consume her thoughts with what he might have in mind than to cloud them with inane conversation. Outside the restaurant, he drew her against his side, one arm casually draped across her shoulders and his fingertips tracing small patterns over the top of her bare arm.

He felt her skin react instantly, tiny goose bumps peppering the surface, and sensed the shiver that ran through her body.

"Cold?" he asked.

"No, not at all," she replied, her voice slightly thick, as if she'd just woken.

He allowed himself a small smile of satisfaction, but it was short-lived because even as he recognized how his touch affected her, so did it in turn affect him. Desire could be a double-edged sword at times, he mused as he led her through the vast, glass sliding doors leading into the lobby of his building.

He guided her into the mirrored elevator and as they traveled to the top floor he marveled anew at just how identical she and Sara were. If he hadn't been aware of that intrinsic spark of difference in his reaction to them, he would never have been able to pick one from the other. From the lush, dark red spirals of hair, the wide-set gray eyes thickly lashed in black, to the long patrician nose and the full, deliciously sensual mouth—Sara and Sarina were mirror images of one another.

On his floor, he swiped his electronic key to open the double doors, again carved with the family crest, and showed Sarina into his apartment. The carefully carved words seemed to leap out at him as he passed through the doors and pulled them closed behind him. Honor. Truth. Love. It was as if each word echoed in his mind. His internal response was instant and emphatic. Of course he abided by all three. How could he do anything else and still hold his head high?

But what of the lie he'd been perpetuating with Sara? a quiet deep voice asked from within. Could he swear that he'd been truthful about that? Could he claim his actions had been fully honorable? He puffed out a breath of frustration at the train his thoughts were taking. He had no time to examine this now.

"Is everything okay?" Sarina asked.

"More than okay," Rey said, gliding across the carpet and gathering her in his arms.

She slid into his hold as if she'd been doing this for weeks rather than days, he thought. There was no sense of restraint, no physical holding back. Her lower stomach and thighs pressed against him and she curved into his body as if it was the most natural thing in the world to her.

And it was certainly the most natural thing for his body to welcome hers, he thought ruefully as his pulse began to beat that bit faster and his temperature rose. The scent of her hair and the fragrance she wore wound their delicate way around him, casting a spell upon his senses.

Sara had never affected him so deeply, he acknowledged as he stroked his hands over the bare skin of Sarina's back. Sure, he'd been attracted to Sara. He was a hot-blooded, heterosexual male with a well-honed appreciation for a beautiful woman, but there was something about Sarina that hit a different chord with him.

Perhaps it was the fact that he knew she was not who she claimed to be that added that extra touch of spice to being with her. He eschewed the thought even as it occurred to him. It had been different from the moment she'd arrived here, not since he'd figured out that she was an imposter.

He tipped her chin up to his and kissed her lightly on the lips before reluctantly setting her away from him.

"I need to check on something in the kitchen. I'll be right back."

He needed to create some distance before he lost himself in her and forgot what he was trying to find out.

"You cooked?"

She followed him into the large and well-equipped kitchen.

"I am capable of it, you know." He laughed at the note of surprise in her voice and lifted the lid on the slow cooker he had on the bench top. Instantly, the rich aroma of the spiced lamb he'd prepared before heading into his office this morning filled the air.

"That smells divine," Sarina said, coming beside him and leaning over the pot to inhale.

She closed her eyes and breathed theatrically, then smiled.

"I didn't think I could be hungry so soon after the tapas, but I'm prepared to be wrong about that."

"Good, I'm pleased to hear it," he said, giving the mixture a gentle stir before replacing the lid. "I'll put the rice on and we'll be ready to eat in about twenty minutes or so."

"Can I do anything to help? Set the table or something?"

"I thought we could eat outside on the terrace. The harbor is beautiful this time of year and when the sun sets fully, it's lovely to see the lights. You'll find place mats and cutlery in the drawers over there." He gestured to a sideboard against the wall. "Would you like a drink while we wait for the rice?"

"Just water will be fine. If I have any more wine, it might go to my head."

"And that would be a bad thing?"

She just laughed and got the utensils and place mats out of the drawer before crossing to the wide glass picture windows that led outside onto his private balcony. The expanse of tiles with the toughened safety glass wall beyond, allowing an unobstructed view of the inner harbor, had been a major selling point for him when he'd bought the apartment.

He'd loved living at the castillo—it had been his family's home for centuries and he'd enjoyed the sense of longevity surrounding him while growing up, even more so when his parents had unexpectedly and tragically passed away. But once he hit his mid-twenties he'd wanted something intrinsically his own, and he was drawn to the busyness of the city—loved being close to his work where he headed up the publicity machine that was responsible for driving the del Castillo brand, in its many forms, to greater heights.

"Wow, that view certainly is something," Sarina said as she came back into the apartment. "It's a good thing I have a head for heights with that wall of glass there."

"It unnerves some people. Are you sure you're comfortable to sit out there?"

"Oh, definitely, I wouldn't miss the sunset for all the world," she gushed enthusiastically.

The phone on the wall gave a discreet chirp, distracting him from her smiling face.

"*Hola!*" he answered, then frowned at the voice on the other end. "*Sí*, I understand." There was another pause. "Well, of course we will manage. You make sure she is well cared for. If there is anything I can do, don't hesitate to ask. Anything, do you understand? *Adios*."

Slowly he replaced the receiver and rubbed his hands across his eyes.

"Is it Benedict, is something wrong?" Sarina asked.

"No." He sighed. "It isn't Benedict, thank goodness, but it is serious. My PA has been diagnosed with a ruptured ectopic pregnancy, she's being rushed into surgery now. That was her husband. He's beside himself with worry about her and apparently all she could think of as they wheeled her away was for him to tell me that she won't be in to work tomorrow." He shook his head in amazement.

"She obviously takes her job very seriously."

"*Sí*, she does. She is like my right hand in the office. I could never have spent so much time at the hospital with Benedict if she were not so trustworthy."

"You must be worried about her."

"I am, but I know the doctors at the hospital are among the best in the world. I'm sure they will do whatever they can. I do fear, though, that she will put more strain on herself fretting about leaving the office at what she knows to be such a crucially important time, aside from Benedict's situation."

"How so?"

"Our company is working on a major publicity push for the resort and the winery. Having to get another person up to speed will cause delays." He shrugged and turned to open the fridge and grab the fixings to throw together a green salad. "Still, there's nothing I can do about that. We'll just have to make do, and reassure Carmella as best we can that everything is under control."

"Do you have a temp agency you can call to fill in someone else's position at work and then second one of your existing staff into her role?" Sarina suggested.

"It's a good idea but we're already operating on a skeleton staff through the summer."

"Perhaps I could help?"

He laughed out loud at the suggestion. "You? There are no horses in my office, and the only time my staff jump is when I make them."

"Horses aren't the only thing I can manage," she replied, lifting her nose in the air. "I've been known to run— I mean, I've helped my sister a time or two back home when she's been snowed under. She sometimes needs an extra pair of hands on a keyboard or a fresh perspective on her ideas."

Reynard noted her near mistake in revealing her true vocation. He pretended to consider her suggestion as he ripped apart lettuce leaves and tossed them into a bowl. If she'd orchestrated a reason to come to work in his office, then he might have been suspicious, since it could have been part of whatever plot she was brewing. But she couldn't have anticipated Carmella's situation. And besides, it might not be a bad idea, he decided, to have her exactly where he could find her every minute of the day. Eventually, she'd be bound to slip up somewhere and he'd be in a position to extract the truth from her, and put an end to her and her sister's plans.

"Do you really think you could?"

"I'm going nuts with boredom at the cottage, Rey, give me a chance. If I stuff up, then you can fire me," she said with a self-deprecating shrug.

He nodded slowly. "Okay, then. Starting tomorrow you can be my temporary assistant. I warn you, though, I'm a hard taskmaster."

"Good," she replied. "I enjoy a challenge."

Oh, she'd have her challenge, all right. But it wouldn't be the kind of challenge she'd be expecting. It would be a challenge of her own honesty and truth, and it would be on his terms. Something he was very much looking forward to.

Nine

A challenge? Rina wanted to grab the words back into her mouth the minute she'd said them. What the heck had she been thinking? Work with him? Sara would never have done anything like that at anytime let alone when she was supposed to be on holiday—or, more importantly, enjoying life as the fiancée of one of the island's leading citizens.

She wasn't kidding about being bored, though. Aside from the strain of waiting for news about Benedict at the hospital, at least there she'd felt useful, as if she'd had something of value to offer and add to the family's comfort. At the cottage there was nothing. She'd met the cleaner and been soundly scolded both in Spanish and in English for risking life and limb on the rickety old bike. Now she wasn't allowed to do her own grocery shopping or any cleaning around the house. And she got the feeling the woman wouldn't be too happy that she'd done some gardening, either.

With Sara not returning her texts or calls, she felt as if she was locked in limbo—and sitting still had never been her forte.

"When do I start?" she asked.

"Is tomorrow morning too soon?" Reynard replied.

His expression remained urbane but she saw something in his eyes that made her think he expected her to withdraw, or find some reason to change her mind.

"That should be fine. How shall I get into the office, though?"

"Good question. The ideal solution would be for you to stay here," he suggested.

Again she had that sense that he was watching her. Preparing to gauge her reply.

"That could work, or I could hire a car so I'm a little more independent."

His eyes narrowed a little. "Are you sure? You wouldn't prefer to do without the worry of driving in the central city, on the opposite side of the road to what you are used to?"

"I'm sure I'll get used to it pretty quickly. I've driven in Europe before. It becomes logical when you're driving in the left-hand seat to keep your left shoulder to the center of the road."

He nodded slowly, but she had the impression he was less than pleased. For herself, as tempting as it was to stay in the apartment with him, she knew she would never be able to resist wanting to be more intimate with him. There was an allure between them that she found more and more difficult to fight. For the sake of her love for her sister, she didn't dare give in to it.

"It will not be necessary for you to hire a vehicle. There is bound to be a spare car in one of the garages at the castillo. I'll call Alex and see what's available if you're set on driving yourself."

"I am, and I appreciate it."

"You like your independence?" he asked.

"Within limits," she acceded.

If she really was engaged to him, she'd have agreed to stay at his apartment in a flash, but that wasn't the case. Besides, for whatever reason, Sara had been keeping a distance between herself and Rey, and until she came back, Rina had to work harder to maintain it.

Reynard turned to check the rice on the stove top.

"Ah, dinner is ready. Would you take the salad and the dressing in that glass cruet to the table? I'll bring the plates."

Rina did as she was bid and Rey followed behind her in a few moments with their meals plated up. They ate in a relatively companionable silence, given the way her mind was now racing. After their meal they watched as the sky turned myriad shades of purple before turning into a black velvet blanket peppered with golden stars.

"I see why you chose to live here," Rina commented. "It's as if the sky is mirroring the lights in the city below."

Reynard nodded. "Yes, I never grow tired of the view. I wondered, at first, whether I would even notice the stars sitting here at night, but you can see everything when you look for it."

Rina shot him a sharp look. Was there a hidden message in there, or was she simply being oversensitive? When Rey didn't say any more, she relaxed a little.

"By the way," Rey continued, "I took the opportunity to phone Alex while I made the coffee. He has instructed a staff member to bring a car around for you tomorrow morning. It is one of their pool cars so it won't be missed."

"I really appreciate that. Will you show me tonight where I will need to go, before you take me home?" she asked.

He nodded. "*Sí,* and we can make a quick call into my offices to get you a card for the parking garage under the building, too. Shall we be on our way then?"

"I think that's a good idea. Wouldn't do to keep the help up too late." She smiled.

Rey snorted a soft laugh and shook his head. "Is that what you are to me now? The help? Is it not enough to be my fiancée?"

"I didn't mean any offense," Rina amended.

"No offense taken," Rey said, reaching for her hand and leading her from the table. "But just so you know I'm clear on this, I heartily concur with office romance."

He wrapped his arms around her and lowered his head, his lips warm and soft against hers, the lingering, slightly nut-flavored taste of their coffee on his tongue as he kissed her. Rational thought fled as he deepened the kiss and as she wound her arms around his neck, holding him close to her. Liquid heat flooded her body, curling around her like a burning silken ribbon of need which then tightened and clenched deep within her womb in an age-old response.

Moisture pooled at the apex of her thighs, her skin there sensitive, yearning for more. Yearning for his touch. Her nipples peaked against the softness of her bra, her breasts full and aching for him. When his hands skimmed up her rib cage and cupped her through the fine fabric of her dress, she moaned, a guttural sound that came from deep within. She arched her back, pressing her breasts against his palms, wanting to feel his possession without the barriers of the layers between his touch and her skin.

He shifted and his hardness pressed against her mound, drawing another moan from her as sensation spiraled with increasing demand from her core. She lifted one leg, hooking it around his, tilting her pelvis so she could flex against him again and again, slow, firm. Firmer.

He dropped one hand to clasp her thigh and the raw heat of his fingers curled around her flesh burned like a brand. He broke off the kiss, his breathing heavy, and rested his forehead against hers.

"Stay."

His voice was thick with desire, the single word more a command than a request. But now that the moment had paused, instinct no longer drove Rina forward. With the slow consistency of molasses, awareness flowed back into her mind. What the hell was she thinking? Here she'd been only just telling herself to back off, to find that elusive level of distance she needed to be able to carry this pretense off and now she was all but plastering herself to the man.

She pulled away, placed her foot firmly back on the floor and unhooked her arms from around his neck.

"I...I don't think I should."

Rey's hand lingered on her thigh, slid upward to cup her buttock and pull her against his hips.

"Stay."

His tone this time was more beguiling, pitched deeper, his eyes now burning with the promise of finding a way that would ease the desperate ache that now threatened to consume her.

"I can't. I shouldn't have reacted like that...led you on."

"You didn't lead me on," he said softly. "You reacted honestly, as did I."

If she'd reacted honestly, it was about the only thing she'd done with an element of truth in it since she'd started this whole thing, Rina thought desperately.

"I'm sorry."

"No, don't apologize. We are lucky enough to share a special spark of attraction between us. If we cannot be truthful about that, then what can we be truthful about?"

Each word fell like a blow on her heart. If circumstances were different, she'd be free to explore that special spark he spoke of. Even as she thought it, a chilling wave of reality swamped her. If circumstances were different, it would be Sara here in his arms or, more realistically, in his bed.

She curled her fingers over his and removed his hand from her body, every nerve screaming in protest even as she did so. Then, she carefully stepped away from his warmth and lifted her face to look him straight in the eyes.

"Please, I'd like to go now. Thank you so much for tonight. For everything."

He gave her a small smile tinged with regret and turned away to grab his car keys from the bench top in the kitchen.

"Not quite everything, hmm?"

She smiled back, a reflexive action that completely lacked humor. "No, not quite everything, but that's my fault, not yours."

"There is no fault, *querida*."

Silence stretched out between them as they left the apartment and traveled down in the lift to the basement car park. Once settled in his car, Rey grabbed her left hand, and held it against his thigh—just where she'd wanted to place her hand when they'd been driving together earlier. Instantly the warmth of his skin and the bunch of his muscles beneath the fine woven fabric of his trousers imprinted against her palm. It felt even better than she'd imagined.

"No one said you could not touch me," he said, his voice little more than a growl.

Rina tried to pull her hand away. "I don't think that's a good idea."

His fingers closed over hers, trapping her hand where he wanted it. "Humor me, please. I promise, I will not bite."

Rina nodded her assent and he lifted his hand from hers and slid the car smoothly into gear.

His offices were on the opposite side of the city from his apartment building. By the time they pulled into the car park, Rina was fighting back yawn after yawn as the strain of keeping her emotions and desires under control took its toll.

"Do you wish to come upstairs with me, or wait in the car while I get you a swipe card for entrance tomorrow?" Rey asked after unclipping his seat belt and turning off the car.

"No, I'm okay, I'll come with you. It'll help me to know where to go in the morning."

They rode the lift to his floor and he unlocked the large wooden double doors. For the second time that night, Rina stared at the del Castillo crest and was reminded of the lie she had perpetuated. And to think she'd had the nerve to challenge him on it over dinner. Where was her normally logical head at?

The answer was simple. Her every thought, her every decision, was clouded by the man standing next to her. Despite everything, all she wanted was to be with him and that fell in total opposition to the love and devotion she owed her twin. A sudden shaft of envy speared her heart. Coveting anything of Sara's felt wrong—so very wrong. But in this she was struggling to keep her balance.

It didn't take long for Rey to find her a key card for the parking garage downstairs and to allocate her a parking space.

"This card will also give you access to the floors of the building from the elevator," Rey instructed.

"Thank you," Rina said, trying to ignore the tiny zap of electricity that shot through her as their fingers brushed briefly.

"I'll show you where we'll be working. Come with me."

Rina followed him past the luxurious reception area and down a thickly carpeted hallway. On each side she could see into a variety of offices. Some individual, some clearly shared in a more open plan environment. Near the end, the hallway widened considerably into a second waiting area. A desk and computer guarded the entry into another office space and as Reynard pushed open the doors, Rina felt as though she was being drawn into the inner sanctum of some medieval master.

Rey flicked a bank of switches on the wall and subtle lighting brought the room to life. As opposed to the modern and somewhat minimalistic furnishings he employed in his apartment, this was all old-world splendor. With her PR background, Rina could acknowledge the clever planning behind the decorating decision. The del Castillo brand resonated with wealth, power and history, all of which were reflected in the richly decorated space.

Highly polished mahogany panels lined the walls and deep leather furniture sprawled over the hand-knotted Persian carpets that covered the floor. A large partner desk dominated one side of the office, with a computer flat screen perched on one side. Judging by the papers scattered over the desk, this was very definitely Rey's work space and he used every centimeter of it.

The contrast between the ordered neatness of his home life and the rich disarray of his working world struck her as strange, at first glance. For most people it was the other way around.

When she thought about it, though, she had to admit to enjoying keeping her semidetached townhouse back in Christchurch in a neat and tidy state so it was an oasis for her when she arrived home from work each day. Seeing Rey's personality so similarly reflected hers, she appreciated more sharply how much she looked forward to coming home to a calm and organized atmosphere.

In this room, she could feel the energy of the workplace even despite its lavish opulence. This was a true representation of the Reynard del Castillo she'd come to know since her arrival here. Focused, determined, but still taking the time to appreciate the indulgences his life afforded.

She wandered over to the large corner window that overlooked the city lights. From here, she could just about see the harbor in the distance, but overall she had the impression of being able to look out over the whole world.

Heat suffused her back as she became aware of Rey standing close behind her. His reflection stared at her in the glass. With the sparkle of the city's lights a halo around him and his features thrown into relief by the office lighting, she was struck anew by the sheer male beauty of him. His eyes burned under heavy dark brows, his chiseled cheekbones high and leaving his cheeks in shadows below them.

She found herself staring at his lips, at the full lower curve, the deeply indented cupid's bow of his upper lip. She doubted even Michelangelo's skill could have captured his near-perfect features. She wished she had the right to touch him, to trace the sharply defined edges, to reach up and kiss him, taste him again.

Rina closed her eyes briefly, unsure whether in doing so she was erasing his image from her memory, or imprinting it there in perpetuity. She started as a warm hand enveloped her shoulders, long fingers gently gripping her bare flesh. It would be the most natural thing in the world to just allow herself to lean back against the expanse of his broad chest. To let his heat infuse her body. To drop her head against his shoulders and to expose her neck to his touch.

Her eyes flew open as Rey lifted her tumbling hair to one side and with that one single movement, exposed the tender skin of her throat and neck. The image she watched now was strangely sensual as the dark-haired man, trapped in the glass, bent to press his lips to the exact point where her shoulder and neck met. She gasped at the contact, trying desperately to quell the throb of longing that pulled inexorably through her body at his touch.

Rey lifted his head, his eyes meeting hers in their reflection again.

"It's quite a view, isn't it?"

His voice was deep, the sound a rumble of air across the shell of her ear. The innuendo in his voice was as sinfully persuasive as the touch of his hands on her shoulders, hands which seemed to have a mind of their own as they skimmed down her arms and over her body, one reaching up to cup her breast through the vibrant blue fabric of her dress, the other skimming down, over her hip and lower.

Heat and moisture pooled in a flood at the apex of her thighs and she squeezed her legs together involuntarily, the sharp clench of muscles making the sensations running through her sharper, clearer, simply *more*.

Rey pressed his lips once more to her neck, his teeth grazing her skin ever so gently, before she felt the warm rasp of his tongue across her skin. She had no resistance left. She dropped her head back, exactly as she had imagined, and allowed him to bear her weight.

She felt him push up the hem of her dress, felt the warmth of his hand as he cupped her mound, his fingers skimming over that part of her that screamed for his touch, screamed for release.

Rina watched their reflection, watched as the man in the glass eased aside the damp fabric of the woman's panties and allowed his fingers to stroke the moist crease exposed there. She could almost fool herself that this wasn't happening to her. That it was someone else reflected there in the glass. That it was anyone but Rey who strummed her body to a crescendo that remained just out of reach.

And in that moment, the exact moment he touched her most intimately and her senses went wild, came the dousing reality that it should not be her. That she had no right to take the pleasure he offered her. She had no right to offer the same in return.

"Stop!" she cried, her voice a fractured facsimile of its usual self.

Rey's hands stilled. "*Querida,* why stop? I can feel you, every part of you. You're so close." His voice dropped to a whisper, his breath a caress against her skin. "Let me give you this, let me take you over the edge. I will not allow any harm to come to you. Trust me."

Every particle in her body shrieked at her to give him the right to continue, to bring her to a climax that she knew would render her senseless, useless to say no to him, to anything he wanted. But her mind knew with damning reality that she would never be able to face herself again, let alone her sister, if she allowed this to carry on.

"No, please. I can't." She shook her head frantically, tears burning at the back of her eyes.

It was pain and torture, yet pleasure of indescribable heights at the same time.

"Please," she begged again, "don't make me."

The words acted as effectively as a drenching shower of freezing rain, and she felt his mental withdrawal as keenly as the physical. His hands, which had continued, slow and gentle on her body, now stilled before he dropped them to his side and stepped away from her.

Rina turned from the glass, unable to look at herself, unable to look at him and the questions that undoubtedly raged in his eyes, even as they remained unspoken on his lips.

"I'm so sorry," she mumbled as she straightened her panties under the privacy of her dress. Her tender flesh still throbbed and ached. "I should never have let things get this far. It's not you, seriously, it's me. I..." she trailed off, suddenly at a loss for words.

How did you explain to the man who had very nearly brought you to orgasm, that you couldn't let him touch you again, ever?

Reynard rested his hands against the back of one of the large leather couches and looked at her. She couldn't hold his gaze, fearful of the recrimination—or, worse, the questions—she might see there.

"Can we go now, please?" she asked, her voice finally a little stronger.

He didn't even speak, only nodded, and gestured to the door to his office. As she accompanied him down the hallway, Rina tried to pull her thoughts together. She could not allow anything like this to happen again. It had come too close to total capitulation on her part. And yet, deep inside, a part of her continued to crave him, crave his touch.

She groaned inwardly. The sooner Sara returned to this

forsaken rock in the Mediterranean and resumed her life here, the better, because right now Rina couldn't wait to resume hers, far away from here.

But, a little voice reminded her, you have nothing left at home anymore. All your hopes, all your dreams for the future—all gone. Sure, she still had her job, but hers was the kind of work she could do anywhere in the world, with her talents very much in demand.

It was past time, she realized, for her to make a new beginning. Step forward in her life, rather than going back to where she'd been before. But whatever she chose to do, her life was not here with this man. That life belonged to Sara, and she'd been mad to even begin to think she could play with the fire ignited within her by being around Rey.

If Sara returned tomorrow it wouldn't be a day too soon.

Ten

Rey drove Sarina home in absolute silence. His body still clamored for her, the taste of her skin remained on his tongue. He'd wanted to see how far he could push her and he'd found out—found out he was just as susceptible to her wiles as she was to his. The knowledge was galling, and yet intoxicatingly exhilarating at the same time. He was man enough to know that, with only an ounce more persuasion, she would have capitulated to him—yet gentleman enough not to force her. The power lay firmly in his hands.

The fact that it had left his body raging with fire and need was a discomfort he would learn to either live with or overcome completely.

He had no doubt she'd been as enraptured as he. What was it, he wondered, that had broken through the veil of sensual pleasure and brought her back to damning reality? He'd wanted to take her all the way—to ensnare her, for want of a better phrase. Beneath the exterior that was identical to her twin's lay a rich and sensuous nature. If he could tap into that, he would ensure she fell completely under his spell.

Keeping her in his life, in his bed, would make things safer for everyone—and, no doubt, prove intensely pleasurable along the way.

Rey snuck a glance at Sarina, sitting next to him in the close confines of the car. Her face was pensive, a tension around her eyes that hadn't been there earlier this evening. Her hands lay clasped together in her lap and even in the dark interior, he could tell they were tightly clenched. Her posture, also, was taut—as if every muscle in her body was poised and ready for flight—and suggested that she hovered on the surface of her car seat rather than sank within it. Would she run from him? he wondered. Would she decide to cease this pretense and cut her losses? While he wouldn't deny that it would be a relief to have this stupid blackmail business no longer hanging over his head, he perversely still wanted to see just how far Sarina was prepared to take this.

He knew she was shaken by the strength of her reaction to him. Truth be told, he was equally shaken. Overriding that, however, was a frustration that went beyond the physical. He couldn't afford for her to run away. Not now, not when *Abuelo* was growing stronger again and would be permitted to return home soon—and especially not while Benedict was still in hospital, his accident all the while feeding *Abuelo*'s obsession with the curse.

It occurred to him that he should never have organized a vehicle for her. It would allow her all too much freedom when he needed to know where she was at any given time. Perhaps, with gentle persuasion, he could convince her to stay with him at his apartment. In her own room, if she continued to insist on such. Yes, she required careful handling, that much was clear. Keeping up the travesty of an engagement was surely taking its toll on her—even this evening, she'd almost slipped and exposed her true occupation.

It would be interesting to work with her, he realized. To watch how she would reveal herself and her experience when exposed to the del Castillo publicity machine. The concept of a new challenge with Sarina sent a thrill of anticipation through his veins. He would keep her close at hand, set her up in his office, in the room where she'd almost capitulated under his touch.

The constant reminder would hopefully be a sensual burr in her side—the images of the two of them in the glass a tangible, visceral thing every time she glanced out the windows. An inner satisfaction spread throughout him. Yes, he still held the ultimate control over this situation, and would continue to do so for as long as she and her reprehensible sister believed they had him hoodwinked.

He reached out and laid a hand on her fisted knot of fingers. She jumped beneath his touch, and despite the faint clawing edge of frustration that still clung deep inside, a small burst of humor settled upon him that she could react so.

"I won't bite, you know," he said softly, injecting as much comfort into his words as he was able. "What happened tonight was my fault. All of it. I overstepped the parameters we set when we agreed to get engaged so early in our relationship. It would be unfair of me to expect more from you than you can give right now."

"Thank you," she replied softly, her face still resolutely turned away to stare out the side window.

But his words had the required effect. He could feel her begin to relax, sense the rigidly bound muscles in her body begin to ease. As they pulled up outside the cottage and he walked her to the door, he permitted himself the barest brush of his lips upon her cheek.

"I'll see you tomorrow, about eight-thirty?"

"Sure, whatever time you need me."

"Eight-thirty will be early enough." He stepped off the stairs and onto the narrow path, giving her the advantage of being taller than him for a change. "Are you sure you'll be able to navigate your way back tomorrow morning? The roads will be chaotic."

She nodded. "I'm sure I'll be fine, but if I get lost I'll call you."

"Make sure you do. I don't want to lose you, *querida*."

He couldn't bring himself to call her Sara, not now he knew the truth about who she was.

"You won't," she replied, her earlier strain audible in her voice once more. "Good night."

He lifted one finger to stroke her cheek before answering, "Sweet dreams."

He waited on the path until he heard the ancient door lock tumble closed, then returned to his car. Once safely buckled in, he opened up the engine and roared back toward the city. As the car ate up each kilometer back to Puerto Seguro, he acknowledged that the thrill of racing down the road was a poor substitute for the physical satisfaction his body still craved, and lowered his speed accordingly. But no matter how he controlled the power under the hood of the car, controlling his feelings for the woman he'd left behind was another matter. *Lust,* he told himself. *It's only lust.* He wouldn't, couldn't, allow it to be anything more.

Rina walked out of the elevator and toward the doors to Rey's offices fighting the urge to turn tail and run all the way home. Last night had been one stupid decision after another and the lack of sleep she'd endured as she'd painstakingly pulled apart each minute of their time together had left her headachy and irritable today. Certainly not the best frame of mind to be beginning a new employment position, however temporary it would prove to be.

As she entered the main office, the receptionist looked up from her desk and fixed her with a beaming smile.

"*Buenos dias,* Miss Woodville. How are you this morning?"

"I—I'm well, thank you. Should I go straight to Mr. del Castillo's office?"

"Yes, go through. Can I get you a coffee?"

"Tea, actually. If it's not too much bother. Just weak and black would be great."

"I'll bring it shortly."

Rina smiled her thanks and carried on down the corridor that led to Rey's office. She hesitated in his waiting area before lifting her hand to his office door and rapping softly before entering.

He was standing by the window. Of all the places he could have been as she entered the room it had to be there. That exact spot. Fire flamed through her body as he turned and smiled in welcome. A slow smile that lifted one corner of his lips before the other, as if they shared something intimate and private between them and only them. And they did, she told herself. Just not what it could have been—and certainly not what her body, even now, demanded.

"From the look of you, I'd say you had about as much sleep as I did," he commented before crossing the room and kissing her cheek.

"I had a lot on my mind last night," she responded.

He gave her a look that said, "I bet you did," as clearly as if he enunciated the words aloud.

"Have you heard how your PA is this morning?" Rina asked, mindful of why she was here in the first place.

"Resting as comfortably as possible, and struggling with the loss of her baby. It will be some time before she is well enough to return to work."

"I'm so sorry to hear that. Losing a child must be devastating."

"Yes, I told her husband she is not to rush her recovery on our account. He is equally upset, of course."

Rey shrugged out of the jacket of the silver gray suit he wore and flung it across the back of the couch nearest him. The pale color of the suit agreed with his coloring, Rina decided, throwing the golden color of his skin into relief against the crisp white shirt he wore teamed with an even paler silver self-patterned tie. She dragged her gaze from him, from the faint hint of the expanse of his chest beneath the fine cotton of his shirt, and sank down into the other couch. Her legs felt weak and unsteady. She had to get this attraction under control.

"So, your first day at work with us," Rey continued. "I thought that rather than pin you down here in the office, we should head out to the vineyard this morning and let you get a feel for the whole setup, then we can lunch and tour the resort in the afternoon."

Tours, great, that meant other people. Someone to act as a buffer against the shimmer of sensual tension that continued to hang between them. She could barely contain her relief.

"I'd love that. Thank you."

A knock at the door heralded the arrival of Rey's receptionist, armed with a tray bearing Rina's tea and a steaming mug of coffee for Rey.

"Thank you, Vivienne," Rey said as she placed the tray on the low table between the leather couches by the window.

"No problem, Mr. del Castillo, and I've rescheduled your appointments for today and let the vineyard manager know you'll be there by ten-thirty. I've also booked your lunch at the resort for two o'clock. I hope that's not too late?"

"No, that will be fine. By the time we've toured the vineyard and discussed matters there, that'll work out. Thank you."

"Is there anything else you need?"

"No, thank you, Vivienne."

Vivienne closed the door behind her, leaving them cocooned in Rey's office. Rina busied herself, reaching for her tea and taking a sip. The cup clattered as she set it back on the saucer, betraying her nerves.

Rey gave her a sharp look. "Still scared of me?" he asked, raising one dark brow.

"More scared of how I feel around you, to tell you the truth."

"Well," he said, an expression of surprise flashing across his features. "Thank you for your honesty, I think."

He reached for his coffee mug and took a long swallow of the fragrant brew. Rina was mesmerized, watching the grace of the muscles working in his throat, the faint trace of moisture left on his lips, even the ripple of strength as he leaned forward and put down the mug.

"I meant what I said last night. I overstepped our boundaries and I shouldn't have."

Rina decided since she'd already been honest about how she felt, she may as well continue. "You didn't do anything to me that I didn't want at the time. But just so we're clear, I'm not ready to explore this any further right now. I know we're—" she hesitated a second "—engaged and for most couples it would be normal for our relationship to be..." She waved her hand, not willing to verbalize the images that filled her mind when she let her guard down. "Anyway, I think we should just keep taking it one day at a time. Yes?"

Rey held her gaze as he slowly inclined his head. "I do not wish to do anything to jeopardize our engagement. One day at a time sounds sensible."

"Good." She smiled, relief breaking through her. "So tell me a bit about the vineyard. How old is it, what level of production, do you export, hold tastings?"

He laughed and raised a hand. "One question at a time, please. I thought you said you were good for ideas and typing, but you're sounding like a professional."

Ice trickled down Rina's spine. She'd overplayed her hand. Just like that, she'd gone and done again the very thing she was trying so hard to avoid. She had to be more careful.

"Maybe a bit more of my sister rubbed off on me than I thought," she replied ruefully, hoping he'd accept her response.

"Okay, it's probably better if I give you the rundown on the way. Finish your tea and we can be off."

By the time Rina drove herself home to the cottage that night she was both physically exhausted and mentally exhilarated. It had been difficult holding back the knowledge and thought processes that were second nature to her, but she'd done it. Now her mind was bursting at the seams with ideas and concepts to help lift the del Castillo resort profile and to promote the vineyard, and the very fine wines they had begun to produce overseas.

Once inside the cottage bedroom, she switched the tones back on for her phone, and dropped it into her bag before quickly changing out of the clothes she'd worn to the office and into a pair of shorts and a tank top. While traveling in the air-conditioned splendor of Rey's car, or during the time at the resort, the temperatures had been bearable but entering the sunbathed cottage after it had been closed up all day was like stepping into a sauna.

She pushed open as many windows as she could, to let the air flow through, and made her way out the back of the cottage where a deep shaded porch looked toward the cliffs. From here, she could hear the sea. Its sound was soothing after the busy day she'd had. On her way through the cottage she'd stopped to pour herself a glass of the Tempranillo wine the vineyard manager had pressed upon her. It was the wine that had stood out the most for her during the tasting session she'd enjoyed and she was anxious to start making notes on the ideas that swam about in her head for raising the vineyard's profile.

A light sea breeze teased the pages of her notebook as she scrawled her thoughts onto the paper. Eventually, her mind ran dry and she put down her pen, reached for her wine and sat back in the wicker armchair to enjoy the moment. Bit by bit, she could feel herself relax.

The vista from this back porch was amazing. Not too far away, she could see the beautiful castillo where Rey and his brothers had been raised. She'd yet to see inside it but if the exterior was any example, she was sure the interior was a masterpiece of old meets new. Had the governess walked the distance between the small castle and her humble cottage that fateful day that she cast the curse? Rina wondered. Had it been a glorious sunshiny day like this one, filled with light and hope and promise? Or had it been dreary and dismal, the castillo the only golden beacon on what must be a forlorn landscape in the depths of winter?

Thinking about the governess and the legend spurred off another string of ideas and Rina put down her glass and lifted her pen, losing herself in the moment. A sound in the distance stirred her from her activities. With a sense of shock she realized it was her BlackBerry—the ringtone the one she'd allocated to Sara. She'd gotten so absorbed in her day and her ideas that she completely lost track of the whole reason why she was here.

She dashed from the chair and ran inside to the bedroom, shaking her handbag upside down until the phone fell onto the bed. Quickly, she hit the talk button.

"Hello? Sara? Please tell me it's you."

Laughter, so like her own, filled her ear.

"Hey, Reeny-bean. How's it going? Are you keeping everything under control?"

It was so good to hear her voice, but Rina couldn't stop to think about that. Instead her mind flooded with questions that demanded to be answered.

"When are you coming back?"

Silence greeted her.

"Sara?" she prompted, and was rewarded with the sound of her sister's sigh.

"It's difficult, Rina. Things aren't going quite like I thought they would. I can't come back yet. Everything's still up in the air."

"*What's* up in the air?" Rina's disappointment at her sister's words, and the sense of helplessness that engendered, pierced her voice. "You have to tell me something. I'm going crazy here. What you've asked me to do—it isn't fair to me and it certainly isn't fair to Rey."

"Oh, Rey, he'll be fine. He's a player, he knows the score."

"That's not the point, Sara. I'm living a lie, for you. I don't know how much longer I can do this."

"Please don't say anything yet. Promise me, Rina? I will owe you forever for this, and I'll tell you everything as soon as I can. You know me. I don't want to say something too soon to jinx this and have it all blow up in my face."

Blow up in Sara's face? Rina thought, with an exasperated sigh. What about the very real possibility of it blowing up in Rina's?

"And when do you plan on telling me? I mean it, Sara, I can't keep this up. I'm terrified I'm going to let something slip, especially now I'm working with him."

"You're what?" Sara's disbelief echoed down the phone line.

"You heard me." She explained about Rey's PA and the pressure he was under with his brother still recuperating in hospital, as well. "I offered to help. I had to. You know me."

Sara whistled, long and low. "Wow, so how am I doing in an office environment?" she asked.

"That's not funny, and you know it. When are you coming back?"

"I...I don't know. Maybe a week?" Sara hedged.

"Are you okay? You're not in any trouble or anything, are you? Maybe I should come to you."

"No! You can't do that. There's nothing you can do for me here. I need you right where you are. I'll make it up to you, Reeny-bean. Truly, I will," her twin implored.

Rina gripped her phone tightly in her hand and counted slowly to ten. "That's it, then. A week. After that, I'm telling him the truth."

"I'll tell him the truth myself—I promise, I will—as soon as I get back."

"A week, Sara. That's my absolute limit."

"I know. I gotta go. Love you, Rina, and thank you. You're saving my life."

"That's what I'm worried about. Is it really that serious?"

"I'm just kidding. Everything's fine. Like I said, I'll tell you all when I come back. Now I gotta go."

Sara blew kisses down the phone then disconnected the call, leaving Rina standing in the bedroom, phone still to her ear, and filled with a frustration that brought tears stinging into her eyes. She'd really thought talking to Sara would make her feel better about the decision she'd made to continue with the farcical sister swap. Instead, she felt even more confused.

Did Sara even love Rey?

How had she referred to him? A player who knew the score? What score? And who referred to the man they had promised to marry as a player, anyway?

Rina threw her phone down onto the bed and went outside to retrieve her glass of wine and her notes. At least now, she had a finite time to look forward to—a date when all this would be over and she could go back to being Sarina Woodville again.

But what of Reynard and her feelings for him? What of Sara and whatever decision she was about to make? Could Rina really stay here and watch her sister pick up where she left off with Rey? The answer resounding in her head was an emphatic no, so where would that leave her?

And how could she tell Sara that she'd fallen in love with her fiancé?

Even as the truth of her words echoed in her mind, Rina tried desperately to refute them. She couldn't be in love. It didn't happen that fast. She'd only been on the island just over two weeks. Granted, she'd spent a great deal of that time with Reynard, but she couldn't love him, could she? She'd spent years with Jacob—slowly building a relationship, setting plans in place for their future. Even as she grasped at those straws, she knew that what she'd shared with her ex was nothing like the inferno that burned between her and Rey.

She tried to call upon the logic that usually dictated her life, but reason had deserted her as effectively as her sister. All she could think about was the way she felt every time she saw him. Every time they touched.

She knew she wanted more. She wanted it all. And she knew she could never sit back as an uncommitted bystander and watch her twin marry the man that set *her* on fire with only a glance.

Rina slugged back a generous mouthful of wine, relished the sensation of it sliding over her tongue and down her throat, before pouring herself some more. She needed oblivion—something, anything, to erase Reynard del Castillo from her mind and from her heart. Even if it was only temporary, she needed the respite from a truth she didn't dare acknowledge.

Eleven

Rey tried to ignore the scent of Sarina's hair and the way it spiraled wildly over her shoulder, touching his shirt as he leaned forward to read what she was explaining. He couldn't believe they'd been working together for an entire week now. An entire week without touching her beyond a light kiss on the cheek, morning and evening, as she arrived and left the office.

It had proven more difficult than he'd anticipated, keeping his hands off her delectable body, especially now that he knew how responsive she could be. He'd spent the past several days in an uncomfortable state of semi-arousal which had left him irritable and short with all his staff. It was soon obvious they blamed Sarina for the change in his usually easygoing mood, and he'd noticed a certain coolness among some of the staff in the way she was treated by them.

Under normal circumstances he'd have put a stop to

it, without question, but these were anything but normal circumstances.

She continued to carry off the pretense of being her sister quite well, he thought, even going so far as to say she'd discussed some aspects of the new campaign with her by phone before presenting them to him earlier in the week. He couldn't mistake her acumen for Sara's, however. Not that Sara was unintelligent—she was completely the opposite—but there was an attention to finer detail that was imminently apparent in Sarina's observations and suggestions that her sister lacked.

He forced himself to tune back into what she was saying.

"So you see, if we introduce the tapas bar to the pool area of the resort, that will keep guests on the grounds, rather than seeing them travel out farther to find light meals, but it won't affect the bistro and à la carte restaurants in any way. It'll also appeal to your younger crowd and I think you need to look at pitching inclusive packages to the twenty-five to thirty-five age group. They have disposable income, they're more likely to be involved in holidays for comfort and leisure's sake than extended overseas trip like the, say, eighteen to twenty-fives. Plus, it'll bring a younger dynamic to the resort and perhaps even encourage them to come back in future years on family packages."

"It sounds good in principle. Let's see what the rest of the family says when we go to the castillo for dinner tonight. You can present your ideas for the vineyard and winery, too."

"The rest of the family—that includes Benedict?" She looked up from the report she'd been referring to.

"Yes, Alex picked him up from the hospital today and brought him back to the castillo to give him some peace.

The security at his house is insufficient to give him the privacy he needs right now."

When news of Ben's release leaked to the press, both local and European paparazzi had descended on the vineyard and, more particularly, the outskirts of Benedict's home in the mountains, eager for a photo of the debilitating scars that were said to mar his once perfect body.

If only they knew, Rey thought, that the scars they sought to expose to the world were nothing compared to the news Benedict had only shared with his brothers the night before his release from hospital. Ben had insisted *Abuelo* not be told—partly because he hadn't wanted to cause their grandfather any more worry, but more particularly because he didn't want the old man to have another reason to bring the curse back into family discussions.

It was enough that the media had, hard on the heels of Alex and Loren's nuptials, exposed the curse for all the world to read about and had drawn their own conclusions about Benedict's accident. If they discovered Benedict's injuries had left him infertile, who knew where the media would take things? More importantly, who knew how *Abuelo* would take the news?

"But he's just out of hospital. Is he up to a family dinner?"

Benedict's release from the hospital had been a relief for all the family. That was not to say, though, that everything was back to normal. He was much quieter than he'd been before. *Abuelo* had waxed long and lyrical about how a man who'd just faced death needed time to make peace with himself and his choices, but Alex and Reynard knew exactly why he was quiet. It was one thing to choose not to have children, but quite another to have that choice irrevocably removed from you. Compounding the issue was Benedict's adamant refusal to consider the idea of marriage—ever. Who would want him? was his argument. A man who couldn't give his wife the children her arms ached to hold was no longer a man at all in his eyes. Nothing Alex or Reynard had said to him had been able to convince him otherwise.

Faced with the same situation Rey couldn't say he'd have felt any different, although his heart ached for his younger brother. And it killed him to see the light extinguished from Ben's eyes, leaving in its place the reflection of a hollow anger.

"It'll do him good to be among us properly again and discussing business. If he tires, he can easily go to his rooms. Besides, for the first time since the accident, he will be able to focus on something other than his injuries and getting strong again."

"Yes, I can see that. Well, I hope he likes what we've put together."

Rina checked herself for the umpteenth time in the mirror before Rey arrived to pick her up for their dinner at the castillo tonight. She didn't know why she was so nervous. Everyone had been as warm and welcoming as you could expect from a family presented with a fiancée no one had met before. More so, if Aston del Castillo's pleasure in his grandson's engagement was any indicator.

Besides, based on Sara's call last week, she only had to keep this up for another day, two tops. The sense of relief she felt was almost overwhelming. Keeping up appearances at the office and controlling the magnetic attraction she had for Rey had taken its toll.

She eyed herself critically in the mirror again. No amount of makeup could hide the ravages of the sleepless nights she'd endured. Even when she had slept, her dreams had been peppered with replays of the night in Rey's office as well as other more adventurous forays where they melded into one another again and again.

She'd woken several times, on the point of orgasm. It wouldn't have taken much, she knew, to give herself the relief her body longed for, but she'd held back, refusing herself even that release because in her heart of hearts she knew it was still all wrong. Reynard was Sara's, not hers. She was merely a fill in. Using him, even in fantasy, to fulfill her physical yearnings was too close to infidelity, even for her.

Rina had already made up her mind to leave Isla Sagrado the second Sara returned. She'd go visit extended family in the United Kingdom for a while, then return home and begin rebuilding a life for herself back in Christchurch. She couldn't bear to remain here and see her twin with Rey. She could only hope that time and distance would make it easier for her to pretend she hadn't done the unforgiveable thing and fallen in love with him. Maybe then this aching need would begin to fade and eventually burn out.

It was probably just a rebound thing anyway. Forced into close proximity with a handsome man she was bound to accept his attentions hard on the heels of being dumped by her own fiancé.

Outside the cottage she heard the roar of Rey's car, followed by silence as he cut the engine. Instantly, her heart leaped uncontrollably in her chest. In the mirror she saw her eyes dilate, a wild flush of warmth spread suddenly across her cheeks. Who was she kidding? This was no rebound reaction. Her feelings for Rey were real. Painfully, intolerably real.

Rina closed her eyes for a second, hiding from the truth reflected in her image. She could do this, she reminded herself for what felt like the thousandth time since she'd embarked on this whole disaster. She'd made it this far. Another day or two was not going to destroy her.

She went to the door and opened it.

"Good evening," Rey responded as she pulled the door wide.

Her heart caught in her throat as she allowed herself to drink in his presence. He was dressed in an impeccably tailored black suit with a pale cream-colored silk shirt beneath it. His hair was still damp and slicked back from his face, exposing the broad, intelligent forehead and high cheekbones that lent a severe magnificence to his features.

She was female enough to be hugely relieved she'd dressed up for tonight. She knew the del Castillos tended to observe the old traditions like dressing for dinner, which was served late—Spanish fashion. Luckily, Sara'd had just the thing in her wardrobe—an off-the-shoulder deep plum-colored satin cocktail dress. Artful pleating both above and below the sash at the waist gave a feminine fullness to the fabric without creating too revealing a silhouette. It was tasteful while still being sexy, and was just the sort of thing she knew her sister would have chosen for a night like this.

Rina had done her hair in an auburn river of curls down her back, and she'd pulled the side sections up—securing them with a cluster of small diamante clips on top of her head—which exposed the chandelier-style diamante earrings she'd chosen from Sara's stash of jewelry. Rey's look of approval as his eyes coasted from top to toe and back again spoke more vehemently than words.

As the dress was fully boned, but cut quite low in back, she'd gone without a bra and beneath the soft silky fabric of the bodice she felt her nipples tighten and peak in response to the flare of desire in his gaze. She fought back a soft moan as he leaned forward and a hint of his cologne filled her nostrils. His lips were cool, impersonal upon her cheek but the look in his eyes was anything but.

"I think we'd better head straight to the castillo, don't you?"

"Are we running late?" she asked, her voice a little breathless.

"No, but we will be if we stay here a moment longer."

Color and warmth flood her face. She hadn't been wrong about that look in his eyes. His comment was the closest he'd come to breaching his word, after that last time she'd allowed things to get out of control.

Rina forced her lips into a smile. "We'd better get along then, hadn't we?"

The journey in Rey's car was short and as they approached the ancient fortress, Rina was struck by the idea that a single family could have called the bastion home for so many generations. It spoke to a permanence and durability she had little concept of. As a family, they must have toiled long and hard to continue their hold on the building and the land surrounding it over the past many centuries. It spoke to a tenacity and sense of unity quite rare in a modern world.

"This is quite some home," she commented as they drove in through the gate set in the outer walls.

"Impressive, isn't it?"

"I don't think impressive is quite the word," she answered, awestruck by the floodlit battlements.

She heard Rey's low chuckle beside her. "It has that effect on people."

"You must be incredibly proud of your lineage."

He gave a sharp nod. "*Sí*, we all are. We would do anything to protect what is ours. Anything."

Rina felt a frisson of caution run down her spine. Was it

her imagination or was there an implied warning in Rey's words? Instantly thereafter he flashed her an engaging smile, sending her worries to the back of her mind.

"Come. If you think the exterior is daunting, just wait until you see inside."

Rey came around to the passenger side of the car and opened her door before taking her hand and helping her from the low-slung vehicle. She was grateful for his steadiness. The black patent leather heels she'd chosen from Sara's shoes were higher than she usually wore, bringing her almost eye level with Rey's hazel gaze. He placed his hand gently at the small of her back. From the heat he radiated she could almost imagine the imprint of his fanned fingers upon her skin.

He guided her up the stairs that led to the impressive front door to the castillo. They were opened as they approached.

"*Buenas noches, señorita,* and Señor Reynard," the liveried man at the door welcomed them. "Please, come in. The others are waiting in the salon."

Rina's eyes grew huge as she passed through the arched stone portal and into the flagstoned entrance hall. Rey was right. It was incredibly daunting. A massive wide staircase curved up one wall, the wall itself lined with gilt framed portraits. Even from this distance she could discern a strong family resemblance. Rey followed her gaze and murmured in her ear.

"I'm lucky, I take more after our mother's side of the family."

Rina laughed. "Lucky? I doubt your brothers would see it that way."

They continued down a corridor toward another arched doorway. Inside she could hear the low murmur of conversation. As they entered the room, Loren rose from her seat and took Rina's hands, reaching up to kiss her cheeks.

"I'm so glad you could come tonight. Now, we are a real family. Come and sit by me and you can tell me what you've been up to since we saw you last. I hear Rey has you enslaved in his office, of all things."

A pang of guilt lanced through her at Loren's words. *A real family?* It should be Sara here tonight, not her. Rina forced a smile to her lips and murmured something vague, allowing Loren to draw her over to the others.

Somehow she managed to make conversation, glossing over the time she'd spent helping Rey and letting him steer the conversation toward the changes they'd been discussing. This ignited a lively debate between Alex and Rey as he brought up the proposed changes at the resort. Eventually, Alex concurred with most of what had been suggested.

"So, you have hidden talents," Alex said directly to Rina. "Maybe you should stay on in Rey's office. Goodness knows he could do with a fresh take on things."

"If I didn't know you loved me already, *mi hermano,* you'd pay for that remark," Rey bantered in return, saving Rina from making comment.

"And what about the vineyard? I can't imagine that you don't have some thoughts on that," Benedict joined the discussion for the first time.

Rina noticed he looked pale, with faint lines of strain around his eyes. Walking with a cane, he'd moved stiffly across the room before, and his sigh of relief as he'd lowered himself into the deep button back leather chair next to hers hadn't escaped her ears.

She looked to Rey, who nodded. "Go on, tell him your ideas. I warn you though, he won't be a pushover like this one," he gestured toward Alex who snorted in mock disgust.

She fought to control the smile on her face. Being here, being around the brothers and Loren, not to mention the old man who'd been avidly listening to his grandsons and interjecting his own opinions from time to time, was a delight. There was a deep love and respect between all of them. She could well imagine how the family code had come about with them as living examples.

Rey crossed the room to pour a glass of one of Benedict's finest wines and brought it over to her.

"Could you bring the bottle over, also?" Rina asked before turning back to Benedict. When he did, she turned the label to face him and pointed at it with the tip of one finger. "I think the starting point for the wine is to have a sense of unity with the del Castillo brand. It's something you need to consider across the business entities. At your offices, at your homes, I'm constantly reminded of your family crest. Honor. Truth. Love. But I don't see that anywhere in your marketing, for the resort or for the wine."

By the time a maid came to call them into dinner, Rina had expounded on her ideas for not only revamping the wine bottle labels, but for an entire new del Castillo look. Her ideas had been met with shrewd observation and many questions but she knew from the tingle in her toes that she had captured them with her ideas. The knowledge was exhilarating but tempered with a pang of regret that she wouldn't be here to see them through once Sara returned.

Rey watched her from across the room and tried to ignore the sense of pride he had in her as she caught the attention of everyone else. Caught it and held it in her palm as she spoke with a passion he recognized all too easily. She might have tried to pretend a lack of knowledge on publicity and development issues in the office, but here, with a private audience, the real Sarina truly glowed.

She was animated as she spoke, and he felt every cell in his body tune into her energy. More than that, she fit in with the dynamic that was the del Castillo family. Strange that a cuckoo in the nest should appear to suit him so much better than the sister he had actually asked to marry him. Would Sara have eased into tonight's conversation as easily? he wondered. He had to answer in the affirmative. She was urbane and well practiced in social mores. She would have fit in as easily—but not as well. He could see that his brothers and *Abuelo* were already completely under Sarina's spell, not just because of her intelligence and insight, but because of the care and consideration she showed them all. Sara lacked the heart of her sister.

A heart he had become increasingly intrigued by.

Before the idea could flower and develop into something more, he reminded himself of the sham the sisters were conducting. No one did such a thing, in his knowledge anyway, without an ulterior motive. Usually a financial ulterior motive. He had to keep his wits about him and his emotions very firmly in check. Eventually he'd get the truth from Sarina, he was sure of it.

Abuelo insisted on escorting her into the dining room, and Rey was forced to acquiesce. But as he watched the long column of her spine as she walked slowly in front of him, he couldn't help but feel the familiar strands of anger pull at him. She was not just taking him for a ride, she was hurting them all. Loren, with her trust and eagerness to form a close friendship with another del Castillo bride. *Abuelo*, with his fear of the governess's curse and his hopes for his grandsons and the family line to extend into perpetuity. Even Benedict and Alex seemed to have opened their hearts to the woman who was supposedly his forever.

Where had their judgment gone? Alex and Benedict had initially been skeptical of his engagement when he'd announced it to them a month ago. Benedict, in particular, had skated all too close to the truth. But now, for some strange reason, they seemed to want to bring Sarina—or Sara, as they thought she was—into the family fold.

Too many people stood to lose too much by her actions. He had to do something to force her hand and he had to do it tonight. There was no other option left to him.

Twelve

Rina was relieved that conversation over the dinner table was wide ranging and relaxed, however it became more and more difficult to acknowledge everyone when they called her by her sister's name. Especially when it was Rey. More than anything she ached for him to call her by her own name, but she knew that was impossible. No matter what Sara's decision was, Rey was strictly off-limits.

As the evening progressed, she noticed how Benedict began to look more and more drawn. It wasn't until *Abuelo* had retired upstairs for the night, aided by Javier, that Alex and Reynard turned their full attention to their younger brother.

"How are you, really?" Reynard got straight to the point.

Benedict flicked a look at Loren and Rina and shook his head infinitesimally. "Tired, sore. It's only to be expected."

"What you need is to get away from here. I hate to say it, but keeping up appearances for *Abuelo* is going to do your head in, Benedict." Alex sat back and twirled his glass of port between long fingers.

Rina watched him, interested that for all the brothers' similarities, they were each very firmly carved individuals. She knew there was little more than twelve months between each of the brothers but Alex clearly took to heart his role as head of the family, appearing older than his years.

"And where am I supposed to go, Alex?"

A trace of bitterness laced Benedict's tone. Rina noticed Rey's brows draw together in concern. Clearly this was not Benedict's usual demeanor.

"He's right," Rey added. "The media are bound to follow him wherever he goes around here. It's not as if he can hide out at the resort or any of our neighboring countries. Besides, he needs to follow his rehabilitation program. He won't be able to do that if he's constantly being hounded."

"What about New Zealand?" Rina blurted before she could think twice.

Four sets of eyes swiveled toward her.

"New Zealand?" Alex asked, raising one brow in a manner all too similar to his brother's. "Don't you think that's going a bit too far?"

"Isn't distance what he needs?" Rina lifted her chin toward Alex before flicking a look to Benedict. She'd expected him to appear annoyed, or at least be ready to shoot her suggestion down in flames, but there was a thoughtful expression on his pale face.

"Sara's right," Loren interjected. "No one would follow him there. He could go by private jet. It would lessen the risk of his travel plans being detected and ensure his travel is more comfortable."

"But what about the personal trainer he's hired?" Rey interjected.

"We do have personal trainers in New Zealand, you know," Rina commented, semi-teasingly. "It might be the other side of the world, but it is quite civilized."

"Why can't he come with me?" Benedict spoke and all heads snapped toward him as if pulled on the same cord.

"You're serious about this?" Alex asked, a note of incredulity in his voice. "But you should be here. Close to home. What if—"

"What if nothing. There's no more the doctors can do for me, I've told you as much. Besides, I can recuperate in New Zealand just as easily as I can here. Better, probably, because I won't need to worry about you all."

"And the vineyard?" Rey asked, sending a confused look in Alex's direction.

Alex merely shrugged his shoulders, deferring to Benedict who immediately started to speak.

"The vineyard has managed without me all this time. What's another month? It's not as if I can actually work there anyway, I'm still too damn weak. Besides, I can work on a computer from New Zealand as effectively as I can here at home. Maybe now that things are financially looking up a bit again, I can complete that research into the new wine varieties I started to explore four years ago."

"You'd be willing to do this, then? Be so far from all of us?" Alex asked quietly.

"If it means having a chance to come to terms with everything, then, yes."

There was an undercurrent between the men that Rina couldn't put her finger on. Judging from Loren's expression, she too was out of the loop. Alex turned to Rina, his dark eyes serious.

"Did you have somewhere in mind that would suit

Benedict's needs at this time? Privacy is of the utmost importance."

"Actually, I do have a place that should work. A friend of mine runs an exclusive boutique hotel and health spa on the shores of Lake Wakatipu, about twenty minutes from Queenstown by private launch. There's a fully equipped gym, aqua therapy facilities, a lap pool—pretty much everything you need. Above all, it's totally secluded. Only a private wharf, or heli access. Of course, being winter there and with Queenstown the tourist mecca it is, it's a pretty busy time of year for Mia, but I could call her if you like—see if she has space available?" Rina offered.

"I know the area. You think you could arrange this now?" Benedict asked, his chocolate brown eyes burning with intent.

Rina looked at the ornate antique ormolu clock on the sideboard. "I can try. New Zealand is twelve hours ahead of us, so it'll be ten-thirty a.m. there. I should be able to get a hold of her."

Loren rose from her chair. "Come with me, Sara, I'll take you to my study. Perhaps you can call your friend from there."

"When would you want to book from, and for how long?" Rina asked as she followed Loren to the door.

"As soon as she can take me, and for at least a month."

Her head spun slightly at the swiftness with which Benedict had made his decision. Clearly he wanted to get away from Isla Sagrado, but why so urgently?

"And, Sara?"

She turned in the doorway. "Yes?"

"I want sole occupancy—well, for me, my trainer and possibly one or two other personal staff. I'll pay handsomely for the privilege."

She nodded. "Okay, I'll see what I can do."

When Rina returned to the dining room she was bubbling with suppressed excitement.

"It's doable," she said as she entered the room. "Provided you agree to her financial terms, and that you pass a credit check, you're all set for next week. I had to do some persuading because she was heavily booked for the time you want, but she's agreed to transfer those to other resorts and spas in the area. She does expect to be well compensated for the loss of trade and for the disruption to her existing guests, of course. I'd told her I'd let you know and call her back."

"And her terms?" Benedict asked.

"The same rate as if she had a hundred percent occupancy of the hotel, plus a premium of twenty percent."

"Make the premium thirty percent. I'll pay half up front, the other half at the end of the occupation."

Rina gasped. "Are you sure?"

"Never more so. Call her back."

"I still can't believe he made up his mind so quickly," Rina said to Rey as they drove back to the cottage.

"He has his reasons," Rey replied enigmatically. "Thank you for supporting him in this. For making it easy for him."

"I'm just glad I could help." She stared out at the dark landscape and worried at her lower lip with her teeth. "His injuries—he will recover from them, won't he?"

Rey sighed. "We hope so. But the accident has taken a far greater emotional toll than we expected. I think his recovery may take a while longer. I'm only sorry he feels the need to be so far from us while he does so."

Rina reached across the interior of the car and put her hand on Rey's thigh, squeezing gently with her fingers.

"He'll be all right. Mia will ensure he's looked after and her staff is exceptionally well trained as far as privacy is concerned."

"They will need to be. My brother's pride has taken enough of a blow with his accident—it would crush him to see pictures of himself, in his less-than-able state, plastered across the tabloids. This way, when he returns to Isla Sagrado, he'll be his old self again."

"He's that proud?"

"He's a del Castillo," Rey replied, as if that should be sufficient explanation.

Rina laughed softly and made to pull her hand away from his thigh, but Rey settled his hand over hers and linked his fingers in her own. Effectively trapping her with his gentle hold. In her heart of hearts, she wished she had the right to be here like this, touching him. Sharing thoughts with one another as genuine couples did.

She'd seen the closeness between Loren and Alexander. Sure, they were still technically in the honeymoon stage of their marriage, but there was a sense of unity between them that she envied. The love they bore for one another had been evident in a myriad of unspoken moments where their gazes had intercepted or their hands had brushed. It was the kind of relationship Rina had always wished for but been too frightened to trust. With Jacob she'd felt secure. No massive highs, no massive lows. Just stability—pure and simple. Now she knew she wanted so much more than that—was ready to take that risk. Except that risk wasn't hers to take. Not with Reynard anyway.

When they reached the cottage he moved swiftly around the vehicle and opened her door, ready to escort her to the front door. His old-fashioned courtesy was something she'd miss when she left Isla Sagrado. It had become all too easy to relinquish the hold she'd so tenaciously made on her life and how she lived it.

Rina pulled the key from her evening bag and Rey surprised her by taking it from her fingers to open the door for her. He ushered her over the threshold and she bent to remove her shoes, letting them drop just inside, before she moved forward to switch on one of the table lamps near the entryway. The golden glow of the bulb flung an orb of light around them, even as it appeared to cast the rest of the cottage into deeper shadow. A draft of air pulled through the house, and a noise rang out from the bedroom.

"Wait here," Rey commanded and flew through the dimly lit sitting room toward where they'd heard the noise.

Rina waited by the door, wondering if she should start to dial the police. Her heart hammered in her chest. The cottage was isolated. If anyone had decided to break in and Rey hadn't been here... She'd been burgled once at her townhouse in Christchurch. Discovering that her home had been violated—every personal effect touched and either broken or stolen—had left a very sour taste in her mouth and a sense of vulnerability that even now she fought to control.

She'd thought Isla Sagrado beyond that kind of thing, especially with the legend attached to the cottage. She'd noticed that few locals wanted to come out this far from the nearest town, especially not after dark. She'd felt safe here, secure. Now, she wasn't so sure anymore.

Another sudden thought occurred to her. What if it was Sara who'd made the noise? What if she'd come back earlier than anticipated? The fist around her heart tightened. How on earth would they explain it?

Relief flooded her as Rey swiftly came back across the room.

"You left a window open in the bedroom. Some creature must have come inside and knocked the bedside lamp off the stand. It's gone now. It was probably just a cat from one of the farms. I closed the shutters and lit the candles on the dressing table for you. The lamp is probably beyond economical repair."

"A cat? It gave me quite a fright. I'm so glad you were here. I'd have been a mess on my own."

Even now, knowing everything was okay, small tremors rocked her body.

Rey pulled her into his arms. "You're shaking. Are you all right?"

She nodded. "I'll be fine. Just give me a few minutes."

"Perhaps you need a distraction, hmm?"

Before Rina could think, his lips were on hers, slowly, gently coaxing hers open. She felt him push the door closed behind her and fumble the key into the lock before turning it with a click but all she could concentrate on was his solid heat and strength, paired with the incredibly gentle touch of his mouth against hers, of his tongue as it stroked across her lips, dipping and tasting as if she were a morsel to be savored.

"There," he said softly against her lips. "You're quite safe now."

Safe? In his arms, with his lips on hers and her heart racing at a pace that no longer had anything to do with fear and everything to do with the man who held her? She ought to push him away, to send him back out into the dark velvet night as far from her as possible. Instead, she slid her arms under his jacket and around his waist and aligned her body against his.

Rey lifted both hands and cupped her jaw gently, tilting her face to his.

"Tell me to leave now, before I become incapable of doing so."

His voice was thick with desire, his accent stronger than usual. Rina parted her lips to say what she needed to say, to send him out the door and potentially out of her life forever, but the words dried on her tongue even as the heat flaring through her body rose and spread. In her head, she knew it was wrong to be doing this, and yet to the soles of her feet it felt so right. For the first time in her life, she stopped listening to the voice of reason and gave over to her heart.

With a groan, Rey kissed her again, drawing her lower lip into his mouth and gently scraping his teeth and tongue across the full soft skin.

"Last chance," he murmured.

Thirteen

And it was her last chance, she realized. Her last chance to give herself over to sensation—to what she wanted right here, right now.

In answer she dragged his head down to hers and kissed him with every ounce of unrequited love she had in her. Rey didn't waste another second on talking. Strong arms hooked behind her shoulders and her knees and he swept her off her feet and carried her to the bedroom. Once there, he reverently set her back on her feet, trapping her with the heat and intensity in his gaze as he yanked away his jacket and kicked off his shoes before reaching for her again.

The shimmer of candlelight reflected from the small mirror perched on top of the tall chest of drawers that passed for a dressing table. Aromatic scents of patchouli and sandalwood blended with the richness of fragrant rose wove their own sensual spell around them.

Rey traced the outline of her lips with one finger, then

trailed the featherlight touch along her jaw and to the hollow at the base of her ear before coasting over her rapidly beating pulse and down her throat. Her heart hammered in her chest, no longer with fear, but with anticipation.

Rey's fingers gently brushed her collarbone before coasting, ever so softly, lower until they grazed the swell of her breasts. Every muscle in her body clenched. The hot tide of desire that clouded her mind sent a jolt of need from her core and forced a soft moan of longing from her lips.

"This gown is very beautiful on you, *querida,* but I'm sure what it conceals is even more so."

He reached around her back for the tab on the zip, and slowly eased it down. The boned fabric of her bodice peeled away from her like a giant petal on a flower, exposing her naked breasts to sight. Her nipples puckered under his gaze, her breasts became full, heavy.

She stood there proudly as he eased her gown over her hips and allowed it to drop in a dark pool of satin at her feet. Rina stepped out of the discarded gown. All she wore now was the sheer scrap of ruby-colored lace panties.

"Ah, I knew I was right," he sighed, his eyes roaming over her form. "You are truly beautiful."

He lifted his hands to slide her earrings from her lobes, tossing the glittering chandeliers to the top of the dressing table with scant care as to where they landed, then slowly and painstakingly removed the tiny clips from her hair. Once each tress was freed, he gently ran his fingers through the weight of her hair, letting it spill across her shoulders in a wave of rippling fire.

Feeling beautiful, feeling incredibly bold in that beauty, Rina reached out and, one by one, slid the buttons loose from his silk shirt. She tugged the tails loose from his trousers before skimming her hands up and over his chest and out to his shoulders, peeling away the finely woven fabric from his body before tugging it down his arms and pulling it away completely.

His chest was smooth and tanned, the cords of muscle finely delineated—his nipples now taut discs punctuating his skin. She lightly brushed her fingertips over them, felt the tight nubs harden even further under her touch. How would he taste? How would his skin feel beneath her lips, her tongue?

She licked her lips, heard his sharply indrawn breath. She looked up and saw the fire in his eyes, felt the answering blaze in her own.

With her eyes still locked with his, she brushed her hands over his shoulders, relishing the strength of bunched muscle beneath her palms even as she coasted her hands down over his biceps and then his forearms before drifting over his fingers. Mere inches separated their bodies but it was as if a live current of electricity sparked between them.

She reached for his belt, fumbling a little at the clasp until the leather finally dropped free from its buckle. Her fingers dealt swiftly with his zip, then eased his trousers from his hips. His erection strained against the black cotton of his boxers and she hooked her fingers under the elastic band at his waist. His skin peppered with goose bumps at her touch, another sharply indrawn breath rasped through his lips.

She carefully eased the fabric from his body, allowing his shaft to spring free from its restriction. Rina backed Rey against the edge of the bed, coaxing him onto its surface, then bent and drew off his trousers and boxers. His socks, too, took only a second to remove.

She rose to her feet again and gently pushed at Rey's shoulders, sending him back on the bed. He was totally naked and hers to revere. Flickering candlelight danced across his skin, showing the shadows and clefts of his body, revealing that which jutted proud and obvious from the nest of dark hair at his groin. Feeling an audacity she'd never indulged in before, she straddled his thighs. The heat of his skin against hers was scorching. The fine hair of his legs lightly abraded the backs of her thighs.

"I want you like I've never wanted anyone before," she said with total honesty.

The words surprised her even as they fled her mouth. She'd never in her life admitted to her personal needs like this. Beneath her Rey smiled, his hands creeping up to clasp her hips and tilting her forward so her mound rubbed against him.

"Then take me, I'm all yours. There's protection in my trouser pocket."

"You expected this?" she asked, momentarily disconcerted.

"Expected it? No. Anticipated? Hoped? Most definitely. I am, after all, a man with needs."

Rina smiled in return. "Then we'd better see what we can do about them, hmm? But first, there are one or two things I'd like to indulge in."

She leaned over him, her hands braced on either side of him, until her breasts skimmed his chest—her nipples rough against the satin smoothness of his skin. She gasped at the sensations it wreaked in her, and repeated the movement before replacing her skin with the tip of her tongue. He groaned beneath her as she swirled her tongue across one distended disc before repeating the action on the other side.

His hand raced over her hips and to her shoulders, finally bunching in her hair and holding her as she continued her tracery of his body. Beneath her mouth, his muscles clenched and flexed, giving her other, even more intriguing surfaces to trace. Inch by inch she tasted him, working her way down the ridges of his abdomen and to the impression of his belly button.

His skin was responsive beneath her tongue, with tiny spasms denoting his most sensitive spots. Spots she committed to memory. When she slid off his thighs and settled between them he lifted his head, dropping his hands from her head to clench the bedcovers beneath him.

"I warn you, *querida,* I am not a patient man," he growled through clenched teeth.

Rina laughed, a slow bubbling sound that rose through her chest and spilled into the air around them. "Then it's time you learned," she teased.

She reached forward with her hand, her fingers lightly tickling the sensitive skin at the top of his thighs, working her way closer until she cupped his sac gently in her palm. With exquisite care she massaged that so vulnerable part of him and reveled in his trust. Then, she leaned forward and flicked the tip of her tongue against his erection. He twitched beneath her touch and another groan ripped from Rey's throat.

His knuckles gleamed white as his fists tightened their hold on the bright colored cotton of the bedcover, his head dropped back as if he could no longer bear to watch and feel at the same time.

Rina pursed her lips and blew cool air where her tongue had been before repeating the action again, tracing her tongue along the veined flesh, relishing the sensation of tender skin over heated rigid steel. She closed her fingers around his base and firmly glided them to his tip, before taking that smooth head into her mouth and swirling her tongue over him.

He tasted of salt and musk and male, and in all her life she had never savored anything so intoxicating.

"No more, you're killing me here," Rey said, his voice rough and breathless.

"You don't like it?" she asked, before drawing him deeper into her mouth.

"Too much, I like it too much. I want our first time to be together. Every step of the way."

Somehow Rey found the strength to withdraw from the heated cavern of her mouth and to sit up. He grabbed Sarina's hands and pulled her upright and stood, length for length, skin to skin. The texture of her was enthralling and he ran his hands over her body before coaxing her back onto the bed. He grabbed a condom from the pocket of his trousers and tossed it onto the rumpled covers before lowering himself over her body.

As her long slender legs parted to allow him to settle between them, he fought with the age-old urge to bury himself in her body—to lay claim to her and coax her body to the heights he knew they'd soon scale together. But strangely this joining between them suddenly meant more to him than he'd realized. He wanted to *make love* to her—to bring her pleasure and delight, to go further than merely indulging in a sexual act. In this moment, it didn't matter whether she was Sara or Sarina. All the conflicting feelings and emotions of the past three and a half weeks coalesced into one crystal clear thought—she was *his* woman, at least for tonight.

Her hair spilled out around her like a halo of tangled copper. Her slender body spread before him, his for the taking. He forced the ravenous demands of his flesh into submission, wanting to take this slowly—to execute every maneuver with intricate care. He smoothed an errant tendril of hair from her forehead and smiled as she turned her face into the palm of his hand and lightly bit the fleshy mound beneath his thumb.

"Who's impatient now?" he murmured, as he lowered his mouth to the pert tip of a breast.

He drew the peachy pink nub into his mouth and rolled his tongue around its peak before nipping lightly with his teeth. She sighed and shuddered beneath him, forcing him to once again take hold of his senses, to focus on giving her some of the teasing delight she'd afforded him.

He ran one hand over her thigh, to the top of her hip and then along the delicate curve that led to the inside of her groin. His fingers ruffled the neatly trimmed thatch of dark auburn hair at the centre of her body. Already he could feel the waves of heat coming from her core. His fingers dipped lower and were instantly wet with the evidence of her desire for him.

He parted her sweet flesh and traced his thumb over her clitoris, feeling her jolt beneath him as if he'd sent a surge of ten thousand volts through her body. He eased a finger into her honeyed depths. She clenched around him—tight, so very tight. It was almost more than he could bear.

He withdrew his hand, laved her nipple with his tongue once more, then pulled away for only as long as it took to sheath himself. Positioning his shaft at her entrance, he linked his fingers in hers, pulling her arms up and settling their hands on either side of her exquisite face.

She flexed her hips up toward him, her thighs open, her knees wide.

"Reynard, please. Don't make me wait any longer," she begged.

Her gray eyes were dark and stormy, reminding him of the seas that raged below the castillo on a harsh winter night. A fine sheen of perspiration beaded her upper lip, her forehead, her chest.

"Please?"

Her voice fractured as he surged inside her, incapable of holding back for another second. Pleasure already began to flood through his extremities as she closed around him, drawing him deep within her, taking him to the ultimate point of intimacy. He withdrew, relishing the tight clutch of her body, and sank within her again and again until he felt her tremble beneath him, heard her cries of pleasure, felt her body tighten and clench about him until she wrought from him a climax that saw exquisite pleasure radiate throughout his body, leaving his frame shaking and shuddering in its aftermath.

Rina lay in the dark, long after the candles had guttered in their holders, long after she'd felt Rey's heartbeat resume a normal rhythm and long after he'd drifted into sleep.

Their lovemaking had been everything she'd ever dreamed of and more. He was a generous lover and after that first cataclysmic joining, they'd made love again. The second time had been slow and gentle, taking their time to understand one another's bodies in intricate detail, yet with a result equally as shattering as the first.

Her heart expanded and all but burst on the depth of her love for him, on how right they'd felt together. But she'd been unspeakably wrong in allowing their lovemaking to take place. It had been her decision—he hadn't pushed or coerced her in any way—and in making that decision she'd betrayed the trust of the one person in the world who'd always been her rock.

How could she face her sister now, having knowingly slept with her fiancé? How could she face Rey, still pretending to be someone else?

It wasn't enough to try and tell herself that Sara wasn't really in love with Rey. Her twin had been asked to marry him, she'd chosen to say yes. It had been her choice to accept a man who offered her the relative safety of a relationship that demanded little beyond peripheral compatibility—plenty of marriages had been based on less—just as it had been Rina's choice to settle for the predictability that had been Jacob.

Inasmuch as it was wrong, they'd made their own decisions. Chosen men who'd offered the security they'd craved as children. That Rina's choice had been proven totally wide of the mark, with Jacob's eventual defection, only made it clearer to her how wrong it was for Sara to go ahead and marry Rey. But that remained her sister's choice.

Rina curled up in a small ball at the edge of the bed, her stomach a tight mass of pain, her chest aching with unshed tears as she tried to come to terms with how Sara would feel when she told her the truth. And she would tell her. There was no way she could hide anything as monumental as what she'd done. She'd made a choice of her own tonight, and again it had been the wrong one.

She could only hope that her sister would forgive her.

Rey shifted on the bed beside her, his arm snaking over her body and pulling her into the curve of his stomach. Her bare buttocks nestled against his lower abdomen and she felt his body stir at her touch. Even in sleep, he wanted her.

Her sister's forgiveness was one thing, but what would Reynard say when she told him that the woman he'd made love to was not who he'd thought? There was no way she could continue the pretense until Sara arrived home. No way she could look him in the eye and not tell him how much she, Rina, loved him.

Eventually sleep claimed her and calmed her mind, but

not before she'd resolved to face Rey with the full truth when he awoke. As much as her sister's forgiveness was vital to her, his meant so very much more.

Fourteen

As cold fingers of light began to poke through the window in the colorless predawn morning, Rina stirred on the bed. Her body was sated but her mind was instantly tumbling with all she had to say today. She slid from the tangled sheets and grabbed a light robe off the back of a chair in the corner of the room. Hers? Sara's? She didn't know anymore. She'd blurred so many lines she'd almost lost touch with who she was truly meant to be.

She went to the bathroom to relieve herself then walked silently to the kitchen, automatically measuring out coffee and water in the percolator and setting the gas burner to heat. She knew it was still ridiculously early but by the same token she couldn't lie next to Reynard another minute with all the guilt that now racked her, body and soul.

Just inside the front door, on the table where the lamp still burned she spied her evening bag. Inside was her mobile phone. She crossed the room to get it. Now that she'd made her decision, she had to get off her chest what she'd done. Was it too ridiculously early to call Sara?

She flicked a glance at the wall clock in the kitchen. 6:00 a.m. Probably too early but she had to shed this burden before it crushed her, and that started with Sara.

As she slid the BlackBerry from its little pouch inside the evening bag, she noticed she had three missed calls already. She'd put the phone on silent mode last night before going out and in the excitement when they'd returned to the cottage, she'd forgotten to change the setting. On checking the log she noted two were last night and one already this morning. All were from Sara.

So, she'd made her decision.

Rina's heart sank. The very fact that her sister had tried so often to reach her meant that she must have made up her mind. Sara had never known restraint. One message would never be enough.

With shaking hands, she started to dial her voice mail, only to nearly drop her phone when it vibrated in her hand. She gathered her startled thoughts together and hit the talk button.

"Sara?"

"Oh, thank goodness I got you this time. Where have you been? Actually, never mind about that. I just wanted to let you know, I'm coming back today—"

Sara's voice faded out on a burst of static.

"Back today? What time?" Rina asked, the weight of guilt in her chest warring with looking forward to seeing her twin again.

"…so excited… I've been so silly but I reached my decision…coming to talk to Rey…getting married…can't wait to see you—"

Rina's heart dropped straight to her feet. She tried to pull words from her mind but nothing would cooperate, and then, on another burst of static, her link to her sister was gone. Rina's legs turned to water and she sank onto the nearest piece of furniture, a wooden straight-backed chair. The cool of the wood seeped through the light material of her robe and into her skin and a shiver ran through her body. The phone fell from her hand to the tiled floor, the back cover bursting off and the battery scattering a short distance away.

Sara was coming back to marry Rey. She'd made her decision without knowing that her sister, her twin, had betrayed her in the worst way possible. Rina began to feel her hold on reality slip away. Not only had she done the worst thing imaginable by sleeping with her sister's fiancé, she would now irrevocably lose them both.

It was time to come clean. First with Rey, then with Sara when she arrived. What she'd done was monstrous, and she could only hold onto the thin reed of hope that her sister could one day find it in her heart to forgive her for what she'd done. Sara had been clear that she hadn't loved Rey, but that didn't make what Rina had done last night any less despicable. Reynard had given her the choice to send him away. She'd chosen not to. Everything—every touch, every sigh, every starburst of pleasure—it was all her fault and it was time she became accountable.

She forced herself to her feet and went to the kitchen, gathering two mugs and pouring coffee for each of them. It was time to face the music.

Rey was sprawled over the bed on his stomach, his dark hair endearingly rumpled, his tanned skin a dark contrast to the white sheet that curved lovingly across his buttocks and obscured his legs from view. The fingers of one hand splayed across her pillow, much as they'd splayed across her body in those moments when they'd slept last night. A painful tug in her chest reminded her that he wasn't hers to view.

She put both coffees on the bedside table and reached out a hand to wake him. The instant her fingers touched his shoulder, they tingled. Even now, knowing he was forbidden to her, knowing she had to deliver to him the painful truth about what she'd done—how she'd deceived him—her body still responded on an instinctual level.

She leaned over the bed and gave him a little shake. "Rey? Wake up, I need to talk to you."

His dark lashes flickered on his cheek before he opened his eyes, lifted his head and rolled onto his side. The instant his gaze met hers, his eyes began to burn with the hunger she recognized, and couldn't help but share. He reached out one hand to touch her face, his fingers stroking her cheek and coming to rest on her lips, still swollen from last night's feverish kisses.

"Buenos dias." He smiled and slid his hand around to cup the back of her head and pull her down for a kiss.

At the tenderness of his touch upon her lips, the burning sting of tears pricked at the back of Rina's eyes. She squeezed her eyelids shut. She couldn't cry in front of him. Not now. Somehow she found the strength to pull away and stand at the edge of the bed.

"Already tired of me?" Rey teased from within the untidy evidence of last night's passion.

"No, it's not that." She grabbed his mug off the nightstand and passed it to him. "Here, have this."

Rey pulled himself upright against the headboard and took the mug from her, his fingers grazing hers.

"I'd rather have you, *querida*."

He wouldn't want her again after what she had to say. Rina took a sip of her coffee and instantly wished she hadn't. The dark brew caught in her throat and she fought to swallow it past the restriction there.

"Sar—" Rey started. "Is everything all right?"

Rina couldn't meet his eyes. Instead she put her coffee cup down and perched on the very edge of the bed.

"I…I'm not who you think I am," she began.

Rey felt the familiar boil of anger start deep in his belly. So, this was it? She had gotten what she was after? That was the only reason he could think of for why *now* she wanted to tell the truth. It had been foolish of him to give her and her sister the very ammunition they needed by sleeping with her last night. Hell, sleeping? They'd achieved very little of that. The sex had been great.

A prick of conscience jabbed at the back of his mind. Great? It had been better than great. And it had been so much more than just sex. He'd made love with her, worshipped her, taken and received pleasure such as he had never experienced with another before. Resolutely, he squashed those thoughts. The Woodville sisters had an agenda. When he hadn't been sexually attracted to the one, they'd delivered on the other—and he'd let them. Did that make him a bastard for taking advantage of the situation?

Not at all. He'd be damned if he'd let them screw one Euro from his family.

"I know who you are," he replied, his voice deadpan.

Shock flew across Sarina's face. "You know?"

"You are Sarina Woodville. Younger twin and sister to Sara Woodville—my fiancée."

"How did you…? When?" Her eyes flew to the bed. "Why?"

"How? Well, you are indeed a perfect replica of your sister but there are some things you cannot fake and your sister's nature is one of them."

"But you never said—"

"Never called you on it? Why would I? I didn't have time to deal with your silly games. At the time my first priority was my brother, my second, *Abuelo*. And then you started helping me at the office at a time when help was badly needed. I suppose I've received recompense for at least some of what you and your sister have cost me."

"How long have you known?"

"I realized that you weren't Sara when I kissed you. I knew instantly you were not the woman I'd asked to be my fiancée."

"How?" The word came out in a strangled gasp.

How? He was not likely to tell her the truth—how kissing her sister had been a pleasant diversion whereas kissing her had been an experience that had blown his mind off the Richter scale.

He did not want to think of that now. Nor of the delight he'd experienced when they'd danced together at the tapas bar, or of the intellectual satisfaction he'd gained while they'd worked together. He especially did not want to think of how she'd made him feel last night.

"How matters not. What's important is that I caught onto your deception early enough to stop you when you tried to capitalize on it."

"Capitalize on it? I don't understand. Sara just asked me to—"

"Just asked you to lie to me? Deceive me? Set me and my family up for scandal and humiliation?" He smiled, although he had never felt any less humor in his life. "You see, the del Castillo family are well versed in the tricks of others. You two are not the first to think you can deceive us into what appears to be a relationship and then subsequently sell our family to the media, or worse, threaten to do so to extort money from us. We are not so dull witted that we will allow this to happen, no matter how much stress we are under."

"But it's not true," she insisted. Her face had paled, her pupils massively dilated, her hands trembled. "We aren't trying to extort money from you. Far from it. Sara didn't want to upset you—"

He snorted. "Upset me? You two have far from upset me. You disgust me with your avaricious lies. I know she needs sponsorship to continue with her horses, she was at least honest about that while she was here. But clearly that wasn't all she wanted, nor you. Tell me, when your fiancé broke off your engagement, was it because he'd discovered just how duplicitous you are? Or did you discover that he wasn't worth the bother and decided to come here for bigger fish to fry?"

"It wasn't like that," she cried, her slender shoulders slumped forward and what appeared to be grief slanted raw and stark across her face.

Oh, she was a good actress. He'd give her that. Even now, some traitorous instinct wanted to reach out to her, comfort her, pull her into his arms and take away all of her pain. He ruthlessly pushed the urge away. She was manipulating him again. He would not allow himself to fall for it.

"Rey, you have to believe me. I could never do what you're suggesting. I love you!"

The anger that had been simmering low in his gut exploded into a red haze of fury. It wasn't enough for her that she'd seduced his body and his mind—now she thought she could play with his heart, as well? He pushed himself up, dragging the top sheet off the bed and wrapping it around his hips. His forgotten coffee mug crashed to the floor and splintered into a dozen pieces, dark liquid spilling across the tiles.

"Love? You *dare* to tell me you love me?"

"It's true, I do love you. I didn't expect to—I certainly didn't want to. You're engaged to my sister."

"*Was* engaged to your sister."

"But we weren't…we didn't… Please at least hear her out."

"I'll hear her out, all right, before I send you both packing off the island. You are no longer welcome here. I think you'll find your visa rescinded by this afternoon."

Rey dropped the sheet and stepped into his trousers, eschewing the rest of his clothing which he bunched into a bundle and tucked under his arm.

"Rey, please don't go. Please don't leave like this. I know I should have told you everything from the beginning but there was no right time."

She thrust out her left hand in an attempt to stop him as he stalked past. The diamond ring he'd given Sara still glinted on her finger, caught in the rays of the rising sun as they filtered through the window. Already the heat of the day was streaming in, but inside him he'd never in his life felt so cold. He looked pointedly at the ring on her finger.

"That is not yours to wear."

"I know, I'm sorry." She bent her head and pulled the ring off her finger before dropping it into his outstretched hand.

Reynard shoved the ring in his pocket. If he never saw it again it would be too soon.

"I will make the arrangements for you to leave Isla Sagrado at once. One of my staff will call you with the details," he said as he covered the short distance to the bedroom door. He stopped inside the doorway and hesitated a moment, then turned to deliver his parting shot in scathing tones.

"Oh, and thanks for last night. That definitely made it all worthwhile."

Fifteen

It was well into the morning before Rina could bring herself to move from the bed. She'd curled into a fetal position of silent suffering in the face of Rey's bitter anger. Finally, the worst of the anguish passed, leaving her blessedly numb. Like an automaton, she gathered the sheets and bedcover off the bed and staggered through to the washing machine, set in an alcove in the bathroom. She shoved the linens into the machine, added soap and turned it on.

Continuing to go through the motions, she took a shower and washed herself thoroughly—washed away every last touch or caress that Reynard had given her.

A while later, back in the bedroom, when she reached for the first thing at hand, she remembered she was no longer wearing her sister's clothes. She was no longer Sara Woodville, but Sarina. She bent and dragged her suitcase from the bottom of the small cupboard, put it on the bare bed and wrestled the zip open. She grabbed the outfit on top—a pair of white capri pants and a mint green T-shirt. It was little comfort but it felt good to be in her own clothes again.

Since she'd been here, aside from her lingerie, she'd hardly worn her own clothing. She turned back to the wardrobe and fingered the fabric of the blue dress she'd worn on the night they'd almost made love for the first time. She should have told him then, she thought.

She'd felt so beautiful that night. So desired, even if it was all wrong. It occurred to her that he'd known even then that she wasn't Sara. And knowing she wasn't, he'd still wined and dined her, had performed intimacies on her that had tested her resilience beyond her expectations. A resilience that had broken under his kiss last night.

He'd meant to make love to her all along. A bubble of anger started to bloom in the pit of her stomach. What kind of man made love to one sister while still engaged to the other? Was he so calculated and so removed from genuine emotion? And Sara still expected to marry him.

She sank to her knees on the cold tile floor. Oh God, Sara. She was returning today. How on earth was she going to tell her what she'd done?

Reynard paced back and forth in his office, his mind tumbling with anger and confusion. His behavior toward Sarina was justified. More than justified, he told himself for the hundredth time since he'd gotten into his Ferrari and raced back to the city. But try as he might, he couldn't ignore the sharp tearing pain in the region of his heart as he considered the woman he'd made love with last night.

He'd been harsh in the face of her confession. Cruel, also, as he'd left. Neither state came naturally to him but, considering what had happened with Estella and then the discovery of the twins' deception, what else was he to do?

He dropped into his leather executive chair behind his desk, put his head against the high back and closed his eyes. Sarina's image was branded across his mind. The look on her face last night when she'd decided not to send him on his way. The passion when he'd entered her body for the first time. The hurt, the shock as he'd let loose his venom this morning—each word an individual blow calculated to hurt her.

He'd known all along about the lies, and yet, when she'd admitted it to him, it had roused in him a new fury. Why? He'd known, even when he'd asked to stay the night with her, that this choice was bound to be exactly what she needed for her plan. He should have expected her to tell him the truth when morning rolled around. Why had he been surprised? Had he fooled himself into believing that their lovemaking meant something to her? That she had not embarked upon a course of treachery and deceit for mercenary gain, but had, instead, shared her bed with him for no reason other than her own desire?

His head began to throb.

He forced his eyes open and reached for his telephone. Whatever his reasons, whatever hers, he needed to follow through and see her leave Isla Sagrado. There was no room in his life for her kind, nor his own brand of foolishness in wishing their time together to be any different.

Before he could lift the receiver, however, his intercom buzzed.

"Señor del Castillo, Miss Woodville is here to see you."

Words momentarily failed him. She had the unmitigated

gall to come to him at his office, even after he'd told her that he never wanted to see her again?

"*Señor?* Should I tell her you are otherwise engaged?"

His lips quirked at Vivienne's unintentional pun. "No, it's okay. Send her in."

The instant the door opened, he knew it was Sara Woodville who crossed the threshold. The two women might be identical, he acknowledged as he rose and walked around his desk to receive her—but to him, Sara was a pale facsimile of the woman he'd come to love. He misstepped on the carpet. Love? No. It couldn't be. The very thought was ridiculous.

"Rey, I have to tell you something." Sara cut through any preliminary greetings and got straight to the point.

"This should be interesting," he answered under his breath.

"I beg your pardon?"

"I'm aware of the deception you and your sister have pulled. You can consider our engagement officially ended."

"Oh, thank goodness!"

Her answer was anything but what he'd expected. She was relieved? What manner of con artist was relieved to have the game ended before payout had been achieved?

"I didn't want Rina to tell you the truth, but obviously she has. Rey, what we did was wrong. What *I* did was wrong. I should never have accepted your proposal. Not when I loved another man."

Rey's head reeled. "You love another man?"

"I do. I met him during the endurance trials near Maureillas. We fell in love so fast that I didn't want to believe it was real. *Couldn't* believe it was real, to be honest. It was all too much for me. I wasn't looking for anything serious, you know that. But he swept me off my feet. It scared me enough to push him away. I said some terrible things to him and hurt him badly before the tournament here. He was supposed to come and compete for France but he withdrew from the team and remained in Perpignan."

"Why are you telling me this?" Rey asked, still thoroughly confused. Had the sisters been setting up yet another mark?

"Because you deserve the truth, and you deserve far better than me. When I arrived here, and we met, I decided you were the perfect man for me. Uncommitted, fun, not looking for forever. And then you asked me to marry you. I was flattered, who wouldn't be? But I said 'yes' for all the wrong reasons. I didn't want to admit to myself that I'd fallen in love with Paul, but then I began to suspect I might be pregnant."

"You stopped drinking coffee and alcohol."

"Yes, I'm surprised you noticed."

"What I noticed was that your sister had not. It was one of the first things that drew the truth to my attention, although I was distracted at the time with Benedict's accident."

Sara's hands fluttered to her face, "I can't believe I'd forgotten to ask you about that. How is he?"

"Recovering at the castillo for now."

"I'm so glad. I never meant to leave you in the lurch at such a rough time—I had no idea anything had happened to Benedict until Rina told me. But by then, I was already in France. It wasn't long before I started to question my acceptance of your proposal and I knew that before I could do anything, I needed to talk to Paul again. Things with us were still so new—I couldn't tell you I had to run off to

France to talk with an old lover, but how could I explain leaving?

"Then Rina called to tell me about her broken engagement, and the timing was just too good to pass up. She needed to get away, and so did I. I asked her to visit, and arranged my flight from France to get in at the same time as hers. We barely had a chance to say hello before I shoved the letter at her, asking her to take my place."

The envelope with the ring, Reynard realized. The one that had had him worried that Sara planned to break their engagement. The one that had triggered their first kiss—and with it, the realization that Sara was not the woman who had been taking over his senses. It hadn't been addressed to him at all, but to her sister—asking her to play along with the charade.

"I know it wasn't fair—to you or to Rina—but I also knew that she wouldn't tell me no. I flew straight back to France. At first, Paul wouldn't see me, but eventually we got together and we've sorted things out. He still loves me and I know I love him also."

"And if he had not wanted you? Were you going to foist his child upon me?" Rey was rocked by her revelations, but his wits weren't so completely scattered to keep him from asking the obvious question. Sarina might not have been using him with financial motives, but Sara still could have been.

"I'll be honest. When I first went to Perpignan, the thought had crossed my mind, but in the end, I know I would never have done that to you. Reynard, I'm so sorry I used you. Sorry I used Rina, too. I should have been honest with you from the start and explained why I had to go away instead of expecting my sister to pick up the pieces."

"I can't accept your apology, Sara. What the two of you

have done—it has made me feel very manipulated and very angry."

"I understand. Look, I haven't seen Rina yet, and I need to tell her what has happened. Can I ask you not to say anything to her until then?"

Say anything to her? He'd ordered her from the island—from his life. He doubted that not speaking to her would be a problem. In response to Sara's question he nodded.

"Rina is leaving the island later today. I suggest that you go with her."

"I'm only here to clear things up with you, collect Rina and get my things. You won't need to worry about us again."

After Sara had gone, Reynard's head began to pound. How could he have been so incredibly wrong about Rina? Had his earlier experience with Estella so poisoned him that he'd been incapable of viewing any woman without suspicion? She'd admitted she pretended to be her sister. Admitted everything, including her love for him. And he'd called her a liar and crushed her with his anger.

Yes, she had deceived him, but wouldn't he have done the same thing for either of his brothers? Of course he would, if asked. In fact, his perpetuation of his engagement to Sara was no less a counterfeit than what the sisters had done to him. He'd done it to put *Abuelo*'s mind at rest, but the fact he had done it at all made him no different from Sarina and her twin.

He loved her. The truth of it pounded at his temples, insisting he acknowledge it. More, that he accept it as the core of his being. As hard as he'd fought it, she'd inveigled her way into his heart with her gentle ways, her quick intelligence and her unreserved passion. And he had sent her away. A deep-seated ache penetrated his chest.

He reached for the phone on his desk once more.

Somehow he had to right the wrongs he'd done her. Somehow, he had to find a way to make her stay.

"Reeny-bean, are you there?"

Rina straightened from the dryer where she was untangling the clean sheets and bedcover in readiness to remake the bed. She dropped everything and ran to the front door of the cottage. Apprehension over what her sister was going to say to her confession flew in the face of her initial joy at seeing her twin again.

Tears flowed freely down her face as they hugged one another tight. It felt far longer than a month had passed since Rina had last seen her sister at Isla Sagrado's airport. So much had happened.

"I've got so much to tell you!" they both blurted at the same time, then laughed through their tears.

"You first," said Sara. "Is everything okay?"

They walked, hand in hand, into the sitting-room area and sat together on the sofa there. Rina swallowed against the fear in her throat. Sara would understand why she'd done what she'd done. She had to.

"I did the worst thing, Sara. I fell in love with him. I'm so sorry. I didn't mean to. I didn't want to. I fought it all the way, but—"

"You fell in love with Rey?" Sara interrupted, her voice pitched high in disbelief. "How? Why?"

"I don't know. It just happened. But he worked out who I was a couple of weeks ago. He's been playing me along ever since." She drew back from her sister and squared her shoulders before meeting concerned gray eyes the mirror of her own. "I slept with him, Sara. I'm so sorry. I broke every promise we ever made to one another. I just…" She shook her head and began to sob anew. "He doesn't want me—he's basically banished me from Isla Sagrado."

"It's okay." Sara pulled Rina into her arms and hugged her tight, stroking her hair like she had when they were younger and Rina had borne the brunt of their parents' anger for one thing or another. "Really, it's okay. I broke our promises first by making you do what I did. I don't love Rey, I never did. I accepted his proposal for all the wrong reasons and I should never have done it. And I never should have asked you to step in for me, to keep a relationship alive that I wasn't even sure I wanted. It wasn't fair to him, to me or to you. I should have been honest with him from the start. You were so right, Reeny-bean. I wish I'd been truthful with you when you arrived here, even if it would only have saved you from being so hurt."

They sat and rocked together until Rina's sobs quieted.

"He's so angry." Rina said when she could speak again.

"I know, I've never seen him so distant before."

"You've seen him?" Rina pulled away from her sister's arms. "When?"

"Before I came here. I owed him the truth about why I went away. I owe it to you, too. The truth is, I met someone a few months ago, during a tournament in France. We fell in love and he wanted to marry me, but I couldn't. It was just all so fast, so intense, you know? And we were already competing against one another in the tournaments. All I could think about was how fierce Mum and Dad were about beating one another at everything they did, how horrid they made themselves feel when one or the other won. I didn't want that to happen to me. So when I got here and met Rey and he was so different, it was a relief to just let myself think we could make a go of things. When he asked me to get engaged, of course I said yes. I figured that when we married, life would just be more of the same.

There was no spark, no fierce need, no impatience to be better than him.

"But then I found out I was expecting Paul's baby, and I knew I couldn't avoid the truth any longer. I love Paul, and I realized what an idiot I'd been. Of course I'd hurt him so badly when I left him that I had some serious roads and bridges to rebuild. But he's accepted my apology. He still loves me and wants me to be his wife."

"I can't believe you didn't tell me about him." Rina placed her hand gently against her sister's lower stomach. "Or about the baby."

"I didn't want to believe it was true. You know what it was like growing up."

"Yes, I accepted Jacob's proposal for the very same reasons. He was safe. I didn't want to run the risk of—" she flung her hands in the air "—feeling like this."

"You poor baby. But don't worry. We'll pack all our stuff and be out of here as soon as we can. There's a flight to Perpignan later this afternoon. We can be on it and you can meet Paul and everything will be okay, you'll see."

Rina wished she could believe in her sister's optimistic point of view, but even knowing her sister had finally found her happiness, Rina knew she would never recover from the searing pain that filled her mind and her heart.

While they cleared their things and finished packing, made up the bed and emptied out the refrigerator, they discussed Sara's pregnancy, which had been a breeze so far. By the time the taxi arrived outside the cottage, Rina knew that at least she'd have something to look forward to. A niece or nephew to spoil and love—and to distract her from the empty sense of loss she carried deep inside her.

They'd just wheeled their cases out to the taxi when a cloud of dust came down the road. A cloud of dust accompanied by an all too familiar growl of high-performance motoring.

"He's probably just come to make sure we're leaving," Sara said. She stood in front of Rina as Rey alighted from his car. "You needn't have bothered coming to check on us. We're leaving Isla Sagrado for good."

Rey slid his expensive sunglasses off his face and took another step closer. "You might be leaving, but Sarina is most definitely not."

"I have no reason for staying here. In fact, you couldn't pay me to stay a minute longer," Rina said, and opened the back door on the taxi. "Come on, Sara. We don't want to miss our flight."

The two women got into the backseat, but before the driver could close the trunk of the car, they heard Rey bark an order in Spanish.

"Did he just tell him to take my case out of there?" Rina asked her sister.

Not waiting for a reply, she jumped out of the taxi. "What do you think you're doing? Put my case back in there."

"The *señor,* he asked me to take it out," the taxi driver said, looking uncomfortably between both Rey and Rina.

"Well, you can put it straight back in."

She stepped forward to do it herself, but at the same time, so did Rey. Her fingers tangled with his on the handle of the case.

"Please. Listen to me," he said with a quiet intensity that thrummed along her veins.

Even after everything he'd said and done to her, her body still leaped to life at his touch. She snatched her hand away, closed her eyes for a moment and swallowed against the tangle of words that lodged in her throat. She couldn't trust herself to speak.

"Rina?" Sara called as she exited the car.

"It's okay. Let him say what he has to say, then we'll go," Rina answered.

"Thank you," Rey said. "Can we go inside, for some privacy?"

"No." Rina shook her head emphatically. "Whatever you have to say to me you can say in front of my sister, as well."

"So be it." Rey nodded, but gave the ogling taxi driver a fierce look that sent the man back behind the wheel of the cab so he would not be able to hear. "I've treated you abominably."

"Yes, you have."

"I've come to beg your forgiveness."

"I don't know if I can do that. You played with me, with my feelings for you. You hurt me." Rina's voice wobbled and she saw a shaft of pain streak across Rey's face at her words.

"I know. I was proud and angry but that is no excuse—I should never have treated you so. I recognized you were different, right from the start but I refused to listen to my heart. I'd been attracted to Sara when I met her, but it was nothing compared to how I felt when I met you. The instant we were together, you completed me. Offered me calm when I most needed it. Lit a fire in me when before, the most I'd ever felt with any woman was a mild fascination. Yet despite that, I pursued my agenda without considering what it would do to you—or what it would do to me.

"It doesn't excuse me but I had reason to be suspicious. Our family had a near miss with a money-hunting opportunist only six months ago. A woman I'd allowed in my employ, thereby making my family as vulnerable to her schemes as she'd planned on making me. It very nearly cost us a small fortune, and I vowed it would never happen again. So when I realized you and Sara had exchanged places, my immediate thought was that you were taking up where the last one had failed."

"I tried to tell you, it wasn't like that," Rina said quietly.

"I know, but in my arrogance I thought I knew better. What I did was reprehensible. I chose to blur the truth with Sara when it suited me and I reacted unreasonably when faced with the very same thing in reverse. You asked me once if I lived by my family creed. I'm ashamed to say I haven't. Not for a very long time. But I aim to change that, if you'll let me."

He wiped a hand across his eyes, then looked directly at her again. She could see the sheen of tears turning his hazel eyes to green, saw the raw hope etched on his face. She didn't understand.

"Let you?" she asked. "Surely that's up to you."

He nodded. "It is up to me, but I need to be reminded from time to time of what a conceited, unfeeling ass I can be. I need someone to keep me on track, to remind me of what's most important in my life—to prevent me from falling back into the trap I've allowed myself to live in these past years. You said you loved me. Were you telling the truth?"

Rina looked at Sara who nodded. "Yes, I was."

"Then will you accept my remorse, my heart and my love?"

He dropped down onto one knee on the dusty road and pulled a ring from his pocket. A new ring, totally different from the one he'd given Sara. One Rina fell in love with almost as much as she already loved the man who offered it to her. The large central diamond—flanked by matching shoulder-set, emerald-cut stones—flashed fire in the sunlight.

"I never really understood what love was until I realized this morning that I'd sent away from me what was most true and precious in my life. Will you let me spend the rest of my life making my foolishness up to you? I love you, Sarina Woodville. Will you marry me?"

For the second time today, she heard her name on his lips and this time, it sounded as sweet as she'd ever imagined. Her heart, broken and shattered only moments ago, began to beat strong again in her chest. Hope filled her, making her light-headed, as if this wasn't real. As if she was only dreaming.

She stepped forward and knelt on the road in front of him, the stony road digging into her knees, reinforcing that she was very much awake. Tears, this time of joy, ran down her cheeks.

"Yes, I will marry you. I love you, Reynard del Castillo and don't you ever forget it."

"I won't," he promised, reaching out to wipe away her tears and to cup her face tenderly in one strong hand. "I love you. You and only you. And I will love you forever and remind you of it every single day of our life together."

He took her hand and slid the ring—her ring—upon her finger. It was a perfect fit. Then, he helped her to her feet, brushed the road dirt and grit from her knees and kissed her. It was only the sound of sniffling that drew them back to reality. Together they turned to Sara who was wiping tears of her own from her cheeks.

"Rina? Are you sure?" she asked.

"I've never been more certain of anything in my life," Rina replied.

"Then I wish you both the best of luck."

Sara dashed forward and hugged her sister tight before

doing the same with Rey. "You have a lot to live up to," she admonished. "You had better treat her right or you'll have me to answer to."

Rey smiled and looked at Rina. "Don't worry. She is my everything."

Rina and Rey stood together, arms entwined about one another, as Sara got back into the taxi and it drove away. Rey reached for Rina's suitcase and dragged it behind them as they went into the cottage.

When the door closed firmly behind them, an apparition—a woman in eighteenth century dress—straightened from the flowers she'd been tending, and smiled gently before fading away.

* * * * *

Benedict's story is next!
Don't miss For the Sake of the Secret Child,
the enticing conclusion of Yvonne Lindsay's
WED AT ANY PRICE *trilogy,*
from Mills & Boon® Desire™.

A sneaky peek at next month...

Desire

PASSIONATE AND DRAMATIC LOVE STORIES

2 stories in each book - only **£5.30!**

My wish list for next month's titles...

In stores from 16th September 2011:

❑ Ultimatum: Marriage — Ann Major

& For the Sake of the Secret Child — Yvonne Lindsay

❑ Expecting the Rancher's Heir — Kathie DeNosky

& Taming Her Billionaire Boss — Maxine Sullivan

❑ The Billionaire's Bridal Bid — Emily McKay

& Million-Dollar Amnesia Scandal — Rachel Bailey

❑ At His Majesty's Convenience — Jennifer Lewis

& Her Little Secret, His Hidden Heir — Heidi Betts

Available at WHSmith, Tesco, Asda, Eason, Amazon and Apple

Just can't wait?

Visit us Online

You can buy our books online a month before they hit the shops! **www.millsandboon.co.uk**

0911/51

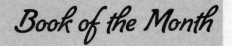

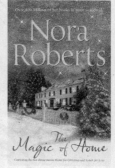

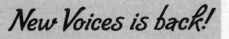

Avoiding the dreaded cliché

Open your story book with a bang—hook your reader in on the first page and show them instantly that this story is unique.

A successful writer can use a conventional theme and twist it to deliver something with real wow factor!

Once you've established the direction of your story, bring in fresh takes and new twists to these traditional storylines.

Here are four things to remember:

- Stretch your imagination
- Stay true to the genre
- It's all about the characters—start with them, not the plot!
- M&B is about creating fantasy out of reality. Surprise us with your characters, stories and ideas!

So whether it's a marriage of convenience story, a secret baby theme, a traumatic past or a blackmail story, make sure you add your own unique sparkle which will make your readers come back for more!

Good luck with your writing!

We look forward to meeting your fabulous heroines and drop-dead gorgeous heroes!

For more writing tips, check out:
www.romanceisnotdead.com

Visit us Online

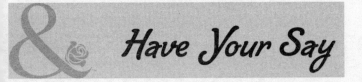